Appalachian Spring

A Novel

By

S.L. Baer

1663 LIBERTY DRIVE, SUITE 200
BLOOMINGTON, INDIANA 47403
(800) 839-8640
WWW.AUTHORHOUSE.COM

This book is a work of fiction. People, places, events, and situations are the product of the author's imagination. Any resemblence to actual persons, living or dead, or historical events, is purely coincidental.

© 2005 S.L. Baer. All Rights Reserved.

No part of this book may be reproduced, stored in a retrieval system, or transmitted by any means without the written permission of the author.

First published by AuthorHouse 02/04/05

ISBN: 1-4208-2080-X (sc)
ISBN: 1-4208-2079-6 (dj)

Library of Congress Control Number: 2004195266

Printed in the United States of America
Bloomington, Indiana

This book is printed on acid-free paper.

Where references to registered trademarks appear in this book, they have been distinguished by the use of initial capitalization.

Where once ancient lightning bolts danced on preeminent mountain peaks towering above the clouds, where once the soles of Cherokee moccasins, then cloven hoofs of the cattle of the first white ones tread, now the Vibram prints curse over worn-down peak and windy gap, in search of life more simple than that below. From Georgia to Maine or Maine to Georgia, the Appalachian Trail snakes up and over and through the remnants of the past glory of the North American continent, reaching its highest points within a range of mountains named for the surreal rising of morning mists shrouding their hoary heads in hues a painter feigns to capture, the top of Tennessee and North Carolina. Once raped and left for dead by the profit-hungry hoards that shaved its head and disemboweled its body, its life was nursed back to health and nurtured by the sacrifice of those who work without fiscal motives…

To them, the rangers of Great Smoky Mountains National Park and the many volunteers, this book is dedicated.

They are the fortunate ones who, in the context of a vast universe, came face-to-face with their smallness and impotence and grew larger because of it.

Thursday

1
Fontana

The wedding was now five days past. Intimacy and the Florida sun had fanned the flames of romance, and, during the drive north, she basked in the warm thoughts of their future life together. There was, however, an anxiety growing within her, which she tried to ignore until they stepped out of the car on the flanks of Fontana dam and felt the chill of the March mountain air on her cheeks and in her soul. The compromise had seemed fair when they planned it, and now she was determined to live up to her end of the bargain without complaining.

He had read in a magazine about a couple spending their honeymoon on a wilderness trail, just the two of them and nature, and he knew immediately that this challenge was the way to begin a marriage. She countered that everyone she knew spent their wedding trip in the romantic surf and sand. Besides, neither of them had ever spent a night out with only what they could carry on their backs. They were both determined in their own ideas, however, and it seemed they had reached their first marital impasse even before saying their vows. Then the answer was clear: they agreed to honeymoon half in the sand, half in the mountains.

They bought a book. It listed all the things they needed, and they dutifully purchased and packed them, only to find that neither of them could lift their packs. They whittled and deleted until the weight was manageable. They tucked their packs away and thought no more about them until today when they pulled the packs from the tail of their Toyota. He helped her pack onto his bride's back and hefted his own. They attempted a few adjustments, though they understood neither the pack literature nor the salesman's explanation. Those skills would be hard-learned along the way.

After the first wobbly steps, they regained some balance and set off across the parking lot, encouraged by the ease of walking on flat pavement.

Before them, the Appalachian Trail crossed Fontana Dam and followed a paved road gently ascending into the trees frocked with pale green leaves of early spring. Beyond the serpentine lake to their right, the hillside rose steeply toward the peaks and balds of Great Smoky Mountain National Park.

Both were now confident that they could do this thing, maybe even enjoy it, the weight on their backs and the burning in their legs and lungs notwithstanding. After following the road for thirty minutes, they came to a sign spelling "Appalachian Trail" with white-painted letters routed into brown-stained wood, pointing them left to a path leading into the woods and away from the paved road. Immediately the trail climbed steeply. Neither of them was willing to show weakness or humility, so they plodded upward until at last their legs would not take them another step. They rested on a fallen log with packs still on, drinking from brand-new Nalgene bottles and forcing complements to the beauty of nature surrounding them. The spring sun filtered through the infant leaves of the spring canopy, but the spring wind chilled them. So onward they went, remembering the feel of unbroken Sanibel sun on nearly naked bodies the day before, dreading the four long miles to go to the first shelter listed on the backcountry permits flopping at the tops of their packs.

The trail steepened with each step. They said little. Both focused on the rebellions developing in mind and body, losing the battle to maintain a positive attitude, barely succeeding in maintaining the façade of one. Their packs became heavier, shoulder straps and hip belts relentlessly rubbing and gouging. Rest stops became more frequent as they gasped for air, rubber limbs dragging over rocks and roots and fallen logs. She felt the wear in her ankles, which twisted powerlessly on the uneven earth. He felt it in his lower back.

She slowed to a stop. She turned around, leaned against a tree and waited for him to appear in the bend of the trail behind her. He looked up and caught sight of her pitiful blue green eyes, and a feeling of remorse swept over him. He had been too preoccupied with his own discomfort and embarrassment to be aware of hers. As he reached her, he started to pull her to himself. Instead he froze, his eyes widening as he looked over her drooped shoulder toward the trail beyond. She turned and gasped.

Not thirty feet away stood a large whitetail buck, frozen in his tracks, staring back. His black muzzle twitched as he sampled the wind, but it carried their scent away from him. The three stood transfixed timelessly until the buck broke the stalemate, turned and stepped slowly and silently up the trail, looking over his shoulder every few steps in distrust. Then he snorted and left the trail, his great antlers scraping the twigs overhead as he went.

They exhaled and became aware of the pounding inside their chests. The man looked at his wife and saw excitement and happiness on her face, where defeat and despair had just been. He felt better.

"Brian! He was…hardly…afraid of us!" she gasped. "Why didn't he…run away?"

"I don't know, Carrie. God, that was awesome! Did you see those antlers?"

"See his antlers? I could almost smell the beast!"

"I didn't think deer had antlers in March."

"Apparently this one does!"

The two stepped quietly, arm-in-arm toward the point where the deer first stood. There in the mud, in the middle of the trail, were the plain fresh tracks of cloven hooves. Brian and Carrie strained their eyes to see through the woods, but the buck now was as invisible as he was silent, dissolving into the woods to which he belonged.

This gave the novices new energy and drive, and they reached the end of the endless incline by early afternoon. They had hiked only three miles, but the last two and a half seemed straight up, climbing two thousand feet.

They stopped for rest and lunch at the first fallen log. As Carrie began to unpack their provisions, Brian took a water bottle in one hand and his map in the other, and sat down to study it.

"Looks like we're sitting on top of Little Shuckstack."

"It sure didn't seem little getting up here! Do we have to climb Big Shuckstack?" Carrie asked, half-jesting, half-fearing.

"Yeah, it looks like Shuckstack is next, but it's not very far."

By the end of lunch, the Ralstons were more reclining than sitting, having melted slowly off the log and onto the ground, the rotting trunk now serving as a moss-upholstered backrest. They leaned toward one another. Brian placed his hand upon her shoulder and began to massage the muscles Carrie was discovering.

"Brian," she spoke affectionately, "I'm glad we decided to come on this trip. I had my doubts, and I'm still scared, but I'm starting to see what people see in it. I can't describe what it felt like standing there with that buck. And right here, no one in sight but you and me. I almost wish it could stay that way."

"You wouldn't rather be back in Florida?"

"Florida was great. Being there with you was great. But the only place we could get alone was in the hotel room. We haven't seen another human being today since we crossed the dam."

"Maybe they all have better sense. I was afraid you were mad at me, dragging you out here and all."

"I was. I was ready to turn around and give up."

"You may yet!" Brian poked her rib.

"We've come too far to turn back!" Carrie answered.

"We've got to get going, Carrie," Brian said. "If this is Little Shuckstack, we have two more miles to go."

Brian stood up first and held out a hand. Once securely on her feet, she leaned over to pick up her pack. Brian began to laugh.

"What's so funny?"

"Your tush is soaked!" Brian chuckled as he looked at the dark wet circle encompassing Carrie's backside and the matching double impression in the wet moss she had used as a cushion. "Can't you feel it?"

She felt it as soon as the cold wind hit the wet spot. Of all the places to be wet and chilled, she thought. Bad choice, blue jeans for a wet-country hike. It felt as if she had two pounds in each pocket as the wet denim and panties sagged.

"I have to change," Carried said blushing. She rummaged through her pack for replacement garments. She pulled off her boots and stood on a rock in her sock feet.

"You gonna do it right here? What if someone comes along?"

"No one's come along yet, but if they do they'll get an eyeful!"

Brian glanced nervously up and down the trail, then at his wife as she pulled off the wet jeans and panties, still amused by the incident and now by the fact that goosebumps covered every bit of exposed flesh. But his amusement gave way to adoration as he saw his wife's nakedness again for the first time, illuminated in the soft primeval sunlight flickering through the branches of oak and fir, her form framed by the backdrop of wispy green branches of young hemlocks dancing in the breeze. He wanted her now, but instead reiterated the advice that it was time to move on.

Carrie tied the wet clothes on the outside of her pack. The soft dry warm-ups felt good against her skin. The Ralstons were soon enjoying a brief section of downhill trail, before beginning the short steep ascent of Shuckstack, which they conquered with new enthusiasm. The worst was behind them. Carrie replayed her vision of the deer and felt the comfort of dry and lighter clothing. Brian replayed his vision of Carrie's nakedness in the outdoors, and his hope grew that his fantasy of fully enjoying her in the openness of nature would be fulfilled. Faith replaced doubt. Exasperation and drudgery vanished. The afternoon sun banished the damp and chill, and few clouds punctuated the deep blue sky, bluer than the young couple had seen or could remember. The air was fresh and thin, scented faintly with springtime. At the top, they found an old fire tower where they enjoyed a brief respite.

Beyond Shuckstack's mitered crown, the ribbon of trail lay lightly on the ancient range's spine, traversing each vertebral prominence and the subtle depressions between. The trail across these higher points was still walled in by trees on either side, but in the gaps, a view opened to either side where the strongest winds had concentrated, limiting the growth of trees to dwarfed and gnarled forms. Carrie and Brian stopped awhile at each opportunity, where they rested, talked and looked out upon the mountains of which they were beginning to feel a part.

"Here's home for the night," Brian said as they came upon the sign to Birch Springs shelter.

Shed of their packs, the two stood, arms around each other, drinking in the scene before them. The shelter and its surroundings were far more rudimentary than either had imagined, but quaintness and charm held disappointment in check. The shelter, built in typical fashion for this part of the Appalachian Trail, had only three walls and a roof, the fourth side fenced with chain link. The crude cabin hugged the hillside and tucked itself among the hemlocks so unobtrusively that it became part of the natural scene, not an intrusion of man into it. The spring gurgled from the fern-lined bank in front of the shelter. They could smell its earthy cleanness and feel its cold, damp emanation in their bones. They stood transfixed, all their senses and thoughts engrossed in ethereal wonder, swilling one long draft of the soul-purifying elixir.

"Join me for a drink?" Brian said, breaking the spell and nodding toward the spring.

"I'd be delighted, kind sir," Carrie mimed with a curtsey, offering her hand. By it she was led to the water's edge.

They dipped their plastic mugs into the icy water. Brian raised his upward.

"To my beautiful bride. I'm a lucky man to have her!"

"And she's happy to be had."

They touched their cups and intertwined their arms to sip their toast, just as they had last Saturday before God and dearly beloved witnesses. The water that now passed their lips was more precious and fine than the champagne at the wedding, which now seemed so long ago. The couple lingered on a kiss. Then practical considerations returned.

"I've got to find the bathroom," the blushing bride mumbled. She looked around the clearing and found a small toilet area sign pointing toward the woods. She walked briskly past the sign. The trail fanned out and seemed to lead nowhere. There was no bathroom in sight. She looked about until she saw remnants of tissue here and there, and it dawned on her what "toilet area" meant.

Brian opened his pack, found his camera and began taking pictures of the shelter. He heard Carrie returning. He aimed the camera and snapped just as she emerged from the trees. She stood there with the most pitiful look upon her face. He started to inquire and then noticed the dark streak from the left waistband of her sweats almost to the knee.

"I lost my balance."

Brian started to laugh, and Carrie started to cry. He went toward her to comfort, but she stepped back.

"Just get my jeans from my pack! And toss 'em to me."

Brian obeyed.

"Go up toward the trail and make sure no one comes. I've got to wash up."

"I don't get to watch?"

"Go!"

Brian went.

Carrie's jeans were still barely damp from her poor choice of seating earlier but were far drier than the sweats. She had one dry pair of sweats in reserve, but she dared not put them on now. Another accident would leave her with nothing for sleeping. So she washed and dressed. She was almost over her embarrassment when it hit her.

"Brian, give me the roll of film."

"What! Not on your life, Carrie. Don't you think it's funny now?"

"Hell no, Brian. You think it's funny because you could pee on every tree between Fontana and here. You oughta try my way once. Then you can laugh. There's no way we're getting that developed."

"Carrie, it has all our other pictures on it. I promise I won't show it to anybody."

She protested further but let it die.

Once inside the shelter, they began setting up home. Along the back wall, there were twelve wooden bunks, six below and six above. The bottom bunks weren't far above the dirt floor, and the top ones weren't much below the log rafters and rusty sheet metal roof. Integrated into the stone of the wall to the right was a fireplace, as well-crafted as any they had seen. The left stone wall was bare. A half dozen cords hung from the rafters overhead, each with a stick tied on the end. About a foot or two above each stick, a tin can with a hole in the bottom had been threaded upside down and suspended curiously on the cord by a knot.

"What are these for?" Carrie wondered.

"Beats me. If someone comes along, we'll ask'm. Do you want top bunks or bottom bunks?"

"We might have a little more privacy on the top."

"*If* someone else comes."

"I want to sleep against the wall so I won't end up with some strange sweaty man snoring next to me."

"I don't snore."

"I wasn't talking about you. And yes, you do snore. I just don't want one on both sides of me."

Brian laid out the food and cooking utensils and fired up the stove. Having achieved a fine blue flame, he placed a pot of water over it. Carrie was fascinated to see the stove work. She grabbed Brian's hand in both of hers, shrugged her shoulders and giggled with a child's adoration. Brian caught the reaction and puffed up.

Carrie opened a foil pack.

"It looks like a scoop of dirt and pine needles," Brian observed.

Carrie poured boiling water into it and let it sit as directed. The smell and appearance of spaghetti with meatballs slowly developed. The reconstituted dinner vanished in minutes. They finished cleaning up with enough daylight left to gather wood and start a fire in the ring of blackened rocks outside the little hut. Carrie made cocoa, and they were set for an evening for two around the fire. Carrie had learned well from her first mistake: she laid out a poncho on the ground between a section of log and the fire. The couple sat down on the poncho, backs against the log, and snuggled up to their cups and each other.

"It doesn't get any better than this," Brian sighed.

"You sound like a commercial."

"They ought to make commercials about this."

"No they shouldn't. Then we wouldn't be here alone." Carrie looked up at Brian, smiling coyly, firelight dancing in her happy eyes.

They leaned toward one another and stared silently into the flickering fire, sipping sweet hot cocoa. They lingered in silent contentment for some twenty minutes. Brian spoke first.

"I wonder how long we should wait to make sure we're the only ones showing up tonight."

"Why do you ask?" Carrie teased.

"I was wondering what you would look like in this firelight."

"I would look like one big goosebump! Promise to keep me warm?"

Carrie set both empty cups aside and sat up on her knees facing Brian. His eyes were fixed upon hers. She gazed back and began to sway subtly, hypnotically until he was entranced like a cobra before its charmer. Without taking her eyes from his, she unzipped her jacket, slipping it sensually off each shoulder, letting it fall to the ground behind her. Her graceful fingers found the top button of her soft cotton blouse and loosed each one with painful slowness. When the final one was unfastened, her blouse fell open, and firelight spilled across her small firm breasts, red nipples small and hard with cold and excitement. She stood with the fire behind her, sliding her jeans and panties off her hips, and letting her blouse fall to the ground, her feminine form now in silhouette with glowing aura tracing her curves. The heat of the fire quickly warmed her bare back, and she turned her freezing front to the fire to chase away its chill, then turned again and again, a slow, spinning ballet. When she was warmed on all sides, she returned to Brian, who was still frozen in awe. She sat upon his lap and slid her arms beneath his jacket and around him, burying her face against his chest where his heart beat wildly. Brian pulled his jacket around her and wrapped her nakedness in his warmth.

"Did you like me?"

"You are…"

Carrie stopped his answer with a deep, passionate kiss. They both tore frantically at Brian's clothes, removing them with no attention to order. Their sharing of love was as feverish as his undressing. They did not separate for some time, but pulled over themselves whatever clothing they could reach for the little warmth it might provide.

"I never knew…I didn't think…God, this is it! I couldn't have dreamed making love could be like that!" Carrie struggled.

Their lovemaking had always been with more compassion than passion. Each time before, Carrie made love with the apprehension of a virgin. This time was different. She only felt desire.

"It was like our first time," Brian said.

"It wasn't anything like our first time," Carrie said. "I was so afraid then."

"Afraid? Afraid of what?"

"I was afraid I would disappoint you."

"Disappoint me how?"

"Well, you know, fat, flat and clumsy."

Carrie looked at Brian with sensitive sparkling blue green eyes, her face plain and pleasant, framed with mousy-brown, slightly frizzy hair worn shoulder length and shoulder width when not pulled back. Her figure was young and alive, just a little wide in the hips and meager-chested, and she carried herself well.

"Carrie, how could I be disappointed? I love you. You're the most beautiful creature I've ever seen or touched. I keep being afraid I'm going to wake up."

"If you told me that this morning, I wouldn't have believed you. I was sure you were ready to dump me as soon as we got back to civilization. Or dump me over the side of the mountain."

"It *was* true this morning. That's why I was so afraid of failing you after I dragged you all the way out here against your will."

"Well I sure was mad at you for dragging me out here then, but not now. I felt like a failure, and it was your fault for making me feel that way, for putting me in a situation where I could fail. I thought we'd ruined our marriage in the first week."

"I thought I had ruined it, Carrie."

"Well now I'm glad you made me do something scary like coming out here. I feel like I grew ten feet today."

"I wouldn't like you if you grew ten feet."

"You said 'For better or worse.'"

"Yeah, but not for taller."

They stared up at the stars, clearly visible through the leafless trees and thin cold atmosphere.

"Brian?"

"Yes, hun'?"

"I'm glad we had those bad thoughts today."

"How come?"

"We worked it out. We talked. We were honest with each other. You told me about your weakness. And feelings. And we still love each other, don't we? That's why making love was so intense tonight."

That may be part of it, he thought, but for me it was ninety-nine percent seeing you dance naked in front of the fire. He didn't dare say it.

"Can we promise to always be that honest with each other?" Carrie continued.

"Yes. We'll be like two open books," Brian promised, unaware that he had just hidden his thoughts from her. They returned to stargazing. The moon was nearly full and was starting to pour its gray-blue light into the clearing, replacing the waning glow of the dying fire. The temperature was dropping. Brian started to get more wood for the fire when Carrie thought she heard a noise in the woods and suggested they retreat to the stone and chain-link sanctuary. They both heard a second sound, so they quickly gathered cups and clothing and entered the shelter.

2
UT Campus

Andy Young glanced up at the clock above the lectern. Only ten minutes left to finish. But what was the use of sweating any longer? Ten more hours and the paper would still contain many blanks. History of the U.S. was of little interest to him, and now he would pay the price. Glancing out the classroom window, Andy could see the edge of Neyland Stadium and the Tennessee River beyond. Hidden behind the bluffs on the other side were the mountains where he knew he could forget about academics and other troubles. Andy shook his head, and bubbled in 'b' for each of the still blank answers, carried his papers to the front and walked out the door to freedom.

A sophomore now, Andy was still undecided in his major, though he had declared Finance to please his father. He had thought much about majoring in Broadcasting. His easy manner, generic charm and pleasant voice had earned him approval from peers and mentors alike, and he had used them in the past to compensate for his mediocre academic skill. Those assets would lead to success in broadcasting also, but his father never saw it that way. His father, having built his medical practice with hard work and business acumen, determined that his contribution to his son's education insured his say-so in his son's future. His father had wanted him to go into medicine also, but Andy's grades made that impossible. A business degree would be an honorable way to guarantee a financial future for his son, or so he thought, and Andy had agreed to this compromise in order to obtain his father's financial support. Andy's heart was not in it.

In fact, since enrolling at the University of Tennessee, Andy's heart had been more in fraternity life, parties and recreation in the absence of parental scrutiny, than anything related to his future. Even his dating life had little of permanence about it. Andy met people easily, and dates were easy for him to obtain. Beneath his soulish exterior, however, was a coat of armor. He had dated many different girls, but as soon as they got too close, they scraped their feelings upon that barrier. If they tried too hard to pierce it, he dumped them, if they had not dumped him first, preferring relationships with men who were not endowed with an exoskeleton. That is how his last relationship ended, and, though he really did not care that he had lost Leigh, being dateless would interfere with the weekend plans. This mountain trip would be awkward since it had been planned as a double date. He was afraid that Paul and Connie would be reluctant for him to tag along. He'd just have to wait and see what they said.

Andy arrived at the Student Center and went downstairs to Smokey's. He chose the barbeque line, paid the cashier and carried his tray about looking for his friends. He found them at a corner table.

"How'd the exam go, bro'?" Paul asked, knowing his friend had not spent much time studying.

"It went, and now it's gone. That's the last I want to hear about it. Hey, Connie. You're looking beautiful as ever."

"Where's Leigh? She gonna meet us here?" Connie inquired.

"Guys, we gotta talk. Leigh and I broke up last night."

"What happened this time?" Paul asked coldly.

"Paul! You'll hurt his feelings!" Connie chided.

"Hurt his feelings! Wait'll you know him better. Andy ain't got no feelings. Ain't that right Andy?"

"I guess this means you two oughta go on to the AT by yourselves tomorrow," Andy tested.

"No Andy. Paul and I wouldn't feel right if you didn't come."

Paul rolled his eyes. "Yeah, you can still come."

When Connie went to refill their drinks, Paul leaned over and stared at him with squinting eyes.

"There ain't no way you're gonna come with us, friend. Three's a crowd." His scowl changed to a smile as Connie returned and slid back into the booth.

"Andy here was just saying how he just didn't feel right coming along without Leigh. He's still pretty torn up over her dumping him and all."

Connie assumed a serious look, leaned over to Paul and whispered something in his ear.

"Well I gotta go, guys," Connie announced. "I'll meet you two back at Paul's apartment around fourish." She leaned over and kissed Paul then smiled at Andy. She spun around and sauntered away, and Paul and Andy both watched her leave. Neither said a word until she was gone.

Paul turned to Andy and said, "She's great, isn't she. I could get serious about this one."

"Yeah, that's a fine one you got there, man. You'd better keep her happy or she'll figure out she can do a lot better than you, punk. By the way, what's she think I'm gonna do, come pack your groceries just so I can watch her smile?"

"That's just it, Andy. She says she's not going unless you're going. So I guess three's company, eh?"

"Why won't she go if I don't?"

"She doesn't like the way it looks."

"Well my being there isn't going to stop anything, is it? I mean this won't be y'all's first time together will it?"

"No, but she's got friends from home here. She's afraid they'll talk. Like sleeping together is OK as long as you don't actually *sleep* together! So you'll go?"

"Sure I'll go. But I won't promise not to be bored."

"Bored? You said yourself that no one could be bored in the Smokies."

"No, but it would be easy to avoid if Leigh was goin.'"

"What happened there, anyway?"

"She insisted on some higher plane of commitment before she'd spend the night out in the woods with me. I didn't say everything that was in her script about it. She got mad and cried. Then when I didn't get shook up and all and nurse her feelings, she flew."

"No chance of patching it up with her before the trip?"

"She's already left for home. I've gotta pick up some hiking socks at Appalachian Sports. Wanna come along?"

"Sure."

After packing, they headed for Stefano's, which was crowded with students celebrating or mourning the results of midterm exams.

"I wanna eat big tonight," Paul announced, "I'll be craving pizza on the trail long before I can get another fix."

"Eat big if you want, but don't drink big tonight, or you'll be dehydrated on the trail tomorrow," advised Connie.

"Yes, Mom," Paul mocked, but he knew she was right.

As soon as the orders were placed, Andy was up and across the room to another table where three girls were seated.

"I can see he's torturing himself over what's-her-name!" Connie observed with sarcasm.

"He holds the UT record for rebounding. You wait. He'll work his charms and have a date for this weekend before you know it."

"Oh, he has charm? I didn't notice," Connie lied.

"Don't tell me you haven't noticed."

"Yeah, I noticed, and I was about to run away with him. Then I remembered that I don't split up friends. I have a policy against it. If you ever stop being friends, tell me right away so Prince Charming and I can go for it!"

Andy returned to the table just as the pizza arrived. He thanked the waitress and grinned with dimples, causing her to smile and blush and waltz away.

"So Andy. Who are your new friends?" Paul inquired.

"They're not new. They're in my English class. See the blonde? That's Leslie. Her friend in the middle is…."

Paul interrupted, "Which one is coming with you this weekend?"

"Well, I've been thinking about asking Leslie out…"

"While you were dating Leigh?" Connie broke in.

"Well is she coming?" Paul repeated impatiently.

"No. But we're on for the first Friday after Spring Break."

Paul sank.

The three ate, drank and entertained friends visiting from other tables until eleven when Connie insisted it was time to turn in and left. Ten minutes later Paul's cell phone rang. Andy could tell there was bad news. The trip was off. Paul's grandmother was hanging in the balance. They returned to Paul's apartment, and Andy helped Paul get on the road.

"Just lock up when you leave. Sorry about the trip, man," Paul patted him on the shoulder, then left.

Andy crumpled amid the packs on the floor. What a letdown! Emptiness crept in from all sides. He soaked in it for a few minutes, then thought about going back to Stefano's to get plastered. To hell with that, he thought. I'm heading to the mountains anyway. He repacked for a solo trip and hit the sack.

3
Pigeon Forge

A chill morning mist drifted over the hotel parking lot, obscuring the surrounding mountains. Louise Leonard scurried about, trying to rouse her sleepy teenage charges slumbering under the influence of adolescence, late bedtimes and the knowledge that these warm beds were to be their last for several nights.

Kevin McGinnis was first to show his face through the motel door, but only long enough to test the weather. Among the youth, he alone had some knowledge of the activity before them. He was eager to begin. This tourist trap had been of little interest to him. Most of the group had loved it. *His* adventure was just now beginning.

The others felt both the excitement and insecurity of facing something new. At the moment, the challenge of pulling themselves out of bed required total concentration. Daniel Dozier, the youngest, was winning, but Brad Busby's success was still in question. Both Kevin and Daniel were dressed by the time Brad had sat up in bed, his coal-black hair shoved to one side, heavy eyes submerged in his puffy face. Kevin and Daniel found Lori Wong already in the van, which Glen Leonard had warmed for them.

"Morning, Lori," the two boys said in unison. Lori looked up and smiled her good morning. "Where are your two suite-mates then?" Kevin quipped.

"They're reapplying their faces, and you know how long that takes. Never know which wild creature of the forest's going to be looking to see who's the fairest."

Lori's mother had vehemently protested her coming on this trip, as she had protested her every involvement with the church. Lori's parents emigrated from Taiwan when Lori was ten months old. By hard work, they had built a life in Memphis, hoping for a college education and a secure place in the technical world for each of their six children. When her father died, her mother took on the work of three people to keep their dream alive. She viewed Lori's passion for church as a threat to her carefully planned future. But Lori was grown up, she was eighteen, a senior, and had a will of her own, and her mother dared not force her will for fear of losing her precious child. She could only protest.

Mrs. Leonard returned to the van with a tray of juice and coffee carefully balanced on a white cardboard box of donuts. Kevin had looked up to Mrs. Leonard since she taught him in second grade Sunday school. He had admired Mr. Leonard since the time his father was critically injured at the plant. He not only had stayed with, prayed with and comforted Kevin's whole family, Mr. Leonard had understood the turmoil occurring in the twelve-year-old Kevin as he wrestled with tragedy. The wise church elder had taken Kevin aside, laid upon him softly the hard responsibilities of manhood. From that time on Kevin sought and earned the Leonards' approval.

Christie Jenkins and Tammy Day reached the van with an air of importance, with hair styled and makeup applied, ready to impress and conquer in their new outdoor fashions. Christie sat in front of Kevin, pretending as usual not to notice him while certain he was noticing her. Tammy sat down beside her and looked about. Her confident guise crumbled; a frown spread across her face.

"Where's Pastor Dave?" she asked, attempting nonchalance.

"He's gone to get the drinks. We'll saddle up as soon as he gets back. Open the door for Brad. I think he's finally with us," Mr. Leonard said. Tammy watched the parking lot.

Brad lumbered up, a duffle under each arm, earphones in place like a miniature life support system.

"I brought the stuff from the guys' room like you said, Mizz Leonard." His attempts to flatten his hair were obvious but unsuccessful, accentuating the awkwardness aptly supplied by his size, both vertical and horizontal. At eighteen, he was already the tallest of the group and weighed in at over 220 pounds. His lack of interest coupled with his lack of coordination had kept him from using this endowment in sports, and, at this point in life, it was hard to determine where any of his interests or abilities lay. He had been raised in the church and participated in the activities, but that was all. He rarely volunteered any information about what he thought or felt, and when asked, his clumsy answers communicated little that would encourage further conversation. The leaders and the boys were nice to him, and Lori was tolerant, but Christie and Tammy ridiculed him, mostly between themselves, though sometimes openly.

A red sixty-five Mustang pulled in beside the van. A young man, tall and thin with dark hair and skin, stepped out and strode to the van.

"Morning Bro. Dave," chimed several of the youth. Tammy said nothing, watching her finger as it traced the rim of her orange juice cup.

"Y'all ready to become backpackers? Let's ask God's blessing on our trip before we go." His deep reverent voice petitioned for safety and fun and the glory of God. Everyone said "amen." He climbed in the seat beside Brad, and the van pulled away.

As they passed the entrance to Dollywood, some were missing it already, some never would. Hotels, restaurants, tourist shops and water slides passed by the windows, giving way to forests and stream banks on the way toward Gatlinburg. Behind them, the clouded sky glowed orange, and before them to the east, the sun rose tentatively over the mountains, shining brightly through a gap in the clouds. The Gatlinburg bypass deposited them at Sugarlands Visitor Center where they stopped long enough to obtain the requisite backcountry permits before proceeding up the curves and grades of Newfound Gap Road. The shoulder, streams and valleys fell away as they climbed and climbed, the church van complaining loudly. Its occupants were silent, eyes glued to the windows as they beheld the beauty of the Great Smoky Mountains National Park passing below and looming above, transfixed as if they had never seen it before, though most of them had several times. At last, they reached the gap, and the passengers piled out and retrieved their packs.

"Gather 'round people. Let's review the map so you'll see where we're going," the elder summoned. He showed them the Appalachian Trail, the shelters and distance between them. He laid down his rules of engagement, concluding, "And nobody goes anywhere alone. Clear?" He reviewed the rendezvous at Elkmont with his wife and kissed her goodbye.

Mrs. Leonard drove away waving, and the group looked at the trail disappearing into the dark woods of the mountainside. They each took a deep breath, shouldered packs and pushed forward, absorbed into the hemlocks and the Fraser Fir corpses. A few looked back. After thirty steps, no one could even tell a parking lot was anywhere near.

The wind was blowing steadily from the northwest, sending waves of dreary ghost-like figures of fog up one side of the ridge line, across the trail and down the other side like eerie bands of foot soldiers, assaulting enemy positions through the smoke of battle, dim characters from the dreams of children and the nightmares of old men. Glen Leonard remembered such scenes from Vietnam; the others had no such associations, but marveled at the haunting beauty.

The early going was not difficult, a fortunate breaking-in period for the green youth. Mr. Leonard led, setting a slow steady pace, stopping frequently to make sure his charges did not miss a detail along the trail. David Wilkes took up the rear of the column to contain the stragglers. For even at the slow pace Glen had set, Brad, Christie and Tammy began to lag, Brad because of his bulk, Christie and Tammy because of the effects of little sleep the night before. Kevin stayed close to Glen, his mentor. Lori and Daniel walked together in loneliness and conversation about the birds, trees and weather. Daniel would have preferred a male companion his own age, and Lori would have preferred a conversation with Kevin. She admired Kevin and detected a like-mindedness in him, a seriousness of purpose rare in any boy her age. There was no one else her equal in conversation. Unlike the other teens she knew, she was acquainted with hardship and had learned to fight to overcome it. When she embraced Christianity, she paid a price higher than the risk of peer ridicule, for in doing so she had turned her back on her ancestors and her family, as her mother had so often reminded her with bitterness.

Christie and Tammy hiked together. Christie wanted to catch up to Kevin where she was sure he would take notice of her. Most boys did. She was pretty. When she was around Kevin she felt especially so and therefore liked his company. Feeling pretty aroused sensual longings neither her morals nor her upbringing would allow her to admit, so she projected them onto Kevin and believed that he felt them for her instead. In truth, he had scarcely noticed her, and the interest she felt he had in her was merely another perversion of reality forged by her complex and contradictory imaginations.

If Christie could not admit her attraction for Kevin to herself, she certainly could not show it to him or even admit it to her closest friend, Tammy, who had no such inhibition and embarrassed Christie constantly by sharing her interest in forbidden things. If Christie protested, Tammy merely said she was kidding or that it was not a sin just to think about them as long as they remained thoughts and not deeds. Such a situation had occurred the previous night when Tammy told Christie there were things she would like to do with Pastor Dave. Christie first blushed and stared.

"Tammy, you don't mean that. You shouldn't even say it!" she said, feeling the heat in her cheeks.

"I didn't say I was going to do anything. I was just imagining what it would be like to be his wife was all. Besides, there's not a girl in the church that doesn't think he's cute. I just *said* it, that's all."

It was true. Most of the girls and many of the young women, single and married, had thought at least once what a catch he would have been. But he came to the church already taken, and now his wife was going to have a baby. His good looks and his inaccessibility combined to fan the flames of infatuation, and Tammy had been nursing one colossal crush for some time. Now Tammy had begun to toy with him flirtatiously as Christie had always done with Kevin. Nothing overt of course, and no one but Christie suspected her of design, especially not Dave. Her wiles were subtle. This morning as they hiked, she had allowed others to pass, complaining that she should have slept more last night. In position now ahead of the young pastor, she was sure his eyes could not escape the little things: the fanning of her hair so it fell around her pack and onto her shoulders, the frequent application of lip balm, the coy little smile tossed over her shoulder when he spoke.

David Wilkes had not noticed. He had been transfixed all morning at the wonders of God's creation unspoiled save by the ribbon of trail man had carved. Never did David feel closer to his creator than when in nature, and never had nature been so lavish before him than now. As he walked, he prayed and gave thanks silently. When he spoke to the others, it was to point out a red squirrel or a chipmunk or massive hemlock, acknowledging God as the author of each.

Not that Pastor Dave was unaware of his physical prowess, for in high school and college he had used it to fill his social calendar with dates that were both beautiful and devout, and even to charm the little old ladies who spoke to him after his student sermons were delivered. But in his senior year, he had met a young woman who seemed to see past it all, and drew from him a vision for God, his ministry and life. He felt his strength increase when he was with her, and he found himself wanting to grow, to please her, to deserve her. Her name was Susan, and one week after graduation, they were married. He attended seminary while she taught school and made their home. They had lived on love and her puny teacher's salary, but they were happy. After graduation, the school helped him find his present place of ministry, and they were able to buy a little starter home. Now they were expecting their first child in May. Wilderness was not her element, so she was grateful for this excuse to stay home; otherwise, she would certainly be at his side.

The group came upon one of the rare clearings on the trail, and Mr. Leonard called for a rest stop. Eight packs hit the ground simultaneously, and each novice backpacker stretched and rubbed muscles they each were sure they had not started with this morning. Two sections of log provided seating for Mr. Leonard, Tammy and Christie. The others seated themselves on the damp earth and leaned against packs, trees, or both. Mr. Leonard pulled from his pack a Ziploc filled with gorp and passed it around. Energy from the nuts and M&Ms revived the young, and they began to move around, while those older rested where they were and only observed.

Glen leaned toward David, his face posed in the kindly seriousness that foretold a consultation of spiritual importance.

"David, we must look after Brad. I'm afraid he's being left out as usual."

David glanced at Brad across the clearing, standing, finishing the last crumbs from the bag of gorp.

"I had a chance this morning to spend some time with him, but Christie and Tammy dropped back, and he passed them. He seems to be having a good time anyway," Dave said.

"He seems to have a good time no matter what," Glen said, "but I'd like to see him get more from this trip."

"I'll see what I can do, Glen."

The group gathered their packs and proceeded upward. The day was becoming warmer. Nylon shells and fleece jackets came off. The sky was clear above, and the last of the morning fog had climbed the ridge and disappeared. Spring leaves had not yet arrived at this altitude, and, where the evergreens were not dominant, the sun found many paths to the ground and to the hikers who felt the warmth upon their cheeks and shoulders, a relief from the early morning chill. As the hikers fell into their previous order, David called to Brad to wait for him. He yelled three times before Brad lifted the earphones from his ears. He stood still in the trail, his bulk and his pack a formidable obstacle for Christie and Tammy to pass. Christie eased by, but as Tammy began the maneuver, her shoulder strap caught a loose buckle on Brad's pack and stopped her motion, nearly twisting her off her feet.

"Help!" she yelped, and David rushed forward to steady her until she found her feet.

"What's goin' on?" Brad asked. He had scarcely felt her weight and started to turn around to investigate, nearly whirling her off her feet again.

"Stand still, Brad!" David commanded. He found the point of entanglement, and noting the potential hazards inherent in its anatomical location, called upon Christie to perform the extrication, which she did between fits of laughter. Once freed from her fetter, Tammy quickly tucked away her embarrassment so as not to miss an opportunity to express heartfelt gratitude to Dave the rescuer, laying a hand lightly on his upper arm, a gesture she suddenly revoked when she saw him struggling to contain his laughter. She clinched her pouty lips and punched him squarely in the chest, turning his pent up titter into a full-blown guffaw. Upon this, Tammy spun about on one foot and proceeded up the trail, punching Brad in the upper arm as she passed, eliciting from him a pitiful, "Wud I do?"

David, now back in composure, put an arm on his shoulder.

"Come on, Brad. I'll explain it to you."

David could see the two girls ahead talking and giggling and looking back at him occasionally with smiles or smirks upon their faces.

"Brad, how's it going with you in school these days?" he asked.

"OK, I guess."
"Have you decided what you're going to do after high school?"
"Naw."
"Are you going to college?"
"I dunno. My old man wants me to."
"Do you want to?"
"I dunno."
"If you go to college, where would you want to go?"
"My old man says I oughta go to State Tech."
"But where would you want to go?"
"I dunno."
"Have you prayed about it and asked God to show you what to do, Brad?"
"Yeah, I guess."
"Well, I'll pray for you."

David could see that he was getting nowhere. Besides, the trail was getting steeper, and he felt his lungs begging for air. He would keep trying to talk to Brad – later.

Glen Leonard was also feeling the burn in his chest, so when he led the group out into another clearing, he ordered a halt for lunch. There were no complaints from anyone about stopping, for even those who had not felt the strain of climbing and altitude were feeling the want of a substantial meal in their stomachs. Mrs. Leonard had said that donuts and gorp were inadequate fuel for the labor of backpacking, and these eight now knew she was right.

Mrs. Leonard had packed sandwiches of various types, and Mr. Leonard had carried them. As the hungry youth took their places on the ground and against trees as before, the sandwiches were passed around, and though most were flattened or distorted by the shuffle of Glen's pack, there was no complaint. David had carried a can of soda for each, and he was glad to have the weight out of his pack. The famished tore into the food as soon as it was received. David interrupted the feeding frenzy long enough to say grace. Just as the after-lunch sedation descended, Dave took out a weathered Gideon New Testament and began a talk about the temptation of Christ in the wilderness. After a skillful exposition and a few personal anecdotes, Dave asked the group for examples of how they might apply these truths. Typical teen temptations were named, but Christie had the misfortune of naming the sexual one. Her gaze fell immediately to the ground as she felt the judging gaze of the others burning on her face, and she knew her comment had been taken as a confession. Dave saw her blush and came to her rescue, but it was too late to save her.

The long lunch break had rested the youths but had also allowed *rigor mortis* to set in. Each donned his pack moaning. The trail continued upward now without even a short level or downhill diversion. The hikers were too focused on gulping thin mountain air to bother with conversation, too focused on placing one heavy foot in front of the other to think of anything else. Except one.

Christie was still feeling the pain of her embarrassing blunder more than the pain in her body. After all, I was not thinking of me, she thought, rolling it repeatedly in her mind. I was referring to Tammy and her crush on Pastor David. But everyone thought I was saying I was horny. Besides, lots of kids at school don't think of anything else, especially the guys. She thought about Tammy, how she was always wondering what it would be like on her wedding night…or what it would be like to do it with this person or that…or with Pastor Dave. Christie liked the way it felt when she knew some boy was attracted to her. There wasn't anything wrong with that, was there? Being pretty was a gift from God. That's what her parents said. And her mother taught her that it would be a sin for someone so naturally pretty just to let herself go and not fix her hair or her makeup or wear pretty clothes. But why should anyone think she is a slut, just because she made a comment about a teenage temptation everyone has?

Christie's mind raced from one scenario to another. What did Pastor Dave think of her now? Did he pick that story about temptation just for her? Would Mr. Leonard tell her father what she had said? What did Kevin think? Was she going to the top of Saint Lori's prayer list? Would Kevin think she was something to avoid, a youthful lust to flee? Somehow the worries kept returning to Kevin. Why was she so concerned about him? Christie decided to put it all out of her mind, but Kevin still filled her mind's eye. Her heart pounded with anxiety;

adrenalin pulsed through her veins, accelerating her pace. In her huff, she nearly ran into Kevin's back, where he had stopped to tie a bootlace.

"Whoa, girl!" Kevin jumped up and took a step back.

"Sorry." She didn't know whether he was referring to hiking or sex drive.

"Where'd you get all that energy? Got some secret energy bar?"

These were the first unsolicited words he had spoken to her that she could remember. She stood and stared, doe-eyed. He had such a kind face, such a gentle voice. Christie's embarrassment was quickly forgotten, supplanted by a queer balmy feeling in her core, a visceral emotion that made her feel warm within but spread goosebumps without.

"Are you OK?" Kevin probed.

Christie pulled herself together.

"Yeah, I'm great. You just startled me."

"I startled *you*? I was tying my boot. Did you think I was just another boulder in the trail?"

"Yeah, a redheaded boulder." Christie's wit was returning. "I was going to sit on you."

"We better keep moving or someone's going to run into you."

"I think Brad's behind me. I'd be the loser if that collision ever occurred."

"Where's Tammy? I thought she was your shadow. Your Siamese twin."

"We're just friends. I do lots of stuff without her."

"I've never seen you two apart for five minutes. I thought your name was Christie-n-Tammy!"

Christie smiled inside. She was talking to Kevin. Talking to Kevin! Now that was a novel idea.

"Kevin, you really seem to take to this woods scene. Have you done this sort of thing before?"

"Several times. I was in the Boy Scouts, and my family has done some hiking and camping together. But this is my first time on the Appalachian Trail."

"There's a first time for everything." Christie blushed when she realized she had just set herself up to be misunderstood again...if Kevin was still thinking about that incident at lunch. But he wasn't.

"Yeah, I've always dreamed about this, and now I'm here doing it."

"Is it as good as you expected it would be?" Christie noted the sparkling in his eyes as he spoke. This was serious to him, so she'd best be serious, too.

"Better. Pictures can't do the AT justice."

"The AT?"

"Appalachian Trail."

Way to go Christie. That should have been obvious.

"This is my first time to do anything like this."

"You're kidding, Christie. I wouldn't have guessed. You seem to fit right in. Especially the way you were just zippin' up the trail a minute ago!"

"I was just thinking about things."

"What things? Uh, sorry. It's none of my business."

Christie fumbled around for an answer, but couldn't find one she could say, so she lied.

"I don't remember."

Conversation and the steepening trail slowed their pace, and soon Tammy overtook them.

"Hey Christie, wait up."

Christie was at once disappointed and relieved to regain Tammy's company.

"I thought you were with Pastor Dave."

"Brad is with Pastor Dave. I was alone. Who were you with?"

"Kevin."

Christie turned. Kevin was gone. Oh God! He was embarrassed to be seen with me after my big mouth!

"Kevin who?" Tammy's sarcasm was biting.

"He was just here."

"Sure."

Tammy laughed, Christie pouted and they both continued plodding up the AT, reaching Mt. Collins shelter with daylight to spare. Both had much on their minds, and they were accustomed to telling each other everything. The trail had kept them quiet, and confession was overdue.

"Did I make a fool of myself today or what?" Christie started.

"What are you talking about?" Tammy half-knew, but wanted the confirmation.

"You know. When Pastor David asked for teenage temptations. You could hear a pin drop!"

"You mean when you said 'Sex'?"

"Yeah. When I might as well have stood up and told everybody to watch out because I was in heat!"

Tammy was trying to hold back a giggle. She was truly enjoying the fact that her prudish friend had embarrassed herself in mixed company – church company – about the subject of sex and now was suffering in Victorian fashion for it.

"Christie. I don't think anybody thought that about you. It's just an embarrassing subject to all these puritans. It's such an obvious answer. Everyone was already thinking it. You were just brave enough to say it."

"You mean stupid enough." Christie paused. Maybe Tammy was right, and she was being stupid now. "You didn't think I meant I was tempted to *have* sex did you?"

"Well aren't you? Don't you ever think about it?"

"Not as much as you do, Tammy. Are you really tempted to have sex?"

"Not really. It would be a sin and all. But sometimes I wish it were OK. I don't understand why God made us to want to do it and then would tell us not to," Tammy confided, enjoying the new openness Christie was displaying. Usually this subject shut her up tighter than a clam.

"What do you mean by wanting to do it? Isn't that the same as being tempted?"

"Well, you know. Sometimes when you are near somebody you're attracted to, their looks, their voice, their cologne, just kind of turns you on, and you think about it, and you get those feelings. Like when I'm around Pastor Dave. I can't help it. He gives me chill bumps, but I'm all warm and melting inside. And then…"

"Then what!" It began to dawn on Christie for the first time what had been happening to her. With Kevin.

"Then I get all warm and kind of wet. You know."

Christie knew, and the shock of it left her momentarily speechless.

"What? That's not a sin is it? It's just nature isn't it?" Tammy asked sincerely, seeing the consternation frozen on her innocent friend's face.

"I don't know." Christie gazed blankly past her confidant. Not only had she just realized that she had sexual feelings, but that the feelings had an object. What she had felt with Kevin today was not innocuous schoolgirl affection. It was grownup attraction. Feeling pretty in his presence suddenly ceased to be innocent; it took on ominous, malignant qualities. She would never feel the same about herself or Kevin, as if a small portion of her virginity had passed. Her heart beat rapidly with guilt and fear.

"What's going on, Christie?"

"Kevin Ginnis makes me feel that way."

"Kevin Ginnis? For real? I thought you'd been kind of flirty with him. Do you like him? You gonna try to get him to ask you out?"

"I don't know. I don't think so."

Christie was not really thinking about Tammy's questions or answers. She was thinking about Kevin. He was respectable and good, but she had never thought of dating him. He wasn't the dating kind, was he? She caught sight of him in the clearing laying wood for the fire, gesturing to Daniel, the master firestarter and his apprentice. What was it about him had done this to her? He hadn't tried to woo her as most of the boys at school and church had done. She enjoyed their advances, even encouraged them, but kept them carefully controlled, safely distant, consenting to date only those who met her standards – and her dad's. She had always imagined that Kevin also wanted her but was too shy to show it. Now she wondered if he had even noticed her. Maybe he was too spiritual to care about her good looks. Or maybe she had scared him off, her flirting having created in him the same sense of danger she now felt. But if he felt nothing for her, what of her newly identified feelings for him? What was it about him that was different from her other male interests she now viewed more apathetically than ever? She studied him from this safe distance. His reddish hair, green eyes and boyish countenance; his slender athletic build and the confidence with which he carried himself…

"Christie! Hello-ew! Anybody home!"

"What!" Christie snapped, her cheeks ruddy with sixteen-year-old infatuation.

"Christie's in luv!" Tammy teased, but she knew not to take it any further.

"Promise you won't let on to anyone about this. I've got to think."

"Form a chow line," Glen ordered. Dinner was served and consumed without a word. Talking and complaining did not return until someone mentioned dish crew.

"How do you wash dishes out here?" Daniel asked innocently.

"Volunteer with me and I'll show you," Kevin offered.

"*Carpe Diem!*" Tammy suggested with a nudge to her ribs. Christie ignored her.

With no other volunteers, Lori obliged, and the K.P. went to work. Meanwhile, Dave produced a harmonica, and led the disciples in a few familiar ditties as darkness enveloped the camp. Then he started a prayer around the circle, closing it himself when it returned. The exhausted hikers readied themselves for an early bedtime. They were all sound asleep in no time, hard wooden bunking notwithstanding.

Friday

4
Elkmont

Four o'clock came early to three young women still on California time, but when the alarm blared, the energies of healthy youth overcame the warm soft sleeping bags that fettered them. All three tried to sit up at once, but quarters were too tight in the three-person tent with room for two. Amber poked her head tentatively through the unzipped fly, looking left then right into predawn darkness. She crawled from the tent and stretched, now fully awake in the near freezing air that pierced her polypropylene longjanes. She poked her head back through the tent door, nearly butting heads with Michelle who was preparing her exit.

"Toss me my warm-ups or something. It's freezing out here!" Amber begged through chattering teeth.

Michelle obliged. She and Kim donned theirs while still in the relative warmth of the tent, making use of the extra space Amber had left them. Soon the three were shivering together in the darkness, huddled and bouncing up and down to fire their furnaces. The activity helped, and the excitement of the arrival of the day for which they had longed warmed their bodies even more. They made quick work of dressing for the trail and breaking camp, then piled gear and bodies into the rented Topaz. Michelle took the wheel, and Kim and Amber began to sort their things they had hastily tossed in the back in disarray. They found the juice and energy bars and consumed them on the way, so that, arriving at Newfound Gap, only the stuffing of packs remained. They had planned it this way so that there would be some daylight by which to do the work, rather than fumbling around in campground darkness. Everything moved like clockwork, and they were on the trail shortly past first light.

The packs felt light to three young females so lean and fit. Energy burned in their legs and in their well-tuned hearts and lungs. Arms, legs, hearts and lungs pumped in harmony as they hiked. They were warm now even to the extremities, despite the near-freezing temperature and rising wind. How much better the air felt here than down below, where it was humid and thick, liquid-feeling to breath compared to the California air to which they were accustomed. At this altitude, it was thin, much dryer, and went in and out with ease, energizing, life-giving, insidious pollutants notwithstanding. Michelle called for a break to stretch.

Amber watched with envy as her friends extended their legs above their shoulders as if they had hamstrings made of rubber. Amber did likewise, and no observer would have seen the difference. To Michelle and Kim, it came easily, so naturally, but for Amber it felt like work. They stretched and contorted for fifteen minutes, and all three felt ready to fly.

"We'd best be moving on. We've got twelve to go, guys," Michelle prodded.

Twelve miles to walk. It seemed like a cinch. They could run it in less than three hours. Kim might be able to do it in two. Not with packs of course.

The only thing that would distinguish the three lean, golden-haired athletes from each other at a distance was the color of their fleece jackets. Kim wore cobalt, Michelle a multicolor, and Amber stood out with a bright citrus yellow. But when these came off (and they soon did due to the pace that Kim was setting) they were identical, same tights and jog bras. Even their Jansport packs were the same, bought the same day. They looked like triplets down to their boots, except that Amber was a little shorter than the other two, with sharper curves.

Onward they went, their pace quickening now that all their muscles were loose and primed. Perspiration began to flow, replaced regularly by sips from their biker's bottles conveniently holstered at their hips. Endorphins also began to flow, intoxicating, euphoric; the girls felt on top of the world. It was all they had dreamed it would be. No, they hadn't seen the plants along the way, nor had they noticed the rare views wherever the tree cover broke. Their pace made certain the wildlife kept far away, concealed from view. But they saw, or rather felt, the thing that they were conquering, their eyes trained not to see the details, but to look unerringly toward the finish line.

"You know, I'm surprised we haven't seen anyone else on the trail," Kim observed.

"Me too. Everything I read said this was going to be like a super highway. There weren't even many cars back at the parking lot," Michelle puffed, the longer sentences adding to oxygen debt.

"Maybe it's still too early in the morning."

"Yeah, maybe. Or maybe it's because it's a weekday."

"Well it is OK by me. I don't miss the crowds at home," Kim reflected.

"I would just as soon see a lot of people," Amber chimed in.

"You mean a lot of guys?" Michelle jabbed.

"What's wrong with guys? You have one. I want one," Amber quipped.

"Do you ever think about anything besides guys?"

"You sound like my mother. 'Forget about boys! Get a job! Go to college! Make something of yourself! Don't take any chances! Well, hell. What is life if you're not going to take some chances and live a little?" Amber said.

"Calm down, sweetie! I didn't mean to touch a sore spot," Michelle soothed. "That spot is pretty sore, isn't it?"

"Yes it's sore. That's all I've heard since our senior year. I will do those things when I'm ready in a few years. And I'd do them sooner if she'd stop nagging about them."

"Amber, I just worry sometimes that you're hornier than you are smart," Kim said with friendly compassion.

"Don't you have any interest in men at all, Kim?" Amber parried.

"When the right guy comes along, there'll be nothing that can hold me back. In the mean time, I have plenty to be passionate about. And I'm not wasting this on just anybody!" she said, patting her ass.

"Well I may die tomorrow. I don't want to waste any chances I have waiting to find my Mr. Right. How am I going to find him if I'm not looking?"

"Just don't do anything stupid Amber," Michelle chimed in. "Besides this was supposed to be a trip for us. Can't we think of something else?"

"That's easy for you to say, Michelle, with Greg sitting at home waiting for you, planning to make passionate love to you the minute you get back to his arms! Besides, you know it's just talk anyway. Jesus!"

"How do we know it's just talk when you talk about jumping on every guy you see that fills out his jeans? We know you could use a little affection now and then, what with your mother and her cold ideas and all. I just think that makes you vulnerable," said Michelle.

"Michelle, that's a bunch of bull shit! When was the last time I jumped on a guy? A little flirting never hurt anybody. I have sense enough to know when it's right. I don't need three mothers!"

Michelle turned around just in time to stumble over a large root. Amber cocked her head and laughed.

"You'd better pay more attention to your feet and less attention to my social life!"

"How far do you think we've come so far?" Michelle asked, once they had hiked a little longer.

"There's no way to tell. Two or three miles maybe."

About that time, they came upon the sign to the Road Prong Trail. It indicated they were 1.7 miles from Newfound.

"Only 1.7 miles! We're not making the kind of time you thought, Kim," Michelle said critically.

"Well then. Let's pick up the pace."

They did, not slowing again until they reached Mt. Collins shelter, where it was agreed that a pit stop was necessary. Kim led the way down the side trail to the shelter. Suddenly she slowed, turning her right ear toward the front, her normally fluid movements changing to stiff and tense ones, the muscles in her shoulder and neck defined in the golden morning light.

"What's up?" asked Michelle, sensing that Kim was on full alert.

"I thought I heard voices."

"There are probably people at the shelter."

"People?" chimed Amber with obvious hope in her voice.

A few more paces confirmed the presence of other humans ahead. As the three sauntered into the clearing, they saw a number of teenagers, male and female, scurrying about the place, obvious in their fatigue and confusion. One by one, the teenagers stopped what they were doing and looked up at the newcomers, stunned and silent as if seeing some new specie for the first time.

"Mornin'," Pastor Dave broke the silence, drawing out his vowels in his smooth, friendly, disarming way. He had a triple dose of it, being Southern, a minister and uncommonly good looking.

"Morning," the three responded, amused that their 'morning' was half the length of his.

"Where you ladies from?" Dave asked, knowing it wasn't from 'around here'. The others returned to their work of breaking camp, but not without an occasional glance back at the strangers, sizing them up before risking a social exchange.

"California," Kim answered, "LA area."

"Really? Y'all've come a long way. We're from Memphis. Only took a seven hour drive to get this bunch here."

"We've got you beat. Only took us three hours on a plane and another hour in the car. California must be closer than Memphis!" Michelle teased.

Michelle tossed her pack down and stepped forward into a stretching lunge. Kim and Amber followed. Dave couldn't help thinking this looked like some TV exercise show straight from Hollywood.

"Y'all look like pretty serious hikers."

"No, this is our first overnight. We've just done a few day hikes in the Sierras to get ready for this one," Amber answered. She switched to stretching the other leg, tossing her blond locks onto her back where they slowly slid off her shoulder while she gazed at the young pastor to see if a hook was set. It wasn't. He wasn't even looking.

"Are all you guys together?" Michelle asked.

"Yes," Glen responded.

"Are you some kind of club or something?"

"We're on a youth trip from our church. Dave here is the youth pastor. I'm Glen, just helping out. There's Lori, Brad, Kevin. Over there are Christie and Tammy. Oh, and Daniel." Each acknowledged with a nod and a smile.

"I'm Michelle. This is Kim and this is Amber."

Amber no longer looked confident. She was still blushing from the realization that she had just tried to pick up a minister. He still had not noticed.

"Y'all go to church in California?" Dave asked.

"I go some with my mom," Amber answered, then wished she could reel those words back in. What a setup!

"What kind of church does your mother go to, Amber?" Dave pressed.

Amber resented the question. In fact, she resented being talked to at all at this time by this person.

"Catholic."

"Do you girls have a personal relationship with the Lord Jesus Christ?"

The teenagers were all listening now, shifting slightly closer, circling.

Amber stood up and said, "We really need to be moving on. We've got ten more miles to go today."

While the three were putting on their packs, Lori stepped forward, handed Amber a New Testament and said, "Amber, I want to give you this. Maybe you can read it some tonight. I'm going to pray that God will open your heart while you read it."

"Maybe I will," Amber said sarcastically.

"You guys have a good trip," Kim waved, as the three started up the trail away from the shelter.

"God bless you," they heard behind them as the clearing disappeared.

"Why did they single me out?" Amber asked, eyeing the little green book as if it were a tumor.

"Maybe you need it more than us," Michelle jabbed.

"What a bunch of losers!" Amber said.

"I don't think they are losers at all," Michelle retorted. "Everyone is free to believe what they want to believe, right?"

"Why can't they just keep it to themselves and leave other people the hell alone!"

"Because they don't believe they're supposed to," Kim answered. Kim always had a way of ending controversy.

"I think they're pitiful," Amber said, picking up her pace. "And annoying. I hope they stay way behind us."

From Mount Collins shelter, the trail descended only briefly, before resuming its relentless upward bearing in search of the summit of Clingman's Dome. They talked less and kept their faces forward, set like flints to the wind. Their legs and hearts worked hard, intoxicating their bodies and minds with the excitement of adrenaline and the euphoria of endorphins, their chosen addictions. On they went until perspiration wet their tops and their crotches and left white crusty salt lines about their faces and their armpits. They were beautiful in their bodies, masterpieces over which they had slaved to bring the art to perfection, yet out-of-place, so out-of-place on the trails tunneling through the trees, through nature herself. They were out of place but had not yet discovered it.

With Mount Collins peaking through the leafless trees at the hikers' backs and the Dome disappearing into the clouds in front of them, there Kim, Michelle and Amber first encountered snow. It was patchy at first, but to their surprise, the patches soon began to coalesce into sheets of packed snow deeper than the two-foot holes punched in places by hiking boots when the snow was fresh-fallen. Snow of any amount was beyond their expectation. This was the Southeast, the temperate land, and late March was upon them. This was a photo-op, and they took turns standing in the knee-deep holes and documenting this phenomenon to have proof for the unbelievers at home.

It was here also that they first began to encounter day-hikers, mostly pairs or families of four. Generally, the day hikers passed without a word or even eye contact as strangers do in a shopping mall. One older couple paused to comment on the unseasonably warm weather on the Dome this day. That puzzled the girls further as they had thought already that the air had more bite than they expected in the middle South. They did not know that altitude was equivalent to latitude, and that though they started in Tennessee early this morning, by now, as far as climate was concerned, they had hiked nearly to Canada where the tyranny of winter was not fully overthrown.

The trail led constantly upward, folded into switchbacks to soften its steepness. The girls felt burning in their lungs, hunger for oxygen, weakness of limbs. They were above six thousand feet now, and all their training could not compensate for the scarcity of oxygen and the weight of their packs. Their vulnerability surprised them, angered them and bolstered their resolve to press onward through the pain.

After two miles, the trail leveled, and they found themselves on a ridgeline from which they looked down in all directions. Ahead and to the left there was a bump on the line of the ridge, and upon that bump perched a strange object like a rock. As they neared, it took shape and revealed itself as the concrete observation tower atop Clingman's Dome, recognizable from the photos they had studied. They took the side trail that led to the base of the ramp spiraling up to the mountain's artificial pinnacle. They walked silently up the ramp, upward above the trees where the view opened in every direction. The sky overhead was a deep ocean blue. The sun shown down from its late morning position, glancing off the snow-splashed peaks stretched in two directions, bumpy and disorganized like a huge logging chain laid upon the ground, connected link after link to opposite horizons. In all other directions were other peaks, lower and smoother, arranged like folds in a blanket, diminishing until they gave way to the distant farmlands in the Tennessee Valley. Toward North Carolina, the peaks did not give way, but continued to the horizon, beyond which it seemed the world dropped off to nothing.

The girls from California stood mesmerized by the soft beauty of the eastern mountains, too soft, too subtle, too ineffable for the imperfections of pen or camera to express. There the girls experienced it, saying nothing but knowing everything, sad that it could not be shared with others, joyous that it now was theirs in their hearts to keep.

After the Dome, the trail dropped quickly beneath their feet. Their boots pounded the rocks or slid on snow and mud. When the trail bottomed out at Double Spring Gap they saw the last pair of day hikers they would see that day, and they felt the remoteness. The trail spilled into a clearing, and, in the center of the clearing, nearly on the trail itself sat another three-sided stone shelter. Lunchtime was declared. Three packs hit the ground beside the log bench outside, and the stretching ritual began again.

"Time to check out the toilet area," Michelle said, bending over long legs, straight, blond hair falling forward and brushing the ground in her final hamstring stretch.

"Why don't you two go on? I have the lunch in my pack. I'll have it out and ready to go for you when you get back," Amber said.

"Thanks Amber. My bladder thanks you, too," said Kim.

Michelle and Kim followed the sign to the toilet area, moving lightly now without the weight of packs. Amber meanwhile, dug into her pack and pulled out a large Ziploc containing a pack of StarKist, a boiled egg, a fast food packet of fat-free mayonnaise and one of relish, a stack of crackers and a smaller Ziploc with various cut raw vegetables. She opened the tuna and set about mixing the other components for tuna salad, trail-style. Engrossed in her work, she neither saw nor heard him approach.

"Are you making enough for me?" he asked, startling her so that she nearly sent the delicately balanced containers to the dirt.

Amber turned toward the voice, her translucent face reddening with both fear and embarrassment. She saw a young man standing over her, with an impudent grin between two large dimples, looking at her with dark disarming eyes. She smiled too, and her fear and anger were gone.

"I'm really sorry if I scared you," Andy Young said as he slid his pack from his shoulders.

"You didn't scare me," Amber lied, and nervously brushed a golden strand from her reddened face.

"Are you alone?" Andy asked before he realized the insolence of the question.

"No, there are three of us."

"I didn't think someone like you would be out here all alone," Andy said.

"What do you mean someone like me?"

"Pretty girls are not usually alone. Anywhere. Especially out here," Andy disarmed her thoroughly.

"Am I in some kind of danger? You don't look like one of the bad guys."

"I assure you I'm not."

"Do you go around telling all the girls that they are pretty?" asked Amber.

"Only the pretty ones."

"Are you out here all alone?" Amber asked.

"No. I'm just out here pining away for lost love, the girl who was supposed to be my date on this trip," Andy said with his dark eyes now turning sad, appealing to her pity and receiving it.

Kim and Michelle returned to the clearing, surprised to find that Amber had company. Amber and Andy were too engrossed with each other to notice them until they spoke.

"I think introductions are in order," Michelle stated.

"Michelle, Kim, this is…uh…I don't know your name!" Amber giggled.

"Andy. Andy Young. Glad to meet you, Michelle and Kim." They, too, noted his easy charm. "And I still don't know your name," he said, piercing her once again with his dark eyes.

"Amber."

"Where are y'all from?"

"California. LA," Michelle and Kim answered together. Amber was still entranced by his dark eyes, which Andy had not taken from her even when the others spoke.

"You're from the south, right?" Kim asked.

"Clarksville, Tennessee. But I'm in school at UT."

"UT?" asked Kim.

"University of Tennessee."

"Lunch is served, ladies," Amber said. "I'm taking my turn in the bushes. Keep this guy here, OK?"

"You'll be glad to know, there aren't any bushes. Another one of those high-tech outhouses," said Michelle.

Andy watched Amber walk down the trail and disappear into the trees. She felt his eyes upon her, and channeled all her energy into her stride for him to enjoy, which he did. He then turned toward his pack to retrieve his lunch.

"So Andy, are you out here by yourself?" Michelle asked, forking tuna salad onto a cracker.

"Yes." He did not see a need to beat around the bush. He had already picked the object of his intentions. "Your friend Amber. She got a boyfriend?"

"We wish she did," Michelle quipped.

I am not alone anymore, he thought confidently. Inside Andy smiled broadly, but only a little of it showed on his face.

There were two logs at the fire ring. Michelle and Kim occupied one, so when Amber returned, she had no choice but sit by Andy on the other. Her portion of lunch was passed to her, and she ate it, not saying much. Andy said or did nothing that Amber failed to observe. When Andy had finished the last bite of his bagel and Swiss, he took his water bottle and washed it down, turning his head back so the veins and muscles in his neck stood out. Amber watched his Adam's apple as it moved up and down with each swallow. Amber swooned. Michelle and Kim saw her falling for him, but withheld their usual tactless mockery. This felt different.

"Where are you staying tonight?" Michelle asked for Amber, knowing the question was on her mind but could not ask it.

"Silers Bald. That's just a few miles west."

"That's where we are staying tonight, Andy," Amber said with muffled enthusiasm.

"Great. Now I know I won't be alone there with a bunch of drunk yokels," Andy said.

"Is that much of a problem around here?" Kim asked.

"Only where they can easily tote a cooler from a car. This shelter and the next few are too far from any roads. You're stuck with mostly serious hikers now. Where did y'all start?"

"Newfound Gap. This morning," Michelle said.

"I must have been just behind you the whole way." Andy smiled and added, "You're three tough women, looks like."

"Tough as nails, sweet as honey," Kim answered, and they all laughed.

"Did you run into that bunch of church kids?" Amber asked.

"Yeah, saw them crawling up Clingman's Dome. They were moving pretty slow. They are supposed to make it all the way to this shelter tonight. Hope they do," Andy answered with genuine concern in his eyes.

He could say anything with his eyes, just his eyes, she thought. Her heart raced.

"Did they try to convert you?" asked Kim.

"They might have if they'd had enough breath. Why? Did they try with you?"

"Just a little. Not obnoxious like some. They seemed like pretty nice people. I hope they make it all right," Michelle said.

"Andy, you could hike with us to the shelter if you want to," Amber invited, laying a hand lightly on his arm.

"How could I turn down an invitation to walk with three beautiful California women? Reckon I'll be safe with you three?"

Only as safe as you want to be! Amber thought.

After a rest, four hikers left the clearing at Double Spring Gap, Michelle and Kim taking the lead, followed by Amber and Andy who slowed their pace considerably.

Silers Bald shelter was only a mile and a half up the trail from where they had eaten lunch, but the addition to their party had already upset the balance and flow the three young women from California had been experiencing on the trail until now. The three had hiked together like appendages of the same creature. Michelle and Kim maintained the pace to which they were accustomed, pausing only to insure they were not leaving poor Amber behind entirely, and that only grudgingly, perturbed that the newcomer had distracted her focus from the race to which they were committed.

"Your friends are hiking like this was a marathon. Do they always hike like this?" Andy asked.

"Yes, and I'm glad to have you as an excuse to take it a bit easier," Amber answered.

"So that's what I am, an excuse! Well, I've been an excuse for a lot of things, but this is a first. I'm not so sure I'm honored."

"What if we say you are rescuing a beautiful damsel in distress?"

"Well you are beautiful. Are you distressed?"

Amber wallowed in the compliment while Andy pondered the veracity of it. She was not beautiful in the sense that many of his former girlfriends had been. She was not model-perfect, but there was truly something attractive about her, something that he had latched onto, or rather had latched onto him, something he could not quite form into words. Usually, when confronted with a girl who attracted him, he would well up with confidence. He would feel the powers of his charm come alive, the intensity of this confidence in direct proportion to her physical beauty. With Amber, he felt differently. Her face was plain, her cheeks low and chin slightly withdrawn. Her thick blond hair was no more beautiful than Leigh's. Nor was he seeing it at its best. Her figure was attractive and trim, but he had seen better. He had slept with better! Yet he felt himself drawn to her with an attraction that increased slightly with every step she took and by bounds every time she spoke. She didn't bring out his confidence. In fact, the very vision of her or the sound of her voice weakened him and made him feel as if he wanted to be weak, to be controlled. He shook his head as if to come to his senses, but he could not, nor could he understand what was happening.

The trail began its ascent of Silers Bald, steepening considerably, though the distance to the top was not great. Conversation gave way to labored breathing, but Andy continued to ponder his plight, watching Amber's every movement as her legs reached out, her well-defined muscles clearly visible beneath her tights, flexing to propel her body forward and upward, the powerful yet graceful movements rhythmic like those of a trained dancer.

Andy tried to change his mind about pursuing her, but it was too late. Amber had decided to pursue him the moment he entered the clearing. The hunter had become the prey, and he could not resist. He had never been at the mercy of a woman, but he was now and resigned himself to whatever that meant. He did not wish to win her but to be won.

Shortly, Andy and Amber reached the summit of Silers Bald and the two somber faces of Michelle and Kim, the unwilling forced to wait, who dealt out their chastisement and left the Bald to descend to the shelter tucked below on its other side. Andy sat alone beside Amber.

"Look out there, Andy," Amber said, her green eyes sparkling with life as they surveyed the mountainous horizon clearly visible for three hundred degrees.

"There's the trail we came up, and you can see almost back to the shelter where we ate lunch!" she said gleefully as a child enthralled in new discovery.

"Do you see that big mountain in the middle? That's Clingman's dome."

"Really? What's that one just to the left of it, just behind it?" Amber asked, pointing, and leaning toward Andy so they could both look down the line of her arm, bringing their cheeks perilously close.

"That's Mount Collins. That's the first mountain we climbed after leaving Newfound Gap."

"There's a shelter on that mountain. That's where we saw those church kids."

He could smell her scent as she talked.

"Andy, don't you wish you could just stay out here forever and never go home?"

"I've been thinking I might just do that."

"Wouldn't you get lonely, though? I would. Unless I had someone like you with me."

Andy turned his gaze from the horizon. She was looking up at him, into his eyes, her eyes serious and expectant, demanding a response. He couldn't think of the right words; he couldn't even think. He was frozen in her gaze, transfixed. He couldn't get away. She drew closer and kissed him. They looked at one another, neither saying a word, both surprised by the power of one first kiss.

"I didn't plan to do that," Amber said, breaking the silence at last. "But…"

"But what?"

"But I'm glad I did. I…"

"I'm glad you did, too," Andy said, putting her at ease.

"I didn't want you to think that California girls go around throwing themselves at men. Do Southern girls ever kiss first?" She was blushing and looking at her muddy boots.

"What Southern girls?" Andy said, and drew her chin upward in time to see her pouting lips spread into a dimpling smile. This time he kissed her gently and warmly. Amber felt the heat building in her middle and starting to spread its urgency outward. She pulled away, catching her breath. She kissed him quickly to let him know her withdrawal was only temporary.

"We'd better go catch up with the mother hens before they cut a switch," Amber said, rising and pulling on Andy's arm. He followed obediently, and the two walked down the trail to the shelter, arm-in-arm, but as they found it, they separated, guiltily, as if spying parents awaited their return.

"So we finally caught up with the gazelles," Andy said to Kim and Michelle as he and Amber approached the fire ring.

"It's about time, too," Michelle jabbed.

"The view from Silers Bald was incredible. We just had to take it in for a bit," Amber explained.

"We had to take it in for awhile, too," Kim said, thinking of their forced wait upon its crest, while Andy and Amber caught up.

Andy entered the shelter, and, noticing that Kim and Michelle had already taken the bottom bunks, tossed his backpack on the top, unpacked his bedding and opened the valve on his Therm-a-Rest, which came alive with a hiss and began to crawl toward the end of the bunk as it unrolled itself. Andy wasn't ready to cook, so he poured himself a cup of water and headed to the fire ring to watch the girls in their labors.

Michelle had taken charge as usual since the cooking skills belonged to her. But this evening's fare required little skill: boiling water, opening a vacuum-sealed pouch, emptying its contents into water, letting it sit, serving. It required a little courage to eat however, for the result was unrecognizable, and each one of the girls picked up the empty package to remind herself what the dish was called: Thai Vegetables with Chicken.

Andy watched the proceedings with mild interest while he sipped his water and munched a handful of gorp. He watched Amber, still seeking to learn what had him so hooked. Was it her smile that was so beguiling? No. Was it her green eyes that flashed with mischief that were so bewitching? Maybe. He decided it was something deeper. Something he had not seen in the Barbie-doll dates to which he was accustomed. Amber was alive, confident, on fire. These attributes glowed in her eyes, on her countenance, even on the skin of her arms. They were in her voice. He could feel them. Smell them. Taste them. There was more to discover here than merely what was beneath her clothing. He wanted to undress her soul, to discover its secrets, to know her. And the most amazing thing to him was that he wanted her to do the same with him. He wanted to *be* known. That was a first for Andy Young. Here was a perfect stranger, and he already wanted her to search out and discover his inner secrets. Sure, they had kissed, and it was passionate. But they were still strangers. That would change, though. He could not wait to be alone with her again. But he knew he must put her friends at ease first, so he resigned himself to some social intercourse with them.

"So Andy, you go to Tennessee? What's your major?" Michelle asked.

"Finance."

"Do you get to hike here much?" Kim asked.

"Not as much as I'd like. I could spend all my time up here, but then my grades would drop even lower, and my old man…"

"You have parent-pressure?" Amber picked up the scent quickly. "I have it badly."

"My father just wants me to be as successful as he is. And he measures success with dollar signs."

"How else would a finance major measure success?" Michelle probed.

"I'm not a finance major at heart."

"What then?" Kim asked, and Amber focused all her attention on the forthcoming revelation.

"I want to major in broadcasting."

"Why aren't you, pray tell?" Michelle asked.

"My father doesn't see it as a sure thing. So his support depends on doing what he thinks is a safe bet. Hence finance."

There was an awkward moment of silence as the girls thought over Andy's pitiful position. They were accustomed to making their own decisions in life, Michelle and Kim with the blessing of their parents, Amber exercising her freedom over the protests of her mother. He was unaccustomed to divulging such things where female conquests were at stake.

"Why don't you tell your father you aren't interested and do what your heart says to do?" Michelle asked.

"Simple. He pays for it. Money is control."

"Can't you pay for it yourself? Work your way through?" Kim asked.

"Don't think I haven't thought about it. I'm still thinking about it. My father makes too much for me to get any financial aid, so I'd have to lay out of school a year or more to save enough to go back. I've thought about that a lot. It seems easier to finish this way: get a well-paying job instead of flipping burgers and then go back to school for broadcasting."

"Have you ever talked to your father about it?" Amber asked, sitting close to him, pitying him with her green eyes.

"We've yelled about it together many times. What you don't understand is that you don't talk to my father. He lays the law down. Either you obey it, or you are in rebellion. There's no democracy there. There's not even negotiation. He says do it, and you do it." Andy looked off in the distance, seeing nothing. His smile was gone. His dimples were gone. The confidence was gone from his face. Even his broad shoulders drooped a bit.

"So what do you girls do at home?" he said, brightening up by an act of his will.

"We're gym people," Michelle said with a smile.

"So you are like independently wealthy, and you live at the gym because there's nothing else to do?"

"No, we work at the gym. Kim and I do. Amber's the one who just hangs out."

"So you're independently wealthy then, Amber?"

Amber's embarrassment ran deep.

"No, Andy," she said with a solemnity uncharacteristic for her. "I'm in a position similar to yours, see. My parents want me to go to college. I don't. Not yet anyway. Not until I decide what I want to major in. They want me to go just to be going. Seems an awful waste to me. So I just hang out at the gym, and every once in a while I try to decide what to major in."

Michelle wanted to say that Amber would major in guys. She didn't.

"Andy, you look like you are in pretty good shape. What do you do to stay that way?" Kim asked.

"This. This is my gym. I get up here whenever I can."

Andy made his dinner while the three girls went down the trail toward the spring to clean dishes and bodies. When they returned, they made a clothesline between two trees where they hung dripping black running pants, black Lycra bras and T-shirts in triplicate. They sat down just as Andy began to eat.

"Why did y'all come all the way east for your first backpacking trip? We always think about how we'd like to go west," Andy asked.

"We thought it would be nice to start out somewhere where it wasn't so cold this time of year," Kim said.

"And somewhere there was plenty of water," Michelle added, "so we wouldn't have to carry so much."

"Don't listen to them," Amber said. "The grass was greener, that's all. You don't think much of the place where you grow up. We just wanted to go somewhere different. This is it."

CONVERSATION CONTINUED, BUT as the sun sank and the woods darkened, Andy asked Amber if she would care to go for a walk. She accepted. They excused themselves and headed up the trail in the direction of the Bald. They returned to the spot where they had first kissed. The trees were now black silhouettes, but the sky overhead glowed in ever changing shades of orange, increasing in intensity from east to west as the sinking sun set the fast-moving clouds afire. The sunset itself was not visible behind the trees to their backs, but the hulk of Clingman's Dome lay plainly before them in the dying light, the shape and gray-blue color of a humpback whale.

The peaceful scene served only to augment the frenzied beating in the chests of the two young and virile seekers. The wind was merciless, each gust biting deeper, and the two huddled for warmth and passion. They kissed with deep and prolonged kisses, and held their pounding bodies ever closer. Andy's hands found entrance to Amber's clothing, cupping her bud-like breasts. Once again, she pulled away.

"It's way too cold here to finish this, Andy. Besides, the others said they were coming up here, too. What can we do? I want you so much. You know that, don't you? But not like this."

Andy pondered awhile before answering.

"I've got a tent. Tomorrow we can separate from the others and catch up with them later."

"Where would we go?"

"In the morning we'll look at my map and figure out a place. I don't care where it is as long as I'm alone there with you. Amber, I've never felt like this about anyone before. It's so strange, because I just met you today."

Andy wished he could pull back those words.

"Andy, I feel like I've been waiting for you to come along for years, and when you showed up today I knew it was you."

"You seem different from your friends, Amber."

"They think the world would be just as fun without men. Their idea of an orgasm is running faster than ever before…or doing more reps than they've ever done on the butt machine."

"They've got boyfriends don't they?"

"Michelle does. Kim probably won't ever have one."

"She's not a lesbian is she?"

"She's asexual. It's just that plain."

"What's Michelle like with her boyfriend?"

"She runs him. He's like a lapdog. But she's as excited about sex as she is about wearing a tampon. You know. Something you do when it's time to do it."

Andy laughed, and then Amber laughed too.

"It's really sad, you know. She wouldn't know what love was if it hit her in the face."

"Two great bodies going to waste," Andy mused. "But you've had a great love life, right?"

"No, not so great. Wanting and having are two different things. I just haven't found the right guy I guess."

She looked up into his face to read his responses. Desire was in his eyes, and she determined at that moment that they would figure out how to make this happen.

"What about you?" Amber asked, still watching his eyes.

"What about me?"

"You've had a great love life, haven't you?"

"I've had dates. But I've never been with anyone I felt like I wanted to stay with. I always thought something was wrong with me. You make me feel different, though."

"You tell everyone that the first day you meet them!"

"I've never told anyone that."

He was telling the truth. Amber believed him, and the pounding began inside her again.

"We'd better get on back," Amber said. "So, we're going to plan to run away together tomorrow, right?"

"I'm for it."

"Well, let's go back and dream about it," Amber said.

"What are your friends going to say?" Andy asked as they descended toward the shelter.

"They won't like it. We're inseparable, like triplets. Plus they'll say it isn't sensible. But I don't care. Life's too short to be sensible, right?"

"Right. I hope your friends have a fire going. I'm frozen."

"There won't be any fire with Kim and Michelle around. It's bad for the wilderness. So we don't do fires."

Amber was right. There was no fire, and all were preparing to turn in. After a short public goodnight kiss, Andy and Amber turned in too, but sleep would not come for either of them. The passions in their organs would not rest, and their minds raced with anticipation of its fulfillment. When fleeting moments of sleep did come, they dreamed of each other, only to awake sweaty and out of breath.

5
Birch Springs

Throughout Thursday night, there were sounds about the shelter at Birch Springs. But inside the shelter, Brian and Carrie slept soundly, deaf to the single black bear who had awakened prematurely this early spring, awakened hungry and restless, with the clear memory of food from a careless backpacker found at this location last summer. He paced back and forth and circled the shelter making low guttural sounds as he sniffed the earth and air with his supersensitive nose, reading the story of who and what had passed this place in recent days. He did not attempt to enter the shelter where the two young lovers dreamed of lovemaking and beaches and weddings, hiking and homemaking, and what was to come in their lives together. He did not try the strength of the heavy galvanized mesh and posts guarding the entrance. In his three seasons he had not yet lost his fear of humans, but with that single meal at a backpacker's expense he had begun to associate hikers with food, starting down the path that would lead to nocturnal visitations at a popular campground, then to daylight raids as boldness would grow, unstoppable by entrapments and relocations perpetrated upon him by park rangers who would eventually perform the tragic deed of destroying this magnificent animal.

Brian and Carrie slept on, neither hearing the bear nor feeling the hardness of the boards under their exhausted bodies. It was nearly eight o'clock when the sunshine finally roused them from deepest slumber. Carrie at once felt an urgency and jumped down from the bunk without Brian's help, hastening through the gate and into the woods.

Brian roused slowly, feeling more than she the stiffness in his joints and muscles. He climbed gingerly down the notched post, and headed for his pack containing breakfast. He noticed at once a circle of litter about it, a mixture of rice and trail mix and bits of paper and plastic. He reached into the pack, blindly found the food sack and pulled it out by its draw cord. As he did so, more rice and trail mix showered from a hole in the bottom of the nylon sack, adding to the mess already on the dusty ground. He cupped his hand over the hole and carried it to the bottom bunks where he poured the sack's contents upon the planking. The bag of rice was nearly empty, and the remaining trail mix was not in its Ziploc at all but scattered among the more secure items in the stuff sack. And in addition to the scattered trail mix and rice were the telltale droppings, the signed confession of the nightly thieving shelter mice.

Carrie returned. Together they assessed the damage, which they counted as slight. They still had enough food for the duration of the trip, but they would have to devise something to prevent a reoccurrence.

"What if we could hang it up at night?" Brian asked, and they both looked up toward the rafters. Suddenly the meaning of those cords with sticks and tin cans became painfully obvious.

The two ate breakfast, refilled water bottles and packed their packs. They were on the trail again by ten, much later than planned. Their packs were lighter by far than the day before, lighter by the food they and the mice had eaten, Carrie's wet clothes, Brian's extra clothes and several other items deemed unessential during their grueling uphill struggle the day before. These extras they had stashed at the shelter, planning to retrieve them on their return trip. Still the hip belts and shoulder straps dug painfully where bruises had formed from yesterday's weight, torturing the two during the first mile of hiking, bringing back all the negative and discouraging thoughts of the previous day. But then their muscles loosened, their bruises ceased to cry out and their positive spirits returned.

THE TRAIL CLIMBED gently, gradually toward Doe Knob, a welcome respite from Thursday's grueling uphill battle. The sun was shining down harshly through the cloudless blue sky and leafless trees. There was little wind, just a slight breeze blowing, and the warmth of the sun felt good after a chilly night. Brian was the first to discard his jacket and then his long sleeve shirt as perspiration began to flow. Not long after, Carrie did likewise, stripping down to her spandex sports top. The slight chill spread goosebumps over her body as the crisp air dried the sweat from her skin. But soon her skin was dry and all she felt was the sunshine upon her face and shoulders, warming her muscles and energizing her mind. The heat from the sun was concentrated in the fabric of her black sports bra, encircling her torso in its warm embrace. She thought how nice it would be to find a rock on which to lie down, baring every inch of her tired, sore body to the massaging strokes of sun and breeze. Instead, she pushed onward, following Brian's plodding steps.

As Carrie entered a clearing, she had a sense she was not alone. She glanced over her shoulder and saw, to the extreme right of the clearing, a form, sitting on a stump, alone. The trail was a semicircle around it. She moved slowly, cautiously. At first, he was a boy, then an old man, and finally he appeared as something in between, adolescent qualities mingling with aging ones. He became ageless, timeless. She could imagine that he had always been there. A smallish man, lean and fit, eyes full of youthful energy and awe, their gaze alternating from the trees above to something in his lap. Stroking a grayish goatee, concentrating so hard on his work, he still did not see or hear her. There was an intriguing quality about him, a mystery, a contradiction, beckoning yet unapproachable. She moved closer, and she could see he was typing on a laptop, still oblivious to her presence. Somehow she knew he was writing. A funny place for an author to work, she thought. She smiled nervously. Hi, she said. Hi, he answered. She wanted to say much more to him. To make him say more. But there wasn't any more to say. She suddenly wanted to know everything about him and at once knew that she could know nothing. When she mentioned him to Brian, he denied seeing him. She would think of him often, wondering, and she would feel a little guilty when she did.

Two birds were traveling with them. Overhead a hawk circled, great wings spread wide, lifted up and up by invisible thermals, unnoticed by the couple who were more intent on careful placement of their feet upon the trail than on looking skyward. The other bird followed at a distance, flitting from tree to tree, his song heard first by Carrie who awakened Brian's ears to its beauty. They looked and looked, but they never saw the little music maker, though its canticle followed them for a half mile before they heard it no more.

Near the top of Doe Knob, the wind returned, chilling the hikers, forcing them into long sleeves once more. Each time the wind broke, the sun bore down and sweat rolled. Each visit of the wind chilled them. So the cycle went until mid afternoon when the wind died and did not return, intensifying the heat. Brian and Carrie again shed layers of clothing for the descent into Ekaneetlee Gap. Unlike other gaps on the Appalachian Trail, the land broadened into a large flat area covered with deciduous trees so thick that even though there were no leaves yet at this altitude, they could scarcely see through them. The pitch of the mountains thus hidden, this could be any wooded flatland in Florida. They stopped briefly, and then plodded onward.

As trail fatigue set in again, Carrie's enthusiasm began to wane. That is, until something caught her eye up the trail. Like a mirage, the image of a shelter emerged through the trees.

"We're here already!" Carrie cheered.

"No, hun', this is Mollies Ridge. We're going on to the next one," Brian corrected. Carrie's heart sank. It was just a mirage after all. She stumbled after Brian into the clearing.

They were overdue for lunch. Brian dropped his pack beside a large mossy log, sinking to the ground beside it. Carrie sank beside him. They drank water and ate their pitas and cheese in silence. Carrie's spirit began to revive.

The silence was short-lived, broken by the sound of voices approaching from the direction they had just hiked. A little fear and a little perturbation piqued them for a moment as they watched the trail to see who would emerge. They had gone a day and a half without seeing many other human beings. They weren't sure they wanted to see any now. Two figures with huge packs passed between the trees. Then it became obvious by their size and smooth, lumbering gait, they were men. They were traveling rapidly with long strides, both using twin hiking poles and moving with easy controlled movements, all combining to give the observing couple the sense that the men were skiing rather than hiking. As they neared, details emerged. They were both tall, well built and in their twenties. The one in the lead was white, and the one following was black. They entered the small clearing.

The white man was clean-shaven with a slightly longer-than-military length to his thick sandy brown hair, cropped high above his broad, flat forehead. His brow was thick and bony, his blue eyes set dark and deep above his high cheekbones and long, strong jaw. There were no lines upon his face, yet it was not expressionless. It was calm and self-assured, alert and missing nothing, without fear. His head was carried high by a thick and muscular neck firmly rooted in broad, strong shoulders, clearly visible beneath a Capilene Henley. He was sweating profusely, but showed no signs of fatigue as he set his bulging pack down gently against a tree, and introduced himself as "Railroad." Well Roy Richmond, that is. "Railroad" was his trail handle. His friend was "Spike."

"Railroad Spike. That's cute," Brian said as they shook hands.

"We didn't plan it that way. It just happened," Spike countered. "My real name is Dwight Tucker."

Dwight was a couple of inches taller than Roy, not quite as stout, though obviously well kept and athletic. His coiled black hair was also cut short. His skin was medium brown, smooth and shone in the sun. His dark brown eyes were deep-set. He smiled widely, and his young beardless face already showed deep lines from his nose to the corners of his mouth, and ripples at the corners of his eyes. He was more animated than Roy, but likewise calm and strong.

"I'm Brian and this is my wife Carrie."

"Glad to meet you," Dwight said.

"Where did you start?" Brian asked, wondering how they could look so fresh.

"Fontana," Roy answered.

"I mean this morning," Brian said.

"We did start at Fontana this morning," Dwight said, amused because he knew what Brian was thinking. "Where did you start from?"

"Birch Springs," Brian said sheepishly.

"We're new at this," Carrie said. "You two aren't though, are you?"

"We are thru-hiking," Roy said.

"What's thru-hiking?" Carrie asked.

"We started at Springer Mountain in Georgia, and we'll keep going 'til we get to Maine," Dwight answered.

Brian thought about their day and a half on the trail and marveled.

"How long will it take you to do all that?" Carrie asked.

"We figure three or four months. We started, what Dwight, two weeks ago?" Roy answered. "The first week of March. We're taking it pretty slow right now, about twelve miles a day."

Twelve miles a day! thought Carrie. We're not making half that!

"We'll speed up to about fifteen when spring comes on a little more. We don't want to be too far north this early," Dwight added.

"Yeah, we spent several nights in snow already in North Georgia. We didn't really have any snow gear with us," Roy said. "We've had some pretty cold nights, too. Did you guys bring some warm clothes, I hope?"

"Sure," replied Brian, but he was thinking to himself whether they were warm enough. "It was pretty cold last night."

"Last night was warm compared to a few nights ago," Dwight said. "My water bottles froze in the shelter. I forgot to turn them upside down, so I couldn't get anything out for a couple hours. Roy remembered, though."

"Yeah, and I was good enough to share."

Brian took note of that trick and tucked it away for the future.

"Are you guys section hikers?" asked Dwight.

"Section hikers?" Carrie shrugged.

"Just hiking a piece of the AT," Dwight explained.

"Oh, yes. Just out for four nights," Carrie replied. Brian nudged her with his elbow to remind her of the advice not to tell too much of their itinerary to strangers.

"Well, we'd best be heading on. We like to be in camp while there is still some afternoon left. You know, so we can do our chores. Maybe we will see you guys later," Roy said, stuffing his water bottle back into its pocket.

"It was good meeting you. Good luck," Brian offered.

"Good luck to you, too, Brian and Carrie, right?" said Dwight.

"Right," Carrie smiled and waved. The couple watched the thru-hikers disappear into the woods and silently wondered what kind of people these must be to take on such an adventure and to look as though they were accomplishing it with such ease.

"I read about the people doing that," Brian commented after a while, still looking toward the path that carried them away. "There are quite a few that start out, but a lot of them wash out along the way."

"I would think so. Wouldn't that be embarrassing to tell all our friends and family we were going to do that, have them think we were crazy, then for us to wash out. I wouldn't want to go back home after that."

"I wonder what those guys do that allows them a hunk of time off from work like that," Brian pondered. Carrie knew that temptations were brewing in Brian's competitive mind, but she felt safe that they were but fleeting ones. She sensed that he was embarrassed to find someone doing something better than he could. His ego was challenged.

"I guess we'd better be moving on, too," Carrie said, and tried to stand up. Her muscles had stiffened and refused to cooperate. Brian gave her posterior a push on her second try, and she was successful. He rose to his feet slowly, his muscles also stiff and sore. They hoisted their packs and found that the pain in their bruises had returned. They ignored it, and a few hundred yards down the trail, it went away as before. They wondered what it would be like to do this day after day for four months. Surely the body would adjust, and it would not be miserable every day.

Onward they went, happy to be mere section hikers, happy that the next shelter they would see would be theirs for the night, awaiting them after only two and a half miles. They took it very slowly and rested often, and Carrie was never so glad to see home as she was when she laid eyes on Russell Field shelter. She had taken the lead since lunch because her pace was slowing, and it made it easier for Brian to stay with her. As she came into the clearing, she saw the closed side of the shelter to the left, identical to the ones at Birch Springs and Mollies Ridge, but this one was drier and sunshine glinted off the corrugated metal roof and bathed the grass that grew around it. A welcome relief from mud and dampness, she thought. As she approached the front, she could see that it was occupied. Well, no love in the outdoors tonight, she thought, and she approached with apprehension, straining to discern in the darkness beyond the chain link what manner of strangers these were who would be sharing her abode this night. One of them noticed her reluctant spying.

"Hello there, Carrie. You made it."

"Roy?"

"Yes, come on in."

She was relieved that her sheltermates for the night were not complete strangers. She glanced over her shoulder to make sure her mate was behind her.

"Honey, it's Roy and Dwight."

"Great!" Brian said, blocking his disappointment from creeping into his voice. He too was thinking of the night before.

"We took the top bunk, but if you'd rather switch, it doesn't matter to us," Dwight offered.

"No thanks, the bottom's fine. Carrie had trouble getting up and down at the last one," Brian said.

"We're headed for water, so the place is all yours. Come on Dwight."

"Thanks," Carrie said.

After the two men left, Brian looked at Carrie with a blatant expression of disappointment.

"It's all right, Brian," she said, hugging him. We'll have a lifetime of nights together. Then, realizing her filthy condition, she pulled away.

"What I really want is to get washed up. When they come back, find out where the water is, please. Then you can stand guard for me, OK?"

"Sure," he said with the indolence of a fourteen-year-old who's just been asked to take out the trash, and he turned to begin unpacking his bedding. Carrie did likewise.

Roy and Dwight returned, both bearing a cluster of Nalgene bottles in each hand.

"The spring is down that side trail," Roy said, pointing.

"We're going to wash up," Brian warned.

"It's all yours," Dwight said with a nod and covered his eyes mockingly.

Carrie had gathered her toiletries, warm-ups and a towel, and the two descended to the spring, just hidden from view by the hillside. Carrie felt less than secure with the knowledge that the two men could spy on her if they wished, but the feeling of dampness and dirt in every part of her made the risk acceptable. She removed boots and socks, then peeled her top, pants and underwear from her sticky wet skin. She dipped her pot into the spring, and began to pour its contents over her shoulders. She gasped for breath and shuddered as the icy cold water chilled her torso. She worked with urgency, though, after the initial shock, the water began to feel good, as she was aware of her freshness returning.

Brian watched laconically as she lathered her body with soap. He should have been aroused, but he was not. He was too tired, too sore and too disappointed to allow himself to be drawn into going nowhere. So he watched and sulked and wished she would hurry up.

Carrie dried with the towel and slipped into dry clothes, an act she prolonged as if indulging in the greatest of luxuries, a mundane experience made sublime by two days of trail life. She gathered her things, and the two walked silently back to the shelter.

"You clean up real nice, Miss Carrie," Roy imitated the dialect of a southern black slave.

He did it just to annoy Dwight. Dwight was only slightly annoyed, having grown up apart from the stereotypes Roy was mocking. They were good friends and had been for some time, and they both knew how far they could go with each other in good humor. They both knew that the respect they had for each other superseded their differences, and racial realities were no longer taken seriously between them. Brian and Carrie did not know this and were extremely uncomfortable.

The next hour was spent in preparations for the evening meal, and not much conversation ensued. What little that did was between Brian and Roy with an occasional comparison of cooking equipment or methods. After dinner, Brian watched as Roy and Dwight repacked their food and waste, hanging it from the peculiar ties dangling from the rafters. Brian imitated them, careful not to repeat his accidental offerings to the shelter mice the night before. Brian mentioned building a fire in the fireplace, but Roy and Dwight showed little interest. They suggested that if he wanted a fire, he'd do better to build it in the fire ring outside so they wouldn't turn the shelter into a smokehouse.

So Brian, with Carrie's help, gathered what wood he could find and soon had a warm fire flaming just as the retreating sun allowed the spring chill to rule the air for the night. Soon Roy and Dwight decided they were interested in the fire after all, and brought hot water and tea bags as their offering for admittance into the ring of dancing light.

"I've been wondering since we met y'all back there...what do you two do that allows you this kind of time off?" Brian asked, a little sheepishly.

"I just graduated from college in December, and I don't start work until fall," Dwight answered. "I'm going to teach high school, so, you see, they won't let me work until fall. And they kick you out of the dorm when you graduate, so I'm really homeless. Couldn't think of anything better to do this summer."

"What about you, Roy?"

"I just finished my tour in the Air Force. Since Dwight had this time off, I decided to put off starting work until we could do this hike."

Brian thought about his job at the bank, how that new finance majors were graduating all the time and looking for work, and about the house payments that would begin as soon as Carrie and he returned from this honeymoon and found the home they both wanted. This kind of time off did not seem included in his foreseeable future.

"What did you do in the Air Force?" Carrie asked.

"He's a fly-boy," Dwight answered for Roy.

"A pilot?"

"I just fly transports. Don't start thinking Top Gun or anything exciting," Roy answered.

"Are you going to fly in your new job?" Carrie asked.

"Fed Ex. I flew cargo in the Air Force, so Fed Ex thought they could trust me with theirs."

"Sounds interesting."

"No, Dwight here is going to have the interesting job, teaching teenagers. I'll just be bouncing back and forth like a ping-pong ball. Baltimore to Memphis, Memphis to Baltimore, Balt…"

"Don't whine about boring," Dwight interrupted. "I'll trade paychecks with you any day."

"What are you going to teach, Dwight?" Carrie asked.

"Phys-Ed, health and biology."

"See what I mean about interesting? He's going to teach teenagers about the birds and the bees," Roy chided.

"The teenagers already know about the birds and the bees and a lot more," Carrie defended.

"I'm going to an inner-city school. There's a program that forgives my student loans for doing that," Dwight said.

"Don't listen to him, Carrie. He hasn't talked about anything for years but wanting to go to an inner-city school so he can make a difference," Roy said.

Carrie looked at Dwight with admiration.

"Are you scared?" she asked and made eye contact.

"Scared white," he answered and grinned from ear to ear. "I know what I'm going back to," he added and looked away.

Carrie shifted a little uncomfortably.

"How did you two meet?" Carrie asked in order to change the subject.

"You mean what are a white boy and a black boy doing together in a place like this?" Roy responded with a calming half-grin. "I was zoned to an inner-city school. We played football together. We just got to be good friends."

"I guess that's easier in Baltimore than in Atlanta," Carrie said with a little embarrassment in her blue green eyes.

"Tell her about your father," Dwight prodded.

"My father is bigoted enough for any ten Southerners. So needless to say, he didn't like it when I brought Dwight home. Practically threw him out of the house and me behind him. You would have thought we were getting married or something. I told him I was colorblind. He said I was just plain blind. So we just stayed away from him."

"See, Carrie? No place has a monopoly on prejudice," Dwight said with the gentlest of voices. "And my mother wasn't any better about Roy. I sure wasn't bringing any white boy to my house, or she and my uncle both were going to beat me silly."

"So what about you two? Have you been married long?" Roy asked with his eyes fixed on Brian, forcing him to join the conversation.

"Just married. This is our honeymoon," he said.

"Congratulations," Roy said in concert with Dwight. "Have you two backpacked much together?"

"This is our first trip," Carrie answered.

"First trip together, or first trip?" Dwight probed.

"Both."

"You've got guts, man," Roy said to Brian.

"We compromised and spent the first half of the week on the beach before we came up here," Carrie said.

"You've got guts, too, Carrie. So how do you like it so far?"

"Well, I have to tell you. It's been hard but definitely worth it. I was afraid at first, but I know now I can do it. Brian's been real easy on me, too. That helps. Besides, if we can do this together, we can do anything together, right?" Carrie cast an expectant look at Brian, and he nodded in affirmation.

"How do you go about gearing up for a trip like yours," Brian asked, shifting the attention away from Carrie.

"What kind of gearing up do you mean?" Dwight answered.

"Your food and stuff. You can't carry enough for two thousand miles, can you?"

"We resupply whenever we get close to a town. Sometimes the trail goes right through a town. We can buy stuff there, and we have things mailed to us by friends at home," Dwight answered.

"Mailed to you?" Carrie laughed incredulously.

"Sure," said Roy. "They send the package to the post office in the next town we're due to be in. The postmaster holds it for us until we pick it up. They're really good about that…used to it I guess."

"That makes sense," Brian said. "Will your gear last you all the way?"

"Hope so," Dwight chuckled. "Socks and boots probably won't though, so we both broke in a couple of pairs of new boots and left them with friends. They'll send those only if we ask for them."

"Why all the questions, Brian? Are you going to become thruhikers?" Roy asked.

Brian wasn't sure if he were serious or mocking.

"We might, but we'll just see how the rest of this short trip goes first."

Carrie sipped the last of her tea and pulled her fleece around her, moving closer to Brian for warmth.

Roy, not missing anything, said, "Dwight, why won't you keep me warm like that?"

Carrie blushed.

"You're not as pretty as she is, Roy," Dwight said.

Carrie blushed deeper.

"No, and if I leaned on your cold shoulder, I'd probably freeze to death!"

Dwight looked to the sky. "We've got some clouds moving in tonight. Maybe it won't be so cold."

Carrie looked up at the sky. Countless stars glittered through breaks in the clouds. An eerie bluish yellow glow lit the clouds to the east, faintly at first but growing brighter as a full moon rose behind them. They watched silently for a time.

"Did you ever see a sky like that in Atlanta?" she asked Brian rhetorically.

"Not in Bal'more, either," Roy cut in.

"Balmer?" Brian asked, but quickly understood.

"These clouds are leading some rain in," Dwight said.

"Dwight's my meteorologist. That's why I brought him on this trip."

"Let it rain all it wants to tonight, so long as it's dry and warm for hiking tomorrow," said Brian.

"Spoken like a true section hiker," Roy said.

"After you've been on the trail a week or two through these mountains, you know getting wet is going to happen. The Smokies are a rain forest, you know. Yeah, there's as much annual rainfall here as there is in the Amazon," Dwight said.

"Class, listen up!" Roy said, forever mocking.

The wind interrupted their conversation with a cold biting gust.

"Well, guys, we're going to leave it to you. We'll be up real early tomorrow. We have a bigger hike to do before we get to our shelter for tomorrow night. We'll be crossing Thunderhead too, and it's supposed to be a little tougher. So we may not see you tomorrow. Where are you guys going next?" Roy said.

"Spence Field, just a few miles from here. That's where we turn back," Brian said.

They said their good nights, and Roy and Dwight buried themselves in their down bags. Brian and Carrie stayed awhile by the fire, watching it burn down, watching the wind whipping the embers up and away, watching the backlit clouds flowing by, not feeling a need for words, content for the moment with hypnotic surroundings and the warmth they found in each other's arms.

6
Clingman's Dome

At long last David and Glen had their troops packed and on the march. Sore bodies and tired cranky minds sapped any enthusiasm left from the previous day. As the trail snaked upward toward the Dome, and the sun rose toward its zenith, the youthful brigade became strung out for nearly a mile. Rest breaks became random, further separating the hikers from one another. No one hiked alone; that was against the rules. But they stayed together in slightly cohesive groups of two or three. They found the same patches of snow that Kim, Amber and Michelle had found, but no one marveled, and scarcely a comment was made. They weren't conscious enough.

The top of Clingman's Dome was the designated rendezvous, and the group came together one fragment at a time. When all the fragments were accounted for, lunch was passed out. Fuel, water, rest and the knowledge that the trail descended from this location were enough to revive and awaken each somnolent soul to take in the unsurpassable beauty of the sweeping mountainscape encircling Clingman's Dome.

"It feels as though you're on top of the world," Daniel mused from the top of the concrete monolith projecting above the trees.

"You are on top of this part of the world, Daniel," Mr. Leonard said, ruffling Daniel's brown mop with his hand.

"It would be cool to watch the Rapture from here," Daniel mused.

"The only cool place to watch the Rapture is from right in the middle of it," Kevin said.

The eight stayed for some time admiring the work of their Creator, until the sun was slipping downward into the afternoon sky, and pragmatism prompted the leaders onward toward their destination for the night.

The trail at once turned downward, relieving those sets of muscles so overused now for two days. Downhill hiking also relieved the oxygen demand. Everyone felt some measure of energy return, and the group hiked together, conversing along the way. Glen had to fight to hold back the teens who wanted to let gravity have its way with them, for his knees constantly reminded him that he had known better days for downhill hiking.

It wasn't long before Tammy felt a misery beginning in her right ankle. A faint pain began to nag, and each downward step, driving the weight of her body and her pack into that ankle, increased it. She began to lead with her left foot to avoid the pounding shock. Dave, who was taking up the rear, noticed her peculiar gate and slowing pace.

"Is something wrong, Tammy?" Dave asked when he had nearly run into her.

"It's my ankle. It's getting sore," she answered, hanging her head and pursing her lips.

"Let's try tightening your boot laces," Dave suggested.

Tammy sat on a rock in the middle of the trail, while Dave tightened her laces from the bottom up.

"That's not too tight, is it?" he asked. The pain was gone from her face, replaced by indulgence.

"It feels fine. Shouldn't we tighten the other one too, just in case?" she said after an awkward pause during which she was extricating herself from a fantasy in which Dave was proposing on bended knee. He tightened the other, and they continued on, her discomfort vastly improved.

Christie slowed to allow Tammy to catch up.

"What was that all about?" she asked with a mother's scowl.

"My ankle's been hurting, and Pastor Dave was fixing my boot," she said as blandly as she could. "Quiet or he'll hear you."

"Ankle my eye! I've been wondering what kind of excuses you were going to come up with to get his attention," Christie accused.

"I didn't mind the attention, but my ankle really was hurting."

"And now it's all better right?"

"Well, some better."

The afternoon journey was three miles, and the downhill pace brought the hikers from Clingman's Dome to Double Spring Gap shelter with much less time and energy than it took to get them up from the other side. They arrived weary and hungry, with just enough daylight left for dinner.

After dinner was consumed and dish duties were done, the group settled themselves about the blazing fire in its ring of light: tired, sore and contented, the day's discomforts behind them. They reveled now in their accomplishment. Dave led the group in a devotional, and initiated a chain of praise and prayer that began with him, circled counterclockwise and finished with him again. There was no need to encourage an early bedtime this night; the need was self-evident, and everyone was ready. Glen latched the gate, and the sounds of sleep began immediately.

Saturday

7
Double Spring Gap

It was past midnight before Tammy fell asleep. She lay awake thinking about Dave, how he stooped before her, took care of her ankle, made her feel special. He had asked her how it was feeling a dozen times since, including just moments before he told all good night. He was the kindest, warmest person she had ever met. God, what a hunk that man was! And he had taken special care of her on the trail. She wondered if he fell asleep thinking of her, thinking about kneeling before her, holding her foot cradled in his hands, wishing he could touch more, but could not…not then.

A firm hand jostled her shoulder.

"Tammy, are you awake? We need to talk."

It was Dave. Her heart leapt. He held his finger to his lips and motioned for her to follow. She rose and did as he bade her. She followed him barefooted through the gate, which was already standing open. The full moon shone brightly through the black sky, and she could see plainly that he was leading her down the moonlit path into the woods. The moonlight flickered through the trees and onto her long white nightgown, which fluttered with the breeze, the warm breeze, which tousled her hair. David led her silently, on and on, until at last they came to an opening in the trees and out onto a stone outcropping, which overlooked the valley beneath, flooded with eerie blue light dancing off the mountains surrounding it. The stars were innumerable, bright, twinkling.

David took her by her willing shoulders, looked into her eyes and spoke of his love for her, how that he knew she wanted him, how in the morning all the world would know that she was the only woman for him, the one true love of his life. Then he kissed her, and slipped her gown off her shoulders, laid her down and kissed her everywhere, and made love to her under the full moon, on that great stone cushioned with thick cool moss, high above the valley beneath.

When Tammy woke, her heart was pounding. She pulled herself out of her confusion. What was real and what was dream? Oh, the letdown of reality! She looked and listened for the others; they were all still sound asleep. This was her secret she would share with no one, not even Christie. Not even God, for if she talked to him, she would have to feel that this was a sin, and confess and repent. And it felt too good to be a sin. She felt a void, a longing, a disappointment, first that it was merely a dream, second that the dream had ended. She tried and tried to go back to sleep if perchance the dream would continue. She could tell Dave how wonderful he had been, and she could hold him and feel it all start again. But she could not sleep. She felt the blood racing in her head and down her arms and legs. She dreaded the morning all through the blackness of that night, for then the dream would be lost forever, and she would have to face the boredom of reality, another day on the trail trudging step over step with her pack on her back, Dave behind her where she could not see him or talk to him, Christie's very sight reminding her how bad she was, rotten with sin, condemned by every glance, judged by every word.

No, she could not face another day like that on the trail. She thought and strained for some idea, some stroke of creativity, how she could turn her dream into reality. Yes, she wanted him. She would be content no more with fantasy. He was now the object of her designs. But how? A plan did not come, but morning did, and with it, a dark blanket of despair spread over her and gripped her. She shook it off, determined she would have her way, someday, somehow.

When the others began to stir, Tammy unzipped her bag, struggling to pull herself out of it as a butterfly emerging from its chrysalis. She placed her feet upon the ground and stood, but when she did, a pain shot up one leg, and she crumpled to the ground with a cry of agony. This brought Glen, Dave and Christie abruptly to full consciousness as the three rushed to her aid.

"What's the matter, Tammy?" Dave asked.

She did not speak, but answered by pulling up the leg of her warm-ups to reveal an ankle swollen twice its normal size.

"You poor thing!" Christie exclaimed, panged now with guilt, for she remembered accusing her yesterday of malingering.

"Let's get her outside where we can get a good look at the situation," Glen suggested, and he and Dave each took a side. She hopped along with each arm on their shoulders. They brought her to the log outside the shelter where the ankle could be examined in the dim gray light of a foggy dawn. Christie thoughtfully placed her jacket around Tammy's shivering shoulders.

"This ankle's got a bad sprain," Glen said, looking up at Dave with the concern of a country doctor. "I don't think it's broken, or she couldn't have continued walking on it."

Dave looked at the swollen thing, purple on the outside, puffy all the way to the toes.

"She can't hike on this foot today, Glen," he said, sorry he had not taken it more seriously the day before.

"What it needs is some ice," Glen said.

"Where are we going to get that out here?" Dave asked.

"The spring," Kevin said, who had now joined the crowd.

"Yeah, the spring," Christie said, her adoration of Kevin increasing again.

"We'll have to get her down to it. We don't have a container big enough to bring water back in," Glen said.

"How's it feeling now, young lady?" Dave asked with his characteristic concern. She had been feeling like a patient surrounded by doctors discussing her case as if she could not hear them.

"It doesn't hurt unless I put weight on it. I didn't even know it was like this until I stood on it when I tried to get up."

"Sometimes sprains are like that. We should have soaked it last night. But we didn't know…" Dave said, lifting her to her feet again.

Glen and Dave helped her down the hill toward the spring. Tammy stumbled a few times, each time in Dave's direction.

As soon as they came over the edge and started down, a strong wind met them, nearly causing them all to lose balance and blowing a cap off one or two heads. The buttresses of the mountain channeled the wind like a wind tunnel, blowing forcefully up one side of the gap and down the other. At other gaps, the wind was strongest at its top. At the top of this gap, there was no wind: it blew up and overhead by a trajectory that missed the gap itself. So no one expected the wind until starting down toward the spring. All the youth except Tammy were studying this phenomenon. She was studying how to catch her breath as her ankle was thrust into the icy water.

"You need to keep it in for twenty minutes," Glen prescribed, and he and Dave began to discuss the implications of the injury. They thought they were out of earshot, but through tricks of the wind, Tammy heard every word.

"I don't think she'll be hiking on that for at least a day or two. And even then it will be very slow going," Glen said.

"We've got to keep to the schedule though, or we won't reach Elkmont before the food runs out," Dave said.

"We'd better take a few on schedule, and the rest stay here until she's mobile."

"Glen, if we do that we'll still run out of food. The only answer is for most of the group to go ahead as planned, and Tammy and one of us stay here until she's mobile. Turning back is no solution either. We're pretty close to half way and the hardest hiking is behind us," Dave reasoned.

"OK, but I think I'd better stay behind. It would be more proper, don't you think?" Glen said.

"You're right, Glen. Besides, I've got the devotional planned for each day," Dave said.

Tammy sank.

"Dave."

"Yes, Glen."

"I can't stay. I have to be in a meeting on Monday. There is no way I can miss it. You'll have to stay. If it comes down to it, Louise can take me to the airport in Knoxville, and I'll fly back. She can wait until the whole group's together and drive everyone back."

Tammy nearly jumped out of the spring and danced a jig.

"Then it's decided, Glen. I will stay with Tammy here. You take the rest of the group on, and we'll catch up when we can. We'll keep someone else behind for a chaperone, OK?"

"G<small>ROUP, GATHER</small> 'R<small>OUND</small>," Glen called out. "Looks like Tammy's not going to be traveling today. Dave is going to have to stay with her. We need one more person to volunteer to stay behind and help. Lori, would you be willing…"

"I'll stay behind, Mr. Leonard," Christie volunteered.

Glen looked at Dave questioningly.

"Thanks Christie. You'll be a big help. Tammy will need a lot of help and company, too, I think," Dave approved, relieved that Christie would be staying. He knew the two were close, and having her there would take the social pressure off him.

Glen and Dave led all but Tammy and Christie back to the shelter where they repacked according to the anticipated needs of the two parties and reviewed the new plans with everyone. Then Glen returned to the two girls at the spring and helped the crippled one up the hill to the shelter to rejoin the group, which was preparing to down breakfast and hit the trail. After breakfast, Dave prayed and asked God to watch over the sheep that were scattering, to give courage and protection and to heal Tammy's wound quickly. And thus they parted, Kevin in the lead and Glen bringing up the rear. Dave, Tammy and Christie watched silently as the column marched out of sight.

8
Silers Bald

In the predawn hours on Saturday, a thunderstorm, creeping up the Appalachian Trail from the west, let loose without a warning directly over Silers Bald shelter, with thunder that vibrated the corrugated sheet metal roof like a large bass drum, and with lightning that flashed about from all directions at once, and no direction in particular, diffused by the rain and the fog that whipped by the open front of the shelter at the speed of the flight of doves. By the time the hail began, the occupants of the shelter were fully alert, neither desiring nor possessing any reason to come out of their sleeping bags.

They sat and watched, hoping nature's anger would come to a quick end. Soon it did with the first light of dawn, the storm changing abruptly to drizzle and fog so dense that it seemed as if the world had ceased to exist beyond the trees whose silhouettes were barely visible. Those who ventured into the soup to heed the morning calls of nature wondered whether they would find their way to the shelter again. They did, and in its protection, preparations for breakfast were underway.

"I hope this fog lifts soon," Michelle said. "We can't afford to hang around the shelter, today of all days."

"Why is that, Michelle? Today's hike is a little shorter than yesterday," Kim asked, trail map in hand.

"Today is the roughest terrain that we will cover, so it will probably take longer," Michelle answered.

"You'd better hope this storm moves out. A lot of that rugged terrain is out in the open where you don't want to be in a thunderstorm," Andy said. "They don't call it Thunderhead for nothing."

The fog began to lift by the time breakfast was finished and packs were packed, but the visibility was still too poor for the hikers to set out. So the group sat, waited and talked. Amber headed to the spring to fill her bottles, and Andy decided it was time to fill his, too. He caught up with her at the water source.

"Good morning!" he said as he slipped his arms about her waist from behind, startling her.

"Morning to you! Did you follow me just to scare the hell out of me?"

"Yes, and to tell you I've got a plan."

"A plan? Really? Tell me."

Andy unfolded his trail map and laid out his scheme to Amber.

"See this valley as it falls away on the right side of the trail? Down here we pick up a stream. We can make camp beside it here in this valley. Nobody on earth will know we are there. We'll be as alone as Adam and Eve," Andy said with boyish excitement.

"Coo-wool," Amber said, feeling that she couldn't wait to have him alone to herself. "But then what?" she asked, under the influence of a little bit of practicality.

"Look at this stream. If we follow it further down, we'll pick up a trail that will lead us here, then here and finally to Elkmont. I can call and get a friend to pick us up at Elkmont."

"Andy, our plan had us hiking down from Spence here, spending the night at campsite 19 then 24 and looping back up to Newfound where the car is. We could join back up with them here at 24. Look how close we would be to it! That's a great plan, Andy!" she exclaimed and kissed him on his stubbly cheek. "Ouch! I'll do it only if you promise to shave!"

"I don't have a razor with me."

"I've got one. You can use it. Deal?"

"Deal. Let's go tell the others"

Amber looked downcast, her pouty lower lip extended.

"What?"

"They're going to give me hell for this," Amber said.

"You what?" Michelle flew into a rage. "You slut! You're not splitting the group up for a roll in the hay, are you?"

"It's not like that, Michelle," Amber protested, turning away, tears pooling but not overflowing.

Michelle stood firm, erect, arms folded across her chest, foot tapping impatiently. Her face was drawn into a point, making her look much older and more mature than her twenty-one years.

"I'm sorry, Amber, I didn't mean that. It's just not right for you to split the group up like this."

"Amber, it's dangerous what you're talking about doing," Kim stepped in with much more understanding in her voice. "Leaving the trail is not wise. And besides, I know you like Andy a lot. I wouldn't mind following him into the woods either. But you don't really know him…"

"I know him! You wouldn't understand. I know him like I haven't known anyone else. I've always known him!"

Michelle and Kim realized that their entreaties were futile: Amber had made up her mind. So the three reviewed the plans and agreed that a separation of only two nights was not so bad and that they would finish the hike together.

They donned their packs and headed down the trail into the thinning fog. Within moments they came to the parting place.

"Are you sure you want to do this?" Michelle asked one last time.

"Yes," Amber stated firmly.

"Take care of her, Andy," Kim said, and hugged Amber.

Amber followed Andy as he made a right turn off the worn trail, downward into the trees where no path existed. Michelle and Kim watched them disappear, and then continued down the well-traveled trail toward the west.

THE WAY DOWN the valley was much steeper and more treacherous than Andy had imagined from the map. The route was littered with mossy stones, slick and wet from the morning rain, and they rolled when stepped upon. Much of the way down was spent sitting and sliding. The peril only served to intensify the couple's senses of anticipation. What they were doing was dangerous, forbidden and foolhardy, but at its end lay ecstasy.

When they were beginning to doubt the map's trustworthiness, they finally reached the stream, albeit a tiny trickle. They followed its course over root and boulder, its magnitude growing as it meandered downward, fed by the leaking heart of the mountain. Along its way, the ubiquitous rhododendrons grew, so thick in places that they could hardly pass. After an hour, they had covered very little distance, but that did not matter, for they wanted to make camp and have each other before they neared the developed trail that would extricate them easily from the wilderness when their soiree was over.

At last, a small flat place was found above the stream, hemmed in on all sides by hemlocks and rhododendrons. The sun had broken through the fog still hanging lightly overhead, and its rays, like spotlights from heaven slicing through the branches, scattered itself upon the ground where layers and layers of hemlock needles had been building a thick soft mattress for decades.

"It looks like a cathedral," Amber said, framing a memory in her mind: shafts of sunlight shooting from windows in the dome of St. Peter's to the alter beneath. The picture was well imprinted while on her pilgrimage to Rome with her mother in three years before.

"This is what we are looking for," Andy said, considering its pragmatic merits: close enough to water for convenience, high enough above it for safety from gully washers, private.

Andy began to lay out the bedrolls on the ground, and bade Amber to lie beside him, but she refused, desiring first to wash, then for Andy to keep his promise to shave. She returned to the stream and removed her clothes, shivering in the chill morning air, taut muscles quivering and tensing. She sat down in a pool of icy water, formed where the tiny stream dropped two feet over a huge hemlock root, its flow dammed six feet downstream by another. It was just the size of a hot tub, but it didn't feel at all like one. Amber gathered all of her willpower to submerge herself. As soon as she did, she began to feel refreshed and rejuvenated. She stood and washed her body until she felt clean again. She shaved everywhere, the razor seeming to yank half the hairs out by the roots, and she was left with several reddening patches of razor burn. She walked naked back to Andy and handed him her razor.

"Your turn," she said.

He stood mesmerized. She was no leaner than others he had dated. Curves no rounder, breasts no bigger. But never had he seen the muscles of a woman toned so well, not hidden by even an ounce of fat. Even her buttocks flexed when she moved, with just a hint of a quiver. But she still had the shape of a woman, muscles rock-hard but small, round, agile.

"It's your turn, Andy," she repeated. He took the razor and left, and Amber lay down in the sun to warm her frozen flesh. Andy returned, naked, shrunken from the cold.

"I can make you grow big again," Amber said, and pulled him to her on the mat. When she made good her boast, she asked him for the protection she was sure he had brought. He hadn't. Something inside her said stop, but the rest of her brushed the caution aside while her passion flared and engulfed her. There was no future any more as she gave herself completely to this moment. She felt Andy enter her, and primeval forces within her rushed outward and over her, her back and pelvis rocking in clonic undulations as though the parts of her were independent, rocking to and fro' to his thrusts, until she froze, arched beneath him with every muscle contracted in tonic ecstasy, gripping her, holding her, until at last the forces released her in one final explosive moment.

The two fell apart, gasping for air like fish out of water, sweat dripping off their youthful bodies in the cold mountain air. Neither had known this kind of passion. Neither had been so hungry for another, and neither had felt the anticipation grow so powerfully that the wait, though less than a day, had seemed eternal. Neither had touched another without latex between.

They lay beside one another, not speaking, until their breathing returned to normal. Then Amber rolled her body over against Andy's, her breasts pressed against his chest, her lean thigh lifted over his. She kissed him, their tongues entwining, the taste of him and the feel of his body under hers igniting her again. Her free right hand searched his body and found the part of him she wanted and stroked until he began to throb with new life in her hand. She raised her leg over him, and spread her lips over him engulfing him, rotating her hips forward, pressing bone against bone so that she felt him deep in her core. She moved her hips back and forth, in and out, and around, the rippling muscles of her abdomen enabling her to move her hips in ways Andy had never imagined, as if she were performing an ancient and exotic dance on top of him. This time she felt his climax explode inside of her, warm, wet, forceful. She had never felt that before, and it brought her quickly to climax again, not once or twice, but in a series of crises so gripping that she thought she would break him. One final yearlong minute, and then she relaxed. They did not part. She lay on him, kissing him, until he slid from within her, and it was over.

Moments later both felt a chill sweep over them. The sun that had warmed them had again hidden its face behind the clouds, and a cold damp breeze rushed up the valley and raised goosebumps on their perspiring naked flesh.

"We'd better get dressed, I suppose," Amber said as she began to look for her clothing with no clue where to find it.

"We'd better get a tent up, too. Those clouds look like more rain on the way," Andy said, and a clap of thunder sounded distantly in agreement.

The site they had chosen was just large enough for Andy's tent and a little room to move around it. Andy pitched the tent while Amber watched and admired her new lover, proud of herself for such a find. She could still feel the fullness of him filling her, and the wetness he had left behind. Her pills would keep her safe from pregnancy, but what of disease against which she had always been so careful to protect herself? Why had she been so unconcerned this time? She brushed those worries away with the thought that she could think of nothing else worth dying over.

With the tent set up, Andy tossed their packs inside, and all was ready for the couple just as the leading raindrops from the coming storm began to fall. This storm was not as violent as the first, but it was followed by wave after wave of smaller storms, sequestering the couple in the close quarters the tent provided. There was scarcely room for Andy to sit up, so the two lay close to one another and talked.

"Andy, when this trip is over will you still want to see me?" Amber asked, looking into his eyes and running her hand over the strength of his shoulder.

"Of course, Amber. This ain't no one night stand for me."

"You mean we will stay together? What do you think of long distance relationships?"

"I've never had one. But we'll work it out somehow."

"Andy, you know my parents have been hounding me to go to college. What would you think if I enrolled at Tennessee?"

"Your parents wouldn't like that."

"Sure they'd rather me go somewhere close to home, but they're so desperate for me to go to college, they'd let me go anywhere, no matter the distance or the cost."

"There aren't many Californians at UT."

"You sound like you're trying to talk me out of it, Andy," she said, her green eyes demanding a response. "Do you love me Andy?"

Those words had always caused Andy to bolt. This time he did not bolt but carefully considered his response.

"Amber, I've never met a girl that does me the way you do." The answer was uncharacteristically honest and from his heart.

"You mean you've never been fucked like that before?" Amber pulled away to pout. Andy held her tight.

"No, Amber. Sex was great, but I'm talking about inside. I've never been torn up inside like this over anyone I've met. Hell, I feel like I'd follow you anywhere just to be with you, and here you are talking about coming to Tennessee."

"So you do love me?"

"I really care about you, Amber."

She looked downcast again.

"Yes, I love you."

These were virgin words for Andy.

"Andy, I love you."

They held each other in tight embrace, both feeling the pounding of two hearts, the warmth of breath on the cheek, drinking in the smell and taste of each other. They remained entwined but not speaking for half an hour, contented.

Outside the thin walls of the tent, the rain had stopped, and nature was strangely silent as if listening to their beating hearts. Then the wind began to blow, whispering gently through the hemlock bows, steadily growing to a moaning crescendo that shook the sides of the tent and pelted it with twigs and needles from the trees above. The air was warm, then cold, then warm again. The wind rose in a howling cry and the trees pitched wildly back and forth, sending fear into the souls of the two huddled in embrace below.

"It's just a storm, Amber. There's nothing to be afraid of," Andy repeated and held her tight. But he too was afraid.

The thunder began, distant guttural rumbling at first, quickly transforming itself to ground-shaking violence as the tempest spilled over the valley wall to unleash its fury on the floor of the hollow where they lay clinging to one another, avowing to each other aloud that there was no place they would rather be.

The rain came in sheets. Then there was a loud crack above, distinctly different from the thunder, for the wind had torn from the trunk of a mighty hemlock a limb that swung from its attachment as it fell and grazed the tent in its path, shredding the fabric with the spears of its broken branches. Wind and rain burst through the tent's torn roof, drenching the occupants and their possessions. Andy and Amber scrambled for their rain parkas, but it was too late. Their clothing and bedding were soaked. There was nothing they could do but huddle beneath their parkas until the storm left them, which it did as quickly as it had arrived, swept away by the winds to wreak havoc elsewhere. The storm rumbled away in the distance, and the chaotic wind calmed itself, shifting from the west to north, steady and cool, filling the valley with fog.

Andy and Amber emerged from the shredded tent shivering. They marveled at the close call that the huge branch had given them. The tent was useless, and their bedding was soaked. The clothes they were wearing were dripping. They assessed the condition of their packs. When they had removed their bedding, they had left the packs open, and now the contents were sopping wet. Amber's fleece jacket, her cotton tee and her sweats were all soaked. At least her synthetic tights and jacket would dry quickly. All of Andy's clothing was cotton except his rain parka, and everything was dripping. His sweats that he used for sleeping were in a plastic bag, though, and were dry. He gave these to Amber, and she put them on.

"We'd better set up a clothesline and start a fire," Andy said. "It's going to be OK, Amber," he added, when he saw that her eyes had welled up with tears and that she stood hugging herself and rocking aimlessly.

So the clothing was hung to dry, except what they had on, which afforded little protection against the dropping temperature and the persistent wind. With shivering hands, Andy attempted to light a fire using all but one of his matches trying. The wind blew them out before he could kindle the wet tinder.

"Amber, have you got any matches?"

"Yes," she said, but then she returned with a look of utter dejection holding out a box of strike-anywheres that were so wet that the red from the tips bled down over her trembling fingers. Andy's had been in a watertight container. Neither had brought a lighter or a candle.

"We'd better save this last match until the wind dies down," Andy said. "If it doesn't, we can walk out of here this afternoon."

"Everything's ruined, Andy! This was heaven!"

"Nothing's ruined. I've got the keys to my friend Paul's apartment. We can go there and be alone. Or we'll get dry things and come back. It's not ruined. OK?"

"OK," she assented and indulged him in a deep kiss.

"Hold me. I'm still cold." Her sweats were soaking up the dampness like a sponge.

Andy cut some hemlock boughs and made a pallet where they could huddle together for warmth. He was sure the tent would dry out by night and he could drape the ground cloth over the top. If they could get a fire going later, they would stay. Lying on the pallet, they kindled their youthful passions again, though it was too cold to remove clothing. With passion came optimism. Everything was going to work out just fine, they told themselves.

9
Thunderhead

Michelle felt something die inside her as she watched Amber following Andy, picking their way down the steep embankment into the trees below. Even after they disappeared, she stood planted, staring at the place she last saw them, staring at their afterimage in her mind, trying desperately to hold on to it as it faded into nothingness.

"Are you waiting for her to come back?" Kim asked pointedly.

"Maybe. You know what she is doing is stupid."

"When did that ever stop Amber from doing anything she'd made up her mind to do? Remember that time…"

"I guess you're right. Let's get going," Michelle conceded, but as they started on their way down the trail, Michelle could not keep herself from looking over her shoulder two or three more times.

The fog continued to thin, and sunshine attempted to pierce the clouds in several places, but no sooner than it succeeded, the escaping rays were quickly cut by the swirling clouds, and the landscape remained closed in, pewter and surreal. Thunder rumbled distantly in all directions, but to Kim and Michelle's relief, it seemed to be waning in the direction they were traveling. Worries for their wayward friend and Andy's comments about Thunderhead weighed heavily together. These anxieties and the still fresh pain of Amber's desertion damped their usually buoyant tempers, and the barbiturate effects depressed their pace. At a time when they should be pressing toward their destination with quickening steps, they felt the growing distance between them and Amber pulling backward, slowing their forward momentum like an inseverable elastic cord that connected them. But they pressed onward, bucking at it as they had been trained to do as athletes, when the body says 'No!' and the mind must push through to the other side.

The trail passed downward from Silers Bald for another mile, and Amber's treason still gripped the girls, slowly, imperceptibly transforming their inner feelings from worry and hurt to anger. The anger worked in their favor: they converted the energy it fostered to speed, reaching at last their racer's pace at which mind and body, heart and lungs, muscle and joints, worked efficiently together as one, covering the greatest distance with the least energy. By midmorning, the wind, which had been at their faces, shifted to their right, and, though increasing in its force and decreasing in temperature, it no longer hindered their movement. The cool air served to invigorate, and at last, they willed Amber from their minds and returned to the full enjoyment of their circumstances.

At Buckeye Gap, the trail upturned steeply, leading them to the pointed prominence of Cold Spring Knob. Its top would have been a natural resting place, but the wind bit through their tights, spurring them quickly onward. Then the trail turned somewhat toward the southwest, putting the wind mercifully at their backs. From Cold Spring Knob, the trail took them up and down over short humps in the ridgeline where it became razor thin. At other times, the trail hugged the side of the mountain, which rose steeply to the left and fell steeply to the right. Sometimes the trail went down, but mostly it went up, the girls comparing the experience to the 'hill' program on the steppers at the gym.

One final steep ascent followed by a short descent brought them to the shelter at Derrick Knob. Within its walls there was no wind, and there the girls rested, stretched and ate their meager lunches of energy bars and dried fruit. With 5.4 miles behind them and 6.0 before them, including Thunderhead, the rest break had to be short, and soon they were again moving quickly toward their goal.

After lunch, the trail grew even more rugged. The steep parts were steeper, the rocky parts rockier. It was their second day on the trail, and, despite their youth, they were feeling the wear and tear in their bodies. But disciplined minds trained to ignore pain pushed the girls onward. The distance covered was their reward, the nearing finish line their motivation. This portion of the hike was the highlight they anticipated, and their bodies were functioning as designed, as sculpted, as trained.

The trees became shorter and shorter, contorted into eerie shapes by years of strong winds. They crossed two very steep peaks, which had no trees at all, their tops crowned with rhododendrons, short-growing, huddling near the ground to shield themselves from the battering of the winds to which they had been exposed the entirety of their tumultuous existence. The winds were strong here even on a moderately calm day, but this day was not such a day, and the wind blew meanly, bitterly cold, having fully shifted now to the north. From one peak to the next, the girls could see the trail laid out before them, leading them toward the greenish-gray mass that was Thunderhead. When they reached the base of the mountain, the trees grew thick again, somewhat protected from the prevailing winds by the bulk of the mountain. The wind this day was not prevailing, and it whistled and moaned as it tested the trees' ability to stand against it. The clouds roared by, dark and heavy, and there at the base of Thunderhead, a mist began to fall, or rather float, for the wind did not let the droplets reach the ground before traveling some distance horizontally.

Kim and Michelle shivered against the combined assault of cold wind and rain stinging their faces. The quantity of rain was not great but enough to wet the trees and rocks, rendering each step on Thunderhead a treacherous one. The trail turned right then left then right again in inexorable switchbacks, but always upward. And then it happened.

Kim was leading. She heard behind her a thud and a cry, which hit her like lightning from her ears to her soul. She turned, and there lay Michelle crumpled on the ground, pinned by her pack, writhing, her face red and contorted with pain. Kim leapt to her and started to roll her over, inducing another cringing cry.

Kim saw then to her horror that Michelle's right boot was caught between two roots that held it firmly, and her foot pointed in an impossible direction, her leg angled one way and her body another like a broken doll.

Something in Kim gained strength from the moment, focusing her mind, making appropriate action immediately clear. In a calming voice, she exhorted Michelle to relax, stroking her face with a soothing touch. She then reached and released her sternum strap, then her hip belt, relieving Michelle of the pack's weight.

"Do you hurt anywhere besides your leg?"

"Only the leg," Michelle forced the words through gritted teeth.

"I have to free your foot. It's going to hurt like hell."

Michelle nodded approval, her face still pinned to the wet cold earth by the unnatural twist in her leg. Kim sheepishly grasped the boot with one hand and one root with the other. With all her strength, she tried to move the root without moving the boot but failed. The root gave some but not enough. Kim took a deep breath and did what she knew she had to do. She moved the root as far as she could, then twisted the boot just enough to release it as Michelle let out another inhuman cry. Her pain subsided somewhat as the leg relaxed, and she lay still face down, quivering and sobbing. Kim covered her with her own parka and held her hand.

"How bad is it?" Michelle whimpered. "I know it's broken."

"I don't see any blood, so it's not compound. It only seems broken in one place."

"What place?"

"Half way up the lower leg."

"Roll me over please"

Kim did so, and another smaller cry emanated from her friend's contorted countenance.

"What are we going to do now?" Michelle asked, knowing that Kim was fully in charge now.

"We'd best get a splint on that leg."

Kim fished in her pack for the first aid kit. She took the wire splint from the kit, carefully wrapped it around the break and tied it in place with two triangular bandages. Then she wrapped the whole with ace bandages. When Michelle moved her leg, the foot flopped almost as independently as before the splint was applied. There's no way she can walk on that, Kim thought. She began to look around for a more old-fashioned splint. Finding nothing that was not too rotten, she was about to cut a green sapling when an idea occurred to her. She returned to her pack and picked up her two hiking poles. These would make wonderful splints, she thought, and measured the size they would need to be, collapsed them accordingly and carefully bound them on either side of Michelle's leg leaving the wire splint in place. The foot was now stabilized.

"Let's see if you can put any weight on it," Kim coached.

She helped Michelle to her feet. She was able to take a few assisted excruciating steps, but quickly she gave out.

Kim and Michelle sat on the ground a few yards up the trail from their packs, trying to think of the best solution to their predicament.

"We could try making crutches out of some tree limbs. Then you wouldn't have to put weight on it."

"If Amber was here, one of you could simply go for help," Michelle said with considerable scorn in her voice.

"There's no use worrying about 'what if,'" Kim admonished. "Why don't I simply stay here with you and wait for someone to come along. Michelle! Are you all right?"

Michelle had lain back on the ground, her face ashen, her eyes glazed over. Kim picked up her wrist. Her pulse was faint and slow. Her hands felt clammy and cold.

"Michelle," she said loudly and lightly slapped her cheeks.

"I'm too…weak…to…"

"Don't try to talk. Just rest."

Shock! That's what was happening. Let's see. Get her warm, that's it. Kim took off her fleece jacket and draped it over Michelle's legs and she tucked her parka around her. Kim was down to her running tights, sports bra and tee shirt. God it's cold! she thought. But Michelle needs these things more. What are we going to do? Somebody will be coming along shortly, right? If they don't stop at that shelter for the night. Oh, God, anyone would stop at that shelter. Get a grip now, Kim. You have to be strong. You have to decide what to do.

Kim lay on the ground close to Michelle to help warm her and herself. She looked at her friend. How could this be happening to them? Michelle's eyes were closed, but the color was returning to her cheeks, faintly. Kim reached to snug the parka around Michelle's neck. What is this on the parka? She looked as little translucent things bounced and disappeared. Her first thought was insects, but it was too cold. Sleet! It was beginning to sleet!

Kim watched for a few moments to see if it would last, but she saw snow mixed with sleet and both were increasing. The ground was turning white. The wind was churning clouds of snowflakes fighting their way downward, melting where the ground was wet, sticking where it was not. The temperature must be right at freezing, and this is the middle of the afternoon, Kim thought. I have to get Michelle where we'll be more protected from the weather. But we have to stay on the trail in case someone comes along. I'll never get her up the trail. We'll have to go down. She kissed Michelle on the cheek and walked alone down the trail. When she came to the first switchback there was a large round boulder as tall as Kim's five-foot-seven stature in the acute angle of the switchback. The boulder curved inward at its base, and the ground was still dry in the hollow beneath its inward curving. The boulder also provided some protection from the north wind.

Kim retrieved their bedding from their packs and made a pallet for Michelle in the crook of the trail under the boulder. She placed their packs on either side of the hollow to block the wind. Now for the hardest part, she thought. Now I have to get Michelle down here. It was not as difficult as she thought it would be, for Michelle had returned to a state of semi-consciousness and giddiness, in which she did not feel the pain of movement so sharply. In fact, she seemed less interested in the pain and more intent on discovering whether Amber had returned and whether her mother had called to check on her leg. Kim was both amused and terrified by her friend's delirium. She helped Michelle to the pallet and zipped her into her sleeping bag. Then she covered her with her own. Snow was now falling hard, and the trail was quickly being covered. Kim could barely even see their footprints in the snow from the spot she had dragged Michelle. With Michelle going into shock rapidly, snow falling so hard, and the day nearly spent, Kim knew she had no choice. She quickly made necessary preparations, and braved herself for the ordeal she faced alone on the trail. She roused Michelle, who seemed a little more lucid now, showed her the food and water she left within her reach, and said goodbye. Michelle objected and reasoned that someone would be along shortly.

"No one will be coming onto Thunderhead today in this weather. They'll stop at the first shelter on either side, and we'll never see them. You rest. I'll be back with help in no time."

"Kim. Which way are you heading?"

"Toward Spence Field."

"That's over Thunderhead. Why don't you go back to that last shelter? What's its name?"

Michelle's voice was trailing off.

"It's downhill after I reach the top of Thunderhead. Besides, it's going toward civilization at Cade's Cove. The other way is getting more remote."

Michelle never heard Kim's answer as she drifted away again.

Kim grabbed the fanny pack she had stuffed with some food, water and dry socks. She took back her fleece and parka and put them on. She left Michelle's parka draped over her sleeping bag. She took the one tarp they had between them and wrapped it carefully around Michelle and under her, knowing that if she got wet, she wouldn't make it through the night. Then Kim started up the trail, and, feeling lighter without the burden of her pack, broke into a slow jog wherever the slippery ground allowed, desperate in her heart to reach help and return in time, fighting back dreadful imaginations and her tears.

The joyful trio of hikers loving life on the trail in the boundless energy of youthful prime yesterday, had become a lone hiker, tired, cold, scared, with one friend broken and freezing in shock, the other hidden off the trail who knows where, with some strange guy who may be a serial killer or escaped mental patient for all they knew. Get a grip, Kim. It's going to turn out all right, but you have to keep your head on tight. It all depends on you girl. Pump those legs, pick'm up now.

Michelle sleepily opened one eye in time to see Kim disappear around a bend in the trail.

10
Russell Field

The crash of thunder brought the four sleeping souls to full wakefulness simultaneously. They peered through the chain link wall into the black darkness beyond. They could not even make out the fire ring just a few feet beyond it.

"You were right," Roy said to Dwight. "You're still my main weather man."

Lightning flashed and rain began to pelt the tin roof of the shelter, slowly at first then bursting into a full drum roll as distant thunder rumbled seemingly from all directions at once.

"What time is it?" Carrie asked sleepily.

"Five thirty," Brian answered after consulting his Indiglo for what seemed an unnecessarily long time.

Too groggy to get up but too disturbed by the storm to go back to sleep, the four lay awake listening to the awesome displays of nature outside. The shelter shook with the torrential rain, wind and the voice of thunder speaking repeatedly with high earsplitting cracks followed by long low guttural reverberations the occupants could feel in their chests. After each flash of lightning, the world was as bright as daylight before fading again to the blackness of night. The storm seemed to last forever, hanging on the very mountaintop where they huddled.

Finally, the storm began to dissipate just as the light of day brought some of the nearby objects into barely recognizable forms. Thunder and flashes continued all around but more distant now, and the rain decreased to a trickle. It was light enough now to see that they were shrouded in fog so thick that even the trees were visible only as dark shapes in the whiteness, which intermittently hid them completely from sight.

"So much for our early start," Dwight said. "We might as well eat and pack up so we'll be ready as soon as this lifts." Roy agreed, and shuffled out of his bag to join Dwight on the dusty dirt floor of the shelter.

Brian and Carrie watched the preparation from the warmth and security of their sleeping bags. They were in no hurry to rise, having only a few miles to go that day.

"What's for breakfast?" Brian asked as Dwight placed a pot of water on the hissing stove.

"Oatmeal. It's always oatmeal. Sometimes the flavor changes, but it's still oatmeal." Dwight bobbed his head in time with his singsong answer.

"Why always oatmeal?" Carrie asked.

"It's very lightweight but good protein and carbs," Dwight answered.

"Keeps him regular," Roy said. "That's the real reason."

By the time breakfast was consumed and packs were repacked, the fog had only thickened and the distant thunder was not so distant. So Roy and Dwight made themselves comfortable sitting on the ground using their packs as backrests. There they sat and talked and waited for the whims of the weather to play out.

Another thunderstorm rolled through, neither as long nor intense as the one that woke them before dawn. When it was past, Brian and Carrie rose, semi-dressed and made their way through misty fog to tend to morning necessities. Returning to the shelter, they prepared their breakfast of cereal and powdered milk, which they ate sitting half on and half in their sleeping bags. The air was quite cold, but eerie spells of warm air came and went.

"This is quite a front," Dwight said, assuming his meteorologist role again. "When all this gets by us, we can expect a beautiful day and a freezing cold night."

"How long will it take to get by?" Brian asked, brushing a damp Cheerio from his sleeping bag.

"The mountain will decide that. In the low flat areas, I can predict that, but the clouds hang on the mountain. How long they hang depends on how fast the upper air currents are moving, how high they are and how deep this storm line is. I've seen them hang around for days."

Brian didn't really listen to the answer.

"It will thin enough for us to hit the trail in an hour or two though," Dwight added.

In that prediction he was right, and by mid-morning Roy and Dwight shouldered their packs, said goodbyes and well-wishes, and the thru-hikers were once again bringing themselves step after step closer to Maine. Brian and Carrie waited in the shelter though, still in no hurry to venture into the uncertainty with only a few relatively flat miles to go before they would reach Spence Field. They decided to wait until after lunch to start for the next shelter.

"Those were pretty interesting guys to spend a night with. I'm glad they were here last night," Brian said.

"I thought you hated having them here," Carrie probed.

"I would rather have spent the night alone with you, but if I had to spend it with someone else, I guess those guys were the next best thing."

"I would rather have spent it alone with you, too," Carrie said, approaching Brian for a proper good morning kiss.

"Really?"

"Yes," she said and ended that part of the conversation with her lips pressed against his.

"We are alone now," Carrie invited. The couple continued the embrace and re-established their lines of communication but did not carry the initiative to the point of lovemaking. After lunch, they, too, hit the trail eastward toward Spence Field.

THE TRAIL BEGAN a slow upward climb immediately as it left Russell Field. The terrain took on a very different look from what Brian and Carrie had traversed in the previous two days. The trees were thinner and grass grew in places beneath them. The land seemed to fall away from each side of the trail, though not dramatically. Even though the trail moved steadily upward, it was not a grueling climb like before, just a gentle slope interspersed with flat expanses. These were swampy even on dry days, but after the torrential morning rains, they were like small ponds. Most of them were spanned by series of three-foot lengths of logs arranged like railroad ties except that they were so close to each other they were touching. This was not easy walking, but they were preferable to the ankle deep mires Brian and Carrie had to cross wherever one of these corduroys was missing.

The wind blew harder as they went, and the air steadily became colder. The fog rushed by them as they hiked. Gradually it thinned until just wisps of fog floated by occasionally. Overhead thick billowing gray clouds darkened the sky. Brian and Carrie came to a place where the land began to slope downward to a relatively open area, a small pass. There the wind howled through the pass and bit into their shivering bodies despite the layers of clothing with which they had armored themselves.

"Snowflakes!" Carrie exclaimed, examining the crystals on the nap of her jacket.

"That's just mist," Brian said incredulously.

"No, it's snow, see?"

A few flakes were now visible in the air swirling about them. Then they heard something rattling on the old fallen leaves that blanketed the forest floor all about them.

"That's sleet, Carrie," Brian observed.

They both removed their packs and donned their raincoats. The sleet fell furiously, stinging their faces and covering the ground quickly with a translucent white icing that crunched beneath their boots. Snow mixed with the sleet. A muffled clap of thunder rumbled over the mountain and through the couple's feet as they stood transfixed with indecision in the small mountain pass.

"Thunder and snow?" Carrie marveled.

"I've never heard of that before," Brian exclaimed. "Anything is possible in these mountains."

The tiny flakes of snow swirled about them, hypnotizing them with random choreography, increasing wildly in number minute by minute. The boiling air filled with them, closing in densely like the morning fog. The distant trees were now obliterated, the near ones blurring into sameness with the surroundings.

"We'd best turn back, Carrie," Brian said.

"Why turn back? We don't have far to go, do we?"

"We're closer to Russell than to Spence. Besides, Russell is closer to the car if this turns really bad."

With shared disappointment, the couple left the pass in the direction from which they came. Traveling was more challenging now as the sleet and snow mixed with mud, and each step became a test of balance. Still the air grew colder and each gust of wind brought more flakes of swirling snow, filling the air and blanketing the ground so that it was becoming difficult to see the trail. In several places, Brian and Carrie had to rely on the blazes, but the wind, which was at their backs since they turned, was depositing a coat of snow on the north side of each tree trunk, obscuring the white rectangles of paint on the trees. They had to resort to looking over their shoulders every so often to see the blazes intended for hikers moving the other way.

Carrie almost fell several times before slipping altogether, landing unmercifully upon her backside and her pack, only the cushion of soggy snow and mud saving her from injury. She lay and whimpered, wanting and needing Brian's comfort, fear spreading in her so that she could feel it in every part. Brian approached cautiously, lest he join her in a heap in the wet snow.

"Are you all right, Sweetheart?" he asked, hand on her shoulder in concern.

"I don't know. Just help me up. This muck is soaking through my pants!"

Brian helped her to her feet and brushed off the clumps of muddy snow from her pants, and he held her as she shook and quivered with little sobs she was trying to suppress.

"Are you hurt, Love?" he asked.

"No," Carrie sniveled.

"Why are you crying?"

"I'm afraid.

"Afraid of what?"

"The shelter seems so far away. I just want to be there and to be warm. I just want to go home."

"There's nothing to be afraid of, dear. This is just a little spring snow. Like at home. You know how it comes and melts. I'll build a big fire for you when we get back to the shelter. It's not very far."

Nevertheless, Brian was afraid, for even as he held his bride, he looked over her shoulder and counted only ten trees still visible down the trail. He thought of the National Geographic special he had watched where mountain climbers were caught in a whiteout, and one of them even walked over the edge of a cliff a few feet from their tents. He pushed those thoughts out of his mind. These are the Southern Appalachians, not the Himalayas, he reasoned, but he knew they'd better press on now.

"Let's go, Carrie. The shelter's waiting for us."

The snow deepened beneath their shuffling feet, and the little pools of water that earlier had melted all the snow that fell into them were now covered over too. All the ground was white, the sky was white, even the air around them was white. Only the faint figures of the trees and a rare blaze on the leeward side of the bark led them on. Finally, the trees disappeared also. All became white except the two hikers themselves; they stood clinging to each other, trembling from cold and fear, not knowing what to do, just knowing they could not continue blindly, so they stood. After the eternity of a few moments in this terror, a strong gust of wind parted the boiling white air just enough that they could make out the faintest outline of Russell Field shelter not thirty feet away from them. It disappeared as quickly as it had emerged. They stumbled toward the place where they had seen the vision. Fear that it was just a mirage mounted until they scraped their frozen hands on the rough cold stones of their refuge.

Once inside the three walls, they could see again and felt some relief from the unrelenting wind. Brian quickly built a fire inside, not caring now whether the chimney would draw or fill the place with smoke. He had wet feet and Carrie's lower half was soaked; they must be dried and warmed. There was still firewood in place, and it was dry. His shivering hands managed finally to light a match and ignite the kindling. He added and added wood until the blaze was roaring. Carrie took off her jeans and two layers of wet warm-ups, and put on a pair of Brian's warm-ups over ashen-white gooseflesh thighs. His warm-ups swallowed her, but they were dry. She could feel the ice in her blood melting as she toasted herself by the fire. When at last her shivering stopped, she asked Brian to roll out her sleeping bag. She slipped into the dry bag, zipped it up and huddled fetus-like as close to the fire as the flammable synthetic womb would allow.

Brian hung her wet things by the fire to dry, then went outside to the fire ring to retrieve what firewood he could. When he returned with the last load, he took off his wet boots and socks and warmed his feet at the fireside until the feeling returned. He retrieved his dirty socks from his pack, happy enough that they were dry. He crawled into his sleeping bag, pulling it up around his shoulders like a garment and sat beside her on her windward side, taking on himself the freezing gusts that blew freely through the chain link.

"How are you now, Love?" he asked affectionately.

"Fine," she answered, but her thoughts were running deeper. She was once again warm and safe, content in feeling Brian's doting.

"When we were engaged…" Carrie said, and then paused, staring into the dancing flames of the fire.

"Yes?" Brian indicated his attention.

"I used to fantasize about being snowed in with you."

"And now here we are."

"Well not exactly. In my fantasy, we were warmer than this. And the cabin had four walls." She paused. "But there is no one I'd rather be here with than you."

"I'm glad of that."

"Thank you for taking such good care of me. I really love you, Brian," she said, turning her eyes from the fire and affixing them to his.

"I love you, too."

"I can really tell."

"I was afraid something bad was going to happen to us out there. And it would be my fault if it did," Brian confessed, his emotional defenses softened.

"I was afraid, too, but I never thought it would be your fault. What is going to happen now?" Carrie asked.

"This will probably stop tonight, clear up and the sun will melt it tomorrow. This is where we are supposed to be tomorrow night, so we are really ahead of schedule, see?"

"Or we could hike out tomorrow if we want to go home?"

"I suppose, but it will probably be slippery most of the day. We should go back on Monday as we planned."

"I'm hungry. Let's eat," Carrie suggested, and Brian agreed.

They fired up the stove and melted snow in a pot. They made Swiss Miss and a dehydrated dinner. The warm food and drink brought further contentment, security and sleepiness. They zipped the two bags together, and made love, while keeping as many clothes on as the act allowed. Away from the fire, the shelter was icy cold, and even their sleeping bags and shared body warmth were insufficient. They covered the tops of their sleeping bags with their raincoats, placed their packs on either side of them and draped their poncho over the end of the bunks to provide some wind protection. Still each gust of wind emptied the shelter of any accumulation of warmth, and the two spent a long miserable sleepless night shivering together waiting for dawn and the warming sun.

11
Double Spring Gap

Glen Leonard and his under strength platoon marched leisurely over Jenkins Knob and into the gap beyond it, enjoying the nearness of Silers Bald, a mere 2.8 miles from Double Spring Gap. All would have been idyllic except for their wounded comrade and her caretakers left behind…and the impending storm. The distant thunder, which had rumbled all about the church leaders and their charges as they tended to Tammy's ankle and deliberated a course of action, now grew nearer and nearer until the storm clouds shrouded the tops of the two peaks on either side of Double Spring Gap, unleashing their fury as if the artillery of two armies were firing salvo after salvo at each other over the heads of the innocents in the pass between. Kevin and Brad, Daniel and Lori huddled together under the tarp Glen spread over them as a mother duck gathering her offspring under the protection of her wings. The storm was intense but mercifully brief, and soon the squad was again underway, shaken a bit, but dry and happy. Silers Bald cleared its beclouded head as the jaunty youth made their way up its graceful shoulder. They reached its crown, and the earth unfolded around them in every direction, as it had upon Clingman's Dome, only in an entirely different mood, colors muted and soft-focused by the clouds, some thin and some heavy and gray, all sweeping swiftly across the puckered earth as if hurrying toward some destination to the east. The darkest ones bellowed thunderous threats as they sped by, and soon the small creatures on Silers' craggy bald heeded the warnings and made their way down to the shelter tucked safely amidst the trees on the leeward side of the bald.

* * * * *

When the last of his severed youth group had disappeared down the trail, Dave turned and started to speak to his two female charges.

But, uncharacteristically for Pastor David Wilkes, he didn't really know what to say, so he hemmed and hawed and said, "Well." He scratched his head and kicked some dirt, and soon a plan came to his mind.

"Y'all make yourselves at home, you know, dress or whatever. I'm going to get firewood."

When Dave was gone, Christie looked at Tammy, who had the complexion of victory. Christie had a look of scorn.

"What?" Tammy snickered.

"You know what! You've been bad. Now you're planning to be bad some more," Christie said, half-joking, half-scolding.

"I didn't do anything. I just sprained my ankle is all. What, you think I'm faking the swelling like you thought I was faking the pain yesterday?"

"No, and I told you I was sorry about yesterday. But things sure have worked out comfortably for you now, haven't they? Somehow, you always get what you want. And this is what you wanted, isn't it?"

"Well, I think it's pretty cool how things are working out, don't you?"

"For you, maybe. The least you could do is to thank me!" Christie answered with a growing agitation in her voice.

"Thank you. Thank you for what?"

"Well if you don't know… There's some real ungratefulness going on here. You could be here with Lori, you know. That wouldn't be so nice, would it?"

"OK, so thanks for volunteering to stay. Listen, I would like to get some time alone with Dave some during this, if you don't mind."

"Oh, I don't mind. But just what do you plan on doing with Dave that you can't do with me around?"

"You are so not trusting. I just want to talk with him, you know. As long as you're around, he'll just be the pastor. He won't really talk to me."

That made sense to Christie, though she could not see why that was so important to Tammy, as if any of her fantasies could go anywhere. So she agreed to give Tammy some space, but feelings of uncertainty nipped at her insides. As she pondered these feelings, she heard Dave returning.

Dave had built quite a pile of branches behind the shelter. Since the early morning storm, the thunder had been growling all about them distantly as if the mountain itself were hungry, but now it grew more insistent and more directional as though preparing to storm again. Dave called to the girls from the blind corner of the shelter.

"Is the coast clear, ladies?"

"All clear," Tammy responded.

Dave entered the shelter wiping sweat from his forehead.

"If there's anything you need to do outside, better get it over with, 'cause I think we're gonna get some rain out there."

Tammy whispered something in Christie's ear. Christie laughed and said aloud, "That's your problem!"

"Is there a problem?" Dave asked.

Tammy blushed. "I, uh, I need to…"

"She needs our help getting to the outhouse," Christie said forthrightly, and Tammy elbowed her in the ribs.

"Uh, of course. Sure," Dave stammered. He put his arm around her waist, and, with her arm around his shoulder, Dave helped Tammy to the privy while Christie smiled and shook her head.

"You're not going to stand out here are you?" Tammy asked when they reached the door.

"Uh, no. Just holler when you're ready. I'll hear you at the shelter."

Dave returned to the shelter to find Christie sitting on a lower bunk, her face cradled in her hands, looking down at the laces of her boots. When he entered, she looked up, started to speak, shook her head and returned to studying her laces.

"You wanted to say something, Christie?"

"Naw, I was just thinking of something."

"You know you can ask me anything."

"Do you love Susan?" she blurted out as if she would explode if she didn't ask.

"Well yes, Christie. I love her very much. She's my wife and soon to be the mother of my child. God commands me to love…"

"I mean do you really love her."

Dave sensed that the depth of her question went far beyond its words.

"What do you mean by love, Christie?"

"I know you love her like the Bible says, but I mean…like in movies?" Christie's eyes were fixed on her boots, but her blush was visible even through the part of her hair.

"Do you mean romantic love, Christie?"

"Yeah."

"Well, yes, we love each other that way too. Can I ask you why you are asking these things?"

"I just wondered."

"Christie, are you becoming involved with someone?"

"No! It's not me!" Christie responded with a tone of conviction too strong for the circumstances. She quieted her voice, looked down and said through pursed lips, "I've got a friend that is, though."

"Is your friend a Christian?"

Christie nodded, and then said, "I don't really know for sure anymore. I'm afraid she's about to get herself in trouble. If I let her, I'm not being a very good friend, am I?"

"I think you have proved that you are a very good friend to be this concerned about her. Does she talk openly to you about these things, Christie?"

"She used to, but not so much anymore. I think she's started lying to me now."

"That makes it tough to help her, doesn't it? Is your friend thinking about having sex with someone?"

Christie sat up, eyes widening with surprise as she looked over Dave's shoulder toward the door.

"Am I interrupting something?" Tammy asked, staring into Christie's eyes with piercing anger.

"Tammy! How'd you get back up here by yourself?" Dave asked.

"Nobody came when I called, so I figured it was hop or sleep in the latrine. And I didn't want to stay there in the storm."

"I'm sorry, Tammy. I didn't hear you call. We're going to fix you a crutch, though, so you can at least get there and back without being dependent on me."

The storm broke over the ridge, a few flashes of lightning followed by thunder, a little wind and rain, and it was over. No words passed between Tammy and Christie, though much was said without them. By the time the storm passed over and Dave had excused himself to look for the makings of a crutch, the tension between the two friends was drawn taunt as a piano string and badly out of tune. When he was well out of earshot, Tammy turned to face Christie and unleashed the fury of the storm seething within her.

"What do you think you're doing? I thought you were my friend!" Tammy yelled softly through gritted teeth.

"I wasn't doing anything. I didn't say anything…"

"The hell you weren't! I heard what you were saying," Tammy's voice grew louder.

"I didn't say anything he would think was about you. I just had to know something…"

"You just had to butt in. I trusted you and you betrayed me. You're not a friend, you're a traitor." Little flecks of spit sprayed as she talked.

"I'm a traitor? I'm only here because I'm your friend. I could be with the others. And you could be here with Lori. What would that do for your little plans?"

"At least Lori wouldn't have been a tattletale."

"I was only trying to understand. Why don't you chase someone who could be a real boyfriend, not just a dream? You're making a big mistake, Tammy!"

"You think Kevin is a real boyfriend? You'll never have a chance with Kevin. He hardly even looks at you. Why don't you just go be with Kevin? You're all talk. You don't understand my feelings for Dave, and you never will. You're just not grown up enough, I guess. Go on! See if Kevin will have you. But stay away from me."

"All right then. You make your big mistake. It's between you and God…and Dave. But I'm not sticking around here to help you do it. You…don't…need my help…to screw…up!" Christie's voice broke as the tears came.

Christie haphazardly stuffed her things and her anger into her pack. When it was filled, she stood firmly and faced her friend, and said with complete composure, "I will pray for you, Tammy Day!" Then she headed down the trail toward the rest of the group, crying for her feelings and her friend as she went.

DAVID RETURNED EAGER for Tammy to try his workmanship. She feigned a smile and accepted his gift as an expression of his love for her. Actually, the crutch worked pretty well, but she dared not show it. So she stumbled in the direction of his arms and fell softly into them after tripping over nothing. This little dance brought their faces together. Once Tammy was firmly on her feet, she kissed Dave on the cheek, said her thanks for the crutch and the catch, and backed swiftly away, smiling coyly and innocently, her intuition guiding her in the fine art of seduction.

"Steady now, girl. You'd better take it easy until you get used to using that. Is it the right length?"

"Yes. Perfect."

"We need to ice your ankle again in the spring. Then you'd better stay off that foot and elevate it awhile. Where's Christie?"

"Uh, she left."

"What? You mean she went to the bathroom?"

"No. She left to catch up with the rest of the group."

"No way! Why did she do that?" Dave began to pace and scratch his face.

"Something you two were talking about upset her," Tammy said cautiously, probing the extent of Christie's breech of confidence, studying Dave's face for signs of suspicion. Seeing none, she continued, "She likes Kevin a lot. She wanted to be where he was. Is there something y'all were talking about that I need to know about?"

"She was telling me about a friend she thought might be about to get in trouble in a dating relationship. You don't think that she was really talking about herself, do you?"

"Well it sounds like it. She's pretty immature about those things."

"I'd better head up the trail and see if I can catch up with her. We can't have her out there alone." Dave stopped himself. "But then you would be here alone…and with that ankle and all. Well, I hope she'll be all right. The next shelter is not all that far."

"I think she'll be all right. She wasn't scared at all."

"What possessed her to strike out like that?"

Dave continued to pace, and Tammy knew she'd better lay low until he recovered from his agitation. Dave turned some of his nervous energy into preparing lunch. After they ate, Tammy decided to sleep since she had gotten little the night before and curled up in her sleeping bag, which Dave had moved to the bottom bunk. Dave went outside the shelter with his Bible and brought his concerns to God until the bright spot behind the clouds passed its zenith, the wind began to blow and the temperature dropped. He retreated to the shelter chilled and ready to build a fire.

When Tammy awoke, it was still bright, so she knew she had not slept long. She saw Dave huddled before the fireplace breaking and adding sticks as the flames licked upward against the gray stones. With each gust of wind, a large black puff of smoke billowed from the chimney as Dave moved back out of its reach. Then the chimney would again inhale, sucking the smoke and the flames upward, and the fire would burn hotter and brighter. Tammy wondered why David had built the fire so large, until a gust of cold wind rushed through the chain link wall, forcing her to retreat into the warmth of her sleeping bag, shivering.

"It's really turned colder!" she said to Dave.

Dave turned around and smiled.

"So you're awake. Yes, it's getting really cold out there. I thought you might need the fire when you woke up."

He's so thoughtful, he's perfect, Tammy said to herself. She smiled at the idea that now she had him all to herself. A sudden fear yanked the smile from her lips, and she looked around to make certain that Christie had not returned. It would be just like her to storm off down the path, get afraid as soon as she was out of sight, then return and screw everything up.

"Any sign of Christie?" she asked sheepishly.

"No. I figure she's had time to reach the others by now. I prayed, and God has given me faith that she made it safely. So I'm not worried anymore," Dave said. "I prayed for you too, and asked God to take away your worries."

Tammy smiled.

"Well, He answered your prayers. I'm sure she's just fine. I'm going to try out that new crutch you made me."

Tammy got her fanny pack that served as her cosmetic bag, fastened it about her waist, donned her fleece jacket and hobbled with the crutch into the blustery wind toward the spring. The wind was howling now up the hollow, biting through her warm-up pants, and covering her body with chill bumps. When she reached the spring, she gathered her resolve and slipped off her moccasin and her sock from her swollen ankle, inspecting its size and color before plunging it into the frigid water. While it soaked, she brushed her teeth and hair and washed. She then opened a perfume sample towelette, daubing it everywhere. Thus freshened, she reached beneath her sweatshirt and removed her bra, pulling one arm through at a time until she was free of its encumbrance without removing her shirt. She shivered as the cold air found its way in, touching the tender skin now relatively exposed, spreading goosebumps once again all over her. She opened her jacket and looked, pleased with the appearance of her liberated breasts with nipples chilled rock-hard pressing forward in two lively points in the soft stretchy fabric. Dave can't miss these, Tammy thought, and he will want them. They have to look great compared to Susan's old pregnant ones. Tammy pulled her thoroughly numb foot from the spring and dried it, replaced the sock and slipper and struggled back up the hill toward Dave. At the top of the hill where the air stilled, she stopped.

"Coowell!" she said, holding out her hand to catch one of several white flakes floating by. A sense of joy swept over her, a joy rooted in the earliest memories of school days, when, peculiar to the temperate regions, the first flakes of snow spelled the hope of unplanned holidays, a conditioned response persisting beyond the circumstances that created it, not yet squelched by experience of adulthood with its incumbent fears and responsibilities. Forgetting her ankle, she rushed to share her childish joy with Dave. He, however, met the news not with relish but with trepidation. He had reached adulthood.

"Don't you like snow?"

"When I'm at home with central heat and no place to go."

"Where's your sense of adventure, Mr. Pastor?" she asked playfully.

Dave envied her naiveté, her unbridled spirit, her spontaneous expression of simple joy. He remembered a verse, "Except ye become as little children…" He was not so far removed from such an unspoiled time himself that it was not easily recalled. But duty had changed him. He wondered whether it was possible to hold on to more childlikeness and still discharge the obligations of maturity. He tucked these thoughts away for future meditation, Bible study and perhaps a sermon. Tammy was still frolicking outside the shelter, attempting to turn circles balancing on her good foot, white flakes of snow now thicker in the air than summer moths flitting about a streetlight. They were sticking in her hair and on the shoulders of her jacket, and she was catching them in her mouth.

"Come on, Pastor Dave," she beckoned. "Come on, Dave. Have some fun." The deletion of his title was deliberate.

"How about some hot chocolate instead?" he countered, and, to his relief, she accepted. She entered the shelter, pulled off her fleece and sat down beside him at the fire. She sipped the cocoa he proffered and watched his eyes to see when they found her points, but he only gazed longingly into the fire. She desired to plumb his buried thoughts and discover the source of his somber mood. He was never so melancholy at home. Was he homesick for Susan, or were his responsibilities killing the life in him? Or did he simply despise his present company. The truth, could she discover it, was that he had taken note, not of the perkiness of her breasts, but of her personality, and her presence had called to light in him a certain blackness in which he felt less alive by contrast to her, anesthetized and paralyzed, condemned to only observe that in which he would willingly take part. In his yet immature theology, depression was less a luxury to be afforded than a sin to be renounced, so he shook himself from its grip, replaced his shepherd's cloak and said, "Well, I had a devotion planned for this evening. There may be but one lamb to feed, but I wouldn't be much of a shepherd if I turned it away hungry. So, let's get our Bibles and we'll feed our souls before we feed our stomachs. OK?"

"OK," Tammy unwillingly consented, feeling some of her hope depart.

Dave directed the congregation once again to the passage on the temptation of Christ in the wilderness, expounding further its finer points with eloquence and conviction commensurate to his calling. They prayed and ate, drank chocolate and talked, watched the snow pile higher outside all afternoon. Supper was early. Then they went to bed, she on the bottom bunk and he on the top, and he never noticed the emancipation of her breasts.

* * * * *

Forcing her way over the rocks and through her tears, impatient to increase the distance between her and her wayward friend, Christie Jenkins compelled her legs to carry her faster than they wanted to go, until they ached like her heart, broken from the dual wounds of rejecting and being rejected. She prayed aloud in repetitive mumblings, at first for God to let Tammy fall on her face with such humiliation and pain that she deserved, proving her wrongness irrefutably, so that she would come back begging for forgiveness and restoration of friendship, which Christie would deny. Her prayer changed, directed more toward her own feelings, that God would give her strength and a new friend, and help her reach the group quickly. Her thoughts turned again to Tammy and feelings of remorse swept from her festering heart. She prayed for Tammy to be saved from her evil intentions. This released a flood of emotion, and she stopped still in the trail, clutched hands to her breast, sank to her knees and leaned her whole weight on a dank and rotting log. There she sobbed with sobs that shook her whole body, clenching her repeatedly in little convulsions. At last, she let go of hatred and prayed bitterly for forgiveness for herself and for Tammy, begging God to show her what to do. No peace came, and God answered in the storm as it struck, as she knelt alone and rocked herself, caring not for the wind or the rain, lightning or thunder. There she knelt and soaked up the downpour and the wrath of God who had abandoned her in her need as she had abandoned her friend. But the storm passed, and she lived. Christie stood on her feeble legs and trembled with cold and emotion, her hair and her clothes and pack dripping. Forlorn and alone, she felt drawn forward to the others where there was a chance of solace, rather than backward to the source of her pain.

She walked on, down off Jenkins Knob, missing by minutes the rest of her tribe where they had huddled in the gap against the onslaught of the storm. She plodded upward toward Silers Bald, but, with her face downcast, she never saw her comrades as they viewed their world from its top. As she climbed, her spirits rose, and she felt there was hope in God for her yet. She resolved in her heart to find the answers and to be faithful in commitment to what she found. When she reached the top, however, her body began to fail her. She had pushed it beyond reason by her cruel pace earlier. She had eaten and drunk nothing. Her frail strength had been drained by emotion, and she was chilled to the vitals of her small frame. Her judgment became clouded as her body drew blood from her brain to warm its core, and hypothermia quickened as the temperature of the post-storm wind plummeted. Christie stumbled along the trail leading down from Silers Bald, her legs supporting her tiny weight tenuously, the coordination of their movements decreasing as her confusion increased. She saw neither the shelter nor the sign pointing to it, stumbling westward on autopilot.

* * * * *

Kevin perked up, his shoulders and neck tensing to lift his head upward as his eyes focused, locking on to some distant object.

"What is it, Kevin," Glen asked, unable to resolve with aged eyes what Kevin had discerned.

"That hiker is not walking right," Kevin answered, rising to his feet. He walked forward, abandoning the pile of firewood he was making. He neared the trail as the figure disappeared into the trees. He shrugged his shoulders and started to return to the shelter, but something would not let him let it go. He turned again and trotted toward the trees. Just beyond a bend in the trail, he caught up with the staggering figure.

"Christie!" he called, but she did not respond. She stumbled forward, pulled by gravity alone. Kevin was unsure whether he would reach her before she lost balance completely. When he came to her, he grabbed her arm.

"Christie!" he said firmly, and she turned to look at him and giggled. His first thought was that she was drunk, but he saw the purple in her lips and the snow-white face where this morning had been a tan nurtured carefully in beds of artificial sun all winter.

Hypothermia! He knew its signs and symptoms. "Christie, come on. I'll take you to the others."

She stood and giggled. He reached out his hand and took hers, ice-cold and trembling, and started her in the direction of camp. He took off his fleece and wrapped it about her wet shoulders. Somewhere in the recesses of her mind where blood was still in sufficient supply, she dreamed of the date with Kevin, which she had dreamed of many times in both sleep and wakefulness. She leaned her teetering body on his, and they moved deliberately toward the shelter until her legs would no longer support her and buckled beneath her. She did not fall, for she clung to his shoulder with the grip of death, and he supported her about her waist, so that her legs, when they gave way, simply dangled beneath her as if made of supple rubber. Kevin reached downward with one smooth movement and caught the wayward appendages behind the knees, sweeping her upward. Christie giggled again and buried her ashen face into his collar, surrendering to the wave of unconsciousness that inundated her.

"Mr. Leonard!" Kevin called as the camp came into sight. "It's Christie. She's hypothermic. Everyone out of the shelter but Lori!" he called, taking charge as the young leader Glen knew he was becoming.

"Lori, you're going to have to take her wet clothes off. All of them," he said as Glen prepared a sleeping bag. "And get her in some dry ones, then into this bag."

Glen and Kevin left the shelter and herded Brad and Daniel to its blind side, there explaining the situation to them. Lori began to undress the small white figure. When Lori sounded the all clear, Kevin entered followed by Glen.

"Now what?" Lori asked.

"Get in your sleeping bag. Huddle close to her," Kevin said, as he approached and checked her pulse and breathing. "Mr. Leonard. Would you get something and raise her feet." He checked her pulse again. He found it, but it was very weak.

"She's slipping," he said somberly. "Lori, I've got to..."

"Got to what? Whatever you want," Lori responded.

Kevin didn't answer. He lay down with them, huddling close to Christie's side. He pulled his sleeping bag over the three of them and reached his arm over both girls, pulling Lori tighter toward him, sandwiching Christie firmly. They lay like that for some time. Meanwhile,

Mr. Leonard heated water, filled several water bottles and placed them between the sleeping bags.

"Her pulse is stronger, Mr. Leonard. What we're doing is working, Lori."

"Her breathing is stronger and more regular, too. I can feel it."

They felt Christie begin to shake violently between them. Presently she spoke in scrambled words, waking in a dream, befuddled. What a strange place to awake.

Christie lay like a fetus in her bag, still shivering, though less violently. Her lips were still blue, but the color of her skin began to return to something consistent with life. Mr. Leonard made hot chocolate, and began to spoon it slowly into her mouth. She was still shaking too much to hold the cup. She seemed lucid now. She remembered nothing. She became preoccupied with how she came to be in the shelter dressed in clothes she did not recognize. As Lori began to relate to her the story of Kevin's rescue and first aid, Kevin rose and walked out. Glen took his place, intent on learning what she was doing on the trail alone and what had become of the others. Christie said the others were fine, but that what happened she could only tell to Mr. Leonard privately. So Lori and the others left the shelter. Christie confessed to the Elder her fears and angers. She felt better. He prayed with her, and she fell asleep before he could scold her for her foolishness.

"Kevin!" he called. Kevin entered. "Kevin, I've got to go back to the other shelter. They're all right, but they are going to need me there. You will have to take over here."

"But Mr. Leonard...I just..."

"Kevin, what you are is the leader you proved yourself to be just now. You did much better than I could have, and I'm very proud of you, son. So I know you can handle it."

"Mr. Leonard," Lori said, from her place outside the gate. "It's snowing. Really hard."

Mr. Leonard walked as far as the main trail to assess the snow and the fog that was blowing in with it. By the time he got there, he couldn't see but a few feet up the trail, and the shelter dissolved completely into the white blankness. He made his way back to the shelter by following the rut of the well-worn trail, which he could feel with his feet more than he could see.

"We will have to trust the others to God," he said, and led them in prayer.

While Brad returned to his earphones and Daniel returned to daydreaming, Glen, Kevin and Lori continued to tend to Christie as she recovered through chills, headaches, weakness and nausea. At the first opportunity, Lori sought Kevin's private company to communicate to him that he should feel no uneasiness for what he had done. And that she felt no shame, and he shouldn't, either. And she felt no resentment toward him. On the contrary, he had grown in stature in her eyes, and she would submit willingly to his leadership anytime God called upon her to do so. When she had finished, there was something in his heart he wished to say to her, but he could not frame the feeling into words. So he stood speechless with his mouth open as if something were caught in his throat. Though his young heart was more tuned to God and the sensitivities of others than most twice his age, he was slow to recognize a transformation at work in his own heart and a door swung wide open in the heart of another. Among all his companions, he was the last to see it. Lori smiled knowingly, touched his arm, and walked away, out of the whiteness that hid them and into the orange glow of the fire dimly illuminating the interior of the shelter. From her bunk, Christie had heard the whole conversation without hearing it, and agreed with its rightness in her heart, and knew from that moment on that Kevin was not to be hers. Strangely, all of her feelings and wants aligned themselves peacefully with that knowledge.

12
Spence Field

Roy and Dwight made it to the cutoff for Spence Field shelter just as the sky broke open again, this time with torrential rains, which quickly turned the rutted trail into a small stream. They walked to the side of the rivulet, across the grassy field to the shelter tucked just into the woods at its edge. Once inside they slipped quickly out of their ponchos, hanging them on the chain link wall to drip.

"You ready for some lunch yet, Dwight?" Roy asked, knowing that Dwight was always ready to eat something, whatever name might be applied to the time of eating it.

"Sure. What else do we have to do? We have five months to make it to Maine. I don't think that calls for hiking in this trashy weather, do you?"

"I'd still like to make it to Derrick Knob today. We may just have to hump it over Thunderhead once this passes."

Dwight stared at Roy until he had Roy's attention.

"What?" Roy asked impatiently.

"We aren't going over Thunderhead if there is any thunder or even a chance of thunder. I'm not getting struck by lightning today, got it?" Dwight said, emphasizing every word.

Roy studied his friend's face for any sign of willingness to negotiate, and, finding none, consented to wait at Spence Field until three o'clock. If the storms were not completely gone by that time, they would spend the night there. Roy knew in his heart that Dwight was right, but he always preferred that Dwight appear the cautious one. Roy, wise and cautious enough for his years, preferred a daredevil persona, carefully developed since junior high and reaching its peak when he was a pilot-in-training.

Dwight and Roy complemented each other in that regard as well as in others. Dwight grew up in poverty surrounded by people for whom sensibility made no sense and for whom tomorrow was a concept too uncertain for which to make provision. That society produced a surplus of live-for-the-moment characters, arrogant, impetuous, with no regard for their own lives, let alone the lives of others, willing to risk all because they had nothing at all to risk. In the midst of that environment, Dwight grew wise and calculating, determined to create a future from nothing, an escape from this self-perpetuating cycle, which consumed generation after generation. Growing up with purpose among the purposeless, Dwight had suffered much abuse, mostly verbal, occasionally physical, creating in him patience and strength, which kept him steadfast against any opposition.

Roy admired these qualities in Dwight and could hide behind Dwight's sensibility while wearing his own reckless façade. Dwight knew that Roy was not the gambler he appeared, but could afford the luxury of appearing so, having developed from a community of boys that, though as poor as Dwight's peers, were not, owing to their whiteness, as impoverished in opportunity to better themselves. They admired, even venerated the Overcomers, the heroes of local mythology, the legends, sometimes emulated, their stories oft repeated. Roy first stood out among his fellows through his boldness and individuality. Then he excelled both academically and athletically, but always in unorthodox ways. When completing his academic assignments, there was always something unexpected, something creative, something of himself. Many a teacher, taken by surprise by this son of a disabled line worker, would stand back and scratch his head and wonder what depth of talent lay yet unfathomed. He was the bane and blessing of his coaches, for his style of play had too much individuality for their comfort, as he would cut back across the field away from his blockers, or stretch the ball forward with one hand, risking a fumble to gain a first down. But Roy's nerve never extended to risking his life or his future. He really had nothing to prove to himself or others, as exemplified by his choice to fly transports when he had qualified to fly fighters. He saw safety and future in one while his compatriots saw adventure in the other. So Roy maintained his reputation as a risk taker but underneath remained fully unwilling to take unnecessary ones. He would not have crossed Thunderhead under risk of lightning unless there was a compelling purpose in doing so, but he did not mind allowing others think that he would.

Dwight and Roy ate their lunch and waited restlessly, huddling in the shelter during waves of storms and pacing outside it in periods of calm, watching the clock. Several storms came and went, but the rumbling in the direction of Thunderhead was continual, validating its name. Disappointed, the two men resolved to wait another day to mark that milestone and settled down in their spirits as they settled in to camp early.

Roy sat on a bunk studying the topo map and field guide, memorizing the features of the land in store for them in coming days. Dwight was also on the bunk, eyes and pencil in a book, his logbook of the miles and memories they were making. The sound of footsteps approaching drew their attention. They saw a pair of hikers coming through the drizzle, both slightly stooped, clad in green Army ponchos and Red Wing work boots, with hiking sticks fashioned from wood, unique in shape and color. One hiker was larger than the other, and it was not until they reached the gate of the shelter and pulled back the hoods from their heads that Dwight and Roy could see an older couple, both gray and weathered, alert blue eyes smiling from sunken sockets ringed with baggy skin as folded and contoured as the landscape.

"Ev'nin,'" the man greeted.

"Come in, come in," Roy beckoned. "Are you soaked?"

"Only with sweat," the old man quipped. "These old ponchos keep the rain out and the perspiration in. So we're poached, ya see," he said, his local heritage evident with every word.

"I'm Roy, and this is Dwight," Roy offered with his outstretched hand.

The man shook it, and introduced himself and his wife as Howard and Kathleen Ramsey.

"That's a mighty fine handshake you've got there young man," he said.

Dwight held out his hand, and the man took it tentatively and looked him up and down.

"Where are y'all from?" Mr. Ramsey asked, directing the question at Roy.

"Maryland, Bal'more," Roy answered, casting a knowing glance at Dwight. "And you two?"

"Wear's Valley, this end of it," Mr. Ramsey said, in a final sort of way as if everyone in the world should know where that was.

"That's down below on the Tennessee side, in the foothills," Mrs. Ramsey spoke for the first time, adding the phrase to her husband's answer just as she had done for years. She had a sweet voice to match her kind face.

"Do you hike these mountains much?" Dwight asked, encouraged by the smile Mrs. Ramsey had cast his way.

"Grew up on these mountains, son," Mr. Ramsey retorted. "Know every trail like the back of my hand." He held out his brown-spotted hand as proof, studying its back as if something new might have occurred on it.

"Used to hunt some up'ere when I was a boy. Sure it weren't legal, but hell, that was the Great Depression and then the War, and we did what we could to get by. Ya know, we couldn't buy meat then. Well, the Mrs. came along, and she loved the wild flowers, and I took her and her friends up here when I was courtin' her. Ya know, a man'll do just about anything a good woman wants when he's awooing her."

He paused in his monologue long enough to put his arm around her boney shoulder, giving her a little shake and a smile. Then he went on.

"She's a goodun too, mark my word. Well, it got to be a habit and we started coming up here all the time. My boys and I used to come up here and camp like you'uns, but now me and the Mrs. just walk. Pardon me boys, we got to come out of these ovens."

Mr. Ramsey helped his wife remove her poncho, and he removed his, hanging them on the fence wire like Roy and Dwight's. He fluffed his red and black flannel shirt until it fit his frame more comfortably. He was wearing Walls brown canvas jeans with some kind of waterproofing so that the raindrops just beaded and ran off. He had an old cotton duck rucksack on his large shoulders, and when he slipped the straps off, they allowed his shoulders to droop forward where they wanted to go. Mrs. Ramsey too wore flannel with large black and white squares and a brand new pair of off-brand blue jeans from Wal-Mart cinched tight above her boney hips. She laid aside her fanny pack imprinted with the name of the eye clinic where her cataracts had been removed. Her husband retrieved their jackets from his rucksack, both red waffle-weave, thick and lofty, and he lovingly helped her into hers.

"Don't get too comferble, dear, and stay too long, or we're going to have to spend the night here tonight," he said. "We got the same number of miles goin' down as we had comin' up, ya know, and not as much day left. But, goin' down sure goes faster than coming up for us old folks. And twice as painful."

Roy offered them some hot tea, which they gladly accepted.

"So, are you boys thru-hikers?" Mrs. Ramsey asked.

"Yes, ma'am," Roy answered.

"Ooh! That sounds so exciting. I love to meet the thru-hikers up here. You've got to tell me all about your trip so far."

Roy told the Ramseys the highlights of the trip, when they started, what the weather was like, the wildlife. Mrs. Ramsey prompted him for more each time he paused, until Mr. Ramsey spoke up and said that it was time to go. It was then that the sleet began, rattling the dead leaves and pattering like the feet of a thousand mice on the corrugated roof above their heads.

"Oh, no! I was afraid the mountain would do this today the way the air was chilling off during the rain. Smells like snow, too," he said stretching out his bumpy red nose to catch the scent like a weary old bloodhound. "Looks like we are going to spend the night after all."

"Maybe this will quit in just a few minutes," Dwight said hopefully.

"Boy, you don't know much about weather in these mountains, do you?" Mr. Ramsey sputtered. "It may stop in a few minutes or it may cover the ground and the trees like glaze on a donut before we get outta sight of this here shelter. The temper'ture has reached freezing and there's precip. Don't ever strike out in these mountains in those conditions when you've got a shelter over yer heads. That's good advice you kin count on."

"Are you prepared to spend the night?"

"We don't go no where up here this time a year without a few extras," he said as he pulled an old dingy olive drab goose down bag large enough for two from the rucksack. "We've got some extra food, and you can get just about anything burning with these candles. And watch this boys."

He then removed from the bottom of the bag a nylon tarp, bright blue, which stretched the length of the shelter when he unfolded it.

There were hay strings tied to the grommets, and with these, he began to tether the tarp over the chain link side of the shelter.

"All right!" Roy and Dwight exclaimed and jumped down from the bunk to lend a hand in tying up this most welcome windbreak. Once it was in place, it became obvious that this tarp had been altered for just this purpose, its dimensions just right in height and length, with an upside down "L" cut in the middle so that it opened and closed with the door when tied to it.

"Some of these shelters have Visqueen, but the wind eventually shreds it, so I come prepared. All the shelters up here are the size of this one or smaller," he explained with pride as he stood hands on hips and admired his ingenuity. "What do you think of that, boys?"

The shelter became more comfortable instantly with the wind blocked. By now, it was clear that Mr. Ramsey had been right, for enough sleet had already fallen to form a coating of ice on the ground, which crunched beneath their feet. Now snow was falling and, insulated from the heat of the ground by the sleet, accumulation began at once. Mr. Ramsey set to work immediately to gather what firewood he could before it was covered, adding it to the small pile that was already in the shelter. Dwight and Roy joined in helping, and before long, they had a large pile ready for the fire inside and a mound of downed branches and saplings piled as high as the shelter along its sidewall. They reentered the shelter, and soon Mr. Ramsey had a warm fire popping. The four gathered around and began to toast themselves, refilling their cups with hot tea.

No sooner had they settled than they heard voices outside.

"Mommy, how do we get in?"

"Knock, knock," a young woman's voice called through the tarp wall. Mr. Ramsey opened the gate. A small boy, followed by a smaller girl, entered sheepishly, herded by their mother. Dad entered last, shaking the snow from his shoulders, and kicking it from his boots.

"Welcome," Mrs. Ramsey said, and rose to help the children remove their wet raincoats.

"We didn't make it any too soon," Richard Bobo said, lifting the pack from his wife's back. "The trail was getting hard to follow and we just about missed the cutoff. There's a thick fog moving up the north side."

"Where'd you guys start from today?" Roy asked.

"Cade's Cove," Rochelle Bobo answered. "We were camping down there this week, and we came up here for tonight and tomorrow night just to give the kids a taste of backpacking. Well, this isn't the taste we wanted to give them."

"So much for the weather forecasts around here," Richard complained. "They only called for a fifty percent chance of showers today and tomorrow. It wasn't supposed to turn cold until we were on our way home."

"Where's home," Mrs. Ramsey asked.

"Indiana," the boy volunteered with pride.

"Indiana! Why y'all've come a long way, haven't you."

"Yes ma'am," he said. The girl stepped closer and looked up at Mrs. Ramsey's warm countenance, but did not speak.

"What are your names?"

"I'm Adam. She's Ashley. She's my sister. She's only five. I'm *seven*."

"I'm Richard Bobo, and this is my wife Rochelle."

Introductions were continued around the shelter. Mrs. Ramsey took over care of the children, patiently drawing out their confidence with the skill of a grandmother, giving Richard and Rochelle a chance to settle in and warm up.

It was mutually decided that there was wisdom in preparing an early dinner and being done with all the chores that would require outside activity well before darkness descended. The activity helped to keep hands and feet warm and took minds off the worry brewing among those most responsible for others. Some small talk took place during these activities, but the group as a whole postponed becoming better acquainted until all were comfortably seated around the fire, a cozy situation given that the little space about the hearth was shared now by eight people and a pile of firewood. The children were given deference to sit closest to its flames, so close in fact that the sole of Adam's boot began to smoke, scaring him with visions of cartoon characters hopping about with their feet on fire. He jumped up and hopped in that fashion, spilling his mother's chocolate and nearly upsetting Mrs. Ramsey's as well.

In the cause of advancing familiarity with one another, Mrs. Ramsey began to tell of the work on their farm in Wear's Valley below, which now, with Howard having had his sixty-seventh birthday and her approaching her sixty-fourth before summer, was scaling down. He had sold half the herd of beef cattle, and had reduced his hay production to meet only his own needs. So now they had more time for the mountains, for each other and for the grandchildren produced by their younger daughter and those soon to be produced, hopefully, by their son, should he finally choose to settle down to marriage.

The Bobos told of cold Midwestern winters and lake effect snow, of choosing to start their family late after Richard's law practice was stable and his partnership secured, and after Rochelle's antique fabric studio was flourishing. With him at thirty-seven and her at thirty-nine, they wished to return to backpacking extensively as they had done when they were younger and childless.

Adam sat in awe and Ashley dozed as Roy told about the training he had received in flying and the places he had seen around the world. Dwight had little to say and the others had little to ask him. Ashley was fascinated with the color of his skin and wished to touch it, but Rochelle drew her hand back and whispered 'No' into her ear. When Rochelle's attention was drawn elsewhere, Ashley stretched again and reached her goal, surprised that it felt the same as her own. This amused Dwight and he laughed aloud, and someone finally asked him for his story. Mr. Ramsey offered him an awkward compliment, stating how he should be proud that he had lifted himself by his bootstraps out of the gumbo that held his brothers down and that he was an example of how not to sponge off the labor and welfare of others while laying up in bed drinking all day, fathering fatherless children and committing crimes all night. Mr. Ramsey was just warming up when Mrs. Ramsey pinched his arm, and, though he had much more to say, he chose silence, for he always preferred Mrs. Ramsey happy and never mad.

They talked on through the afternoon and evening, preparing, downing and cleaning up their suppers. While the wind played its doleful tune, the weary band of wayfarers tucked their bodies into their sleeping bags and shivered until their body heat had warmed them sufficiently for comfort. Before sleep had overtaken them all – and it did so quickly – Mrs. Ramsey complained to her husband that, though she felt none too comfortable sleeping under the same roof with a black man for the first time, that he would do best to keep his own feelings about it to himself. He said he would, but went on to say how that in all his years of hiking, he had seen few enough niggers in these mountains to count on one hand, but lately he was seeing more and more, and now they were even going to start sleeping in them. It would be no time before they took over, and these mountains wouldn't be fit for good white folks anymore. His complaining changed to grumbling, then to snoring with scarcely a transition between.

13
Thunderhead

Kim fought her way up the snowy trail, foot by foot, slipping once for each two or three steps forward, taking baby steps, barely able to discern the location of the trail itself. The trail had been well tended by volunteers, though, and Kim followed the trail mainly by the tunnel pruned through the trees. She hugged the uphill side, lest she place a foot on snow that concealed a drop-off beneath its crusty surface, which could at best twist an ankle and at worst send her head-over-heals down the steepening slopes of Thunderhead. She was moving now by pulling herself along from tree to tree, except where they were spaced too far apart or where the rhododendrons grew. Their outer branches were too pliant to provide a boost forward, their inner sturdier branches protected from Kim's grasp by the large shiny leaves that grew thick and folded themselves against the cold. Odd, she thought, these wild bushes everywhere, worthy of the most formal garden landscape, growing in this most inhospitable place, bestowed with the wisdom to close themselves against the winter weather. She was grateful to them for shielding her from the icy wind where they grew thickest.

After endless climbing, Kim knew the day was growing short. She came to a place in the trail where, at the end of the tunnel of trees and rhododendrons, there was nothing but white. She hoped with every sinew of her being that it was the top of Thunderhead, but as she reached that place, she found it was not. Instead, the trail had reached the edge of the mountain, exposed and windy. From that point, it angled left, with steep rocks and twisted low shrubs on the left, and nothing on the right above or below that could be seen through the blizzard's white cloak. Kim assumed it a severe drop-off, and the trail was narrow and slippery with rocks beneath the snow and ice. The trail was steep as far as her eye could dissect the fog. *Dare I go on here? What good am I to Michelle if I should find the bottom of this abyss with my broken bones?* The white air was turning dingy gray as the last light of day was slowly snuffed.

Kim knew she was beaten, at least for this day. She wisely retreated a few yards back into the thick arms of the rhododendrons. She found a part so thick it made a virtual cave where she felt the wind bite no more, and the snow barely filtered through its roof. She should have prepared for a night on Thunderhead, but she had no more than the clothes on her back and a spare pair of socks. She had a little water and some food, enough for this night alone. She knew that at first light, she must get over the mountain to Spence Field, for she could never survive a second night in these conditions with her meager provisions. Sleep overcame her quickly as she burrowed in and curled her long flexible body into the smallest coil she could.

* * * * *

Michelle awoke with a start. She peered outward from her bivouac as she heard a crash below her. Then she heard a pop like the report of an ancient musket echoing from the trees and the mountainside and the very low hung clouds overhead. It too was followed by a crash, the breaking of branches and the dead muffled thud of a heavy object striking the snow-covered ground. In the surreal and eerie twilight, made more so by the fog in her mind, Michelle could see the branches of trees heavy-laden with snow bending downward, the tops of some smaller trees likewise drooping with the weight in their crowns. She heard more pops and crashes, these more distant than the first. Is the whole forest going to break and bury me? She remembered a time from some distant part of her childhood (just when, she could not say), a New Year's night, snow, fireworks. Her father had wrapped her in a blanket against the cold so that just her eyes showed as they did now. It could not have been at home in Los Angeles for they had no such conditions, but she could not remember from which vacation perhaps these reminiscences came. Maybe they were but a dream. Her leg did not hurt now. She tried to move it, but nothing moved. Sleep came again before she could remember to worry about it.

* * * * *

Kim woke after a few hours. There was little light and what light she saw was without direction. Clearly it was night now. Enough snow had filtered through to cover her lightly so that the Cobalt blue of her parka barely showed through. She tried to look out from her rhododendron cave, but everywhere she moved the branches, there was a wall of snow. Trapped! Buried alive! were her first thoughts. No, there could not be that much snow, so she chose the spot in the branches where she thought she had entered the sanctuary, gathered her fortitude and pushed her way through as if she were swimming through surf, until she touched the cold night wind with her hands. She looked back at the refuge from where she emerged, the womb that had just birthed her, and found it covered with scarcely a foot of snow. The snow still fell, now in great globs that came straight down despite the wind and landed with a splat like bird droppings wherever they hit. She could not see ten feet in either direction. She slipped off a glove, and touched the rim of her watch, and an eerie glow like a mass of lightning bugs illuminated its dial. One-thirty. She had slept for a while. She did not feel like returning to sleep, but what choice did she have now? She re-entered the sanctuary, thankful for its warmth.

Kim tried to go to sleep again but could not. When she closed her eyes, she saw Michelle twisted upon the trail or bundled under the boulder as she had left her. Or she saw Amber, happy in herself, triumphant and arrogant, but happy, as she left the trail and her friends, following that Andy. Had they hiked out to safety, or were they sequestered safely, better equipped than she, less wounded than Michelle? Amber had searched so hard for a boyfriend. Now she had found one, such as he was, and was somewhere with him; Kim, as usual, was alone. She wondered now would she die out here without having experienced the love of a man, which Amber placed in importance above all else?

But I have experienced the love of a boy, she thought, remembering her single short-lived tryst with a childhood friend at fourteen, which started beside her pool when newfound feelings snuck up on them with warm spring sun and baby oil, magnetized them, disabled thinking, seeming natural, ending a month later when his family moved. Suddenly alone, waiting for the promised calls and letters that never came, she kept her wounded heart to herself and turned her passions to running, which was, she made herself believe, much more satisfying than love or sex or anything boys had to offer. She gave up on dating but not on marriage and henceforth saved herself for the man she would love someday.

A little tear formed in her eye as she thought, should she die on this frozen mountain, she would never meet that man and never know his love. Perhaps Amber had it right after all. No! she thought emphatically, marshaling the strength within her. Sentimental weakness. Tomorrow she would wake, and her years of training would pay off. Michelle was depending on her. She was depending on herself. She would bring herself off this mountain if she had to swim through the snow to do it.

* * * * *

Michelle dreamed of Greg: she was following him through the city. He was walking, and she was running, but she could not keep up with him. Her broken leg flopped helplessly beneath her weight. She did not fall, but she made little forward progress, as if she were running on a treadmill. Greg was looking over his shoulder, encouraging her to continue. They were going somewhere urgently, somewhere important. There were people in the streets. They stood still and watched, with smiles on their faces. They were strangers but somehow very familiar ones. There was snow falling, but it never touched the ground. The air was warm like summer, and she was wearing nothing but her running shorts and top. Why won't Greg stop and wait? she wondered, but she kept plodding forward. Finally, she reached him, and it was not him anymore. It was herself.

* * * * *

Kim fell sleep again at last, but her sleep was not sound. She had put herself on alert, but she did not know for what. She felt as though she were watching, listening for something, and each time she drifted off to sleep again, some sound, real or imagined, would wake her. She would sit up and listen, but she heard nothing save the sound of the wind, like dogs howling, and a sound she could not identify, like the sound of babies crying, only more melancholy and less strident. That sound came only occasionally, and she lay and wondered at its source, whether it was an animal or something inanimate that came alive only on nights like this one.

During one such waking moment, Kim caught herself talking to herself, though only in hushed, whispered tones as if someone might overhear. She wondered if this was one of the signs of insanity or, more likely, incoherence brought on by hypothermia. She shuffled through the list of symptoms mentally, and the only one that she could say for sure that she had was uncontrollable shivering. The temperature inside her refuge had dropped since she first found it to be a warm shelter from the wind and cold. Her body heat had melted the snow slightly that had filtered through the incomplete roof overhead onto the mattress of dead rhododendron leaves, and the surface of her fleece pants were damp, though her layers of wicking fabrics were doing their job of keeping that moisture from reaching her skin, thereby keeping her alive. Her legs, though, felt the cold severely, and numbness was creeping into her calves. They ached from the cold and the grueling climb she had forced on them against their will. She felt them with her ungloved hand. They were not entirely numb. She massaged them tenderly, partly to restore circulation and partly with the kind of affection bestowed upon a pet. Strange but true, she thought, I do have affection for these. They are my friends and have served me well. I must take care of them, for tomorrow I am going to ask them to do the impossible.

She ran her hand over the back of her calf, feeling the rippled smoothness of the muscle just under the skin. She could feel where its two bellies divided and rejoined, merging into the Achilles tendon, hard and tight as bone. All these years I've trained, readying myself for race after race, but really I've just been training for this, this great test of my strength against the best course nature could lay out for me. Just as in every race, the key is ninety-percent mental. I just have to focus and follow my usual preparations. I must keep myself hydrated. I only have a little water left, but I can eat snow. I have to keep my muscles warm and loose. She continued stroking, pushing the blood through from her feet to her calves, her thighs and her buttocks.

Several more times she drifted to sleep, but each time when she awoke, her legs ached. She continued to massage them, and she ceased feeling the numbness that she had felt before. She continued to review her running strategy, focusing her mind on the finish, but that was difficult, for she had no idea where the finish line might be, whether there would indeed be people at Spence Field, whether they would be able to help, whether they would be willing. But that did not matter. She would force her mind to focus only on one stretch of trail at a time, exercising the power of her mind over her body to overcome its pains, its whinings as she had always done before so successfully.

She heard noises outside the refuge that she had not heard before. It was the sound of voices, and when she pushed her head through the snow, she saw three men on horseback, dressed in uniforms, park rangers. They said she was safe now. She tried to tell them about Michelle and Amber, but they would not listen.

One said to another, "She is out of her mind with hypothermia. If we are going to get her out of here, it will have to be with force."

So they grabbed her, cuffed her hands behind her back and laid her facedown across the haunches of one of the horses, and started to ride on up the snowy trail.

Suddenly Kim awoke again; the sound of her own voice protesting had wakened her from her dream. She was still huddled in her hideaway, and her arms were asleep from her laying on them. She twisted until her arms were free, and she lay there waiting for the pins and needles to begin. When they did, she lay as still as she could, avoiding the anguish any small movement would bring until the full flow of blood was reestablished to her appendages. She knew she could safely move again once her arms began to feel hot as if the sun were radiating on them. She rubbed them until they felt normal again, and then she repeated the massage treatment for her glutes and legs. Would morning ever come? she asked aloud, and the babies cried their woeful song again in reply. She looked at her watch and it was just three.

Kim lay back and employed her relaxation techniques, gently commanding with tender voice each of her muscles to let go, to let the tension fall out of her like melting butter, until she felt heavy and liquid upon the ground, her breathing smooth and relaxed. She fell asleep once more and slept soundly until morning.

Sunday

At three-thirty on Saturday, snow had begun to fall on the Great Smoky Mountains, laying itself down upon the range of peaks the Appalachian Trail traversed, laying itself down from west to east, from one end to the other as a white sheet pulled up to cover a brown-suited corpse upon a bed. It fell on Brian and Carrie nearly halfway to Spence from Russell, before they made their way back to the shelter. It fell on Roy and Dwight and their new companions huddling for warmth inside Spence Field shelter. It fell on Kim and Michelle as Michelle lay broken on the stony trail winding up the eastern side of Thunderhead, Kim hovering lovingly more as mother than friend, before striking out to garner help. It fell on Amber and Andy as they shivered against the cold clinging to each other inside the remnants of their shredded tent, hidden within a fold in the mountain beneath Lower Buckeye Gap. It fell on the youth of God as they were warm and safe but divided between Silers Bald and Double Spring Gap.

14
Thunderhead

Kim awoke again at first light. She drank the last of her water and ate a PowerBar and made her way through the branches and the snow until she reached the open air. Snow blanketed everything so that the world was white, and somewhere lost in the whiteness was a mountain, and over that mountain was a trail that she must find in order to survive and save her friends. The last hours of sleep had returned the stiffness and numbness to her muscles and joints, and she rubbed them and moved them until they felt warm again. She could see nothing to show her the direction, but she remembered that up the mountain was left, so to the left she began. She could not tell if she were in a fog or whether the snow was still falling that thickly. Which one did not matter; she had only to find her way by feel, and she ended up spending more time on all fours than she did standing up.

After what seemed like an eternity, she reached the place where she had been the day before, where the trail turned sharply to the left and clung tenuously to the windswept side of the mountain. There the wind began to bite, but she welcomed it, for in its relentlessness, it had kept the trail swept clean of snow so that it showed through the white air like a gray stone walkway at least ten feet in front of her at a time. She increased her pace, concentrating with all her fortitude upon her footsteps, for she had no idea where one missed step might land her. In short time, this dark ribbon of trail led her to a place where several stones were piled on top of one another, a carne clearly marking a place of significance. The land sloped away in all directions, and Kim correctly deduced that she was standing on top of Thunderhead. She had no idea that she had spent the night so close to its top.

Kim continued a few more feet in the direction in which she had been traveling, when suddenly she was nearly swept off her feet by a gale of a wind coming from her right. It stung her face with powdery snow picked up from the crags about the summit of the mountain. She stood resolute against its force, determined not to give an inch. Anger for its insults welled up from deep within her. She tucked her head and shoulders directly into its force as a fullback intent on hitting rather than being hit. She could take no steps, but neither would she give any. In respect for this courageous defiance, the same wind that assaulted her began to sweep away the veil on the mountaintops. She looked and forms appeared out of the blizzard, faint and intermittent, but increasing until she could see not only the trail before her feet but also the mountain that was her next obstacle – Rockytop.

Unwilling to let the opportunity slip away, Kim plunged forward and downward. With the momentum afforded her by gravity and increased visibility, she overcame the force of the wind that held her. No trees or rhododendrons were on her side now, only scattered trees, dwarfed, twisted and leafless, and knee-high scrub and brown grasses that anchored the snow that nearly covered them. Each step she took was a race in itself, with the same sense of victory when it was accomplished. She felt as though she were harnessed to a plow that she must drag behind her through fallow ground for the whole distance, or as if she were in a dream where the goal is in sight but cannot be reached for some surreal force preventing forward motion though every effort is applied to it. She felt something tickling her nose, a subtle sensation, strange that she would even notice it, given that she was, at the same time, inundated with a flurry of resounding stimulations. Then she realized that it was the formation of ice crystals in her nostrils. How cold did it have to be for that to happen? She pulled the collar of her fleece jacket about her ears and pulled her sylph-like neck down into it like a turtle retreating from danger. There was a white frosting of ice on her cobalt parka and her hair. She held her mittened hands upon her cheeks to shield them from freezing. They were already chapped and puffy, and her lips were cracking. She tried to lick them, but they were too rough and her tongue was too dry. She tasted the salty sweet taste of blood.

Step by precious step she moved forward, keeping her eyes upon the trail immediately before her and her heart fixed on the peak of Rocky Top, which was a half- hour hike in better conditions, so close the two mountain peaks were. At long last, her weary legs carried her to the stony top of the mountain where they went to rubber. She collapsed like a marionette whose puppeteer had let go of its strings. There was no windbreak at all on Rocky Top, and the wind blew over her crumpled form with force unequaled that day. She cried, but only a little tear came forth, stinging the battered skin as it rolled down and off her cheek to melt a tiny spot of snow where it landed. She cried for the pain, she cried for her friends, and she cried because, for the first time in her life, she had serious thoughts of defeat. But those very thoughts provoked her to cry out, "I will not die on this mountain!" Those thoughts were the tender that ignited her last reserves of inner strength. She gathered her wayward limbs and rose feebly upon them. They strengthened as she rose, for she commanded them, and they obeyed. Despite the numbness in her feet and the fog that shrouded Thunderhead once more, engulfed the peak upon which she stood and stole from her again the sight of the world around her, she pressed on, for she had seen the trail. Its contours were in her mind, and she picked her way down the path from touch and memory. She reached quickly the elevation where the wind was less fierce and the visibility grew, but there also the snow had been allowed to accumulate to drifts at least as high as her thighs and higher in places, and she could only guess where the trail actually was, hidden beneath the blanket of white.

The trail crossed another steep knob and then followed the arching ridgeline as it sunk lower toward smaller peaks. Kim knew from the map she carried that she could follow the sinking ridge all the way to Spence Field regardless of where the trail actually was, and she knew she was on the ridge as long as the land sloped downward to each side. Knowing the direction and moving in it were two entirely different things. As she lifted each leg high and forward through the drifts of snow, Kim remembered running the hurdles in high school, how she felt like a leaping gazelle with each fluid stride, clearing the top with perfect timing. She wished she could do the same now, bounding over the snow stride by stride until she broke the ribbon, and hugged her teammates, Michelle and Amber. The very thought of these beloved friends pushed her forward.

Two more times she faltered. Her feet now ached with numbness. She wondered whether she would loose her toes or even her feet from frostbite and whether she would ever run again free as the gazelle. Her eyes streamed tears, but they were not tears of emotion. The wind had burned them, and she could barely open them to see where to plod next. Sleep was hovering over her like a buzzard waiting for its moment.

Why must I go on, why don't I just go to sleep right here? she wondered, thinking of the relative warmth and safety of her refuge from last night. She tried again to stand, and again her worn-out legs crumpled. She remembered then two years ago when she had run her first marathon. She had over-trained in the days just before it and had paced herself badly so that in the last hundred yards or so, when the finish line was in sight, her legs had gone to rubber just as they were now. She had lost control of them, stumbling and walking a few yards only to collapse again. The early lead she had taken was in serious danger as the second and third place runners behind her were now in sight. When all seemed lost, she saw Michelle, running along the sideline toward her from the finish line, behind the onlookers, her face mouthing out in all its expression, "Get up. You can do it. You're the one!" Kim did get up, mustering enough strength to cross the line just ahead of the nearest challenger.

Kim saw that face again in her mind and felt those same last reserves well up within. She rose to her feet in the snow and pressed onward until shortly she came to a place where she could see, not fog, but smoke, its source just over a hillock. She had made it to help. She gathered her strength and dragged herself over the hill and into the clearing in front of Spence Field shelter.

15
Russell Field

Brian and Carrie huddled together for warmth and security through an almost sleepless night in Russell Field shelter, listening to the moaning wind and to their thoughts during the black hours when black seemed blackest, telling themselves and each other that the sun would be shining through a cloudless sky when it made its morning debut. But they were unable to dispel the dreadful thoughts that returned repeatedly to nip at their minds like a pack of hungry wolves circling and harassing its prey to wear it down, delaying the frontal attack until its victims weaken to the point that no more struggle is possible, persistence, rather than mere strength clenching the triumph in the final struggle of death. They both longed for the sun that would rescue them from these night terrors. When the sky began to lighten, they strained their eyes to make meaning out of the blankness outside the shelter. When the vague patches of light and dark divided into a discernable scene, it was not the scene they had hoped to see, and the wind still howled like the phantom wolves of nighttime imaginations. It still carried a full load of snowflakes rushing through the air as if they had no place to go, for the ground was full of them already, overflowing and penetrating the incomplete barrier of the shelter's chain link wall in a drift fully three feet tall and growing.

"This is no snow like at home," Carrie said at last. She was the first to confess aloud what they both already knew.

"No, this is no Southern snowstorm," Brian admitted, and squeezed Carrie to himself for the sole purpose of discovering whether she would respond by squeezing back. She was indeed reluctant at first but then returned the gesture and sealed it with a kiss on his icy cheek. But her hesitation had done its damage, and he was sure that she held resentment in her heart and blame toward him for the uncomfortable and fearful position in which he through pride had placed his bride.

They lay close together for warmth, staring blankly into the scene that remained unchanged before them as it became fully illuminated with the advent of daylight. It appeared like a window box, or a stage lit brightly before an audience sitting in darkness. Only this was no play. Reality lay on both sides of the curtain. The scene was truly beautiful, and, had they been viewing it through the window in the fourth wall of Carrie's fantasy cabin, they would have seen and appreciated its beauty, but now the whiteness meant blindness, the wind meant biting cold, and the blanket of snow may well have been an ocean separating them from home.

Carrie was the first to realize and to complain that she had held her bladder beyond the point of wisdom.

"I hate the thought of getting up, much less going out there and pulling my pants down, but I'm going to bust if I don't," she said climbing out of the bunk rather sheepishly. She donned her boots, having worn the rest of her clothing all night, hat and gloves included, and she went to the gate to open it. That she could not do because of the snow that hugged its bottom. Brian reluctantly climbed from the relative warmth of the sleeping bag to lend a hand, but even together they were unable to budge the gate.

"We'll just have to dig it out," Brian said, reaching for a stick of firewood sturdy enough and shaped correctly to serve as a shovel.

"There's no time," Carrie blushed, her knees pinched together, bouncing up and down as a child caught in the midst of play by surprise. She headed toward the corner of the shelter away from the fireplace and pulled down her warm-ups. Brian quickly handed her the pot they had used to collect water, and she accepted it, insisting he turn his back and go away. When finished she emptied the pot through the chain link and handed the pot to Brian.

"It's your turn."

"I don't need it," he said, and walked to the chain link wall and stood as if it were a urinal, aiming high for distance. Carrie laughed.

"What's so funny, princess?"

"What if you got frostbite doing that?"

"I'd rather not have that thought," Brian said, a little annoyed, and then he laughed. "I just better be careful not to touch the fence metal."

Carrie laughed too.

"Let's see if we can get this gate open," Brian said. After ten minutes of work, a vestibule in the snow had been created, allowing the gate to swing freely. Once outside the gate, there was no place to go and no visibility, but both felt better knowing they were free to attempt an exit should the need arise.

They were both starving after a long night of shivering and sat down to a cold breakfast. Carrie gathered two energy bars and a bagel to split between them, and Brian rekindled the fire from the live embers on the bottom of a large damp log he had placed on the fire before turning in for the night.

Brian and Carrie ate their cold breakfast in front of the fire, their moods of disappointment and exhilaration alternating as their comfort shifted from the warmth of the fire to the chill of each gust of wind.

"Brian, what if we die out here?" Carrie asked calmly, staring dreamily into the flames of the fire, her hands buried in her lap as she leaned into the warmth from the fireplace.

"We're not going to die out here, Carrie," Brian answered with critical tones. He looked at his wife's face, the warm hues of orange from the fire dancing on her face, a flame reflected in each eye.

"I'm not thinking we will, Brian. I'm just asking what if, you know. We've been rushing around getting through school, getting jobs, getting ready to get married and here we are. All of a sudden we have time to think and…well…that's what I'm thinking of." Her eyes still stared into the fire.

"Why do you want to think of something so morbid when we have so many good things to think about," Brian asked, still annoyed.

"I'm not thinking of it in a morbid way. In fact, I feel more alive right now than I ever have, I think. That's because of two things. One, we've got time to think about life. Two, we've been in some danger. You know it too, whether you want to admit it to me or not. And for me, thinking about death makes me think about life. We're going to die sometime. If we don't freeze to death out here, then maybe a bad trucker will run us over on the way home. I don't know how long I have to live, and you don't either. All I know is I'm alive right now, and I want every minute to count. Facing death makes you kinda prioritize things, you know. It puts it in a new perspective, like, what do I want to do before I die? And what would I change about today if I knew I were going to die tomorrow?"

"OK, Princess. You've got my attention now. Where are you going with all this?"

"I'm not really going anywhere. I want us to talk about something serious. We always talk about work, or the house, or where we want to go for our next vacation. I want us to talk about what is really important to us in life."

"You're important to me."

"What if I die out here, but you make it back?" Carrie asked, finally turning her eyes to Brian.

"I'm not going to let that happen," Brian said, looking away to escape the fire that burned in her eyes.

"Brian. Stop. I'm not saying what will happen out here. I'm saying, what if? Talk to me." She reached for his hand.

"I don't want to think about you dying. If it happens, I'll deal with it. I don't know how, 'cause I really can't imagine life without you. I can't even remember what it was like before we met."

"All right, what if it were the other way around? What if you die out here? What does that make you think about right now?"

"I'd die a failure because I promised nothing would happen to you on this trip."

"Well what if something happens you can't help, like if you got sick or something?"

"I'd be real upset because there are things I haven't done yet that I want to do."

"Now we're talking! What do you want to do before you die?"

"Have our fiftieth wedding anniversary."

"Seriously," Carrie said, now the one acting annoyed.

"I am being serious. When I said I wanted to spend my life with you, I meant a long life. I want to make love to you when you are young and middle-aged and old. I want to watch your tits and your butt sag to the ground and wrinkles grow around your eyes…not very fast of course. I want you to have my children and to see you spoil our grandchildren. I want us to grow old together. So that's why I don't like these questions. What about you? What do you want to do before you die?"

Carrie looked into the fire again as if the answers were burning there.

"I want to feel like my life made a difference in the world. I don't feel like that yet. I feel like everything I've done so far in life is just planning for the future or having fun. I don't feel like I've really made a difference in anybody else's life yet. I haven't even had a chance to make a difference in your life yet. So you'd miss me for a while, and then you'd find someone else to take my place. Maybe someone you like better. Maybe just someone you would like differently. But the point is that I am replaceable. Unh uh, don't interrupt. I know you think that's not so, or you want me to think it's not so, but I can't see you running off joining a monastery just because I'm gone. You like sex too much for that…"

"I like sex with you."

"You're just sentimental. But my point is that if I died now, I wouldn't leave much of a memory behind. I'd be a tombstone, a photo on my parents' living room wall and one on your dresser you stick in a drawer every time you bring home a date and in the dumpster when the next Mrs. Ralston comes along. Maybe someone from high school might say, 'Poor Carrie', whenever they get their yearbook out. Maybe not."

"So what do you want to do about it?" Brian asked, brushing by her to put another branch on the fire. "I mean, isn't that the way things are for most people? You do what you want to do, and then you die, and if you lived long enough to have children they carry on the genes and the family name."

"That may be true for most people, but it's not good enough for me. What makes me different from just the animals? Their whole purpose in life is to mate, reproduce, raise young whose whole purpose in life is to mate, reproduce, and so on, and so on. That deer we saw is doing that, but I'll remember him for the rest of my life. He made a difference in me, and he didn't even know it. He was just looking for something to eat. He was doing just what he was made to do, and that was what was so beautiful about him, a wild animal in the wilds, in his place, carrying on the species, fulfilling his destiny. But aren't we made for more than just that? Aren't we supposed to leave a mark on this world, even if it is just a small one?"

"And how do you propose to leave a mark, Carrie? We can't all be famous."

"I'm not talking about being famous. I'm talking about something that continues when you are gone. It's not good enough just to have children. When we have children, I want to give them something that helps them make a mark on the world. Maybe I'm just going to be the grandmother of someone famous." Carrie added her own stick to the fire.

"While you're making your mark, I'm going to be making sure you and your kids have a good roof over your heads in a good neighborhood with a good school, a couple of good cars, braces and college for the kids. That will be my mark. Something to retire on. Retire early on."

"And season tickets to the Braves. And a boat. And a weekend place at Lake Lanier…"

"And some great vacations the kids will remember," Brian added, completely unaware that Carrie was being sarcastic.

"And where does it all end, Brian?" Carrie took his hand again. "I don't want to see you use yourself up trying to be happy, trying to make me happy with all those things. Can't we just be content with what we have now? I don't want to be a slave to all those things. They will end up owning us instead of us owning them. I want something simpler."

"Carrie? These are all the things we've talked about wanting together. What has changed?" Brian asked with quivers of hurt in his voice. He felt betrayed and began to calculate the amount they could recover by the sale of their once-used backpacking equipment.

"This trip has opened my eyes, Brian. You talked about this trip with a real passion for months. It's a great adventure for you. A test of your manhood. For me it was something to dread, something I didn't want to do. Something I was willing to do for you because you wanted it so badly. But I was surprised when I got out here – how simple life really is when you get away from all that racket we live in. When I was standing face to face with that deer, he was in his place. I was not. And I was jealous of him for it. He always does what he is supposed to do. He always knows what he is supposed to do. He hears us and smells the air. He sees us and freezes. We get too close, he moves away. We frighten him and he runs. He's hungry, he eats. No one has to tell him what to do. I've never felt like

I knew what to do, so I did what others said. Not what my nature said. Not like him. Now I'm hearing it for the first time. It was like looking in a mirror and seeing, not what I am, but what I could be, if I find my place in life where I have only what really matters to me. And I've discovered out here how very little I really need to be happy. Brian, when we get back, I want to forget about those things that don't really matter so we can concentrate on what really does matter."

"What really matters?" Brian asked, folding his arms across his heart and leaning back on the big old piece of log, the only piece of furniture in the shelter, other than the built-in bunks.

"Our relationship really matters. I'm in love with you, and you are in love with me, I hope, but time is going to test that, and the feelings may fade, and something stronger, some more permanent kind of love is going to have to replace those feelings, or we will end up like everyone else: two BMW's, a lake house and a divorce. I want us to spend more time in nature and forget about the season tickets. And I want kids, when the time comes. Brian?"

"Yes," Brian answered softly.

"I'm going to tell you what I want to do. I don't want to be a bank teller forever. And I don't want to be a branch manager either. I know all those plans we made about things we wanted kind of hinge on me working. But what I really want to do is go back to school." She waited for his response.

"Back to school? What, do you want to be a teacher and 'make a difference' in an inner city school like what's-his-name, the black thru-hiker? I really went out on a limb getting you that teller job. Carrie, you're turning everything upside down." Brian stood and picked up the cooking pot to get snow to set by the fire so it would melt.

"I only want to take a class at the community college. At night. I won't have to quit work yet."

"Nothing's wrong with taking a class, I suppose. What kind of class?" he asked, returning with a heaping pot-full of snow.

"Creative writing," Carrie stated softly.

"What was that?"

"Creative writing," she said again, bracing for ridicule.

"Why creative writing? I thought you hated English in high school."

"I want to write. I want to put things in print. I want to say things that make a difference in people's lives. Even if I'm gone." Carrie hung her head, not for shame, for she was proud of these words, and she had put much thought into this. She hung her head for disappointment, for Brian's shame, that he had failed to grasp the depth within her from which these things had come and the resolute will that was behind them, pushing them to the surface, forging in her a determination to make a decided change in a life so programmed for mediocrity. All her new husband had heard was that she wanted to take a class, make a career change that had no guarantee of income or benefits, to the detriment of mutually agreed upon plans to excel in materialism. She had thought that he, who had been the author of this trip that had created in her the will to change, had planned it entirely for other reasons than he had, the real reasons that she now understood, though he had not yet been open enough with her to express them. Time. She would give him time to let these things sink in. Perhaps he would yet hear her heartfelt desperation and understand it and support her, even be with her, in bringing herself to a fully conscious and purposeful state of life.

"Carrie, if you want to take a class that's fine. Now, I've been thinking about something that's bothering me since you started talking about dying out here."

"Yes, Brian?" she asked, expecting that he would bare some secret part of his soul to her.

"If this doesn't let up and start melting real soon today, we might have to be here a few more nights. We need to see how the food situation is holding out. Especially since we lost some to the mice the other night."

Carrie's heart sank as Brian rose and took down the food bags from their hangers. He poured out the contents on the bottom bunk and sorted the various packets remaining into individual piles, each one representing a meal. Without any allowance for snacks, he had four small piles, four more meals. Unless they rationed their provisions, or unless they were able to hike out the next day as planned, hunger would become a real issue for the couple by evening on Monday. This he chose to keep from Carrie.

"Well?" she asked.

"We've got just enough to get us out of here," he said, a statement not entirely a lie, just a failure to add that the truth to his answer hinged fully on the slim chance that the trail would be hikable the next day.

"I think I'll try a nap. I'm feeling sleepy," Carrie said, which was true, but she really just wanted to be alone to mull over the meaning of the conversation they had and to give Brian a chance to do the same. She kicked off her boots and slid herself into the double bag, hoping that Brian would not decide that he would sleep, too, and especially hoping that he would not get the idea to have sex. But Brian was content to tend his fire and run contingencies through his head of how to get his bride safely down the mountain without letting her lose faith in him entirely.

Carrie reflected on her disappointment at Brian's responses, nursing little flickers of anger at first, but answering them with justifications such as the newness of the marriage, the time it would take to nurture the kind of communication she planned to achieve in it, his justified preoccupation with making provision both in the wilds of the Smokies and in those of suburban Atlanta. She slipped quietly into soft slumber, cushioned with thoughts of his warmness and tenderness and his ability and promise to care for and provide for her and their future children, all the things that had brought her to marry him in the first place.

BRIAN SAT AND nursed his fire. He did reflect, but not as deeply as Carrie had hoped, for he still did not understand that she had initiated the conversation in order to share her heart and her hopes. He only felt that somehow his wife had attacked him and the things that were important to him. Maybe she was just letting loose of some emotions left over from the stress of the wedding combined with the fears she now faced being stranded. She would have to learn how to face crises with him, though. Certainly there would be crises to face in the future, and one of the points of marriage, he remembered his father telling him, was that two are stronger than one when bound together. His thoughts turned from his marriage to his father. His father had a cliché for every occasion. When it came to a man's job of provider, he had many. His father owned an old style hardware store, which he had built by hard work, long hours and the motto that every customer must leave his store happy. A job that is worth doing is worth doing right. Know your business son and keep your nose out of everyone else's. Know your business better than the next guy...

When the discount chains came, Mr. Ralston had taken a beating, but his core of regular customers, who had counted on him through the years to know what they needed for any task, continued to patronize his store, after they had tried the new ones and found that, though the price was considerably cheaper, they usually came home with something that was not suitable for the job or that just didn't fit. Some stayed with him just for the personal attention. So he stayed in business, survived, and managed to send Brian to college, the first in his family to do so. A couple of years later Brian's brother followed, and then his sister. Brian's father had taught him that hard work pays off in the long run when everyone else is cutting corners and getting away with it in the short run. This he bolstered by constant example of a deep-seeded work ethic. Brian went to college knowing that it was his father's hard work and not his socioeconomic birthright that had put him there, and he was determined to make it good. And he did, though he was not a born student. The same hard work had earned him a couple of promotions since he started his entry-level job at the bank. He felt the sky was the limit, and he would go as far as he could with it. For his father. For Carrie. For his children. For himself. Because he had learned to love toys and wanted many of them. And he loved providing them for others. This was so confusing, what Carrie was talking about. It seemed so opposite to everything he felt was important and his father had taught him was important. Well, if she wanted to take a course, fine. She'll come around when they get home. Life will be fun again. Life could be fun now, snowed in together and all. As long as they didn't have to keep thinking morbid thoughts about death and trying to change the world.

Brian looked over at his wife. All the muscles of her face were relaxed in sleep. She looked sixteen. He loved her. Taking care of her and making her happy were the important things. Why had he risked all that bringing her out here? She and he and Mother Nature. It had all seemed so right when he planned it. But then the hiking was so hard that it nearly took the wind out of both their sails. They found the strength to go on, strength they didn't know they had. Being caught out in the blizzard was really scary, but they had made it through that together.

She'll feel better when she wakes up. Everything will be back the way it was, the way it should be.

He put another piece of wood on the fire and strained to see if the snow was beginning to slow. It wasn't. He sighed, and the wind sighed, and he took a long drink from the pan of melted snow.

16
Spence Field

Kim did not know the depth of her tiredness until Spence Field shelter appeared. When she saw it, a sense of relief swept over her like a tidal wave carrying away the last ounce of energy that she had wrung from each cell in her body. She dragged herself to the gate and opened her cracking, bleeding lips to call to those inside. Try as she might, no sound came forth from her parched throat. She tried to open the latch, but her fingers were dead and were of no use. All she could do was lie in the snow and kick one leg against the fence anemically so that barely a rattle resulted beyond the noise the wind was making anyway. It was enough, just enough, to catch Roy's attention. He rose from his spot by the fire to investigate. The others wondered what he was doing. He wondered himself, but his keen senses had been alerted to something he heard or felt, and his training had taught him to give full attention to intuitive stirrings within himself that would go unnoticed by most others.

He opened the gate with some difficulty, for despite his and Dwight's taking turns keeping the ice free in its latch and hinges, they were frozen again. The ice cracked free after a few blows from the heal of his hand. He opened the gate, and there, in the stairwell of snow formed by Roy and Dwight's digging to keep the exit clear, lay Kim. Her eyes of glass looked out from her beaten face, which was incapable of any expression, though inside of her, tears of joy flowed freely. Roy yelled for Dwight's assistance, and the two of them carried her to the fire. All others made room as if the whole scene had been choreographed. Kim was trying to speak, but still could not. She struggled within to make herself heard, for her battle was not over until she had delivered the news of her stricken friends and brought help to them.

Roy first removed the mittens from her hands, which were white and translucent like porcelain. Several of her fingers were frozen hard and stiff, and Roy called for a pan of cold water in which to submerse them.

She resisted weakly, but Roy's manner gave no room for negotiation. Kim let the hands, the frozen hands that seemed not hers anyway, fall limply into the water. Moments passed and nothing happened. Then she felt a distant pain in them that grew until it felt as though Roy were holding her hands over the fire. She opened her blurry eyes to reassure herself that her hands were still in the water. The fire in her fingers increased with each beat of her heart, and soon the pain was nearly unbearable. When it reached the point where she thought she could tolerate it no more, it began to subside, replaced instead by a sensation that her skin was dead and falling off. She relaxed as the pain departed from her fingers. Roy called Dwight to inspect her hands, and Roy went to work removing her frozen boots, for by now the fire had melted the ice on them sufficiently for him to free the laces. Kim felt nothing as he removed the boots and then her socks and held her icy feet in his bare hands. Her toes were as cold as ice, but the skin was pliable on all of them. The only damage her feet had sustained was red raw blisters on toes and heels. He put on her feet a pair of dry wool socks donated by Rochelle Bobo and looked up to Dwight for a prognosis on the state of her hands. Mrs. Ramsey draped her in a sleeping bag, repeating Poor dear! Poor dear! Rochelle spoon-fed her a cup of instant soup.

"Her hands were frozen and are beginning to blister, but I don't think there will be any deep tissue damage," Dwight said.

"You mean she won't lose them," Roy translated.

"I don't think so, but I can't promise it. Time will tell."

Kim looked up at them with pleading eyes. Though she could not speak, she could certainly hear, and she wished they would talk to her rather than about her. She attempted to say something, and this time sound came out, heard only as a squeak. Dejected, she sank back into the down sleeping bag and the arms of Mrs. Ramsey who was holding it. Poor dear! Poor dear! she repeated, and Mr. Ramsey came forth with a sudden idea.

"It's unlikely she was alone! Child, you weren't alone, were you?" he asked. At this, she rose up from Mrs. Ramsey's supporting arms, shaking her head urgently.

"Are your friends all right?" asked Mr. Ramsey. Again she answered by shaking her head. She started to speak again, and words came out: the soup was working. With raspy voice, she managed to communicate with the fewest words Michelle's plight and Amber's unknown fate. While the seriousness of their situation was sinking in to all those gathered around, Kim fell into a deep sleep where she dreamed that the sun came out and the good people around her were lifting Michelle out of her half-cave refuge. They let her sleep, knowing that there was little could be done until she regained some strength. She did not sleep long, and when she awoke, she looked around blankly, her mind straining to separate truth from her dreams. The warming fire, the soup and the short sleep had given her strength, and her sense of urgency returned with it.

She rose to her feet, a simple act that caught everyone's full attention. Her voice was stronger, but hoarseness remained.

"Who can come with me to rescue Michelle?" she asked. The onlookers blinked and cast questioning glances at one another, then they all looked at Roy, who had emerged as the group's leader at least as far as matters of survival were concerned.

"Kim," he said softly but firmly. "You are too weak to go out there again. You won't make it. You tell us the best you can where Michelle is, and we will try to find her."

Kim thought for a long moment on his offer. Then her mind was clear and resolute.

"There is no way you can find her in this mess. I have to show you. Let's go."

"Kim do you know what time it is?" Dwight asked.

A puzzled look spread across her face. No, she did not know.

"It's almost four o'clock. Kim, whoever goes to get Michelle is going to have to wait until the morning."

"She's already been out in this one night. She won't make it through another one…" her voice trailed off as the sense of utter helplessness, so foreign to her, overtook her, and the wisdom and firmness in Dwight's voice made her face the reality that truly nothing could be done until first light.

Kim sank back to a sitting position. She discovered that she could cry again. It even felt good to cry, and it felt especially good when Mrs. Ramsey wrapped her boney arms about her and held her, gently rocking. She could almost feel that everything was going to be all right, but there was a stronger voice within still calling her to do something, do something. Kim had never been one to trust to others what she could do herself. All of her problems before had called for action on her part, and it was all she knew how to do. She thought in her mind, to hell with them and to hell with the time, and to hell with these burning hands. Her body tensed as if to rise again, but she knew they were right. The inward struggle continued until she fell fast asleep again, this time for a couple of hours.

While Kim slept, Mrs. Ramsey held her and Mr. Ramsey held Mrs. Ramsey. Everyone was holding someone, either for warmth or security or both. Except for Roy and Dwight. They were huddling to devise a plan. At first light, they would head out with or without Kim depending on her strength. They would need one backpack between them, and they would trade it off, so that they were not too encumbered to move quickly, but they would have necessary food and medical supplies, dry clothes for Michelle and the tent. Yes, they needed the tent, for likely they would be spending at least a night out, if not more, and it was possible that Michelle could not move at all, in which case someone would have to stay with her until further help arrived. Dwight suggested that Michelle, injured and exposed on the north side of Thunderhead, could not possibly survive one night, much less two nights, but he knew they had to try. Roy said, the hell she couldn't. If she was half as strong and a quarter as bullheaded as Kim, she could survive a week. Amber's fate, they thought, hinged on whether they had found shelter or walked out before the snow. There was nothing they could do for her now beyond speculation.

Meanwhile Mr. Ramsey discoursed on his opinion that women unaccompanied by men had no business in these mountains, or anywhere for that matter. The Bobos would have taken offense had they been listening. Roy and Dwight were too amused by his opinionated ramblings to take them very seriously. Mrs. Ramsey was used to them, but would no doubt make him pay for his monologue later. He was just coming to the point that the women of his day would never have tried it, and how it used to be was how it ought to be, when Roy and Dwight decided that what was really needed for the rescue tomorrow was snowshoes. Mr. Ramsey took their stirring about to be signs of attention to his discourse, so he began again in earnest disparaging the liberated woman and the weakly men who pander to her. But Roy and Dwight heard none of it as they headed out the door to gather the raw materials for making snowshoes. Fortunately they didn't have to go far to find the saplings suitable for bending into ovals, for as darkness began to envelop the shelter, the storm that had not really let up all that day, was intensifying its fury, and the temperature was dropping rapidly.

Upon returning to the shelter, Mrs. Ramsey called Roy to see that blisters were also forming on Kim's cheeks. Roy gave her some salve from their first aid kit, and Mrs. Ramsey lovingly applied it to her cheeks and her lips while she slept. She was afraid to touch her hands. They looked so painful as Kim worked them open and closed in her sleep, and Mrs. Ramsey wanted to do nothing to wake the poor dear. The two children looked on wordlessly as they huddled together, wondering whether she was dead or would die or was she a princess escaped from captivity in some dark castle hidden in these mountains. Kim was a source of both wonderment and fear to the children, for she was a mystery, but she was also an example of what this beautiful snowstorm could do to a human being caught in it. Snow had never before been a potential enemy in the children's minds, and something of their childhood innocence was lost as they gazed at her with disquieted curiosity.

Kim awoke as preparations for an evening meal were underway. Two stoves were going, and a variety of foods waited in line to be heated and hydrated. Were it not for the fact that Roy and Dwight had just re-supplied in Fontana, the group would be perilously short of food and fuel, for the Ramsey's were just out for a day hike, and though they had brought some extra supplies, this meal would finish them off. The Bobos had just enough for one more day, and Kim had none at all. Besides, the rescue party, which would depart in the morning, had need of taking sufficient provisions for four people, and no one knew for how long they would need them. But the group – haphazardly thrown together by fate with nothing in common but the snow, the mountains and the shelter, so different that if they had met in any other way in normal life, they would have passed each other unnoticed or at best with an obligatory greeting before going on their separate ways – the group had begun to function as one. The first evidence of this was their sharing of food and the sense that what anyone had they all had in common.

Kim felt even more alert and energy was returning, but she had awaked with a ravenous appetite and could hardly wait for her portion to cool before she devoured it. It was a rice dish with beans, which her body transformed quickly into energy and strength. After dinner, except for her face and hands, Kim felt no more effects of her ordeal than if she had run a marathon. Her muscles were tense with lactic acid, but her body was relaxed with a good tiredness. Even Roy and Dwight were amazed at her recovery, for all were expecting that she would be an invalid at least until they were extricated from this storm. Her hands now throbbed, and each movement sent searing pain up her arms, but it was superficial pain from damaged skin. Circulation had returned fully even to the tips of all fingers, and the damage was like second-degree burns. Kim borrowed skin cream from Rochelle and greased her hands to keep the skin as supple as possible, for it felt to her as though the skin were shrinking and would split if she moved them. Kim then cornered Roy to ascertain the details of the morrow's rescue plans. Roy and Dwight were surprised that she still included herself in them. Nevertheless, her rapid recovery forced them to reconsider their estimation of her fortitude.

"That is truly one strong girl," Dwight told Roy when she was out of earshot.

"You aren't joking. I'm not going to be the one who stands in the way of anything she's set her mind to do. And she sure has set her mind that not one of her friends is going to perish without her permission, wouldn't you say?" Roy said, rolling his eyes to underscore his incredulity.

"We'd better make that third pair of snowshoes," Dwight said, and they did while Kim was scrounging the cooking area for leftovers to satisfy the deep hunger she still felt in her bones, though her stomach was full.

Rochelle and Richard tucked their children into their sleeping bags. The children whined about their early bedtime just as they always did at home, but they were both quickly sound asleep. The couple then rejoined the others at the fire, which Mr. Ramsey had augmented with several more branches to offset the falling temperature.

"How is it that three kids from California are out here by themselves," Howard Ramsey asked Kim. Everyone groaned that he was going to start up again, and Mrs. Ramsey elbowed him a warning. Kim, having slept through his opinions earlier, took it as a simple question.

"We've done just about everything together for years now. We like the outdoors, but our parents don't, or they don't have the time. So here we are. Well, here I am. We never expected it to end up like this," she said looking down at blistered hands, her voice hoarse but improving.

"A lot of folks underestimate these mountains," Mr. Ramsey said with the air of an old guide. "I've seen snow up here as late as April, and when we have an inch at home we can have a foot or more up here. This one's pretty bad though. I haven't seen too many like this before, 'ceptin' the Blizzard of Ninety-Three. That one caught a lot of folks off guard. Why they even brought out the ol' hundred an' first to rescue folks up here…"

"Hundred and first?" Roy asked.

The others breathed a sigh of relief that Mr. Ramsey's meanness seemed to be melting. Beneath his gruff and rigid façade lay the heart of a loving grandfather.

"Yep. The Hundred and First Airborne. Had them up here rescuing folks and doing airdrops and such," old Mr. Ramsey said, wiping the beads of sweat from his age-spotted forehead with the back of his glove.

"You mean they called out the 101st Airborne Division for a snowstorm?" Roy asked with obvious doubt in his voice.

"Yep, the same Hundred and First that they dropped on ol' Normandy. They're parked up here in Fort Campbell, ya know, straddling the Tennessee-Kintucky border, oh maybe two hundred miles from here. That was a real bad'un, that Blizzard of Ninety-Three was. People were even stuck for days in those trailer campgrounds down low. Didn't have no water nor 'lectricity, an' a lot of 'em didn't have much food, neither."

"That must have been something down here in the south," Richard interjected.

"Boy, you ain't down in the south when yer in these mountains. You may as well be up in Canada as fer as the weather goes. Sure it don't stay so cold so long, and we don't get as much snow, but folks who come here better know what they're gittin' into when they come. Some Yankee smart alec comes down here in March and has seventy degree days and goes home and tells everyone he knows to leave their coats at home when they's comin' south. Bet yer glad ya didn't leave yer coat home, now ain't ya?"

"Well," Richard hawed, "I knew to be ready for the unexpected. But I know what you mean."

"Don't mind Howard, Mr. Bobo," Mrs. Ramsey intervened, "He gits touchy about people gettin' hurt in his mountains. He thinks they are *his* mountains, ya know. Somebody dies up here just about every year, not in a snow storm, but on account of something that caught them by surprise."

"Happens all the time that someone wanders off on one of those seventy degree days, then gets rained on and all wet, gets lost and dies of hypermia or whatever that is. Ya know you can die of that when the air's fifty degrees. Did ya know that? Sure. Ya git wet, and it's as good as freezin' ta death."

Howard Ramsey sighed out those last words, and the tension drained from his muscles. His heavy shoulders drooped, and he suddenly looked very tired.

"It's true," Roy said. "Hypothermia gets a lot of people off guard. When a person starts losing core body heat, he gets real confused and does stupid things, like wandering off the trail or taking clothes off. It's especially easy to get once a person is wet, even from sweat."

"It's a wonder Kim here didn't get it," Howard said, his voice a little shaky, not the deep and loud, forceful one he had used so far. "She's out all night in this blizzard, just skin and bones and skintight leotards."

"I kept moving, and I didn't get wet, that's all I can say," Kim said. "These synthetic clothes wick the moisture away from my skin. So they don't look like much, but you stay dry."

"That and the weather didn't have your permission to give you hypothermia," Roy said. He looked surprised that the words just popped out. "I mean you never gave up."

Satisfied with that response, Kim started to say that she was ready to turn in but then realized she had no bag. So she waited to see what would happen as the others readied themselves for bed. Roy first thought of her need and said that he would donate his for her use and he would use their tent as a cover, but only if he could sleep between two others for the extra warmth. Bedding was being arranged when a commotion began by the fireside.

All looked and saw Howard Ramsey clutching his chest, his face red then white as it contorted, clenched in pain. Kathleen put something under his tongue and before too many moments he seemed to relax and the pain subsided.

"It's just his angina," Mrs. Ramsey said to reassure the onlookers, but her worried face did little to reassure them. She turned back to Howard to reassure herself. He was recovering as usual, and he decided that he, too, was ready for bed. The others returned to their preparations, and soon all were sleeping. For most it was a restless sleep, punctuated by rearranging bedding for maximum warmth, or listening to hear if the wind had died down, or getting up to stoke the fire. Mrs. Ramsey was the most restless, for she found herself staying awake to listen for the sound of her husband's breathing. She didn't have to strain to hear, though, his snores seeming to vibrate the entire bunk. Tonight she didn't mind. Let him snore the tin off the roof, just so long as he breathed and lived. She drew up her bones close against his meaty side. He was warm. He was always warm, and she loved him.

17
Silers Bald

Christie was the last one to awake, and she had slept soundly throughout the night, exhausted by her physical and emotional ordeal. The others were gathered around the fire, and she felt no immediate need to get up. Rather, she felt she needed to lie there collecting her thoughts. She always awoke with a bit of confusion: Where am I? What am I doing in this place? Even when she was at home she needed several minutes of orientation before venturing out of the security of her bed. But this day she felt especially in need of orientation, for the memories of yesterday seemed just like a jumble of trees in a logjam on a raging river, tossing up and down, changing. There were whole parts of the previous day she could not remember, and the rest just tossed up and down in the current. She remembered that she had left Dave and Tammy behind, and why, but she could not reframe the intensity of emotion that drove her to such a rash act of desertion. She remembered that everyone had gathered around her and tended to her, and this had somehow changed her attitude toward the group. She felt respect toward them. And gratitude. Moreover, she remembered that her feelings toward Kevin had somehow changed, though she could not remember a reason or see any logic for such a change.

The latter was a point she pondered for a particularly long time as she lay still in her bag, hugging its top closely around her neck lest one bit of heat should escape, for it was far colder than she remembered it being the day before. She was more conscious, however, of her soul searching than she was of the cold. She had selfishly taunted Kevin, unashamedly flaunting her budding femininity before him, aroused in the belief that she had aroused him, though she had not. Kevin was merely a mirror for her self-admiration. She had seduced herself and become infatuated with herself. Kevin was but a sounding board, and a very poor one indeed, for he had scarcely noticed her growing beauty or her throwing it at him. She had merely imagined that he had noticed and succumbed, and that was sufficient to cause her captivation with herself to grow. It had all seemed so innocent and superficial. That is until Tammy took it upon herself to make it dirty. Always before when she thought of Kevin, her pleasure was in making him want her. After that, thanks to Tammy, when she thought about Kevin, she wanted him, and she knew how she wanted him. She then felt guilt, oddly making her want him more intensely. But this morning all was different. When she thought of Kevin, she wanted him but did not want to have him. And she wanted him less. She rested her hand upon herself. She had always thought of attraction being a thing that resided in faces. Now she knew that it merely began there, and she knew its end and its power. A portion of innocence was lost. Her mind was not entirely virginal anymore, for it had been places it had not planned to go, though not unwillingly. Not that she was ignorant of birds and bees and wedding nights or pregnant teens or sluts and such, but she had not placed herself in that context directly as she did now. Being female did not reside so much in feeling pretty as it did in possessing power and being susceptible to power of another sort, and it scared her. She removed her hand and thrust it out of her bedding into the cold.

I could have lost my life yesterday, she thought. Such was the power of the things she was discovering. She was glad to be alive. Before, she had pretended to live. As though playing house or playing with dolls, though she was playing with real people, with life. She had been too busy toying with the things of life to live. Now she wanted to live, to embrace life in its fullness fully awake, conscious and in control. So why, when she felt an admiration for Kevin stronger than she had before, why did she want him less? She dug deeply into her thoughts and studied him as he sat feeding the fire and smiling serenely at the ridiculous things that Brad or Daniel were saying. Then she noticed Lori sitting next to him, her face smiling that same smile. Then it hit her in a flash of light, a brief but intense light. She saw it plainly, and then it faded like a vivid dream remembered for just a few moments after waking, the details quickly dimming and fading into obscurity. Christie groped in her memory for the scene from yesterday. She had felt it, she had submitted to it, she had perceived but did not hear that which had passed between Kevin and Lori. She had felt Lori's thoughts, for Kevin had not yet understood. She no longer saw Lori as competition for a lover's attention. Lori was the one suited to be close to Kevin. It was the kind of connection seen only those not blinded by their own will, a connection no one would attempt divert, even if they wished with all their heart they could. They are constrained, even obligated, to contribute to its success. Christie knew now what Lori only felt. Kevin had only seen its shadow. What a child I have been, she thought to herself.

Christie joined the group by the hearth. All were happy to see that she had recovered and said so. She received the remarks as encouragement and responded thankfully, even to Brad and Daniel. Her new attitude did not go unnoticed, for each member of the group was well acquainted with her habit of sarcasm, particularly when directed toward weaker members. She took food, and it felt good to eat: the nausea was gone entirely. Her cheeks glowed with windburn and contentment. After she had eaten, Christie thanked each one of them for their help. It was then that she noticed her clothes hanging by the fire, still damp and limp, including the ones that had been dry in her pack. She looked down to see what she was wearing.

"Are these yours, Lori?" Christie asked, and Lori nodded.

"Thank you again," Christie said, and hugged Lori for the first time. She meant it to be a brief hug, but she lingered noticeably. She did not want to let go even when she did.

Christie made a special effort to include Brad in her gratitude, though she did not hug him. Before, she would not even have spoken to him unnecessarily except to make fun at his expense. Brad was pacing, working his hands and mumbling to himself.

"What's the matter, Brad?" she asked.

"Battery's dead," he grunted.

The snow continued to fall, and the temperature plummeted as the day went on. All were huddling close by the fire, but they still shivered, the fire insufficient to keep them warm though all the boys were keeping it fueled as high as possible.

"If we just had something to draw across this open wall," Mr. Leonard said. The complaint didn't sound right coming from Mr. Leonard, so he quickly added, "But thank our Lord that we have this fire and each other."

"I'm really getting cold," Daniel complained.

"What was that?" Brad exclaimed as the whole group shuddered at the nearby pop of a tree limb succumbing under weight of snow and force of wind. The sound echoed over the next moments in all directions with the breaking of neighboring trees.

With each gust of wind, more snow filtered through the open chain link, settling on and around those huddled by the fire, only to be melted by the fire's warmth in moments. With each gust, they huddled closer to each other, shivering more forcefully as the melted snow dampened their clothing and their spirits. Only Brad remained warm, insulated as he was from his ruddy jowls down to his size twelves. He noticed their suffering, and he wished there was something he could do.

BRAD STOOD UP. I have an idea, he said to himself. Then a certain calm joy broke upward within him with the recognition that he had given birth to a thought all his own, an experience entirely foreign to him. He began working to free the frozen gate. The onlookers were so surprised that Brad was taking the initiative to do something that it occurred to no one to ask him what he was doing. In a moment he was gone, disappearing past the hole he had kicked in the snow.

"Should I go after him, Mr. Leonard?"

"No, Kevin. Let's wait and see what he is up to," Glen responded, somehow sensing that something of a momentous nature had just happened in Brad. After what seemed a very long time, Glen was about to relent and to go look for Brad himself, when something clanged against the fence behind his head, startling him and showering him and the others with snow.

"What in the world…?" Glen exclaimed as the fence shuddered again, and snow flew in their faces.

"It's trees falling on us," Kevin said.

A look of terror crossed Daniel's face.

"It's not trees."

Everyone looked at Christie to see what else the calm voice would say.

"It's Brad. He's had a brilliant idea."

Daniel started to argue, but then a third branch hit the chain link, blocking out light and a noticeable portion of wind.

"She's right," Kevin said to Daniel. "It is brilliant. Let go help him."

Soon the front of the shelter was covered with broken limbs from nearby spruces and hemlocks, save an opening left for the gate, through which the hero and his two helpers returned with an air of triumph unrivaled by that of the Caesars returning from conquest. They all congratulated him for his gallant exploits, and Brad's round face glowed as bright as the fire with pride.

Brad suggested that they continue their day with a worship service since, after all, it was Sunday. Mr. Leonard suggested that Brad lead the singing, and they all discovered that he had a rather rich baritone and good pitch. He never sang before above a whisper. This time Brad didn't care if anyone made fun or not. No one was making fun.

Mr. Leonard read some verses from his Bible and expounded on the third temptation of Christ in the wilderness. Christie recognized that this temptation was her own, that she had worshiped Kevin, and she had served her own frail beauty. She knew then what she must do. After the service, she sought out Mr. Leonard who led her in a prayer to God in which she promised never again to let idols take his place.

Monday

18
Double Spring Gap

Sunday morning dawned cold and icy on Dave and Tammy tucked away alone at Double Spring Gap, hidden from all others according to Tammy's design, which had worked beautifully. The weather was cooperating, for all night the wind blew, sleet fell and snow filtered through the chain link where the plastic shower curtain, hung by some enterprising hiker who had passed a cold night there some time before, did not reach. The two slept soundly, making up for the loss of sleep the night before, Dave's due to the thunderstorm, Tammy's due to dreams about Dave. Tammy awoke to the sound of Dave rattling the metal gate in an effort to free it from the ground to which it was frozen by a mere six inches of snow and ice. The winds in Double Spring Gap had kept the drifts from piling as high as elsewhere.

Tammy watched as he left the shelter, leaning into the wind as he went. It was already day and it was bright outside the shelter, but his outline faded into the blizzard not fifteen feet from the gate. Tammy lay still in her bag awaiting his return, considering all the ways that she might employ that day to win his attention and his heart. Within minutes, she heard his crunching footsteps approaching. When she saw the shadow of his body materialize out of the white emptiness, she closed her eyes and turned the corners of her mouth upward slightly in a childlike smile, feigning sleep. Dave noted the peaceful look of innocence; her deception had worked. He moved about the shelter stealthily so as not to disturb her, quietly laying a fire in the fireplace and preparing for a morning meal. Then he settled himself in front of the fire to thaw the chill that had set in during his short excursion from the shelter. With his back turned toward the bunks, Tammy's eyes were free to watch her prize, studying the details of his beauty. The growing fire highlighted the fringes of his hair like a halo that shimmered as the flames danced. His dark brown hair shined softly with warm tones of youth, health and virility, forming patterns of light and dark that changed each time he moved his head.

When he moved his head to the side, there was a look of calm strength on his face. She could see it for a moment before quickly shutting her eyes lest he catch her watching him. When she closed her eyes, she could still see it, a serene countenance, not the usual lively, joyful one he wore publicly while discharging his pastoral duties. This one she liked just as well, maybe better, for she felt as though she knew him now more deeply for having seen it.

His spine was erect, still carrying an air of confidence and authority, though his shoulders were bent forward in a sort of humility that revealed his gentleness. He tended the fire carefully, almost lovingly, the same way he tended the souls of youth, the same way he would tend to her heart once he knew that he possessed it.

Tammy dragged herself out of her sleeping bag and felt the chill from which it had harbored her. She hobbled to the fire, and sat beside Dave on the log, huddling close to him as if for warmth.

"Good mornin'," he welcomed her.

Tammy moved even closer.

"I'm freezing to death!" she complained. He put his jacket on her shoulders and patted it down.

"There, is that better?" he asked, moving a little closer to the fire to compensate for the warmth he had given away.

"Much better. Thanks," she said with a smile and a flash of the eyes. "So what's for breakfast?"

"We've got cereal and powdered milk. Or we could cook some instant oatmeal, but we wouldn't have any way during this storm to wash the dishes."

The two ate their cereal and exchanged small talk about how they had slept the night before. About what they would do all day sequestered in the shelter. About how the rest of the group was making out. Dave inquired more about what had led Christie to strike out on her own like she did, and Tammy responded with designed vagueness that lent no light on the subject whatsoever. He inquired about her ankle, and Tammy removed her sock to reveal an ankle with more bruising but less swelling, no longer firm, somewhat spongy. It was not nearly so sore, nor did she need it to be, for the snow had them bound together inseparably and alone for at least another day or two.

After breakfast, they played a game of 'go fish' with the cards that Tammy had brought along, and Dave played willingly. His background didn't strictly forbid the use of playing cards, though it would have been looked down upon with some degree of reproach. But they needed something to pass the time and take their minds off the bitter cold that was settling into the shelter despite the fire. Tammy was winning almost every hand because she was playing to win and Dave was not, distracted by something that he could not quite identify, a restlessness in him contrary to his normally placid nature. He found himself focusing on the face that was before him, with its mesmerizing liveliness, a face that expressed joy through dancing eyes, glowing cheeks, flashing smiles, though with overtones of shyness and innocence, laughing at the simplest of things like the winning of another hand of cards, or the startling pop from the fire, or his little one line jokes he made without thinking. He saw in her again the joy of life and youth that he felt slipping from himself, and he felt a jealousy that made him uneasy. He was aware of her. Trying not to be aware, he became more aware. The seeds of infatuation had been sown and were germinating, their tendrils and roots tunneling into him. He felt a force turning him as a flower follows the glowing sun to drink in its life-giving rays. These were familiar but forgotten feelings, and they confused him and left him feeling uneasy, needing to be alone. After a while, he excused himself from the warmth of the fire and his companion's personality, took his Bible from his pack and hid himself in the corner of the loft, reading with his eyes and praying with his lips, but feeling her presence with his heart. He tried to exchange her memory with Susan's but Tammy's was fresh and Susan's seemed distant, long ago, from another time and place.

The stirrings within him were without form, disassociated, not yet wearing the label of lust, against which he would have employed at once the countless spiritual weapons he was skilled at wielding against that ubiquitous foe, were they so recognized. After a time of reading from Psalms, the feelings passed, and he began to feel normal again. Shivering from cold, more so since he had left his jacket with Tammy, he rose, climbed down from the loft and rejoined Tammy by the fire, which she had kept going in his absence.

"Tell me about your family," he asked.

"My family? Well, you won't get a chance to meet them, I don't think. There's not a whole lot of Christianity going on there."

"Have you spoken with them about Christ?"

"Of course I have, Pastor Dave. But they won't listen. They say it's fine for me and all now, but when I get older I'll even out. They say they used to go to church when they were young too," Tammy said, pawing the dirt floor with her boot.

"What is your father like, Tammy?"

"Oh, Dad? He's great. He treats me real special, you know, calls me his special little girl and stuff like that," Tammy answered with new enthusiasm. "He's a real man's man. Not a he-man, but he's used to bossing people around and getting what he wants. He runs a hotel, you know. Out east. One of those ones where the business people are always having conventions and stuff. So he has to be gone a lot, you know, all hours. They're always beeping him so he can go put out some fire and boss people around some more."

"What about your mother? Does she work?"

"She works sometimes at the hotel. I don't know what she does there, something to help Dad out. Most of the time she's going to the tennis club or some luncheon or just going out with her friends. If Dad is working late, she usually works late too."

"Sounds like you spend a lot of time at home alone. You've got a brother, don't you?"

"Yes. One brother. He's older. He left home when I was ten to go to college at Ole Miss. After that, he went to law school at Vanderbilt. Then he ended up in Texas somewhere with a big law firm, and we hardly ever hear from him. So yeah, I spend a lot of time at home alone. But I got a car for my sixteenth birthday, so now I can go just about anywhere I want to…Christie and me."

"Don't your parents put limits on where you go?"

"My parents couldn't care less where I go or what I do. Just so long as I don't get in their way, or end up in jail or something. I'm just excess baggage at our house!"

"I thought you said your father treats you real special?"

Tammy looked away.

"He does. He gave me the car, didn't he? He sends me stuff all the time. He's just busy, that's all," she said, recovering her poise.

"Do you ever have serious talks with them?" Dave asked, honing in.

"They don't have time to talk. That's what friends are for, right? So, how about you, Pastor Dave? What was your home like growing up?" she asked, making it clear the conversation about her parents was over.

Dave told Tammy about his Christian home, his Christian parents, how they nurtured him and loved him and taught him the ways of God. How that he had gone through a rebellious time during his teens, which was expressed more through his attitudes than his actions. God had claimed him at an early age and would not allow him to stray too far from the straight-and-narrow. At sixteen he had rededicated his life to God during an alter call at church. Soon after that, he had surrendered to the call of God to ministry, and now here he was.

Tammy asked him details about his family, about school, about ministry, but she really cared more for his future than for his past. She began to pry a bit into his private life, his marriage. She began innocuously with neighborly questions about Susan. How did they meet? What was her family like? Was she pretty when they first met? Then she took him by surprise.

"Is Susan perfect?" she asked, her eyes latched on to his to read every response.

"Perfect? No, no one's perfect. We are all sinners…"

"She seems perfect to me. How is she not perfect?" Tammy interrupted.

"Susan has her faults just like everyone else."

"I don't believe you. Give me an example."

"She's a little selfish at times. Like we all are."

Tammy paused, mulling over Dave's answer as if there were any real information in it. He started to relax, thinking that her personal probing was over. Then she blindsided him.

"Does she care more for her baby now than she does for you?"

Dave received the question like a knife to the chest. His jaw dropped slightly parting his lips, which moved as if attempting to frame the words that would not come. He had denied to himself the sense of rejection he had felt since Susan told him the news, glossing it over to fester and ooze.

Tammy's stab in the dark found its mark, tearing open his heart and all the walled-off infection and scarring from seven months of poorly healed wounds. He started to deny the truth that she had just excised, but he knew the pain in his face had already confirmed the answer. It went much deeper than she could have imagined before she asked.

"Yes, Tammy. The baby seems to be first sometimes, even more important than God," he confessed.

"That must really hurt, Dave," she said, laying a hand on his hand. He let her. The counselor had become the counselee.

"It hurts, but it is normal. All of the hormones in her body are telling her to focus on that baby. That's *our* baby inside her. I'm sure that she loves me no less than she did, and in time, she will show it. And I've got to learn to share her with another person."

"I'm sure she will, Dave. You wouldn't have much of a future if she keeps loving the baby and stops loving you, would you? You've got needs that have to be met. Is she meeting those needs? I mean physically."

"Tammy, I've probably said too much already. You shouldn't be burdened with these things at your age. God will meet my needs…"

"You deserve to have the love of a woman always, Dave."

"God gives me all I need. Let's see what He has provided for our lunch today," he said, rising. He avoided the conversation, but he could not get the questions out of his head. He had not made love with his wife in over three months. It was just too uncomfortable, she said. That he could accept, but all affection had ceased, too. She never kissed him, never touched him, never said endearing words anymore. If he tried to kiss her, she turned away and made an excuse. The baby had kicked or something. When wet dreams began occurring, he had turned to relieving himself just as he had done in adolescence, hiding himself from his wife as he had done from his parents. It was not sin now, though, he reasoned, because he aroused himself only with thoughts of his wife and their times together.

They prepared and ate their lunch without talking. Tammy sensed that he had enough to think about for the moment. She would let it do its work, and she would watch and wait for the right time to play her full hand.

After lunch, Tammy rose to her feet, walked behind Dave, leaned her head over his right shoulder and kissed him on the cheek, allowing her blond hair to brush his face.

"Thanks for lunch," she said before the startled minister could respond. She hobbled over to her pack, got a few things and picked up the crutch Dave had made her. "I've got to brave the elements. If I'm not back in a few minutes, send a search party."

Her playfulness is killing me, Dave thought. If I were her age, I'd be thinking a lot about dating her. She'd have to show a little more spirituality, though, he reasoned. He thought again of Susan. She had once been playful like that...and spiritual. Now everything was prim and proper, and the fun had leaked out of their marriage. Was there a way to restore it? he pondered, but he could not think of a way other than prayer, and he felt silly asking God to make his wife more playful again. A feeling of despair and loneliness crept over him. These were feelings to which he was unaccustomed. The pain he had felt from lack of affection from Susan since she became pregnant was something he had been able to carry to God and to muster sufficient strength to endure, knowing – or at least hoping – that it would improve with time. Tammy's piercing questions had disinterred these feelings that he had buried, and he felt them once more. He could deal with those feelings, because someone else was responsible for them. He still entertained hope that it would change after their baby was born. However, something else stirred in him while in Tammy's presence. She was alive and carefree, bouncing with energy and confidence, and by contrast, he felt dead or dying, archaic, old. This was something for which *he* was responsible, and in trying to please God and succeed in ministry, he had lost passion, squelched vitality, bound his personality, denied expression. He had taken on too much care too soon. He found himself wanting to escape from Tammy and wanting her to return so he could see more of that which intrigued him so.

Shortly Tammy did return, but when she did, he gave her his place at the fire, and applied himself to the job of bringing in more firewood from the great pile he had created the day before. He then began the awkward process of cutting the thicker pieces with his pocket saw, a twisted wire contraption with a ring on each end, which required unnatural movements of his shoulders from side to side and much time and patience to cut through even the smaller pieces. Nevertheless, it gave him something to do without her, and he stayed at it until his shoulders ached and gave out. He returned to the fire, adding some pieces he had just cut, and sat down to rub his abused muscles. Tammy did not miss an opportunity. She slipped herself behind him and began to rub his shoulders, which he seemed to appreciate. She longed to sit behind him and slip her legs on either side of him while she massaged his shoulders, but she restrained herself, remembering how startled he was when she kissed his cheek.

When he grew relaxed and sleepy, she stopped and sat beside him. They were sitting on the ground with their backs against the log. He allowed her to sit close to him, grateful for the heat of her body. The temperature had dropped throughout the day, and the wind and snow showed no sign of letting up. Dave said a prayer for the others, that they would be safe and warm as he and Tammy were. Then he fell asleep and his head fell toward her shoulder. Her heart pounded, and her breath grew deep. Soon he would be doing this while awake, she thought, and drank in the pleasure of every moment. She slipped her arm into his, pressing her breast against its warmth. There she remained, her muscles tense and unable to relax, resisting his weight. She gladly bore it for the pleasure it gave her and for the belief that she was doing something wonderful for him. He slept that way for a long time, how long she could not know, but by the time he awoke, she was stiff from head to toe.

When his eyes opened, he jerked upright, and Tammy could tell that for a moment he did not know where he was or with whom. He became aware that she had cuddled very close to him, almost intimately, and he became aroused, feeling for the first time what he clearly identified as lust for the one for whom he had developed an infatuation. He immediately rose to his feet and excused himself with the pretense that he needed to cut more firewood to get them through the long cold night they were facing. Tammy reluctantly let go of his arm, releasing her grip only slowly, so that she felt the friction of his arm against her breast as he removed it.

Dave returned from the woodpile outside to find her by the fire stretching her stiff muscles. Tammy was aware of his eye upon her, and she slipped his coat off her shoulders, and gave it to him, turned her back to him, and reached forward to stretch to her toes, then side to side, and down again. He broke his gaze and returned to get another load of firewood, seeking the frigid wind like a cold shower.

When he returned, Tammy rubbed her stiff neck by the fire.

"It got really sore holding you up while you were sleeping," she whined, obligating him. He did nothing.

"You owe me one," Tammy beckoned.

Dave reluctantly submitted, placing a hand on each shoulder distantly, and began to massage them. Her arousal was evident through her shirt, so he closed his eyes. She felt the motions of his hands slowing, abating.

"Your hands are so warm," she said, leaning her cheek on his right one. She grasped his wrist and guided it, first up the chains of her neck where it was sore, then down to her jaw. He obeyed like a marionette, entranced.

Double or nothing, she thought. She tilted her head to the left, exposing the prominent strand of muscle. Slowly she guided his fingers down its length from her ear to its insertion. Under her spell, he passively followed, down, down into the warmth of her shirt, silky, warm skin, soft breast, pointing. Suddenly he awoke, jerking back his hand from the red-hot fire, two steps back, holding his hand in the other, feeling its pain. He staggered outside into the snow. Eyes closed, he saw her with his soul, and his very essence splintered, tearing him in several directions at once. A part of his spirit cried run, flee, escape! Something inside him praised God for the work of His hands in the creation of such a beauty, fresh as spring, his for the taking. His flesh yanked against the reins, reaching from within, to touch and grasp, to possess. With such anarchy of wills working within him, Dave could do nothing. He knelt in the snow, leaning against the leeward side of the cabin, gathering his composure as he repeated to himself, "Flee youthful lusts. Flee youthful lusts." The arousal slowly drained from his body, but still in his mind, he wanted her. "Flee youthful lusts. How shall I flee? Where can I go?" He longed to return to the shelter and take her in his arms, to take for himself some of her life to replace his lost one. Then the verses of his training began to come to his mind. Of course, he had lost his life…to find it in Christ. Of course, he was dead; he had died with Christ in baptism to be raised to walk in a new life. This new life had nothing to do with the willing girl in the shelter who was seducing him. His new life was immune to her, for he was dead to sin and alive to God.

At last, he gathered himself and his courage, and returned to the shelter. He walked to where she huddled by the fire. He sat down out of her reach and just looked at her, waiting to see if she were intent on continuing or if repentance had begun.

She looked at him with eyes so full that one blink would send a flood down both cheeks.

"I love you, Dave. I'm not just a slut. I was giving you what I thought you wanted," she said, and the tears dropped into the dust of the floor.

"I'm married, and you are seventeen. God's will must be done," he said kindly.

"I'm old enough to love, and Susan doesn't love you anymore."

"It would be a sin against God *and* Susan," he said gently but firmly. "And you."

"How could something so beautiful and so right be a sin? God put us here, and I believe he wants us to love each other."

"Were you expecting me to leave my wife, my baby and my ministry?" Dave asked incredulously.

"No one has to know. I won't tell any one about us. You won't have to leave Susan. I love you and I will give myself to you any way you want," Tammy bargained. She reached for his hand, and he withdrew.

"Tammy, these are schoolgirl fantasies. You know this is not right. What does God have to say about this?"

"God understands," she pleaded, placing her hand on his thigh.

"God understands and calls it evil," Dave said sharply and brushed her hand from his thigh where he could feel its power creeping toward his loins.

Tammy rose to her feet. Her cheeks glowed with anger.

"It's not evil! You think I'm a slut! Well I'll have you know that I've never given myself to anyone, but I wanted to give myself to you. And you don't want me!"

"Tammy, God will forgive you and help you…"

"Damn God and damn you!" she cried, and ran through the gate into the raging storm. Dave went after her. He yelled her name, but as soon as it came out of his mouth, the wind swept it away into the whiteness where only God heard it. He could see and hear nothing but the swirling snow about his head. Light was failing, and he could not even see his feet. He turned toward the shelter and could scarcely see the fire glowing orange through the white air. He entered, telling himself that if there ever was a time for intercession, it was now. He knelt by the fire, asking his God for forgiveness that he had hesitated at all in the face of any of Tammy's overtures that were now clear to him in hindsight. He sent supplication after supplication rising toward Heaven with the smoke of the fire like a burnt offering in the outer sanctum.

After what seemed like hours of entreaty, Dave heard a voice behind him saying his name. He turned and saw Tammy at the gate, standing downcast, with her head and shoulders bowed forward, covered from head to foot with snow.

"Come back to the fire, Tammy," he beckoned her. "How did you find your way back?"

"I was behind the shelter. I didn't go far. I wanted to just keep going until I froze, but I was too scared," Tammy said, sniveling and shaking violently from the cold. She kneeled by the hearth and leaned her dejected self against the edge of the fireplace. Her insides twisted as if in need of expelling some foreign object that piqued her.

"Tammy, when you feel the need to talk, I'll be listening. And God will be listening when you want to talk to him." Dave had again assumed the pastor's role.

"What is there to talk about? I fell in love with you, and you don't want me," Tammy said to one of the stones in the wall. She studied its form, gray, mossy, hard, cold. She wished she could crawl inside it, become it.

Dave could not get her to talk anymore, nor would she eat when he had prepared dinner. She just sat deflated by the fire. She did not ignore him but brushed aside with minimal response all his attempts to draw her out. He decided on a different approach, and read to her a passage of scripture, the Parable of the Prodigal Son. When he got to the part where the father kills the fatted calf, she began to weep quietly at first, her sobs growing until they shook her all over. He finished and prayed for her, but she would not talk to him. So he left her, climbed up to the loft and into his sleeping bag. He did not sleep, but huddled for warmth, praying and reciting scripture, until he heard his pitiful young charge climb into her bag. He prayed again for her and for his wife, and then he fell asleep, cold and lonely, but feeling as though he had unloaded his heavy burden.

19
Spence Field

In the darkness and cold of a predawn Monday morning, an old man struggles to pull himself out of bed. Great is the pain in his chest, and sweat drips from his pores in spite of the single-digit temperature. His wife, sleeping lightly but ever vigilant, wakes. She knows what to do and she does it, and soon he is still, complaining no longer of pain in his chest, but in his head. He feels no cold, but he shivers. Mrs. Howard is relieved for the moment, but she nervously fingers the last pill they have with them; her jaw stiffens against the impending crisis that will overtake them if the storm does not break. Outside the wind howls, laughing at her.

The short crisis woke Roy first, followed by Dwight and the Bobos. The children slept on, dead to the world but alive in their dreams. It was four-thirty. Roy and Dwight decided to get up and eat, then to wake Kim and ascertain if her strength was sufficient to make the day's rescue attempt. Instead, while they discussed the decision, Kim, dressed and ready to eat, slipped down from her bunk playfully angry with the two men for not including her in their breakfast. She had recovered, save for the pain in her hands and her face. Nothing a little salve would not fix. Roy and Dwight were surprised, but her presence did make the chances of finding Michelle much more likely. They ate their oatmeal silently, watching for the first light of day, which broke grudgingly through the darkness and fog, casting an eerie glow on the snow piled high around Spence Field shelter. As the three strapped homemade snowshoes to their feet (Dwight was helping Kim who could not hold the strings with her blistered fingers), Mr. Ramsey interrupted with a renewed attack of angina pectoris. Mrs. Ramsey placed their last tablet of nitroglycerin under his tongue, and the pain retreated again. This time he was left weak and not very lucid. The look on Mrs. Ramsey's face called Roy and Dwight to her side. Roy comforted her with words while Dwight checked Mr. Ramsey's vital signs.

"What's he doing?" Mrs. Ramsey asked through restrained tears.

"He just making sure Mr. Ramsey is OK," Roy answered.

Roy and Dwight looked at each other and knew each other's thoughts.

"That Kim is all the companion you need Roy. You know I'm going to have to stay here," Dwight said.

"Why is Dwight going to have to stay here?" Mrs. Ramsey questioned with a look of puzzlement. "Why don't you stay with us, Roy?"

"Richard took a CPR class last year," Rochelle offered at the expense of an elbow in the ribs from her lawyer-husband.

"Dwight's had EMT training, Mrs. Ramsey," Roy said. "He can help take good care of your husband."

Her face twisted as though she were a stroke victim attempting speech when nothing would come out. She looked down at the hoary head cradled in her lap and stroked the thin gray strands into place. He was sleeping. She hoped it was sleep.

"Dwight, you're a fine young man. You go with Roy and save that girl. We'll be fine…" Mrs. Ramsey broke into sobs that shook her down to her feet. Roy held her, and his strong embrace helped her regain control.

"I know Dwight wants to help. But…"

"Yes?"

"He's black."

Roy rolled his eyes and looked at Dwight. Dwight shook his head in feigned disbelief.

"It's not me," Cathleen Ramsey went on to say. "It's Howard. He'd rather die than let a black man tend to his body. Please don't think that is as terrible as it sounds. It's the way we were brought up. It is terrible, but Howard believes everything so strongly." She began to sob again. Her conscience was divided, torn between two mutually exclusive moral convictions. Her prejudices had always seemed right until now. Now they seemed silly when everything inside her was willing to sacrifice itself to save her husband. If it were right to let Dwight help, then it was wrong to have ever looked down on a human being for the color of his skin. Such a turning point of the whole life was completely impossible during a crisis such as this. Even if it were right for her to set aside her own bigotry to save her husband, how could it be right for *her* to set aside *his?*

"Mrs. Ramsey, my training is more in survival and rescue. Dwight is the man you need here. He's going to have to stay and Kim and I are going to have to leave now." Roy offset the firmness in his voice with a firm hug to her shoulder.

Mrs. Ramsey solved her moral dilemma with silence, letting the decision be made for her. She felt so ashamed deep down into her bowels. In fact, she had always had a twinge of conscience whenever she had agreed in thought, voice or deed with the forces of society that elevated her above a man or woman just because of categories. But in her complex and contradictory system of rights and wrongs, to act contrary to one's heritage, one's family, one's class was certainly the greater evil to be avoided. At this point, though, she had neither time nor heart to weigh such matters. A girl lay dying in the snow, and her Howard was ailing in her arms. The morality of expedience had taken over and dictated that the Rescuer must go rescue, and the Medic must tend to the sick. Moral argument and repulsion could wait for a more convenient season.

Roy finished lashing his snowshoes, Dwight finished Kim's and the two left the shelter. Dwight returned to the patient and worked in silence, not to give Mrs. Ramsey a cold shoulder, but to give her a chance to gather her own thoughts and him to gather his. Most of all he was silent because he really didn't know anything to say.

"How is he?" she asked sheepishly after a long and awkward hush.

"He's not very responsive, Mrs. Ramsey. His pulse is weak, but that is probably just the nitroglycerin. We'll keep a close watch on him."

Dwight could not hide the pain of this latest act of bigotry against him. The hurt accumulated in his twenty-four years sounded in his voice. His voice, however, was strangely lacking in bitterness. Instead, there was a sort of compassion as one might feel for a child who hurts herself for lack of knowing better, or for one who had been born blind and longs to see the beauty in the faces of her brothers and sisters when it can only be described to her by others.

Dwight went on to get a full history of Mr. Ramsey's heart condition. It had never progressed beyond pain. No, surgery had not been indicated. Two tablets were always enough. He'd always before been weak and asleep after two tablets. His condition was a hereditary thing, a family tradition. Howard would have been disappointed, felt disinherited or suspected himself a bastard if he had not developed the family malady. Mrs. Ramsey said that it was the family vice of eating fat pork he had inherited. With that remark, some of the heaviness lifted. Mr. Ramsey's pulse even quickened about that time as if in response to his loving wife's nagging. By the time the shadows of dawn had turned to the light of morning, Howard Ramsey was strong enough to sit up a bit and complain that his head was hurting again.

When Mr. Ramsey began to come around, Dwight wisely retreated to a dark corner of the shelter. He was not fearful of a confrontation for his own sake, but knew that any agitation could send Mr. Ramsey back into fits of angina, and there was no more medicine with which to treat it. Rochelle made him some soup to sip, and it seemed to do him some good. At least it occupied his mouth and kept him quiet.

* * * * *

When Kim and Roy left the shelter, they found a dim gray world of snow and fog. The north wind had blown fiercely all night and had piled the snow high in drifts, so high in places that the pair would have sank over their heads, had they not worn the makeshift snowshoes. In most places, there was about three feet of snow on the mountain. This they knew by probing into the white blanket with the hiking poles they carried. They had two poles each, for Dwight had donated his to Kim. Having two was a great advantage for balance, for where one pole could find nothing solid, the other one often did.

Roy and Kim tied themselves together with a rope. They could not take a chance on becoming separated in the fog. Roy led the way. All Kim had to do was follow the rut in the snow left by his snowshoes. It was a relief to her to have someone on whom to depend. Previously that had been an odious thought, depending for anything on another human being. This was much easier than going alone. The rope pulled her along a bit, and the idea of making snowshoes had never crossed her mind. Most importantly, dependence freed her mind to focus on the only real quest at this point, not to win a race, but to save a friend. There was no shame in asking for, receiving or enjoying help from another to accomplish this goal.

Not that the going was easy. The trail was buried, and the mountain was shrouded in white fog. They could not see any sign of the trail itself. The topo map showed the land falling off from the trail on both sides almost all the way to the summit of Rocky Top, so they had to follow the ridgeline where the snow was deepest.

After thirty minutes going, Roy suggested a rest. Kim resisted weakly, and then gave in. She knew Roy was right, that they must pace themselves and take frequent breaks to hydrate and replenish their energy.

"It's not snowing anymore," Roy said, sipping from his water bottle. "That's good for two reasons…"

"One is that we have enough snow already," Kim interrupted.

"One is that we have enough snow already," Roy continued. "Another is, if our tracks stay visible, we can make our way back even if this fog stays around."

"Let's get going," Kim said sharply.

"You really love your friends, don't you," Roy asked, ignoring Kim's command.

"I suppose. I haven't really thought about it."

They rose and pushed onward, picking their way up a gentle slope scattered with trees. For the next hour, they only stopped occasionally for Roy to consult his compass and map.

* * * * *

At Spence Field shelter, two children had also discovered that it was not snowing anymore. A long night of deep sleep had energized them. It was beyond their understanding why their parents would be so cruel as to prevent them from playing in the snow, so they sat by the fire complaining of the cold and boredom, whining that if they couldn't play in the snow they just wanted to go home. Rochelle told them time after time to stop their grumbling, but her scolding was ineffectual. The only thing that spared the castaways from the children's droning was a little bird, slate on top, sky-gray below, which hopped through the opening between the tarp-covered wire and the stonewall. He peeped and hopped, peeped and hopped, pecking at crumbs from breakfast mingled with the dirt of the floor. The children became excited and scared him away, but he only retreated a few feet before he returned to peeping, hopping and pecking. The children tried to feed him, but there were enough crumbs on the floor that all their attempts to lure him to their fingers were futile. When he had his fill, he left, but he or another just like him visited many times throughout the day.

"What kind of bird is that?" Rochelle asked.

"That's a snowbird," Mrs. Ramsey said.

"I thought it was a junco," Richard said with the air of a schoolteacher correcting his pupils.

"Some people call it a junco, a slate-colored junco," Mrs. Ramsey responded gently. "But a lot of folks call it a snowbird."

"Why a snowbird?" asked Adam, who was interested not only in the names of all the birds and flowers and such, but also in how they fit into nature as a whole.

"That's a good question, young 'un," Mrs. Ramsey said, glad to have something to take her mind off worrying for her husband. "Down in the lowlands, these birds show up a day or two before it snows. The old-timers used them to predict snow. So they called them snowbirds. But during warmer weather they live and nest up here where it is cool."

"That's the same kind of bird we saw along the trail coming up after we got to the higher elevation. They were nesting in the grass along the trail. When we approached, they would burst out of their nests and fly off making the biggest noise you ever heard, trying to distract you from where their nests were," Richard said.

"Oh, yes!" said Mrs. Ramsey. "They'll scare the devil out of you doing that. But isn't it something what a mother bird'll do to protect its young!"

"I didn't see any do that," Rochelle said, Adam and Ashley echoing.

"Well that's because I was taking the lead then," Richard explained.

Adam announced he was taking the lead for sure when they went down.

"You won't see any going down, I'm afeared," Mr. Ramsey entered the conversation, his voice soft and weak. "This snow's done made 'em have to start their nestin' all over again."

"What a shame," Rochelle said, and the conversation died.

Dwight sat on his bunk and listened, knowing he was neither needed nor wanted now, and, should the crisis renew itself, he would be needed only. He was partaking in a little self-pity, a luxury he seldom afforded himself, never in the presence of his friend Roy. The occasion seemed appropriate, however, and he indulged, though only in small portions.

* * * * *

EVERY TUG ON the rope tied to his waist reminded Roy of Kim's presence behind him. Occasionally he turned to look at her, mainly to see if her stamina was holding out, but also just to look at her. He had never met such a woman before, much less one so young, with the strength of will and body this one had, not even in the service. He was simply amazed, and each time he turned to look, he did so to convince himself that she was real. He felt threatened by her a bit, for though his will had been tested and proven iron many times by adversity, it seemed possible that she would outdo him. She had a head start in adversity by days, and, if she stuck it out to the end, he would have to admit the possibility that she had more mettle than he did.

Her face was beaten, but she was not. It was evident in her eyes and voice. It was even in her step. Roy caught himself wondering what she looked like before her face had become blistered and swollen, but he couldn't tell. He realized in fact that he really knew very little about her aside from her will. She caught him completely off guard when she said, "Do you want me to take the lead so you won't have to turn around so much?"

Roy kept the lead, and kept his face forward, but he saw her still in his mind's eye. He set his face toward a broken friend hidden in the snow, the example of Kim's determination brazening his own.

Kim found the fog easier to navigate than the blinding snow. Snowshoes and hiking poles made the going much easier, even uphill. She felt that they were making good time and was confident they would reach Michelle by dark if not much sooner. As her fears relaxed, her determination intensified, and she drove Roy harder and harder.

Some time passed before he became annoyed, still more before he said something about it. Finally, he stopped, turned and stared her down.

"What?" Kim questioned.

"You want to take the lead? OK, you take it," Roy said sharply. "It will be easier for you to drag me if you are in front."

"OK, I will," Kim responded without a moment's deliberation, and passed him. "Let's go," she ordered as she pulled the rope taunt.

Kim was stopped in her tracks like a dog at the end of a chain. Roy did not budge. Kim turned to let Roy have it when she suddenly realized what an ass she was being.

"I'm sorry, Roy. It's just that Michelle… I haven't acted very grateful have I?" She looked remorseful.

"No, you haven't. But I don't care about that, really. We'll do much better if we keep a steady pace and not push quite so hard. I know you're worried. I don't hold that against you."

"Thanks," Kim said, and let him take the lead again. There was something more she wanted to say, but there were no words. She felt no ability to think about it. Something about his goodness or his understanding or something. It was more what she felt than what she thought, and she had never been any good at expressing her feelings. That was Amber's forte. And Kim had never missed an opportunity to chide her for it. Whatever she wanted to say to Roy would have to wait.

They came to a steep place where rocks were visible protruding from the snow. They picked their way around them, the handcrafted snowshoes useless on them.

"I recognize this place," Kim said, and they felt relief for every confirmation.

The difficulty grew with the steepness. Kim and Roy lost time picking their way up and around the rocky places. Their movements at first caused each other to misstep, owing to the irregular tugs on the rope that connected them. As time went on, they found each other's rhythm. They stepped in synchronized motion; the rope became a welcome friend, and a certain energy surged back and forth along its course. Its presence strengthened those it bound. Kim found it strange. Its benefit exceeded the gentle tugs that helped propel her forward. It became alive – a lifeline to another. It spoke to her and nourished her. By the time she and Roy had made their way up over the rocky place, she felt as if she knew Roy better…through the rope. When, at the top, they stopped to rest, she wanted to say something to Roy about it. She wanted to know if he had felt it, too. She said nothing.

They pressed forward on what they assumed was the trail as it ascended through a stand of small spruce. They were grateful, for it blocked the wind and provided momentary relief.

"We'd better stop here to eat and drink something," Roy suggested, half expecting a rebuke.

"You're right," Kim agreed, and smiled at him through cracking lips.

Roy thought he saw something of beauty, but closer observation revealed only the same red swollen blistered face with slit-eyes that he had always seen before.

"What are you looking at?" Kim asked, sipping from her biker's bottle.

"Nothing. Just you," Roy said, and both looked away shyly.

As they ate, anxiety and contentment mingled in their thoughts, anxious thoughts of reaching Michelle, contented thoughts of the understanding growing between them, a connection accomplished inexplicably with a minimum of words.

"Andiamo!" Roy ordered as they finished their snack.

On the other side of the spruce grove, the wind jumped them again. There the snowshoes were of no use, for the ground was swept nearly clear of snow. Iced-over rocks were the only path, so Roy removed his snowshoes and helped Kim out of hers. Her fingers were still of little use. Even the rope tied between them was of no use. Instead, they had to brace each other, arm-in-arm, taking turns one step at a time. Their progress was almost imperceptible, but they were encouraged at Kim's recognition of the craggy rocks near Rocky Top. They barely averted a fall numerous times whenever one of them slipped on the treacherous ice and the other held firm. One fall was not averted on the very peak of Rocky Top when Roy slipped with both feet, and his considerable weight pulled Kim clear off her feet. They both lay still on the ice, too fearful to move until they were sure they had sustained no injury. They were yet arm-in-arm facing the sky.

"It's about two o'clock," Roy said.

Kim laughed.

"Who the hell cares what time it is right now?" she said, jostling Roy with the arm tangled in his.

"Look at the sun," he said, pointing with his free hand toward a faint light spot in an otherwise featureless sky. "The clouds are thinning."

He said that just as another bank of fog engulfed Rocky Top with the two hikers prone on its peak.

"The clouds are thickening, now," Kim said sarcastically. Then her voice changed to real concern, "Are you OK? I mean, you didn't hit your head or anything, did you?"

"Everything is intact," Roy said, and rose and helped her to her feet. "You?"

"I'm fine."

"You're pretty tough, aren't you?" Roy asked. He expected an answer, but Kim ignored him.

"Thunderhead's just a little way from here," she said. "Then it's downhill and out of the wind to where Michelle is."

Clinging to each other, they slowly negotiated the ridgeline connecting Rocky Top to Thunderhead over rock, ice and snowdrift, so slowly that it took over an hour to cover less than half-a-mile to the summit. Though they never really saw the bulk of Thunderhead due to the fog, nor had they seen Rocky Top, they knew by the stone pillar at her peak that the goal had been reached. Just as Kim had predicted, a short while after leaving the summit, they entered the wind shadow of the mountain, and the trail disappeared beneath three feet of soft virgin snow.

Roy and Kim shod themselves again with their bentwood snowshoes, and the pace picked up as they half skied, half shuffled their way through the powdery snow down the rhododendron-lined alleyway. Kim's pulse increased with every switchback that brought her closer to discovering the fate of her friend. They paused to rest a moment, however, near the refuge in which she had spent a night in the snow. Roy had been interested to see how she had sheltered herself.

"It was a small miracle that such a place like this was right here where you needed it," Roy said, duly impressed, though Kim could not find the exact spot as she remembered it. There were several similar places in the rhododendron thickets.

"It seems as though it were a year ago," Kim said, feeling a little sentimental, a foreign feeling to her.

"It probably seems like two years to Michelle," Roy said. "We'd better get to her."

It took thirty minutes for Roy and Kim to come down the same slope Kim climbed in hours two days before. She was in the lead now, her eyes panning for a landmark to locate Michelle. The depth of the snow increased as the altitude decreased, and they could easily have stepped right over her. When they came to a left hand switchback, Kim turned the corner and almost continued on, but something stopped her. She saw something familiar or a sixth sense, an awareness of human presence, was at work. She turned back to investigate. At the crook in the trail, a small piece of rock protruded from the snow, a small hole below it.

"Michelle?" Kim said weakly, brushing snow with her elbows, enlarging the hole. Roy approached with a flashlight and shined it into the enlarged opening.

"It's her!" he yelled, tossed his pack and hiking poles aside and joined the feverish digging with both hands. Soon they could see Michelle's torso in the air pocket created by the protection of the overhanging boulder. Her lower half was covered with snow.

"Michelle!" Kim cried, reaching out with an ungloved, blistered hand to touch her fallen friend's ashen and unresponsive face. Kim felt no sensation return to her but pain. "You check her, Roy! I can't feel her!"

Kim retreated enough to give Roy room. She clasped her hands over her heart, held her breath and watched with saucer-eyes as he touched her face, then held the back of his hand beneath her nose. He slid his fingers to her neck for an eternity. Kim could hear her own heartbeat in her ears.

"I've got a pulse!" he exclaimed. "Let's get her out of here quickly!"

Kim started to pull Michelle's arm, but Roy stopped her.

"We need to pick her up gently. Brush all the snow away first."

This they did, and they dragged her onto the trail by the two sleeping bags in which Kim had put her.

Roy placed his ear to her nose where he felt a shallow, infrequent breath.

"We've got to get her warmed up," he said, his natural calm returning.

Kim could do nothing with her hands, but she lay down next to Michelle, bringing all of her body she could in contact with her own. Roy covered them both with both sleeping bags and the tarp Kim had placed over Michelle before she left her to keep her dry. The crook in the trail was a lousy campsite at best, but there was no time to find a better one. Roy pitched the tent on the flattest spot he could, and the three of them crowded into the two-man tent. Soon they felt some body heat collecting.

"How can she be wet? The bags were dry," Kim asked, but increasing smell of ammonia was her answer.

"You've got to get her out of these wet clothes. I'll step out," Roy said.

"Roy, this is no time for modesty!" Kim exclaimed, as she attempted to unzip her parka. "Besides, I'm going to have to borrow your hands," she said, holding up two useless appendages as proof.

Roy knew she was right, and set in removing Michelle's damp clothing with the detachment of a doctor. He helped Kim out of her wet outer clothes, too. After getting them both secure in sleeping bags, he unzipped a third and placed it over the two girls like a quilt. That left one for him (for they had brought two from the shelter), and he crawled into it, sandwiching Michelle between them. He took one hand, inspected it for frostbite and found none. Then he took the other. Again, there was none. "We'll check her feet after she's warmed up."

The tent was becoming quite warm.

"I think her color is better," Roy said.

"She's breathing better. Her breathing is strong enough now that I just about have to take turns with her. The tent's too tight for us both to breathe together. This tent sure heats up better than that shelter. I never would have thought…"

"You know you saved her life," Roy said. Silence was the only response. "I know I'll have to tell her too, because you never will."

"She's not saved yet. Besides, you saved her."

"Me? If it weren't for you, I'd still be back at Spence Field."

"I'm trying to say 'thank you', you big klutz!"

"Does that mean you aren't mad at me anymore?"

"I never was mad at you. How could I be mad at you? I think you are the most wonderful man I've ever…" Kim heard herself say it before she heard herself think it. Now she didn't know what to say. He intimidated her. No one ever intimidated her. "Thank you for everything," she said trying to repair the damage.

"Reach down and see if you can feel her feet," Roy changed the subject not so diplomatically. He was very uncomfortable.

"Roy, I can't feel anything with my hands, remember?"

"Oh, yeah."

Roy checked her feet and found them icy cold but not frozen. He put the stove together and heated water. He filled a couple of water bottles with warm water and placed them between the layers of bedding. He made soup, but Kim was fast asleep. He ate the soup himself, then tried to sleep but could not. He found himself laying awake and looking at Kim. She didn't look so strong while she slept. I've seen a phenomenon, he told himself. He wondered whether she was always so strong and independent or was this something the crisis had found deep within her and brought to the surface.

He reached over to feel Michelle's face. It was warm. Her breath and pulse were stronger. Then he reached over and felt Kim's face. He didn't know why he did that. Maybe he felt sorry for how painful it looked. Roy dozed, but something kept waking him to watch the sleeping girls.

20
Russell Field

Carrie woke in a foul mood. She always woke up in a gloom on Monday mornings, and this was no exception, though she really didn't remember that it was a Monday. She had tossed and turned and shivered through the night. Brian slept well, she noted painfully all night, rudely filling all her restless waking moments with snoring. The reverberations irritated her badly. How could he sleep when I am left alone to shiver and think all night? she brooded, and her infuriation grew.

When Carrie did sleep, she dreamed fitful dreams. In most of them, Brian was committing some act of betrayal or another. In one, he was smoking and blew smoke into her face (they both abhorred smoking). In another, she had prepared a candlelight dinner and waited for him in a long black satin gown while Kenny G played on the stereo, but he never came. He was working late at the office and having dinner with his boss. In the most disturbing dream, she found something in his dresser, something like a bracelet. A dozen or so objects, delicate, like dried flowers, were strung on the bracelet like charms. She asked him what they were. He wouldn't say. He just smiled treacherously.

She had one dream, though, that had a calming effect, and it left her more tranquil when she woke from it. She dreamed about the buck she had encountered on the trail. She stood on the trail and admired his beauty for what seemed hours. The buck stood patiently and let her watch. He moved, shifting his weight from hoof to hoof, lean muscles rippling beneath his shimmering hide of tan, gray and black. He carried his antlers high and proud, and swung his head gently from side to side. Carrie was herself in her dream as she watched the buck. Then she dreamed that she was a doe, his doe, then in her dream she became the buck. She was all three at once, though she was not any of these fully.

When she awoke, Carrie pondered the dream. Though its meaning eluded her (and Carrie believed all dreams had meaning), it had left her feeling calm at last, and some of her usual sweetness returned. She could have fallen back asleep, she felt, but she did not want to for fear she would forget the dream and the emotions it evoked, and for dread that dreams of treachery would return. She fought sleep, but at last, it came anyway, and she did dream of further betrayals.

Therefore, when Monday morning dawned, Carrie was in no mood to face the day or her husband. Nevertheless, the breaking of day meant she could get up and get warm by the fire at last. She got up and left Brian in the bag, still snoring. She stirred the ashes in the fireplace, and, finding live embers, began to pile small sticks on top of them. She blew and blew as she had seen Brian do, and at last, when she felt she had not another breath, a wisp of blue smoke curled upward from the sticks, and the sticks burst into a small flame. She added sticks as the flame grew until she had a warm and roaring fire. When her front was fully warm, she turned her back to the heat. When she did, her eyes fell on the snoring shadow on the bunk. Inside, she felt all the emotions as if everything she had dreamed about him were true, and somehow she felt justified in those feelings. She knew something he had done had caused the dreams. Dreams were her mind's way of working out at night what it could not deal with in the day, she told herself. The facts may not be true, but their spirit is, she reasoned. She then felt foolish that she could not make any connection between her dreams and her life.

Brian woke and sat up.

"Good morning," he said, as if nothing had happened.

"Good morning," her lips said, though she had not willed them to do so.

Brian was impressed that Carrie had built the fire herself, so he offered to prepare the breakfast. He took her indifference to be a "Yes" and did so. They ate without many words passing between them. After breakfast, Carrie continued in her quiet mood for the rest of the morning. Brian found plenty to do. He unfolded the sleeping bags to let them air, made frequent trips outside to study the weather (after repeatedly freeing the gate from the grips of drifting snow), and generally tidied the shelter. Carrie sat by the fire, adding sticks to keep the flames high. And she thought. She reviewed her dreams. She reviewed their conversations, and she thought about what she really wanted to do with her life. She had previously thought only of getting married, even before she had met Brian, and marriage had occupied her thoughts and her time all the way up to her wedding day. She had not really thought a lot about life after the wedding, assuming that it would take care of itself, that it would be automatic, that her husband would take over from there, making the decisions and forming the stuff life is made of. She dozed a little by the fire, her head bouncing up and down like a bobbing-head doll in a trucker's windshield.

By lunchtime, Carrie was ready to forgive and to connect with her husband. She longed to have a heart-to-heart conversation with someone, and, since he was the only one present, it would have to be him. In fact, it ought to be him, she thought, married as they were. That's what newlywed couples did. That was the whole purpose of being married, to be together, and being together meant talking. Sharing. The more deeply they shared, the more intimate they would become with each other. Exposing their hearts, melding them. That is why she wanted to marry, and that is why she married Brian. He had seemed willing enough to talk, or at least listen, while they were dating and engaged. Since they said, 'I do', it seemed he was only interested in having sex and making plans for spending the money they had not even made yet. If he talked, it was about those things. She had to admit, however, she liked the sex, and the prospect of owning houses and cars and taking adventurous trips was exciting. However, without communication, none of that was so important now. She must confront him with this, but she decided to give him a few more chances to let down the drawbridge before making a frontal assault on his fortress.

"Brian?" said Carrie after they had eaten their rationed lunch.

"Yes?" Brian perked up from his foxhole in which he had been keeping a low profile, having been vaguely aware something was not right between them.

"Brian, I want you to tell me something about yourself that I don't know already."

"What don't you know about me?" Brian stalled, injecting a little sarcasm into the air.

"If I knew, smart ass, I couldn't tell you, now could I? Tell me something you've never told me. Something you've never told anyone." Carrie sat back and waited.

"Can I have some time to think about that?" Brian asked, hoping that enough time would make her forget that she had asked the question in the first place.

"Take your time. I'm not going anywhere."

Brian took her last response as letting him off the hook, but he felt the hook set deeper when, every ten minutes, she would ask if he had thought of anything yet. Brian's problem was not that he had secrets. In fact, not having secrets was exactly his problem. He felt that he was pretty much 'what you see is what you get'. He had nothing stored away in any recesses that he knew about, and, if he did, Carrie would have had a better chance of discovering it than he would. His life was simple enough, and he preferred to keep it that way. Suddenly an idea came to him.

"I've got something. I was pretty nervous about this trip when things got tough, and I didn't want you to know I was nervous." He sighed, relieved that the ordeal was over.

"I already knew that. You told me."

Brian continued to procrastinate, and Carrie continued to probe. Finally, he thought of something.

"OK. When I was a kid, I broke out some windows in the school."

"Why did you do that?"

"Because Bobby Lewis dared me to. Said I was too chicken. When Monday morning came, they called him to the office. Someone had called the office and said they saw him and another boy do it. He never told on me, but I sure sweated that one out until they passed me up to high school."

"What'd they do to him?"

"I think he's still picking up trash on the school grounds."

They both laughed a bit and felt better.

"Did someone dare you to come on this trip?" Carrie probed.

"Well, sort of. That's what it felt like when I read about people doing this. Really, I just wanted to do something adventurous. Getting snowed in wasn't it, though. And to tell you the truth I was about over these shelters by the second night. We've done it now, and I'm ready to move on to something we haven't done yet."

"So you dare yourself into these things. Still trying to prove something to Bobby Lewis?"

"Nope. Just want to have fun."

"I see."

"So," said Brian. "Fair is fair. You tell me something about yourself that I don't know."

"Well," Carrie said, kicking the black dust in front of the fireplace. "I've always wanted to do something creative. You know, make something or do art or perform or something."

"You sew. That's the same thing, isn't it?"

"Well, it's the same, but it's different," she answered, unaware of any contradiction.

"That's impossible," chuckled Brian. "Either it is the same or it is different. Which is it?"

"It's different, but I don't know how. I tried drawing, but no one could tell what I had drawn, so I gave that up."

"Why? That qualifies you to do modern art, doesn't it?"

"Not when you're ten. I wanted to take ballet classes, but my parents weren't the ballet type, so I never got the nerve to ask them. If you can't eat it, wear it or live in it, it's not worth doing, according to them. So I guess that's why I took up sewing. But that doesn't count. I mean maybe if I were designing what I'm making or something, but buying Buttericks and cutting and stitching is not very creative. It's about as creative as paint-by-numbers. I want to create something. Something that lasts, that people can see when I'm gone."

"Why is that?"

"I told you why yesterday."

"You did?"

"Yes, at length. Don't you remember? I was telling you something really important."

Brian shrugged.

"You don't remember that I told you after this trip I wanted to make some changes in my life, do some pruning?"

"No."

"You don't remember me telling you about wanting to go back to school?"

"Oh that. Yeah, I remember. What kind of class did you want to take?"

Carrie turned to Brian. Her cheeks were reddening and her jaw muscles were popping in and out.

"You haven't been thinking at all about it, have you?" Carrie said, restraining herself from saying what she wanted to say.

"Not much."

"Not much is how much you care, isn't it? I'm trying to get a little communication going in this marriage, and you are like talking to a brick wall. I feel like you have tricked me into marrying you. We could talk before we got married. Why can't we now?"

"I don't remember you wanting all these serious talks when we dated," Brian said, surprised by her sudden torrent against him.

"We talked all the time. About everything. I would talk and, you would listen, and…" Carrie stopped as the truth had hit her between the eyes. "I would talk, and you would act like you were listening. And I thought we were communicating…" She sank back to her place on the ground before the fire. "…and I was wrong."

Brian stood by the bunks, his left arm over the top one, his right hand in his jacket pocket, looking down at the prints his Vibrams were making in the dusty ground. He had no idea what to say to end this craziness. He would even lie at this point just to leave this bumpy spot behind them.

"I came out here to be with you," Carrie said to the fire. "You came out here to prove your manhood. Now I'm trying my best to communicate, and you're doing your best to avoid it."

"I came out here to have a good time. With my wife. And it looks like she wants to spoil it with all this nagging."

"You think I'm nagging? I'm just trying to tell you what's going on inside me, and find out what's going on inside you. But I guess we aren't ready for that. I'm taking a nap."

Carrie rested her case, and Brian was happy that she did. She climbed into her bag but did not sleep. The bag was colder than ever without Brian there to heat it up, but she wasn't about to ask him to join her. She folded her arms, hugged her breasts to herself and rocked. Closing her eyes, she heard the rattling of the gate as Brian opened it and closed it behind himself. Where's he going in this blizzard? she thought, then told herself she didn't really care. But she did care. She cared about him, and she cared about her marriage. She was mad enough to spit on both it and him. Soon he returned, but she feigned sleep. She did not open her eyes to see what he was doing. She just wondered.

With every gust of wind and resulting draft, Carrie pulled the neck of the bag higher and tighter until it was covering her head completely. Her thoughts turned to the day she had met Brian.

CARRIE PULLED INTO the bank parking lot and found a space near the door. That was fortunate, for it was sprinkling slightly, just enough to need the windshield wipers but not enough to keep them from stuttering across the windshield even on the lowest setting. Carrie was not fond of this kind of weather. It made her hair frizzier. She had it pulled back with a banana clip, which kept it from her face. Beyond the clip, it exploded into a huge ball of wiry brown tangles, which had been a great embarrassment to her in high school. Now in her last teenage year, however, the wisdom of maturity had tempered her self-consciousness. Besides, the tellers in the bank had seen her in every state of vanity or lack of it for nearly two years. She deposited her puny but precious paycheck from O'Toole's as she had always done and headed back out into the drizzle. She turned the key, and the car groaned, much as she did when her alarm went off on Monday mornings, and fell silent. She turned the key two more times, each time the groan growing more anemic. On the fourth try, there was no sound except a faint clicking.

Carrie went back into the bank and asked to use the phone. The teller directed her to an empty desk. As she was dialing, a voice behind her startled her.

"May I help you?"

Carrie put the receiver down and turned around.

A blue suited, clean cut young man stood at attention, the corners of his mouth turned up slightly in a stiff sort of way as if saying simultaneously, "I am at your service," and "You're wasting my time." However, his eyes smiled at her from behind gold-rimmed glasses, at once catching her attention. She felt as though they were laughing at her for being startled, while also studying her with warm attention and interest.

She smiled a half-smile and wanted to look away but could not.

"I'm having car trouble. I was just calling someone…" she said, brushing a loose coil of hair from her brow.

"What's the car doing?" he said with genuine interest in her predicament.

"It's not doing anything. I mean it won't start."

"Will the engine turn over?"

"I don't know. What's that mean?"

"Is the starter turning the engine when you turn the key?" he clarified.

"It just makes a clicking noise."

"You may have a dead battery," he said. "May I take a look at it for you?"

"I don't want to take you away from your work. I know you are busy and all…"

"Nonsense," he said, gesturing toward the door.

They looked away for the first time in the encounter, as Carrie walked toward the door and he followed. He held the door for her. She mumbled thanks and led the way to her stricken car. She got in and turned the key. Again, a moan emanated from under the hood, followed by the quiet clicking. She looked up, anticipating a diagnosis.

"Still could be the battery," he said. "I'll pull my car up here and try to jump you off."

In a few moments an old Subaru, once red, now dusty rose, appeared from the opposite side of the building. Carrie couldn't help thinking it was not quite what she expected given the executive suit its driver was wearing. He pulled a pair of jumper cables from the trunk, slipped out of his suit coat and rolled up the sleeves of his starched white shirt. In no time, Carrie's car was running, and he was packing the cables up.

Carrie stepped out of her car and walked slowly toward him as he finished. Once again, their eyes fixed on each other.

"I can't thank you enough. I guess I need to go get a battery right now."

He nodded.

"Well, thanks so much," Carrie said as if she would take her leave, but she did not.

Finally he spoke. "If you would let me call you, and, well, maybe we could go out. I'd like to take you out."

"I…I'd like that," Carrie fumbled for words as she fumbled in her purse to find a pen and paper. She was successful and gave him her number.

"Thanks again," she said as he walked away. "Oh, wait!" she called.

"Yes?" he asked with that same professional half-smile.

"What is your name?"

"Brian."

THINKING ABOUT THESE things helped smooth out her rough feelings. He was a catch that most women would envy. He had treated her well from the day they met, but she longed to get inside him. More than that, she longed for him to feel the same toward her, to want her soul, but he was unwilling. Or unable. Carrie once again corralled her emotions by providing Brian's excuses for him. With time he'll open up to me, she thought. If the circumstances were different. Someone has to look after our safety. The stresses from the wedding. Maybe if we hadn't come on this trip. No, this trip was the very thing that had awakened her, becoming snowbound the very thing that had bade her soul to roam freely.

Carrie traveled through time to her wedding day. How simple everything had seemed then, how complicated it all seemed now. They had planned every word, every step, for the ceremony. It was perfectly scripted, perfectly choreographed. Each character in his or her place. The music, the flowers, the candles, the costumes. The perfect ambiance, a soft-focus dream, oft imagined, played out in daylight and consciousness. She floated, borne aloft, carried through by the strains of Pachelbel and Mendelssohn and the minister's reverent droning, "Dearly beloved…" She scarcely noticed when all her family and friends grinned or grimaced at the glitches that threatened to upset and upstage the fantasy. When Carrie came down the aisle and caught sight of the groom at the alter, he looked as noble and regal as the swashbuckling star of any epic Hollywood film, strong and brave and completely capable of sweeping her off her feet and away from danger. As soon as she had pledged herself to him and he to her, they would ride into the sunset, according to the script. She did not see that his face was deathly pale, and, though he wore that same slight smile with the corners of his mouth turned up stiffly, his lips were trembling. Terror was in his eyes, and his knees threatened to buckle and send him to the floor were it not for the support of his best man. His friends did not fail to point this out to Carrie at the reception. She still did not believe it and looked forward to viewing the video.

Perhaps all of her feelings for Brian and his for her were just make-believe as the ceremony itself had been, she thought. Were they attempting to float through a carefully scripted life just as they had done at the church? If so, much better to discover it now before too much emotional baggage had been accumulated. If their whole relationship was built upon feelings, anticipation of a wedding and a pre-formulated life plan, what then when the feelings change, the honeymoon ends and someone departs from the script? Carrie acknowledged that her feelings were changing and the life-script was flawed. Had they been married just over a week, and a video tape was all they had left together?

Confusion prevailed within Carrie. Shades of right and wrong flickered in her mind. She shuttled the guilt for their present impasse between her and Brian. Was it hers or was it his? In the end, she decided that they both owned a share and determined that in their next conversation, she would make good for her part and effect a reconciliation. Before she could flesh out her plan, however, sleep overtook her. She slept soundly without any consciousness of dreaming.

WHILE CARRIE THOUGHT and slept, Brian tended the fire. The supply of firewood was dwindling, and their cache of food was about gone. Since discovering their food shortage, Brian had pretended to eat his portion, but at each meal, he had returned most of his share to the food sack. This fraud was easily perpetrated, preoccupied as Carrie had been with the fire and matters of the mind. Brian's appetite was large, and self-deprivation was taking its toll. He felt weak. Hunger gnawed at his middle. There was a far more uncomfortable gnawing at his mind. Added to his sense of foreboding regarding their predicament was a different sense of foreboding about his marriage. He had always been a problem solver. He had a knack for understanding a situation and seeing the solution. Half of that talent came to him genetically. The other half his father developed by often calling him to consult over a problem at the house or the store, even when he was very little. His father encouraged him even in the feeblest of responses until Brian had the confidence to believe that every problem had a solution, and he was capable of finding it. This very talent, coupled with his penchant for hard work, accelerated his climb into management at the bank ahead of his peers, but it was not working for him here. As long as he could keep the fire going, he was not too concerned about the outcome of their predicament. He was only concerned that reasonable comfort be maintained so that his wife would not suffer deprivation by his irresponsibility. Hunger would not kill them before the thaw, but the guilt and embarrassment of failing to provide might. The solution to that was simple: he would do without so that she would not be hungry.

What about the rift between them? He understood neither its cause nor its solution. He only saw the symptoms, and they baffled him. He thought through the things that she had said to him. They made no more sense now than when he first heard them. That was due largely to the fact that he had already forgotten many of the intangible points she had made. He remembered only the statements that contained an action verb. She wanted to go to school. She did not want to have the things they had planned to have together. She wanted to talk, but he did not know the subject. He felt her cutting into his unanaesthetized insides, but her purpose was unclear to him. He was aware of nothing inside for which she could be probing. Why did she want to do it? Why would she not just leave good things well enough alone? What was the source of her unhappiness, real or imagined? If she would just stop picking at him, everything would be all right.

He, too, thought back through their short history together. When they had met at the bank, what had attracted him in the first place? Her appearance did, that was obvious. She wore a pleasant countenance and a womanly figure, unlike most nineteen-year-olds he had known. He liked hips. But something less overt had snagged him. Her personality was warm and sweet, shy but with a certain confidence that came not from her appearance but from within, not aggressive but feminine and playful. He thought to himself that she would be both fun and manageable. She was neither just now.

Dating her had been fun. He was comfortable with her from the beginning. He felt that she was loyal from early on, so that he never felt threatened with fear of rejection. So he felt free to be himself. Their time together was light and cheerful. She found joy in little things like flowers plucked from a field or the warming spring sun on her legs the first day she dared to wear shorts after a dreary winter. He wooed her with little gifts each time they met, a bracelet, a hair band or some other trinket, and she was always so grateful. They had not cost much, but she appreciated them as if they were luxuries. She laughed at his jokes, and she joked with his friends. She glowed when they talked of marriage and things they would have and do. He had assumed that she would be the same in marriage as she had been in dating.

Brian could not explain his fear at the wedding. He had never entertained a single doubt. Perhaps if he had, he would have dealt with the seriousness of what he was doing before it hit him at the alter when he saw the people, all from different parts of his life, circled about him as spectators. He was nearly washed off his feet when the first three notes of Mendelssohn hit his ears. He remained in a liquid state through the ceremony and photography, and his strength did not return until he was surrounded by laughter at the reception.

What he had done wrong, he could not say. He did remember advice that his father had given him: Women are often in a state that is not possible to explain. Do not try to reason with them at such times. Do not try to fix them or make them see reason. Just stay the course, be kind, and they will come around. Brian decided that this was such a time. Surely when they got home, she would be herself again.

CARRIE AWOKE FROM her nap feeling rested, warm and able to tackle her fears. She turned over on her back and relaxed her body, letting her arms and legs go limp upon her bedding. She made herself conscious of the hard boards beneath her, feeling their strength securely supporting her weight against the force of gravity. It seemed as if she were supported between the earth and the sky. When she opened her eyes, however, she saw only the tan-gray boards of the bunk above. Never mind. She felt peace in her heart, and her first feelings urged her to include Brian in her contentment. She rose and felt the cold air embrace her, torso first, then her whole body as she sat upright, and her toes found her boots on the dirt beneath.

Brian was tending the fire. It seemed as though he had not moved since she lay down. He studied the orange glowing embers shooting out blue and yellow flames that danced about, licking the blackened stones as they ascended and disappeared into the flue. He was entranced by the life of the fire so that he did not hear Carrie approaching behind him. She wrapped her arms about his neck from behind, rested her weight on his shoulders and kissed him on the cheek.

Not one to question this sudden show of affection after two days in frozen isolation, Brian pulled himself from his suspended state and turned himself toward her embrace. They sat twisted and entwined, gently rocking to a common rhythm of beating hearts. No one said anything for what seemed an hour. It was Carrie who pulled away first to position herself closer to the fire, resting one cheek upon the hearth, dangerously close to the peril of combustion. Brian returned to staring at the flames, while Carrie stared at Brian. He was aware of her gaze but did not find it discomforting. On the contrary, he felt as though she were still holding him. He was afraid for his eyes to meet hers lest she see into his heart more clearly than he was capable of seeing himself, for he was now aware through her relentless fathoming that there were perhaps many strata beneath his sun-baked mantle still unknown to him, meant to remain unknown, his nature disinclined toward inner exploration. He preferred the directness of living in the sunlit regions and had little need of finding depth. His guard was up, and sentries were posted at all the portals of his soul.

Carrie, however, was no longer on an expedition. She was now looking no deeper than what had shown itself plainly when she was attracted to him in the first place: kindness, gentleness, a confident shyness, a sense of purpose and stability. She felt irreconcilable feelings of justification and remorse. They had not fought like this before. She had been the instigator. Now she wished for reconciliation and knew it must come from her. She wanted to put all things back the way she had found them, but to change everything forevermore. Since they had not quarreled before, she had not yet learned how to make up, and it was all up to her.

Being aware of her adherent eyes, Brian resisted returning her gaze for as long as he could. When he could resist no longer, his eyes glanced hesitantly toward Carrie, expecting to see her eyes boring ruthlessly into him. Instead, he saw an embryo smile, augmented by the warm flickering firelight as it glanced across Carrie's face. Her countenance, sweet as the one he had come to expect, set him immediately at ease. He knew that something terrible had come and now it had past. He was not one to go picking at it to discover its cause. He returned the smile, and now the air was clear for whatever light conversation might be introduced.

"Brian, what do you think the weather is going to do now?" Carrie asked, caring not about the weather or Brian's opinion of it, but seeking to communicate any way she could that she was wishing to normalize relations.

"I think it is beginning to slack up some. The wind is not so hard, and it doesn't seem as cold to me. Does it to you?"

"No, I feel a lot warmer. Not warm enough though. Do you think we will be able to get out of here tomorrow?" Half of her was hoping the answer would be no.

"I sure hope so. I was thinking that maybe we could hike down from here to Cades Cove. That's less than five miles and there is a ranger station there. We could worry about how to get back to Fontana there."

"That sounds wise. So this may be our last night snowed in together, then?" Carrie cast a slight mischievous look in his direction. She wished so hard that he would just stand up, take her in his arms and tell her everything was all right. That would make it simple for her. But he just sat there, and furthermore, there was no evidence yet that he was responding to her hints.

"Brian?" Carrie said, having no idea yet what question she would form.

"Yes?" Brian said without any warmth or passion to encourage her. Carrie remained silent.

"What, Carrie?" Brian asked, a little annoyed.

"Nothing." She analyzed the stitching on her right boot. After awkward moments of silence, she analyzed the left as if something there might be different and more interesting.

"Brian?" she said. She really wanted to say nothing at this point. She wanted him to take the initiative to make this awful distance between them go away, but she did not trust him to speak up before her last ounce of patience expired.

"What's on your mind, Carrie?" Brian asked, his attention focused only slightly more than before.

"I still love you," Carrie said allowing the words to fall out of her mouth like gristle or a bone that did not belong there, glad to be parted from them. She did not look up to see his response. She wanted only to hear it, feeling somewhat safer if only one sense was involved. Eons of time lapsed before it came.

"I love you, too," he said. What his response lacked in imagination, it made up for in veracity. It provided Carrie a sufficient opening.

Carrie slid herself into his lap and kissed him. They kissed for a long time before Brian's hand found its way through layers of clothing to a naked breast upon a strongly beating heart. Carrie gave herself to him freely and with passion astraddle him as he sat still upon the same log, her naked front warmed by love as the fire warmed her naked back. After they crested the peak of fulfillment together, Carrie remained in place for a long time, clinging to her husband with arms and legs and everything; she would not let go of him. He stroked her back and buttocks with his hands, fending off the cold, and held her close to him. At last, the cold prevailed, and they parted and quickly dressed.

As Carrie pulled her parka tight about her and shivered, she spoke.

"Brian, I'm sorry for being so pushy with you."

"I'm sorry, too," Brian confessed, but he still had no idea what his crime had been.

"I will learn to take things slower in our relationship," Carrie promised, and they pressed purple lips together in a shivering kiss that lasted until they became warm again.

Hunger reminded them that it was suppertime. Brian ate only a few bites, but this time there was nothing to return to the food bag as he had been doing. Nothing remained for tomorrow. There was little conversation as they ate or as they reclined by the fire, but they were contented for the moment. Brian rested his body and his brain, knowing that the morrow would possibly tax both to the limit. Carrie, unaware that Brian was suffering growing hunger and that the food was almost gone, thought dreamily of their future, how she might change herself and Brian, and how she must do so with much greater finesse than she lately attempted.

21
Double Spring Gap

Tammy spent the night as restless as the weather outside. She was cold and lonely, and depression enveloped her, dark as the night. She could not discriminate between the moaning of the wind and the moaning of her soul. She would have said she hadn't slept a wink, but she had slept a fitful sleep where dream and consciousness bore little distinction one from the other. Tammy relived her whole life that night in thought and dream from her earliest recollections, so when dawn finally came, she was unsure of what had really happened and what she had dreamed. She was still trying to sort it out when she heard Dave stir and slip from his bag. By his sounds, she knew that he had gone outside briefly, returned and was reviving the fire.

She dared not look at him. She let her eyelids part slightly and peeked out through slits. The early morning light was eerie and melancholy. It matched her mood so well that it was somehow comforting to take it in. She felt strange, both warm and cold. She didn't really care. It didn't matter, as if she were dead, and those kinds of things didn't affect her anymore. She wanted to rub the sleep from her eyes but did not, believing that she was invisible as long as she did not move.

DAVE HAD AWAKENED with a sense of victory. He had resisted the onslaught and stood firm. His joy was incomplete, however, for each thought or sight of Tammy was a reminder that home was still an emotional desert and the future held no promises. And Tammy. What devil had led her to this brink? He had been drawn, but she must have been pushed. Was the pushing over? Could her healing begin? He wished he knew, for he found that through it all he had developed a real concern for her. No, more than concern. He cared for her. He wished to comfort her, to help her find her way to full restoration, but there was such danger. Would she try to seduce him still? Would his heart yet betray him, or would he be strong? Would she misconstrue his consolation as affection?

Would she let him help, or would she drive him away? He regarded her simultaneously as a helpless child, a wounded soul, a charming woman and poisonous snake.

This standoff could not last forever. Tammy's bladder brought her to her feet. She rose as quietly as she could, slipped on her boots without lacing them, and scurried through the gate without a word. She did not escape unnoticed, but Dave chose to let her make the first move. She was gone a long time, and he began to worry, debating within himself whether he should go after her. Finally, she reappeared at the door. Snow had dusted her hair and shoulders, and her cheeks and nose were red. She cast aside her homemade crutch, and limped toward the fire, hugging herself for warmth. Dave watched her approach, with a muted smile on his face, and waited for eye contact. There was none. Tammy's eyes scouted the ground before every step until she reached the fire, its blaze filling her gaze. Her vacant face hid a flood of thoughts and emotions behind its blankness. Her eyes were puffy and red from restless sleep and crying, the only trace that any emotion had once resided there. She said nothing.

It was clear to Dave that the seduction was over at least for the time being. Encouraged by the relative safety and drawn to her helplessness, he surrendered his silence.

"Good morning," he said, watching her countenance for a hint of what was happening beneath it.

"Morning," she returned. She did not look away from the fire.

"Are you hungry? I haven't fixed anything yet," Dave asked.

The answer was a weak shaking of the head.

"Well, I'm having some cereal. You're welcome to some if you want," he said, pouring some granola from a Ziploc into his metal bowl. He opened another Ziploc and dumped heaping spoonfuls of powdered milk on top of the cereal. Then he added water from his plastic bottle. When he stirred, the water turned instantly milky. He gave thanks and began to eat. He wanted to shovel it in, he was so hungry, but he resisted.

"It's good," he said between spoonfuls. "Sure you don't want some?"

Tammy shook her head again, but then her stomach almost growled. She involuntarily looked over at the bowl of cereal.

"I'm pouring you some. You can eat it or let it get soggy."

Dave prepared it, and stretched the bowl out toward her. She took it reluctantly like a dog receiving a treat from a stranger's hand. She mumbled something, and Dave assumed she was thanking him.

"You're welcome."

Tammy took a bite. It made her nauseous, but after another bite or two she felt the nourishment creeping into her. Her mood began to brighten with each spoonful. When she finished, she set the bowl on the hearth. Dave reached for it.

"I'll clean up," Tammy said forcefully.

"OK," Dave retreated.

Tammy looked up at him. Tears were streaming down her cheeks. Her face was no longer blank. There was burning in her eyes and her face was in full blush.

"I'm so sorry," she sobbed, leaning forward with her face on her knees. Her body shook silently. Dave sat on the log beside her and put a hand lightly on her shoulder. He let her have her cry. The shaking waned, and she gulped deeply. Then little whimpers began. Once she was still and quiet, she looked up again. Her face glistened with tears, and her golden hair clung like a cobweb across it.

"I'm so sorry," she said, shaking her head and fighting back another flood of tears.

"It's going to be all right," Dave said, and his words seemed true. She knew that she had not lost him as a pastor, at least for now, and that he did not hate her. She had matured years during the night, and she now saw clearly the folly in which she had believed wholeheartedly only the day before.

"You are so good," she said.

"God is good, Tammy," Dave gently corrected. Guilt gnawed at her insides. She felt so dirty, so worthless. She felt something moving inside, something alien, something cancerous, though she could not form these feelings into words. She wanted to cry out to Dave and to God, but without words, she could not.

"Wanna talk about it yet?" Dave prodded. The sound of his voice gently drawling out his words was soothing, inviting. She wanted to say something, but she could not say anything. She sat and looked at him, her mouth open as if to speak, as if she had lost her thoughts in mid-sentence.

"Did you know that God knows what you are thinking before you say it?"

She had heard those words a thousand times, but this was the first time they had meant anything to her.

"What did you say?"

She had heard clearly the first time. She just wanted to hear him say it again.

"God knows what you're thinking before you say it."

"God knows..." she said to herself aloud. After much pondering, she looked at Dave with piercing eyes.

"Do you know?"

"Do I know what?"

"What I am thinking?"

"No," Dave said. Then he added, "I have a pretty good idea that there is a bunch of conflicting thoughts going on in that head of yours. I don't pretend to know what they are, but God does. And you will sort it all out soon."

"I will?"

"You already are," he said.

Tammy repeated his words in her head. They gave her a sense that what he said was true, a sense that soon she would find her way out of the tangle in her mind. She hoped that Dave would help her find her way.

"Tammy," Dave said.

"Yes?"

"I'm not implying that anything is going to be easy when I say it is going to be all right. Did you think I meant that?"

"No."

"You said you were sorry."

Tammy waited for him to say something else, but he was waiting for a response. Why would he say that? Didn't he believe her?

"I *am* sorry," she said, a little indignant.

"Yes, but what are you sorry for?"

"What do you mean?"

"Are you sorry that you sinned or that you failed?"

She started to become angry inside, but Dave's question puzzled her. She thought it over. Dave could tell by the furrows in her brow, her thoughts were running deeply.

"I'm glad that I failed," she said.

"Why?" Dave asked.

"I was wrong. Why should I be glad if I succeeded?"

"You shouldn't," Dave answered, rising to put more wood on the fire. "But that is why some people are sorry when they sin. Like a bank robber who feels all kinds of remorse after he gets caught. He's really just sorry that he didn't get what he wanted in the first place. Another reason he is sorry is now he is going to have to pay the price. There are consequences for what he did, and he is sorry that he is going to have to suffer them."

"Dave, I'm sorry I wanted something that would hurt you and hurt Susan. I was just being selfish. I wanted something, and I didn't care who else got in the way. But I hurt you. I don't know why I hurt people. Sometimes I hurt people on purpose. People I care about. I don't understand it."

Dave started to speak, but Tammy cut him off.

"I hurt my best friend, too." She started to cry again. That was the first she had thought of Christie in two days. Great fear came over her like the shadow of a predator. She heard bass drums beating out the rhythm of her heart.

"What if Christie isn't all right. It's going to be all my fault if she isn't all right. We have to do something!"

"There's nothing we can do now but pray."

Tammy rocked swiftly back and forth.

"She knew what I was doing. She was trying to stop me."

"Is that what sent her out of here? You two argued?"

"She knew how bad I was. She was just trying to make me see."

"She was being a friend. Oh, if our sins were only between us and God…but they aren't. Our lies and our wrongs just spread like a disease. They hurt everyone around us."

"What if she is hurt? Or dead? It will be all my fault."

"She's not hurt or dead. I asked God to take care of her and I believe he did. So she is safe in spite of what you did."

"I hope God was listening to you. I hope you are right. But now she is going to hate me. Now everyone is going to hate me. Everyone is going to think I'm a slut, a whore…"

"I don't think you are a slut or a whore."

"You don't? What I did…isn't that what whores do?"

"If you sin once, you are a sinner. If you murder once, you are a murderer. But if you did this just once, then you are not a slut or a whore."

"I told you last night I've never given myself to anyone," Tammy said with anger in her voice.

"I know you did. I know you did. It is hard for a virgin to be called a slut."

Tammy didn't hear these words. She had already closed her ears. She rose from her place.

"I said I would do the dishes," she said icily. She picked up the bowls and made quick work of rinsing them. She returned them to the hearth. Then she retreated to her sleeping bag, crawled in and covered her face.

Dave did not know what to make of that sudden change of color. It reminded him of Susan's unexpected mood changes during her pregnancy. What he intended as a compliment would be taken as an insult. What he said in care and concern would be construed as an attack. Only a day or two before he left for this trip, he had asked his wife if she would like to go for a walk. He asked it wanting to give her an opportunity to get out of the house. And he wanted the time with her. Her response had been so unforeseen. "You think I'm getting too fat now," she had countered. "Why don't you just come out and say it instead of trying to trick me into exercise? Why don't you just ship me off to a fat farm to have the baby and tell them to send me back when I'm good enough for you again?" Then she had cried inconsolably. The rest of the evening was spent recovering from this breakdown. Only after much discussion had Dave discovered that she had been suffering depression all afternoon after looking at some of her pre-maternity clothes. He determined from then on that he would assume that many snags lay unseen beneath the seemingly calm surface when dealing with Susan. Perhaps that wisdom applied here with Tammy also. Perhaps he had hit a particularly sensitive snag that she would not or could not bring to the surface.

As he listened, he heard quiet sobbing coming from the bunched up mound of sleeping bag. He looked and had to withhold a chuckle, for when she had crawled into her refuge and covered her head, she had failed to hide her hair, and it now dangled from beneath the hood of her bag. It reminded him of the squirrel that found its way down the chimney into their living room, hiding itself under the sofa, the squirrel's twitching tail sticking out from its otherwise perfect hiding place.

The quiet sobbing soon turned into quiet breathing, so Dave let Tammy sleep and returned to the fireplace to read.

* * * * *

CHRISTIE HAD ALWAYS played the life of the party role together with fellow actress Tammy. In the short time following her ordeal on the trail, Christie had learned the value of stillness and was now practicing the beauty of silence. In her tranquility, she found that her senses were quickened to see others in a sharper focus. She enjoyed getting to know the others for the first time by watching and listening. She saw their laughter and fears, the life in each of them struggling to survive, rising upward and outward to express itself and to touch others. It is Godlike, Christie mused, we are in His image. Even during the frequent catnaps her companions took, she could see the life of God in them. Why had she never seen it before? It made each one of them valuable, even the ones who seemed never to contribute much socially. They all contributed, though. Why had she not seen it before? From Brad with his baritone voice, which he had kept to himself until yesterday, to Daniel with his listening and his questions, his laughing. From this time, her heart would go out to the ones on the fringes, to bring them in, the outcasts, the misfits, the underdogs. That was the good she would do with her newfound life. There is a responsibility in coming close to death and having one's life handed back again, she thought. But what of Tammy? How does she fit in? Who will Tammy be when they meet again? She prayed for Tammy. For the first time. She could pray, but could they ever be friends again?

Kevin and Lori were arcing. It was nothing they could put a finger on. There were no intimate conversations. They were not laboring on a project side-by-side. There was just a knowing. When one spoke, the other resonated. When Lori saw Kevin, he was in color; all else was black-and-white. When Kevin saw Lori, she was softly focused; all else was blurred. When their eyes met, there was intercourse of the souls. Everyone knew now, but nobody saw a need to say it. Eventually the couple must say it to each other.

Outside the shelter, the snow drifted to six feet. The wind howled and the air was still white. There was no place to go to be alone. The tiny cabin was full of eyes and ears. Lori longed to converse with him. Kevin knew it must happen, and it was his responsibility to make the opportunity. Then he happened upon an idea.

"Lori," he said, when most of the others were napping, "I'd like to read some verses with you."

They climbed to the top bunk where they could not be seen, though any conversation would still be overheard. Kevin went first and put out a hand to help Lori over the top. There was no headroom for sitting up, so they were obliged to lie on their stomachs. They positioned themselves at just the right angle to be able to share the same Bible and to see each other's faces as well.

Kevin opened his Bible. It was small, bound with a blue Kevlar cover and printed in a font so tiny even good young eyes squinted to read it, especially in the dim light of the shelter. The book was open near its middle, and Kevin pointed to a verse.

Lori read it to herself, "Two are better than one; because they have a good reward for their labour. For if they fall, the one will lift up his fellow: but woe to him that is alone when he falleth; for he hath not another to help him up."

She looked up, smiling with tears in her eyes. Kevin turned four pages and found another verse. It read, "As the lily among thorns, so is my love among the daughters." He started to close the book. Lori's hand prevented him. He opened it again, and she pointed to the verse below the last one. "As the apple tree among the trees of the wood, so is my beloved among the sons. I sat down under his shadow with great delight, and his fruit was sweet to my taste." The two looked at each other, half-smiling, half-apprehensive, and both fully unknowing what to do next. After a long while, Lori took the Bible and turned to Genesis. She found a verse and pointed.

"And they called Rebekah, and said unto her, Wilt thou go with this man? And she said, I will go."

Kevin smiled at her, their eyes locked and he said aloud, "The will of God be done."

Then Kevin took the notepad and wrote. Lori watched, trembling, thanking God repeatedly to herself. Kevin passed the notepad to her. She took it and read eagerly. His hand was messy and not at all easy to read. It was obvious that, as he wrote it, he too had trembled.

It read, "I do not know what God wants us to be to each other. I do know that he has made me think of you differently than the others. I can't say anything for the future, but I believe we should be together now."

Lori wrote beneath his words, in delicate script, small, feminine, pretty. She wrote, "You have described my heart exactly. I am willing to take our relationship slowly and follow your lead." Her position of submission conformed perfectly to the teachings to which they had both subscribed, and to Kevin's ideals of womanhood.

Kevin took the pad and wrote, "Seek first the kingdom of God and his righteousness, and all these things shall be added unto ~~you~~ us."

She wrote, "YES. GOD FIRST."

Then Kevin wrote, "I'm afraid that if we assume anything about the future, we will do things that fit a permanent commitment. Then if God parts our ways we will be sorry. I have only respect for you and will not do anything that might hurt you."

She replied in kind, "I have only respect and trust for you. 'All good things come to him that waits.'"

Kevin scribbled beneath her words, "You should know that I am planning to go into training for the ministry."

"A pastor?" Lori jotted.

"Maybe, but probably missions. Does that change your mind about me?"

"It makes me respect you more."

"We should be spiritual friends first. We should spend our time together with others. And not much time alone."

These were hard words to write and hard to read for two who desired nothing now but to be alone, singled out and separated to each other. But Lori understood the reasons clearly enough and agreed with the wisdom. They were charting new territory together. Others had taught them that this was a dangerous journey. They each knew that they had a good thing in the other, and neither was willing to chance it upon a newfound and powerful weakness. Natural affection must wait, and passion must have its time. Patience could not diminish what was real between them. They would build soul upon spirit, and flesh upon soul, reversing natural order. For them it would work, and beauty would come of it. A rare thing had occurred.

* * * * *

Tammy awoke with a start. A branch had snapped and landed atop the tin roof of the shelter with the sound of a giant cymbal. She bolted upright, and then settled back to a lying position as the picture of what had startled her cleared in her mind. Then she remembered her anger at Dave's words that had sent her in a huff for the refuge of her sleeping bag. She was now as baffled as he by it, for as she played it back on the screen of her mind, she felt neither anger nor need of anger.

Dave was tending the fire and squeezing something from a tube into some pita pockets. Tammy at once spoke to him.

"Pastor Dave, I'm not mad at you. I'm sorry."

"You are forgiven, Tammy. Come to lunch," he said as if nothing had happened. He eyed her suspiciously though as she approached.

"Ever eat peanut butter on a pita?" he asked. Tammy noted that when he smiled his eyes narrowed to slits, and they sparkled. Crow's feet pointed to them like arrows.

"No, Pastor Dave. But I'm hungry enough to eat anything right now."

They ate their pita sandwiches without talking, as by necessity most peanut butter sandwiches are consumed.

"I don't know why I got mad," Tammy said after washing down the last bite with a drink from a cup of melted snow water. Then, at the remembrance of what had set her off in the first place, Tammy burst into tears as suddenly as before. She sobbed violently for what seemed to Dave as hours. He wanted to hold her but he dared not. He sat stiffly, watching and reviewing what he might say to comfort her should the sounds of her crying diminish. Presently they did, but before he could speak, another torrent of tears wet her matted hair and contorted face. She made sounds like a whimpering child as she struggled to take in air and wailed like an Arab widow when she let it out. All this she attempted unsuccessfully to hide by hugging herself into a fetal ball with her head facing the stonewall by the fire. Finally, the sobbing began to die down. Dave breathed easier, too. He knew there was torment occurring in this soul, and he must draw it out of her.

When Tammy had regained her composure, she looked out from under the arm with which she had hidden her face. Dave handed her a towelette he had dipped in the warm snowmelt. With it she wiped away the tears and dirt, but she could not cleanse the look of fear and hurt from her face. She pulled back the dampened yellow hair from her face, securing it with a rubber band.

Dave spoke.

"Tammy, I can see there is a war going on in you, and it is not over. It won't do you good to keep hiding it from me. You have confessed your sin, and I have forgiven you and God has too if you are truly repentant."

"What do you mean 'if'?" Tammy glared with reddened eyes.

"I believe you are, but I cannot speak for you. I am only looking for a reason for your outbursts," Dave defended.

"You think I'm crazy, don't you?"

"No…"

"You probably are planning to have me committed when we get back!"

Having let these words out, she looked remorsefully at the ground.

"The only thing that I would like when we get back is for you to consider a few sessions of counseling. However, I won't pressure you. I just want to help you." The warm sincerity in his glowing eyes would have added credibility to his words, had Tammy looked up to see them.

"I don't think much of counselors," Tammy said softly.

"Have you had counseling before?"

Silence. Tammy studied the ground.

"Tammy?"

"I used to see a shrink," she said still more softly. A tear rolled off the end of her nose, landing in the precise spot on the ground that she still studied.

"A psychiatrist?"

"I don't know what he was. He was a cruel little man who got off on hearing about other people's problems."

"So you don't feel there was any help there?"

"No. No help."

"When was that?"

"A long time ago. Too long ago to remember."

"Or too painful to remember?"

Tammy felt her defenses weakening.

"I remember the pain."

"Do you still have the pain?"

Silence.

"Would you please tell me about the pain, Tammy? It can only help you to let it out."

Silence, then quiet sniveling.

"You can take your time, but I think you should tell me."

Dave waited. Let the silence work in reverse, he thought.

Minutes passed, and then she turned. She looked up, her face splotchy red and shiny, her blue eyes looking resolutely at his. It made him uncomfortable, but he waited without showing it.

She spoke.

"I will tell you why I was upset after breakfast."

"Yes?"

"I told you that I have never given myself to anyone."

Here's where she confesses that she lied, Dave thought.

Tammy looked away, and fell silent again.

"You've had a bad experience with a boy. God can take that guilt off you."

"I knew you thought I was a slut," Tammy said with anger, and then the anger died quickly. "I *am* a slut. A no good used up slut. I can't change it. No mean old shrink can change it. You can't change it."

Tammy looked up at the rafters, fighting back tears again. The whole anatomy of her neck was visible beneath her thin white skin. Her veins pulsed, and her throat convulsed. She reined in her emotions once more, and returned her gaze to Dave. She wished he would understand without having to say it. It was too painful to say it.

"Tammy, I don't care if you gave yourself to one unworthy boy or hundreds. You don't need to use those words to describe yourself. Remember that one of Jesus' closest disciples was Mary Magdalene. He wiped it all away. Just tell me what I can do."

"I told you that I have never given myself to a man," Tammy began again. "You can believe me when I said that."

"I'm sorry, Tammy. I thought you were telling me…"

"I know what you thought. It's all right."

"But why do you keep calling yourself those names?"

The sobbing returned and shook her.

"I…it's…too…hard!" Her words escaped between fits of crying.

"It's all right," Dave said. He let go his cautions and held her. He could feel how small and frail she was as she shuddered. He felt her begin to relax, to let go.

"When I told you I've never given myself to anyone…"

"Yes?"

"You called me a virgin."

"Yes."

"That's what upset me."

"Why's that?"

"I'm not a virgin. That was taken away from me."

"You were raped? Dear God."

Tammy shuddered at the word she could not say. Dave felt her melt. She poured out of his embrace like water. She was a quivering puddle sobbing at his feet. Inhuman sounds came from her throat. They were not loud noises, but they made him shudder. Hell must be something like this, he thought. He searched his mental lexicon of counseling procedures. Nothing came to mind. He would have to wing it.

"It wasn't your fault. You are not a slut." He paused.

"You are a virgin in God's eyes." He paused.

"God loves you. He can heal," He paused.

Nothing but clichés. But he kept saying them and little by little, they seemed to help. Finally, she looked up.

"Please don't make me say it," she said, a pitiful pleading filling her voice and eyes.

"Say what?" How stupid of me, he thought. "I won't make you say it," he corrected, wondering what she did not want to say.

"The shrink kept trying to making me say it. Mean little bastard. But I couldn't say it anyway. I could only remember it at night. Like a nightmare. Momma kept saying it was just a nightmare, that it wasn't true. Finally, she couldn't lie anymore, so she took me to the shrink. But I never remembered anything with him. He kept trying to make me remember."

Dave took her rag, dipped it again and wiped her face for her.

"It was like yesterday. Like last night."

She shuddered.

"I remembered it all last night. I remember everything. It's funny how you can forget what you don't want to remember, until something makes you remember."

She was too exhausted, too weak, too defeated to cry now. Her voice was soft and dreamy, childlike but somehow very grown up, jaded. Her eyes were glazed over as though they saw nothing, but they saw, they saw clearly something only they could see, focused somewhere beyond the stone wall of the hut. Dave let her talk.

"I always felt dirty, but I didn't know why. I felt dirty like a slut, rotten to the core. Strange for a virgin. He stole it from me. He told me I wanted it. He told me it was right, but we had to keep it a secret. Then he told me it never happened. And Momma told me it never happened. And I told myself it never happened. I wanted to believe everyone. That's when he started working all the time at the hotel, so I never saw him. Just presents he left for me."

"Tammy, was it your father?" Dave's insides seized.

"Momma was always home for awhile after that, then she started going out nights, too, to help Daddy, you know."

"Did anyone ever tell the police about this?"

"I've never told anyone but you, Dave. And Momma. I didn't even tell the shrink. I made myself forget then. I couldn't remember again until last night. Now it is all so plain. I was only twelve, Dave. Every time he came to my room…"

"How long did this go on?"

"I don't know. I was thirteen when Momma took me to the shrink. He was so mean, he just tried to make me say it, then he told me I just dreamed the whole thing up. Told Momma not to worry, it was just nightmares from puberty. Told her to be careful what I watched on TV. It's so funny. He tried to make me say it, then told me there was nothing to it. I don't think he was a very good shrink."

"Do you want me to go to the police for you?"

"It's funny Dave. I was Daddy's girl. He used to tell me that all the time. He told me that my body was so beautiful that he couldn't help himself. That I had put a spell on him to make him do it. I guess I was trying to put a spell on you, Dave. Do you think Daddy is a bad man?"

"He has committed a great sin against God and you, and it is a serious crime, too."

"Are you going to make him pay, Dave?"

"That is not my job. I'm concerned about you, Tammy. I will do only what you want me to do, as long as it is right."

"They'll just say that it's some story a crazy teenage girl thought up to try to get sympathy. They'll even say I made it up to get you. You don't think that, do you Dave?"

"I believe you," he said, but the very question planted the seeds of doubt. She had deceived and beguiled her way to this point. Maybe this is just another trick of the crafty little fox. No, the emotions were real. He saw something tearing at this girl.

"I believe you," he repeated this time with conviction.

"I need help, Pastor Dave. I can't face this alone. I don't care about making him pay. I'm all sick inside. I just want to get well. But I do want my mother to admit she knows about it. That's all I want. Can you make her do that, Dave? Can you?"

"I don't know. I think the first thing we need to do is to get a good Christian psychologist to help you heal. Not someone who is mean.

Someone you can trust. Perhaps a woman would be good for you. Then maybe we can think about your mother."

"Dave, I couldn't stand to go through something where they make me dredge it all up. I buried it, and I piled everything on top of it. Don't do anything that will make me have to dredge it all up, please."

"I won't do anything you don't want to do."

"Dave?"

"Yes?"

"My mother knows. I mean I know she knows."

"How's that?"

"She used to come and stand at the door to my room at night. I could hear her crying. She would just mumble, 'Poor baby. My poor baby. What can I do? Dear God! What can I do'?"

Tammy chewed the side of her index finger as she spoke.

"Even after it stopped, she still came at night. She still said, 'My poor baby', and cried. I always remembered those times. I never knew why she cried and said those things. It never made sense until now. Dave, she knows. She remembers. I just want to hear her admit to me that she knows. That she believes me. She doesn't have to protect him now. I want to keep it a secret between me, you and my mother."

"And a counselor."

"And God."

"And God."

A little happiness swept over Tammy's tear-streaked face, starting with her small faint smile and spreading outward from there. Dave felt that healing had begun. Tammy felt as though the clouds were parting, the wind abating and the warm sun breaking through.

"Would you pray with me, Dave?"

Of course he would, and he did, and Tammy prayed, too, a long and grateful prayer that flowed easily from her heart, through her lips, and upward.

Outside, the snow continued to fall, driven about by the wind, scurrying along the ground before drifting below the heights of Double Spring Gap.

22
Spence Field

Not one occupant of Spence Field shelter spent Monday in a state of peace. Howard Ramsey had stabilized, but he was by no means safe. He was still extremely weak and slept most of the day, his pulse faint and his breathing shallow, and his whole body seemed involved in the effort to capture each spare breath from the air like a fish upon the bank. Mrs. Ramsey's cheerful, vibrant face was gone, replaced with an old haggard one, as she labored to heal her stricken husband through the effort of her worries alone. What else could she do?

The need to keep the tiny cabin full of people quiet for Mr. Ramsey's sake was a concept totally lost on the two children, whose boundless energy had no avenue of release. He was not being quiet. If he did not wake himself with his gasps and snores, how could their happy playing be a problem? Richard and Rochelle had their hands full keeping them still and quiet. Richard periodically secreted himself to try again futilely to get a signal on his cell phone.

Dwight entertained devils of his own. Caring for his patient was an act of training, his wanting to, an expression of a heartfelt desire to ease pain where he saw it. Doing it with no show of gratitude in return ground his heart, but doing it anyway was right. Retreating to his dark corner each time the patient roused struck painfully dissonant chords in his heart that piqued his nature until it was raw.

Late in the afternoon, Howard Ramsey awoke suddenly with more clarity of mind and vision than usual. Before Dwight could react, Howard's eyes latched onto him as he took his pulse for the hundredth time. There was a look of shock on his face that faded into puzzlement as if he had seen something unbelievable. He closed his eyes and reopened them, testing, then shaking his head from side to side slowly as if to sling the unwanted image from his brain. Dwight laid down his wrist and arose, taking his place on the bunk. No words passed between them.

When Dwight was out of sight, Mr. Ramsey turned his heavy head toward his wife with the same questioning look.

"What was the darkey doing?" he asked with the innocence of a child.

"He wasn't doing no harm, dear," she said, hoping her non-answer would satisfy him. It did not.

"He was doing something to me. Were you asleep and didn't see it?" His words were strung out among short gasps for air. "Was he trying to get my watch or something?"

"No dear, he was taking your pulse," his patient wife confessed.

"What the heck does the nigger need with my pulse? Don't let him get near me again, Kate, all right?"

"Howard, he's trained to do this. He's the only one here who can help us. He wasn't doin' no harm. Now you rest," she said, patting down his hair and his temper. He seemed to obey for a moment, and then stiffened again.

"Kathleen, I don't want no nigger messin' with me. You know that. Make sure it don't happen," he commanded.

"Howard, now I don't want to rile you none, but don't you think we'd best just let the good Lord use what he's put here?" He did not answer but slipped slowly back toward slumber. His mind did not grasp her words, but the tone of her voice persuaded him to loose his grip and let it go. She had said something about God, and that was his weak point.

The entire conversation had taken place in tones loud enough for all to hear, though neither of the Ramseys knew it or meant it to be heard. Dwight felt everyone looking at him. He cast a tentative glance around the group. His eyes met Richard's and Rochelle's first. Richard looked down as if guilty by omission. Rochelle met his eyes and proffered an exaggerated look of condolence with eyebrows peaked and head tilted to one side. He returned a half-smile as his eyes passed on to Mrs. Ramsey. She did not look down or look away. She looked right into his eyes. Guilt was there in the tears welling up, but instead of shame, there was a helplessness, a pleading, a prayer for forgiveness, a sorrow. These were things she could not say or even find words for, but her heart could feel them and her eyes could express them. Dwight understood what he saw in her eyes, and it was enough for him at the moment. He felt his self-pity fading away, supplanted by righteous pity for her. He smiled his warm half-smile at her, and she felt her absolution.

Mrs. Ramsey motioned for his return. The patient was asleep. Dwight emerged from the bunk and knelt by his pallet by the fire, lifting the wrist once more to measure the life in it. Mrs. Ramsey clasped her arm in Dwight's. Her appreciation had finally come to him. They remained that way until Mr. Ramsey's eyes opened once more. His face awoke with the same look of surprise and suspicion as before, and the furrows between his eyes deepened when he saw his wife supporting the black man in his efforts. But the words she had spoken to him as he had drifted to sleep returned to him, this time with full awareness of their meaning and import. So his wife was determined to use what was at hand and call it a gift from God. For the first time in his life, Howard Ramsey was willing to admit that his mind was just not clear enough to see plainly what should be done in these circumstances. He decided to let go, leaving decisions to Kathleen.

"What are you, boy, some kind of doctor?" he asked. His eyes were closed, but the furrows in his forehead had relaxed.

"No, sir. I'm an EMT. You need a real doctor, but I'm the best thing you've got right now."

"What the heck is an MT?" said Howard between coughs.

"An Emergency Medical Technician. I used to ride on an ambulance."

"I don't want to ride on no ambulance, boy. All I need you to do is get this mule off my chest." Dwight looked at Mrs. Ramsey. She shrugged.

"Are you feeling a lot of pressure on your chest now," Dwight asked, his face close to Mr. Ramsey's to make communication easier.

"Well not a lot. It's a skinny mule," Howard said and smiled.

"Are you having any pain now?"

"None."

"That's good. You just need to rest."

"I don't want to rest. I want that pretty gal to feed me some more of that soup."

Everyone looked at Rochelle who reacted with a feigned 'Who, me?' expression, obviously flattered. She set about to prepare some for him, but when she was ready to spoon the broth into his mouth, he stopped her.

"Not you. The pretty young one," he said pointing at her daughter who was among the circle of spectators. Ashley responded with a sincere 'Who, me?' look and everyone chuckled. Pride pushed her forward (with Adam's help) while shyness pulled her back. Pride was stronger, and the result was that she approached the stricken king with stuttering steps. Her mother whispered in her ear, and she said, "I know!" out loud. Ashley then knelt at Howard's side and spooned broth into his mouth as though she had done it everyday.

"No more," Mr. Ramsey grumbled when he felt his strength fading again.

"Say, no more, thank you," Ashley scolded. Emboldened by everyone's laughter she took her lesson in manners a step further.

"You should be nice to the black man," Ashley said, the precursors of motherhood showing in every tone of her five-year-old voice. "And don't call him nigger."

Even Dwight laughed at this. Rochelle spoke quietly to Ashley, and she returned to her place beside Adam. Richard patted her head.

"Out of the mouths of babes…" Mrs. Ramsey said to Mr. Ramsey loudly enough for all to hear. Mr. Ramsey grumbled something unintelligible, and then sleep overtook him again.

Embryonic instincts were awakened in the small girl, and she remained by his side while he slept and watched each flutter of the loose ashen skin of the weathered face as his breath went in and out as stubbornly as the old man himself. She watched his massive chest rise and fall. When Adam bade her join in a game of cards, she turned and glared at him, clamping her index finger firmly over her mouth. She had more important things to do at this moment than join in childish games.

When Mr. Ramsey woke again – his sleep never lasted long at one time – she was there watching over him. She smiled at him.

From across the shelter, Rochelle saw Ashley talking with the ailing man and spoke her name sharply.

"Ashley Bobo! Leave Mr. Ramsey alone. Come here!" she yelled in a whisper.

Mrs. Ramsey, who was near enough to hear that the conversation between the old man and the young girl was a two-way affair, rose and went to Rochelle.

"It's all right. Howard's always loved children. I think she's doing him some good."

"I don't want her scolding him anymore," Rochelle said with an embarrassed smile.

"Why not?" Adam said, looking up from his solitaire. They assumed he was not paying attention. He rarely paid attention. "She's right. You and Daddy both said she was right."

At that, Rochelle turned the color of a Florida sunburn in early spring. Richard looked away.

"Well, you did," Adam pushed the dagger to the hilt with a twist.

"Adam, you be respectful. That is what we told you," Rochelle chastened, recovering slightly from her abashment.

Adam tucked his chin into his chest with the frustration of a child who knows he is right, though he lacks the position in society to be privileged with freedom of speech. Mrs. Ramsey knew he was right.

"Rochelle, don't be embarrassed. It is Howard and I who ought to be embarrassed. You taught your children what is right, and Adam here knows it." Adam raised his chin from his chest and smiled. "I want to apologize for Howard…."

"If there's any apologizing to be done, Howard will do it hisself!"

Everyone turned to him in surprise. The room was silent but for the moan of the wind outside.

"I may be puny, but I ain't deaf! Y'all wanna talk about me, you kin talk to me."

Kathleen tried to quiet him but he was not to be quieted.

They all inched closer, ready to hear the last proclamation of a dying king, but the king was silent, his eyes closed. Even the wind stopped its howling as everyone waited for what he had to say.

Finally he spoke.

"Where's the boy, the MT?"

Ashley pointed.

"Come'ere boy," Howard said, his voice tired and haggard but still in command. Dwight obeyed.

"I've been wrong about you. I don't know about the rest of 'em, but I judged you wrong. I know a lot of white folks wouldn't do for a stranger what you're doing fer me, and I ain't even thanked you. I...wul what I mean is...I'm sorry boy. I ain't been grateful, and I ain't treated you right. This little girl knowed it, and it took her to make me see it."

Richard hung his head and looked away. Everyone else was smiling.

"I...I just..." Howard's words trailed off. He was asleep again. Not a fitful sleep as before but a quiet and still one. Ashley asked if he were dead.

Dwight held his wrist, placed his fingers on his neck and his ear by Howard's mouth.

"No, sweetie, he's asleep," Dwight said, laying his large hand on her tiny shoulder. He turned to Mrs. Ramsey. His smile was gone.

"His pulse is much weaker than before, but it is regular. There's nothing we can do but let him rest."

"And pray," said Mrs. Ramsey.

"And pray," echoed Dwight, but he knew he was not much for praying.

Dwight rose and went to the gate and looked out. The light of day was failing. His own feelings had been vindicated by a dying man. They were now fully emancipated to focus on the concerns for others. Time was everyone's enemy right now. He was helpless to help really, except to give some measure of hope to the others. Should Mr. Ramsey arrest, he knew CPR was not going to save him. His only hope would be quick advanced life support and transport to a hospital. Arrest seemed inevitable if this snow did not break soon. His thoughts turned to Roy and Kim. Had they made it to the fallen friends, or even just one of them? Were they wandering still through the blank whiteness, and would they find anything? Would they find their way back? Whiteout was mortal danger. They could all be lost easily in these conditions, victim and rescuer alike. Roy was his brother – no, closer than a brother. Here he was safe in the shelter where his only danger was losing his patient. But Roy was out there, exposed, vulnerable. Dwight entertained no doubts. Roy had to go. Dwight had to stay. He longed to know what had become of his friend. If any human being could survive out there, it was Roy. And Kim.

What obstacles had they faced, what insurmountable obstacles? Dwight wished he could change places with Roy, not so Roy could have the safer lot, but because it is so much easier to face adversity for the one who is doing than for the one who is waiting.

He returned to check his patient. Nothing had changed, for better or for worse. Once again, Mrs. Ramsey caught him with her eyes. Those knowing eyes. She knew what he was feeling, and he knew that she knew it. It helped. He was not alone. He had been alone so much in life. But he was not alone now. They needed each other and that was drawing them closer.

"I'll fix you something to eat," Kathleen said, as if somehow food could fix anything. It could, in a way, when mixed with love.

"I'll do it," Rochelle offered, "You've got enough on your mind right now."

"That's exactly why I need to do it. Thanks, but I'll go crazy if I don't do something."

What evening light made its way past Howard's tarp, faded into blackness within the shelter, so that by the time they had all eaten, their only light was the orange glow of the fire casting its eerie shadows on the stone walls, a peaceful setting that bathed the occupants with relaxation and sleepiness, which crept over them and into them like the cold. Dwight moved his bedding to be close to Howard's pallet. No one knew or felt or cared to know how early in the evening it was when they all turned in to sleep. It was only eight.

23
Thunderhead

Two exhausted rescuers and their half-frozen friend lay unconscious to the world, lulled into oblivion by the relative warmth of their collective bodies crammed into Roy's ultra light tent made for two. Snow was falling again outside, half-burying them in insulating snow, protecting them from the wind, which howled in the night.

Kim and Roy woke together to the sound of a nearby hemlock as it crashed through branches that the surrounding trees held out to slow its fall to earth. The snow dampened its impact so that it was felt more than heard. Michelle stirred but did not wake.

"That was close," Kim rasped, pushing the sounds through her parched throat.

"Too close," Roy answered in the darkness.

Limbs popped. Trees firing at each other. A war of trees was the only sound in the night. It was a loud war, but Kim and Roy were exhausted and slept soundly for several more hours. Kim woke, but not to sounds. Her feet and legs were cold and hurting. She reached to rub her legs and felt dampness. Her legs and the foot of her sleeping bag were wet. Her stirrings woke Roy.

"What's the matter Kim?" he whispered hoarsely.

"My bag's all wet!"

"How'd it get wet?"

"I don't know."

Roy switched on his flashlight. The floor of the tent was wet and the lower wall of the tent was, too. In fact, it was damp all the way around, but most had collected at the lowest point in the tent floor at Kim's feet.

"The outside of my bag is damp, but it's dry inside," Roy said. "You'd better check Michelle."

"She's dry," Kim reported. "What's with the tent leaking?"

"It's a three season tent. It's not made for this much snow. The heavy waterproofing only goes up about six inches. The walls are weeping above that."

"Does that mean it's warming up, and the snow is melting?"

"No, it means that the three of us are putting off enough heat to melt the snow against the tent…that and our own breath condensing and making rain."

"What time is it?" Kim asked. She had a watch, but she knew her wind-burned eyes were too blurry to read it.

"It's three-thirty. We've got three hours of darkness left, if that's what you were thinking."

"Yes, that's what I was thinking. What are we going to do?"

"You're going to take my bag… No. No objections. That's an order."

"Why, Roy?"

"Because you've been more exposed. It's not because you're a woman and are weaker or anything. Simple common sense."

Kim could not tell if she were being kidded, bullied or just plain insulted. But his voice seemed firm, and she felt a strange security when he was decisive with her.

"What are you going to do?"

"I'm going to wrap my feet with my parka and go back to sleep. In your bag."

"What difference does it make? We are all going to be wet soon anyway. In spite of your heroics."

"That may be, but we are going to stay as dry as we collectively can for as long as we can. Now let's switch."

The switch was difficult in such close quarters, and, after a couple of clumsy attempts, Kim had to choreograph the movement so they weren't both trying to go under or over at the same time. She started to slip into Roy's bag, but had second thoughts when she realized that her socks were soaked. She pulled them off. Little good they were doing now anyway. She took off her parka and wrapped it around the foot of the dry bag, fastening the snaps to keep it in place. Her frost burned hands were working better. That gave her spirits a little boost, and a moment of hilarity came over her. She lay down in the bag and lifted her legs upward so that the end of the bag with the parka around it looked like a faceless hiker sitting up.

"Good night, Roy," she made the mannequin say and laughed as she pulled the top of the bag over her head.

"Good night," Roy chuckled. What a woman! he said to himself. Playing games after what she's been through.

Kim quickly fell asleep again, but Roy lingered, marveling at one woman and worrying for both beside him. He needed Dwight to let him know what else could be done for poor Michelle. She seemed stable enough, but her lack of full consciousness bothered him. She had been hypothermic, but nothing was frozen. There was shock. She was breathing steadily, though shallow. Her pulse was consistent but weak. She responded to stimuli: their voices, their touches, the sounds in the night. But she had not opened her eyes, and she had not spoken. He lay still and listened to the two women's breathing, sleeping, pressed tightly at his sides, wondering whether he should go outside to see what the conditions were, wondering whether he should risk starting the stove again to warm water. He decided fire or carbon monoxide would be greater risks than the cold for now. He could do it outside, but that would cost all the heat they had built up in the tent. He would reassess that in the morning. Finally he dozed.

Roy did not sleep long. When he awoke, the wetness in the foot of the sleeping bag had crept upward to above where his legs were unprotected by the parka wrapped around them. He felt strangely cold and warm at the same time, a sensation similar to fever, but he was not sick. He loosed the bag from around his neck and head and felt the rush of cold air over his shoulders. This gave him a shiver, but then he felt better. He wanted to reach over and feel Kim's bag, but he hesitated. He felt Michelle's instead. Damp but not wet. He looked at his watch. Only four. He had dozed just a few minutes. Now he did not feel like sleeping. He never felt like sleeping when he was damp.

What could he do to increase the girls' chances? he wondered. If he left the tent, maybe the snow would melt slower, and they would stay dry until morning. Maybe he could go find a stand of rhododendrons where he could find shelter as Kim had done two nights before. However, if he left the tent, the loss of his body heat might allow them to chill, maybe even to freeze. A new thought came to him. That's the answer, he said excitedly to himself. Why didn't I think of this before?

He began to slither from his bag, not an easy thing considering the affinity two wet textiles have for one another. When he had struggled free at last, he found himself half in the tent, half in the vestibule. The fabric of the vestibule was sagging heavily under the weight of snow upon it. He tried to open the zipper, but it was cold enough in the vestibule for the condensation from their breathing to refreeze, sealing the zipper in its icy grip. He pushed against the snow pack. It gave a little as he pushed, so he reasoned that it was not too thick. They were not buried. Not yet. He had no way of knowing what the weather was doing, insulated as they were from both the effects – and the sound – of the wind. Oh, well. It had been a great idea. He was going to dig the snow away from the tent walls. Then their body heat would not melt it and they would stay dry. However, he was now a prisoner in his own tent. If it came down to it, he could at least cut through the tent with his knife, and carry out that plan. If it came down to it.

Roy reversed the process by which he entered the vestibule, slithering backward into the bag. He did so as quietly as he could, but still he did not fail to wake Kim in the process.

"What's up?" she asked.

"I was just checking on conditions."

"Oh," she answered and fell swiftly back to sleep.

She must still be dry, relatively at least, or she would have noticed, he reasoned. Sufficiently satisfied that all was well for the moment, Roy drifted off in restless slumber.

Something he could not identify woke Roy from a dream he could not remember. His brain was fogged. He knew he was uncomfortable and his legs felt restless. He tried to move them but something was disconnected between the will to act and the act itself. Then he realized he was shivering. He felt only like rolling over and returning to sleep, but a vague sense of caution prevented him. He felt his legs with his hand. They were wet and cold as ice. It felt to his hands as if the legs belonged to someone else; they were numb. That concept shot through his mind like a bolt of lightning. It triggered something deeply rooted from his survival training. Action must now occur.

Roy felt about and found his flashlight. Then he felt about the outside of his bag. It was soaked. There was water standing in the downhill end of the tent, enough to splash with his hand. He felt about the bottom of Kim's bag, then Michelle's. Everything was soaked. The rain parkas had helped, no doubt, but the water had persisted until it had seeped through every unprotected portal until the wicking action of the sleeping bags had soaked up seepage like sponges.

Kim was sleeping soundly. Roy hated to wake her, but he knew he must. He tugged softly at the side of her bag to no avail. He spoke her name, but she did not rouse. He rocked her gently by her shoulder, her head bobbing back and forth in an action equal and opposite to his prodding, but still she slept. He did not expect this. He feared that hypothermia already had her in its seductive grip. He took both his hands, one to each of her shoulders and shook her vigorously. Her eyes half-opened, and she struggled to fix them straight ahead, but they rolled upward so that only the whites showed between the puffy slits. Her mouth released a quiet moan. Roy could see her bluish lips in the dim dappled light of the Mini-Mag. He reached for Michelle. Her face felt warm to his touch. Her breathing was shallow. So was her pulse. He unzipped her bag halfway up starting at the toe. He felt first her good leg. It was damp but not soaked, and the skin felt cool, not icy. He then felt the foot below the break. It was like touching ice, except the skin was still supple, even to her toes. She was as warm as he could make her now, so he slid the zipper back to the toe. He gave her a little kiss on the forehead. Why did I do that? he wondered, but he did not know. Hypothermia was confusing him perhaps. He returned his attentions to Kim.

He tried again to rouse her, shaking her by both shoulders. Annie, Annie are you OK? he chuckled to himself. He spoke her name loudly. This time there was just a flutter of her eyelids before settling back to slumber. He unzipped her bag at the toe, and felt inside. Both her feet were wet, and cold…so cold, but still Roy did not feel the terrible hardened feel of frozen flesh. Each toe moved, and the skin felt like skin. Very cold skin.

He removed his pants and Capilene, and drew from his pack a dry pair of pants, light cotton, just right for cool nights, but the best he could put next to his skin now. He unzipped his bag from head to toe and did the same to Kim's, then Michelle's. They had one soaked and three half-dry sleeping bags between them and he intended to use that. He opened his wide at the top. Then he pulled at Kim's bag until she was half out of it, the wet half no longer touching her. He lifted her shoulders and slid the dry half of his under her head and torso. This put her fully onto the dry parts. With an unconscious hesitation, he removed her wet leggings and replaced them with her rain parka, damp but not wet. He pulled Michelle free of her bag and onto the remaining dry spot beside Kim. Then he squeezed himself between the two and pulled them toward him, hugging their limp bodies to himself. Finally, he covered them all with Michelle's open bag. Dry for the moment, he thought, knowing that before morning could break, the relentless water would seek and find them again. This exercise proved to be exhausting, and his muscles ached, robbed of blood by the core of his body, which was slipping into survival mode and considered even appendages dispensable, sacrificing them to make every resource available for the preservation of life.

Relative to one another, Roy was warm and the women were cold. Therefore, as he lay with the girls pulled to his chest, he felt his warmth draining out and their cold creeping in. He felt his strength go until finally sleep was a pursuer that he could not evade. It felt good to let go at last and let it overtake him.

His loss was Kim's gain. Her body warmed until blood flowed into her brain sufficiently to allow her to wake. She woke in stages. During the first stage, she instinctively huddled her body closer to Roy, her source of warmth and security. She then began to move her arms a little, then her legs. Finally, her eyes opened. She wandered through a maze of unknowing until time and place returned to her. Then it occurred to her that things were not as she left them. She pulled away from Roy and felt about, loosening the covering bag, allowing the freezing air to rush in. She shook off the shiver and pulled the bag back into place. She shook Roy.

"What's going on?" she demanded suspiciously.

No response.

She shook him more vigorously, but it hurt her hands to do it. This time he roused enough to answer.

"*Alles ist naß!*" he said in a different time and place.

"What?"

"*Wir sind naß und…*frozen." He returned to the present. "Everything got wet. You were unconscious. Had to warm you…us."

His speech was slurred, but Kim understood.

"Thanks," she said, and settled back down. She smiled a bit and curved herself onto his side, consciously.

Roy did not go back to sleep. He was waiting for morning, though half of the time he could not frame in his mind the reason for it. He was on full alert, though not fully alert, not in full faculty of his mind and senses. He just knew that survival demanded it. He wanted to sleep, but fought it successfully for an hour before it finally took him unawares.

Kim's sleep was restless. She watched for morning while intermittently changing the position of her body in relation to Roy. The cold hurt her feet and legs, and her cracking, peeling hands ached. Each restless shift of her body renewed the pain and brought her back to consciousness.

Kim was still half-awake when she could see the first light of day glowing blue through their colored nylon roof. Never had she so welcomed the light of day. With it, a warming wave of euphoria swept over her battered body. It was short-lived, however, for a deep chill followed in its wake, and with it, the realization hit her that temperatures had plummeted. She shook uncontrollably while she tried to gather her thoughts. Instinctively her thoughts turned to Roy. To see him, she had to move away, her body having been pressed against his and intertwined too closely for her eyes to focus. Movement was difficult with her sluggish arms and legs, tangled as they were with Roy's and the makeshift bedding. When his face became clear, she shook him, gently at first, then more vigorously until his blue eyes shown between half-open lids, eyes made bluer by the eerie tent light.

"Roy, it's morning. We made it. But I'm so, so cold," Kim said.

Roy said nothing but pulled her head to his shoulder and held her tightly. Her shivers stopped for a moment.

"Kim, the temperature has dropped in here. I feel it, too. We'd better see about Michelle."

With his free hand, he found her wrist. He could feel no pulse. He wrested his right arm from around Kim. With it, he felt for a pulse, first the same wrist, and then the other, as great fear shuddered in his core. Kim sensed his trepidation, and sat up on her hip with vigilant eye on Roy's face, seeking any clue. Roy placed his fingers on the side of her throat and put an ear next to her nose and mouth. Seconds dragged through eons as Roy and Kim held their breath.

Finally, Roy exhaled a great sigh.

"It's very faint but it's there. Pulse and breath."

He reached and felt her feet again. The broken leg was colder than the other still, but neither was frozen.

"She's much worse, I think. There's only one choice. I have to go for help."

He began to wiggle free of his bedding, stiffened, then slumped into a dejected heap. In his attention to Michelle, he had neglected to notice his own crisis. There was no feeling in his legs from the knees down. What cover there had been for his legs, he had added to Michelle's, so his feet had been exposed. He reached to feel them. Only the tips of his toes on his right foot were hard like ice. The rest felt like lifeless rubber to his touch. He rubbed the supple places until some feeling – pins and needles – began to return.

"Roy, you cannot go for help. I will have to go."

"Kim, you cannot go if it is still snowing."

"I did it once. I can do it again."

She grabbed her parka, her leggings, and her wet socks and slithered into the vestibule, there discovering the frozen zipper.

Roy smiled and handed her his knife.

"Cut a hole just big enough to see out, high, up where you can see the light coming through," he said through gritted teeth. The searing pain in his foot announced that his returning circulation was thawing some frozen flesh.

Kim cut the hole as he instructed, spread the opening and peered out.

"Well?" asked Roy.

"It's not snowing. It's fog. I can hardly see the trees around us."

"Thank God."

"Thank God what?"

"Two things. One, you can't leave until that fog lifts. Two, fog means the sun is breaking things up. I hope."

"I hope too. But I can go now. I found my way up that trail by feel before. I can do it again. What other chance do we have?"

"I don't know how you did it before. I don't know how we did it. But we are better off staying put until help comes. You won't do me or Michelle any good wandering off the side of the mountain alone."

Roy's admonition only hardened Kim's resolve.

"I'm going now," she yelled quietly, reaching for her hiking boots.

Roy rubbed his legs more vigorously in anger. When he looked up again, he saw Kim sitting, boots in her lap, her head hanging low and dejected. There were tears.

"What is it, Kim?" Roy's anger changed to concern.

"They're frozen."

"What's frozen?" he asked.

"My hiking boots. They are an ice sculpture."

He laughed to himself, half from relief, half from her ability to make humorous analogies in such a crisis.

He reached, pulling her into the tent and to himself.

"Stay warm. That's our job. Stay warm until help comes."

Kim shuddered with the cries of defeat and from cold as she surrendered to his will and his arms. She let him pull her tightly to himself, for security, for warmth. Roy felt her shaking. He knew it was a good thing, her succumbing to her emotions, though he did not know why or how. Then great fear came over him. He felt like crying too. He felt the weight of three lives dangling by a thread…and he held the thread. Michelle already near death, his feet freezing, Kim's not far behind. He felt as though they could hold on just a little longer. Nothing he could do but wait for help, and there was no telling how long that would be. There was little hope for Michelle to live. If he and Kim survived, they would likely do so missing some body parts. His will to live and to keep others alive was stronger than any hope-draining thoughts or emotions. He loved his life now more than ever. Each minute was a year, an hour was a century. He felt the life in Kim beside him; he acknowledged the life in Michelle, faint and precarious. Three lives holding on, hearts beating together. This was stronger than anything he had known before. What the hell. If he died, he would do so knowing he had lived. If they died together, they all had lived. If one died, she would live on in the others, for no one would survive to be the same. Hold on till help comes. Hold on until help comes, the voice in his head said, keeping sleep at bay, and the blue dome glowed brighter over their heads.

Tuesday

24
Double Spring Gap

The evils resident in Tammy's life visited her throughout the night in a series of disturbing dreams. At first light, her eyes opened, and she met this morning with a strange energy. Unlike other nights, her dreams had served to distill her thoughts rather than to confuse them. She was ready to go home and face her world as she had come to understand it. Ah, but the snow. And her ankle. She could not go home, but she could go outside, leaving behind the dungeon of dark and gloom, and greet God's creation in whatever state of fuss she found it.

Tammy rose and quietly put on her boots and parka, careful not to wake Dave, whose rhythmic breathing she could hear from below. She climbed down and stealthily traversed the unseen dirt floor of the hut. She fumbled in the darkness to open the gate, slipped through it and into the ethereal gray light, a world of shadows and mere figments of reality. Tammy crossed the shelter yard with a shuffling gait, stopping when she felt her feet contact the hard frozen log that served as seating for the outside fire ring in more hospitable times. She sat down upon the icy bench, the snow-upholstery crunching beneath her weight as it conformed itself to her shape, serving as a quite comfortable seat so long as the snow did not melt.

This morning the cold felt good. It exhilarated her and magnified the lightness in her heart, which had shed its considerable burden of secrecy and denial that it had carried for so many years. Tammy sat and smiled at nature visible now only in faint hues of blue and gray. As she studied their subtleties, Tammy perceived a difference in her surroundings. Where there had been fury, the air was calm and still. No ice and snow pelted her face and the cold no longer bit at her through her layers of clothing. As the sun ascended, the scene grew whiter, but still no form was visible to her, only the whiteness surrounding her, closing in on her, thickening the air so that it was difficult to move in and out of her lungs. Where her heart had waked beating to life, she now felt tightness. She felt her brief joy slipping away; she tried to hold onto it, but it was gone, evaporating into the fog that had swallowed her pleasantly-painted morning and now threatened to swallow her very life. Tammy began to cry – quiet sobs of self-despair, flash feelings with no cause, vague bereavement, something lost, hope dashed, doubt vindicated.

DAVE WOKE. HIS first thoughts turned to Tammy, wondering how she had faired through the night while he had slept peacefully. He listened for her sounds and heard nothing. He rose and could see that her sleeping bag was empty. The fire had died away to a few faint glowing embers, and she was not beside it. She's only just awakened and gone out, he thought. She'll return in a moment. But she did not, and his thoughts turned to worry. He went to the gate, finding it a bit ajar. He opened it and stepped into the fog. He called her name. From little more than ten feet away came the response. In his relief, he continued talking, his babbling serving as a beacon for her to find her way to the gate again.

Once inside Dave expounded the virtues of fog over snow while he resurrected the fire from the ashes. At first, he did not notice that his congregation was barely paying attention. Tammy's red eyes were fixed on the unseen again, and she was slipping deeper and deeper into depression as he spoke.

"Tammy!" No response.

"Tammy!"

"Uh, what?"

"What's wrong?"

"Nothing." Her eyes were glazing over again. "I'm just tired."

"Let's get something to eat. You'll feel better."

"I'm not hungry."

"I want you to eat something anyway," Dave said as he set about finding some odds and ends for breakfast. The food was beginning to run low now.

"How 'bout some dried apples for starters?" he asked, holding the bag toward her. She protested again that she was not hungry while simultaneously accepting the offering and beginning to eat. Strange, Dave thought, this robotic behavior, as if one being were in control of her mind and emotions, another in control of her body. They ate breakfast in silence, broken only by Dave's few feeble attempts to elicit a meaningful response from Tammy, and the sound of snow falling off branches, landing with muffled thuds in the snow.

Nourishment found its way into Tammy's blood, awakening her sleeping emotions. Tears returned and filled her eyes. She blinked, and they rolled down her cheeks and into the creases of her frown, burning as they wetted the already chapped and reddened skin. She did not fight them back, nor did she hide them from David, who looked on in silent pain, letting her have her moment to feel. The moment was short, and Tammy returned to numbness, staring at the wall. Dave called her back from that place, the place that he feared most, Silence, the place Susan had taught him to fear.

"Tammy, you know that this is something that will never go away. It will always be there, and it is right to feel bad about it…always. But you must not stop feeling. You must not hide inside yourself or bury yourself. That is a form of death. You are going to have to learn to live with it and survive. And conquer…with God's help and his people."

Tammy said nothing, but she inwardly she scoffed. Where was God when I really needed him? And what kind of help have the people of God ever been, the hypocrites! Honing in like sharks every time one of their own stumbles, biting the flesh from one another's backs and tearing each other apart in a feeding frenzy. Descending like flies on shit at the mere rumor of unfaithfulness, spreading gossip in the name of prayer, raising the awareness of their own purity by stepping on the heads of the fallen, all while secretly fondling the details of the sins that they would never, or could never, overtly commit.

Bashing them made her feel better for a moment, then worse than before. Who was she to judge and condemn? They were low, and she was bottom scum. Who is lower, scum or the slimy creatures that feed on it? Tammy continued her slide into complete despair. The answer was clear; the only way to end the slide was to end her life. But how? She looked about her at the three gray walls, the fourth of clear plastic. What means was here to aid her cure? No rope for the rafters, no gun, no pills. She could slit her wrists, but without a bathtub as in the movies, her blood would clot before her life was gone. Nothing to do but bash her own head against the frozen stone until the pain all ran out of her. She leaned into the wall to do it, but she could not. It was not in her to harm herself. Nor was it in her to make a feeble attempt at it for the sake of drama. She already had David's attention; what good would that do? Her purgatory was to go on in life carrying the pain of guilt and anger hemorrhaging inside her, killing her slowly. She would not marry; she could not be touched. No new life could come from her belly, lest she pass to it her poison of death. She would live alone. She would wear gray. Others would stare, and they would talk, circulating a thousand different stories about her, which their evil imaginations would spawn to explain her odd behavior. It would make a good movie. She plunged deeper into the black hole of her heart; she was collapsing inwardly, imploding. In the blackness, she heard a voice.

"You need to talk about these things, Tammy," Dave continued, "It did you some good to talk to me, but you are going to need others. There is plenty of help if you want it. And I can get it for you. But don't close up. Don't bottle it in. You've got to look outside yourself."

Tammy did not hear his words, but she felt the sincerity in his voice. She looked out through the mist in her eyes and into his. They were calling to her, summoning her, bidding her to come back. His voice was warmth itself, thawing her frozen feelings. She basked in it.

"Tammy!"

"What?"

"I said it did you some good to talk to me yesterday."

"Yes. Yes, Dave, it helped."

She remembered what a relief it was to tell her secret at last, that flood of pent up emotion when she let it all go. She had felt like she had been given her freedom at last, freedom to think and feel, to live at last. Then it was gone. She wanted it back, so she opened her mouth to tell him more, but there were no words. There was nothing more to say.

"Go on, Tammy. Talk about it."

Nothing would come.

"I'm just tired," she said at last. That was all. Nothing more to say.

DAVID SENSED THERE was more, something from the deeper layers, places she had never consciously been in her own mind. He fumbled for a key. Something to unlock her iron core. But he found none. The secret rooms must be broken into, but he was not the one to do it.

What she needed from him at this point was basic life support, just keeping the victim alive and breathing until the healers could take over. He sensed the despair that was spreading through her, killing her piece by piece. When it reached her will, she was gone. She desperately needed to talk, forcing her to think and feel. In the winter of her mind, she was slowly freezing to death, the coldness gradually numbing while promising that numbness is a friend and that surrendering to its seduction promises great serenity, all the while stealing life.

What could he do now in this place? She needed activity. She needed to be around other people. Less than three miles up the trail, through fog and God knows how much snow was a shelter full of people who could help. Ah, but they could never make it even if the fog did lift, what with Tammy's ankle and the snow. He gave it serious thought, even planned to attempt it as soon as the fog lifted, but at last, he gave it up as a foolish idea, too fraught with physical danger to be the cure for the peril in her soul. Unable to find the words or the way, Dave sank into a small depression of his own, passively tending the fire and sorting what precious victuals were left.

Dave piddled while Tammy sank deeper. In the end, her world collapsed into the core of her being, her shriveling will now resolute on one thing, ending the pain of a tortured and desiccated life. Her gnarled mind gave rise to an idea for the means. She gazed off into the fog where promise of relief beckoned her. She gathered her resolve, made an excuse to Dave and stumbled through the gate into the blankness that seemed to clear the wailing in her head. Once out of the cabin, Tammy shed her parka as though it were one more weight that tethered her tortured being to earth. Tears of anguish and release streamed down her face, mingling themselves in the chapped and cracking furrows their predecessors had eroded at the corners of her eyes and down the sides of her frost-nipped nose. She pressed onward into the soothing nothingness of the dense white fog, toward the memory of a trail in the woods, a year-old memory from three days past when all was clear and bright and hopeful.

As she went, she shed yet more of her clothing, the cold focusing her thoughts resolutely on her purpose, not to tempt a man, but to tempt nature itself to ravage her to death. She welcomed the biting bitter cold upon the bareness of her breast and the clumsy numbness creeping up her legs with every labored step in the waist-deep snow. Her thighs grew weary as she pressed onward to nowhere, away from the shelter of despair, from Dave, from her life below, from life itself. Her movement became as one in a dream: slow, deliberate, intense. At last, the cold-numbed limbs would move no more and she fell forward into the snow, sinking just below its surface, stretching her arms outward in swimming motions, pulling the snow toward her to embrace it as it embraced her. She felt its icy caress upon every inch of her bare skin as she turned herself skyward in her frigid grave. She crossed her arms upon her chest like an ancient corpse, and laughed, amusing herself in her morbid flirtation with death. In her core, however, were horrors, desperation, voices crying out above the humming of her mind-numbness.

The cold crept inward, penetrating her as she invited it to takes its pleasure, and with it came a sleepy peace, a final lullaby, and she was ready to close her eyes. But she did not or could not close them. They had found something to see instead of whiteness of the fog. A ray of light, a ray of hope, breaking through the mist and casting a warm glow upon her chill blue flesh prostrate in the snow. The sun was breaking through, and as her eyes could discern growing details about her in the woods, her mind perceived the shapes of a world of hope within her, which she had not seen before. Tammy's will to die melted with the sun, and she rose from the sepulcher of ice, reaching out to grab the orange-white orb before it paled to gray and disappeared again in fog. Nevertheless, its brief visitation had been sufficient to renew in Tammy a will to live and a hope of life worth living. God had not forsaken her in her most dangerous moment, and her God-voice inside chanted, "Live!"

Tammy walked in the direction where the brief illumination had revealed her footsteps in the snow, her legs wobbling as she stepped; she could not feel her feet. She had the will now, and she knew the way, but she had no strength to carry on. Great fears rushed in to fill the void where awakening joys had been. One can only fear when one has something to lose, and she feared greatly that she would now perish naked in the snow while hope still beat in her breast. She stumbled often, but kept rising to continue. She came upon her pants and soon her boots.

These she donned with great difficulty for the uselessness of her frigid fingers. She could not tie the boots, but even undone they stabilized her wobbling and the pants kept the snow from biting her legs. Furthermore finding them confirmed she was on the right path; she continued in the way through snow and fog until at last her complete wardrobe was once more in her possession. Where to turn from the place of discovering her parka, however, she could not tell, though she knew the shelter was near. Fear gripped her again, and she collapsed and cried. So useless to die so close to being safe, she sobbed. She called out to Dave, but there was no answer, and she cried and shivered on her knees in the snow. What seemed like hours took only minutes, and a voice out of the void called, "Tammy!" She answered, and the voice grew near, until she could just make Dave's shape out in the fog.

"What on earth?" he cried, as he raised her to her feet, and placed his own parka on her quaking shoulders. "Can you walk?"

"Yes," she meant to say, but could not for the shaking, so she answered with a shuffle of her feet in the direction he had pointed her. She looked ahead and her eyes saw a scene she thought now was a glimpse of heaven. The shelter stood out in the fog, a single ray of sunshine breaking through and illuminating its dingy tin roof as though it were gilded, the whole structure circumscribed by a white halo that faded into the fog around it.

Soon she was inside its relative warmth, seated before the fire, and wrapped in the duel embrace of her sleeping bag and David's arm. Her shaking ceased quickly, and she knew now that she was safe, having been brushed so nearly with death of body and of soul, having survived to count the preciousness of life. She knew now that she would never want to take her own life again, so precious despite its damage at the hands of others when most vulnerable; she would live it well regardless.

"What happened to you out there?" Dave asked, separating himself from her to make warm drinks.

"I got lost," Tammy said. It was a peculiar lie, truer than most truths.

"But you've been to the outhouse many times now."

"The fog was thicker," she said, and Dave's curiosity was satisfied. She would tell him what had happened, but not until later. She had worried him enough already, and there was much housekeeping to do.

"Dave, I'm ready to talk about it," she said.

"Well, uh, what's on your mind?"

"Dave, can we eat first. I've starved."

"Of course," he answered and gathered the remaining food. They ate the last of the peanut butter crackers with the last package of Ramen noodles. Dave hung the food bag back on its string, nearly empty save for a few light snacks. He had seen the sun too and knew help was not long in coming.

25
Russell Field

Brian watched Carrie from the bunk. She was sitting on the log by the fire, where she had sat for much of their time since the snow fell. She stared into the flames with a nowhere look, Brian's eyes glued to her unchanging face, wondering where she was.

"Are you going to study the fire all day again?" he asked.

"I might," she answered without looking away from it.

"Have you hypnotized yourself?"

"No."

"What do you see in there anyway?"

"Nothing," she answered, but she *did* see. In those flames was everything. Everything she had thought about, longed for, planned. They made her feel warm and alive. She felt as though looking into the flickering and dancing flames was looking into the future. Her future. Looking into those flames she could dream, she could remember her dreams, she could believe in them. Everywhere else was just coldness and darkness, snow and stone and dirt. They were dead and cold. But the fire was alive, the flames lived and danced and reached upward, flying like spirits set free to soar. They illuminated her heart, discovered her longings, focused her mind. They fleshed out her plans, though her thinking was neither in details nor in strategy. It was in faith and vision. There would be time for details when they returned home, whatever home was now. She embraced her vision. She lived with the flames. Her passions grew. Just as the flames leaped to escape the wood that bound them, there was a life inside her bursting forth to find its expression. Her insides were like jelly, quivering with excitement though hidden behind her blank expression, which Brian could not read. She purposely kept it blank to protect herself from Brian's insensitive perceptions.

Brian climbed down from the bunk and walked to the gate. He shook it, feeling the ice's grip upon it, feeling, though not seeing, the snow bank's weight upon it and on his freedom. Restlessness jerked in his legs, and uneasiness gnawed at his middle.

"You know Carrie, it's just not right." He shook the gate again, not really trying to open it, for he could have done so as he had before, had that been his desire. He was merely testing his boundaries.

"What's not right, Brian?" She did not turn from the fire.

"The Park Service. They are really to blame for all this." He looked at her form, silhouetted against the fireplace, its orange and yellow glow highlighting the fringes of her wiry hair.

"How's that?" she said, casting a suspicious glance over her right shoulder.

"They should have warned people about this. They should have told us this could happen. Maybe we wouldn't have come. They at least should have provided some better accommodations for us. They have no right to put us in a situation like this," he said, staring with clenched brow at the tarpaulin wall as if he could see through it into the harshness that had incarcerated him.

"How can you blame the Park Service for this? You might as well blame God. Or yourself."

"What? You don't think I'm blaming myself for this already? You don't have to rub it in." He was now facing her, and she had tossed her legs over the log so that she was facing him, too.

"You made the choice to come out here. You wanted adventure. You said adventure would bring us together and give us a honeymoon we'd never forget. But I'm not blaming you. I'm glad we came. I'm *so* glad we came. I'm glad it snowed, and we can't go home. I'm not even sure I want to go home."

"Well, I want to go home…to the home we planned together."

Brian took a couple of steps toward her before continuing.

"What's wrong with the home we planned? It's warm and dry, and there's food, and a nice warm heater…"

Carrie turned back to the fire and stopped hearing him. She sat and watched the fire dance about, shooting upward, and in it, she saw not the sticks and flames and smoke, but poetry. It was not combustion, oxidation of wood, producing heat and light, but it was earth and music, and all sacred things combined. We've lost fire, she thought in her heart, we've passed the job of warming us on to some humming piece of machinery stuck in a dank corner of our brick and drywall box we call a home, and we've become as cold and sterile as it is. This could be home, lacking only a fourth wall and a little food, and a partner who sees it the same as I. Here there could be love and life, and our passions could grow until we bust, and the busting would be glorious.

"Carrie! I said…" He took another step and faltered, falling to his right against the chain link.

"Brian, what's wrong?" Carrie jumped up and went to her husband.

"I just need to sit down."

She helped him to the log with difficulty. She was strong, but he outweighed her considerably. He sat down, his upper body swaying in a circular motion like tall spindly Georgia pines in a gusty wind.

"Brian, what's wrong, hun'?" she asked, holding the palms of her hands on each side of his face to steady him.

"I'm dizzy…weak."

"You need to eat something," she said, rising to fetch the food bag.

"It's all gone," Brian said, his voice weak and trembling. "Gone," he reiterated, his head sinking into his hands.

"Brian, I knew it was almost gone. That's why I didn't have any breakfast yet. But isn't there anything at all left?"

"The mice, remember? And we were supposed to be home by now."

Carrie pondered the circumstances. Suddenly it came to her.

"Brian, I've just missed breakfast. That's all. I'm not weak. I'm hardly even hungry. You've missed breakfast before. What's going on," she asked, her hands clamped to her hips, her lips clamped together like a period.

"Nothing," he said through his fingers that held his head from falling to the dirt.

"Something," Carrie insisted. "Haven't you been eating?"

"I ate whenever you did."

"But you haven't been taking your share, have you?"

"No," he confessed. "We would have run out a couple of days ago."

"I could have been rationing, too."

"I promised to provide for you. I don't mind being a little hungry. I mind your being, though."

Carrie's sternness began to melt. She returned to her husband, encircling him with her arms.

"You bastard!" she said. "You wonderful bastard! I'm sorry I was angry. But you shouldn't keep secrets from me trying to be a hero. I want a partner, not a knight."

"It's ok. I'm feeling better. We just need to rest and not use up so much energy. Who knows how long we'll be here?"

They held each other by the fire until midmorning, Carrie stingily feeding the fire, the firewood almost gone, too. They were warm, reasonably so, and she was content. Brian, though, continued to grumble more than their stomachs.

"We won't take trips like this anymore. We'll stick to cruises, resorts, cities…just the luxuries. The comforts. Places where our money counts, where you can buy people to look after you. No more of this roughing it."

At first, Carrie tried to tell him she didn't want that. She wanted this…well with enough food. But he wasn't listening.

"Carrie, don't hold a grudge about all this. When we get home, I'm going to make it up to you. I've been thinking we can afford that hot tub. When we are sitting in that hot tub, we won't remember any of this. I'm going to bust my butt and get that promotion. And I've been thinking about getting my securities license. Then the more I work the more money I'll make, and the more we can have. I'm going to provide all the things you want, and you won't have to think about this at all."

"When would we talk?"

"What?"

"When would we have time to be together, to love each other, if you're spending all your time making and spending money?"

"There will be time. But we have to pay our dues. We're going to have to work extra. Then we will have what we want."

"Why do we need so much to live? Don't we have everything we need right here? Well, if we had more food. I mean, if we were not so rich or trying to be, wouldn't we be richer inside?"

Brian acted as if he did not hear, but in truth, he did not understand, and his hunger was making it more difficult to think and to speak.

"Let's check on things outside. Maybe we'll be out of here soon," Brian suggested. Carrie conceded defeat. Maybe in time he would learn to hear her. Maybe when they were warmed and filled and in their life together, he would learn to communicate. Maybe in reflection he would learn the lessons she had already learned in their isolation together.

Through a joint effort, they opened the gate. The fireplace shovel, the broken-handled spade left by a trail maintainer, opened the way through the snow. The drifts, where they had piled themselves against the walls of the shelter, were now as tall as Carrie, but past the drifts, the snow was only waist high. The air was white and liquid. Their eyes perceived nothing.

"It's not snowing," Brian said loudly, as if the blinded whiteness had made them deaf also.

"How can you tell?" Carrie, disoriented by the featureless world, responded.

"It's fog. The snow has stopped. The wind has stopped. It's not as cold. Can't you feel it?"

They could see each other, and occasionally the outline of the shelter door broke momentarily through the fog.

"How long will the fog last?" Carrie asked.

"I dunno," Brian shrugged. "The book didn't talk about fog."

Brian and Carrie returned to the relative warmth of the shelter. They huddled by the fire, talking little and napping often. Throughout the day, Brian checked on the weather. Each time his report was the same: no snow, much fog, less cold. After one such excursion, Brian said that he thought he could see the outline of some surrounding trees. Carrie took that news with mixed emotions. She knew that they must get food and that the firewood would be gone by day's end, but she did not long for home or comfort, afraid that, when she left this place of self-discovery, she would somehow lose its revelations, reverting back to the half-conscious individual she was when she married Brian, drifting with the current of social expectations, becoming fat in possessions while her soul was starving to death. Nevertheless, return she must, if they survived, and she determined that regardless of the personal cost, she would set her sights on what she had come to value most, if only she could distill the still raw concepts into practical details to guide her daily choices.

Carrie's thoughts slid imperceptibly toward pessimism as she thought how wonderful this would have been, had her husband been the reflective communicating type, had he settled in to make the most of their time together. She would have told her best friend what a romantic adventure it was, snowed in for days atop a secluded mountain, no interference from the outside world, no bellhop, no waiter, nothing to spoil the romantic mood cast by warm flickering tones of firelight and all the things they did to stay warm together, all the things that they talked about, concentrating a year of discovering one another into a single week. But Brian could not relax, he could not listen, he could not speak. He could only blame and defend and reason as he paced and longed to be elsewhere. He had spoiled it for Carrie in all its glorious potential. Now it was reduced to mere survival, staying thawed, conserving energy, waiting for a break to escape. Nothing more than the animals are doing now, Carrie thought. No, lower than what they are doing because they are home, in their places. For them, surviving is what they were meant to do. Certainly, we were meant for more than mere survival, and even more than comfort. But what? She could not say exactly, but she felt it, and felt deeply that an opportunity had been lost to experience it. She determined, however, that she would speak no more of it to Brian until they were resettled in their home. Yes, she would even *think* no more of it. Brian was right, first things first. They had to survive, and to survive they had to think positively. But when they returned, she would not cease seeking to apply this slippery wisdom to her life. She would not live in a rut, sinking deeper and deeper so that its walls — others' expectations for her — would be all she would ever see and all that guided her as she raised a family and prepared to die.

Carrie slid herself closer to Brian. His eyelids hung heavily like half-drawn window shades. Carrie chuckled.

"What's so funny?" Brian asked, his eyes straining to open.

"You. Your eyes. They look like cartoons. All they need is a little string hanging down, and they would be just right," she said, putting as much mischief and playfulness into her overture as she could. She poked his side to provoke a response. Then she cuddled close to his side. Brian acted annoyed, but inwardly he felt relieved and contented that they were not at odds now, that she seemed happy, and that the credit must be his through his sacrifice and promises of future provision.

"Brian, you are right. We've got to think positively when we are in tough places. Keep a winning attitude. If it works in business, it works here, too. We're gonna get outta here," Carrie said, feeling strangely as though she were right and wrong at the same time, like a recanting heretic who has a change of mind to escape the flames, while the flames of freedom die slowly in the heart.

"Carrie, when we are back at home, things will be different. You will see. Just keep picturing that hot tub. It won't be long now and we'll be soaking in it, thinking all this was just a bad dream." Yes, he was right. Carrie's change of mood was to his credit.

Carrie thought to herself that it would seem like a dream all right, but not a bad one. Think positively, think like Brian, deny reality. She started to object, but quieted the rebel down again. Just think positively and love him now. His way. A hot tub really wouldn't be all that bad right now. She tightened her grip and clung to him silently.

When they awoke from their slumbering embrace, everything at once seemed different. It was the light. Or was it the cold? No, it was the fire, reduced to ashes for having burned all its fuel. Carrie began to panic, feeling the bite of the cold and the emptiness in her stomach. But she felt alive, and she was conscious of it. The panic gave way to bereavement for the loss of the fire, not so much for its warmth, but for its warm light of orange and yellow. Now there was nothing but cool blue gray hues illuminating everything evenly in its impersonal tone. Brian did not panic. He had calculated the rate of burn and supply of fuel, and his predictions were right on target. He shrugged it off with a ho-hum. The fire wasn't doing that much for their survival anyway. Their combined body heat was keeping them warm enough. Food was the crisis, and the loss of the fire had not changed that. He thought of going to the door to check conditions again, but decided that it would be a needless expenditure of assets. He would wait. They could go a long time without food. He had a few pounds stored around his middle. Carrie was no skeleton either. They were dry and out of the wind. No, it was just a matter of time before they could hike out. It was down hill all the way if they went toward Cade's Cove. They wouldn't have to wait for the snow to melt. They could slide on their asses if they had to. If they could find the trail.

"Carrie, when we leave here, we should travel as light as we can. Just take what we need to keep us warm. The rest we'll just leave here."

"You think that will be soon, don't you."

"I'm thinking tomorrow morning if the fog is gone."

They sat staring at the cold dark recess in the stones where the fire had been. That focal point had become a habit in just a couple days.

AFTER NEARLY AN hour of soul slumber, Brian broke the uneasy silence.

"Carrie, I was thinking. When we get back, we need to have a party or something. You know, nothing big or anything, just some friends. Sort of a housewarming or something. Wouldn't you like that?"

"Well, sure, I guess, Brian," she stammered. "Who would we ask?"

"The people in our wedding of course. There's John and Sue from the office, and if we ask them, then I have to ask Derrick and Amy, too."

"Sure, that would be great," she answered before she remembered the Christmas party, how that Derrick and Amy talked incessantly about the stock market and the mall, and presumably John and Sue would do the same. Or would it be the virtues of Beamers and Mercs, or German versus Japanese, or some other god that could crash or rust, or be bettered next year by the guy who got the bigger bonus or inherited his parents' nest egg. I have to stop being bitter, she thought to herself. There will be time for learning and growth.

"Sure Brian, whoever you want. I'd like to invite Linda and Krista, too, if that's OK."

"Krista? She's just a waitress. Do you think she would be comfortable with the others?" he asked, with sincere concern.

Krista and Carrie were close in high school, but time and diverging paths separated them…until the wedding. There was still the same resonance of old friendship, and a sense that, if circumstances were kind, they could take up just where they left off. Krista lost her father in tenth grade. He had not provided well for that contingency, and her mother had to sell the house and move to a distant apartment, though still in the same school district. Krista was pretty in a down-home sort of way, and, with her mother's encouragement, married the first decent-looking guy with a fair-paying job who came along – just months after graduating. He was not well suited for marriage, less so for parenthood. Krista found herself a single parent when she was not yet twenty. She supported herself and her son, and helped her mother by waiting tables at a truck stop on I-24. Sometimes the tips were good, usually at the price of some sort of personal degradation. That left little time for socializing with a high school friend. At the wedding, she seemed haggard and humiliated, prematurely used up. Carrie saw another difference, though, a positive transcendent one. She could not put her finger on it then, but now she saw it clearly as a wisdom acquired through sufferings, a wisdom beyond her twenty-two years, a stalwart strength and confidence declaring that she was up to the challenge.

"Don't worry about Krista. Krista can take care of herself," Carrie professed. She would enjoy seeing her take care of herself among the social elite, which Brian and his friends aspired to be. Don't pity Krista, she thought. Pity the first soul that speaks condescendingly to her.

"If we can get the hot tub installed in time…that would be fun. But we'd better not cater the party. I don't think the budget can quite handle all that at once."

"You're the budget man," she said with a playful smile. Suddenly her ears pricked, and she cocked her head to the side.

"What is it?" Brian asked.

"Didn't you hear that?"

"Hear what?"

"That."

"So now you're hearing things. Pretty soon you're going to be…"

"Shhh!"

"What's it sound like?"

"Crunching. Snow crunching."

"Oh, you're just hearing snow falling off the trees. I've been hearing that for hours. That's because it's warming up."

"No, I've been hearing that, too. This is different. Like something walking."

"I heard it too," Brian said.

"What is it?"

"It could be a deer…or a bear."

Brian envisioned a bruin, as hungry as he, much larger and stronger, unlikely to give up easily when chain link was all that stood between him and dinner.

The sounds were nearing, the sound of something moving slowly and deliberately. The sounds were right outside the gate.

"Any body in there?" a voice called from outside.

Brian and Carrie jumped, and their hearts missed a beat, their bodies and senses drawn tight as piano strings, ready for anything…except a human voice. Then relief swept over them, and large smiles spread across their faces.

"Yes, two of us. Come in," Brian invited, and rose to help open the gate.

"You guys all right?" twanged a New Jersey voice, its owner's form silhouetted by rays of sunlight shining from the setting sun, unimpeded now by snow or fog.

"Just hungry," Brian answered, shielding himself from the unfamiliar light.

Once inside the figure stood erect, having stooped to half his height to slip through the shrinking threshold, now almost a tunnel, like the entrance to a cave.

"I'm Bob," he said, as their eyes adjusted enough to make out the shield and patches on hat and parka. The Park Service had arrived.

Bob attended first to the essentials, making sure his victims were healthy, finding out about their sightings of other hikers and radioing in to headquarters to report his findings.

"Are you going to get us out of here?" Brian asked impatiently.

"It's too late to get a chopper in here tonight. The sun's setting and the fog is just breaking up, so looks like we'll be out of here in the morning," said Bob, digging into his pack.

"We're getting out in a chopper?" Brian asked, his eyes lighting up like a child with the prospect of a new thrill.

"Looks that way," said Bob. "Ah, here it is."

Bob pulled a little black nylon bag from his pack, and withdrew three PowerBars.

"How long since you guys have eaten?"

"Last night," Carrie spoke.

"So you are not exactly starving to death, but you may want to take it a little easy with those. And drink water with them."

Brian looked puzzled.

"Say, Bob. How'd you get up here if there's no chopper out there?"

"Snowshoes."

"I would've thought maybe horseback," Carrie said. She was fumbling with the PowerBar, its sticky wrapper clinging to her fingers.

"Nagh, horses aren't any good in snow this deep. They can't keep their footing or keep on the trail. In some places, the snow would be up to their heads. Nagh, snowshoes are the ticket. It still wasn't easy going. I can usually get up here in a couple of hours. Took me all day."

Bob pulled a couple of green wool blankets from his backpack and offered them to Brian and Carrie. Then he spread out his own sleeping bag on the top bunk.

"I was afraid we'd be hiking out in this mess," Brian said tentatively. He didn't want the ranger to think he was wimpish, but the prospect of escaping the return trip through snow by riding in a helicopter made him brave.

Bob set up a cooking stove and laid out packets of food and cooking pots. Bob soon had the stove whistling quietly with a perfect blue, yet nearly invisible flame. Brian watched, envious of the skill and experience with which he performed these tasks. What had seemed to Brian his great success days before, seemed now to have been obvious fumbling and chaos. Bob gave Brian the same feeling that the thru-hikers had. He was never comfortable with someone who could do anything better than he could. Where there was hope of victory, his competitive nature was aroused. Where there was not, he just turned green and sulked. He kept quiet and comforted himself with the prospect of being lifted off the ground, whisked away to civilization, and home in his own bed by next nightfall. It was going to be a long night, but at least there was something in his stomach now, creeping its way into his blood stream, soon to be joined by a full hot meal.

Carrie helped with the preparations filling the billies with water from Bob's dromedary bag, placing one upon the stove, the other on the hearth. It did not cross Carrie's still foggy mind that she could offer their stove and fuel to speed the process. It did occur to Brian, but he dismissed the idea for some vague reason he could not explain. When the water began to steam, and bubbles formed on the insides of the pot, Bob set that pot off and placed the cold one on the stove. He handed a packet of cocoa to Carrie and a spoon, and soon there were three cups of chocolate to warm their frozen insides. By the time that was gone, Bob was ready to refill their cups from a pot of rehydrated chicken and rice, bland in taste and color but a feast in these circumstances.

"Looks as if you guys just ran out of firewood," Bob said, leaning back against the hearth, stretching his legs out in front of him.

"How could you tell that?" Carrie asked.

He answered by holding his hand an inch or two over the lifeless ashes, and twitching his head upward in a slightly cocky but friendly way.

Carrie had not really noticed the man until now. The presence of a new person, a third person, had shaken her abruptly from a dream, leaving her somewhat in a state of confusion from which she had tried to extricate herself with menial tasks. If he had left, and someone asked her to describe him, she could not have done it. But she saw him now. She saw that his face was not as hard as his voice, and his eyes were softer still, baby blue with tiny pupils staring pointedly from deep within their dark sockets. His tousled brown hair gave him a boyish look, but that was offset by the prominent bones of his cheeks and jaw. She would have correctly guessed his age to be thirty-five. He was not attractive in face or features, but something about him drew Carrie into an innocent infatuation that pressed her to learn more. Here she was, face to face with a man who obviously lived a life very different from her own, Brian's or anyone else she knew for that matter. She was determined to take advantage of this chance to see if, perhaps, she could enrich her own life by peering into his.

"Where are you normally stationed when they don't have you up here in the icecaps looking after stupid hikers?" Carrie asked him. Brian looked up from his bootlaces with a scowl.

"Abram's Creek," was Bob's short response. He was not shy, and didn't seem to mind conversation, but what he had to say was usually to the point.

"Where's Abram's Creek?" Carrie asked the obvious question.

"It's around on the west side."

"I don't really know where the west side is," Carrie shrugged.

"Where did you park to begin your hike?"

"At the dam."

"Fontana? Well, Abram's Creek is not far from there. You take a highway that follows the river below Fontana and then turn into the Park in some of the flatter parts."

"Do you live there?"

"Sure. I've a little house there."

"Do you have a family?" she asked, and knew at once from the delay of his answer that she had stepped a little close.

"I'm sorry, I'm not meaning to pry, but I'm just interested in how a ranger lives," she apologized, hoping she had not set him on the defensive.

"No problem. She just wasn't as interested in how a ranger lives as you are. And she didn't like to move."

Carrie eyed her hands while she considered his answer.

"Do rangers have to move a lot? I mean, how long have you been here now?"

"Seven years. I had to move a lot when I was new."

Carrie perked up as if to call all her senses to attention.

"Where else have you been stationed?"

"I was just seasonal at first. I was assigned to a different place every year…Grand Canyon, Arches, Tetons, Yellowstone…mostly places out west."

"Wow," she exclaimed, wide-eyed. "How'd you end up here?"

"My wife wanted to move back east, so when a place came open we moved here. But she never took much to the Smokies. She went home."

"Where's home?"

"New Jersey."

"I could have guessed! So how do you like it here? I mean, do you like it as well as out west?"

"It's different. You can't really compare. They both have advantages. But I want to stay here, if that's what you mean. It's laid back here most of the time. People are nice."

"What made you decide you wanted to be a ranger?"

Bob chuckled.

"You sure do have a lot of questions. Are you a detective or a lawyer or something?"

"No, just a bank teller. I've been thinking a lot about life since we've been stuck here. I'm interested, that's all. Does it bother you?"

"No, I was just kidding."

"Carrie, why don't you leave the poor man alone? He's tired after getting up here," Brian chastised.

"Really. It's all right, Carrie. Go on."

Carrie looked thoughtfully at the dust beneath her feet. Then she looked up, looked him in the eye.

"You know, Bob, a person can't face a time in the outdoors without the essentials of modern life and not come out a changed person. You certainly cannot face death without coming out changed, without questioning the value of everything you thought was important. I'm just not sure how I've changed."

"Carrie, you'll be sorting that out for months or years after something like this. I've had to face some of those questions lately. I know what you mean."

Carrie relaxed and leaned closer, her confidence bolstered by his volunteering something of himself to her.

"What happened to make you question. Was it when your wife left you?"

"When my wife made me choose between her and who I am, she didn't seem like a great loss. There were no kids, so that was that. No, I'm talking about something more recent. We lost a fellow ranger awhile back. He was the first killed in the line of duty."

Bob looked beyond Carrie, and his eyes lost their sharpness.

"What happened?"

"Something senseless. Just a deranged man with a rifle scaring the visitors on the Blue Ridge Parkway. He was the first to answer the call, and the guy shot him. He was a psychiatric case. The ranger had a wife and kids, and they lost him just like that!" Bob snapped his fingers. "It made us all question if what we were doing was worth it. Every time we answer a call, that's on our minds now. Each call could be the time we buy it. But yes, I decided it was worth it. I decided it didn't matter so much how or when a person dies, it's how they live before it happens that matters."

"How did it change how you live?"

"I remembered the reasons why I went into this line of work, being in nature and helping people. I know that sounds canned, but it sure isn't the money. I don't look at any day as routine anymore. Everyday is a chance to learn something new, see something new or help someone new."

"Like us."

"Yeah, like you. You guys would have been all right without me, but at least you're not hungry now, right?"

"At least we don't have to hike out in the snow as we planned tomorrow."

"Maybe you wouldn't have been all right without me."

"What do you mean?" Carrie said, knitting her brow.

Brian was listening again.

"If you'd tried to hike out in this snow without snow shoes or food, you would have become exhausted and collapsed somewhere under the trees where we couldn't find you. No, staying put would have been the thing to do."

Carrie felt relieved, and Brian felt emasculated. He turned bitter.

"We're grateful you came, then. Stay put. We'll remember that next time," Carrie said.

There won't be a next time, Brian thought.

"We'd better turn in," Bob suggested, "We need to be ready for the chopper at first light."

Tucked inside her bag, Carrie thought of her conversation with Bob, turning their words over and over in her mind. As she did, they rekindled in her the passionate longings that she had tried repeatedly now for Brian's sake to kill, but they would not die. She fell asleep with alternating fear and excitement dashing through her mind, firm in the belief that something deep and unknown was changing her, bringing forth a new life in her with all its rewards and dangers.

26
Spence Field

The Tuesday morning sun rose in obscurity and pushed against the clouds and fog, succeeding only in casting a few diffuse white rays upon the stone and tin shelter at Spence Field, so that the only difference its inhabitants could discern in their world was that night had ended and there was light. As weak as this morning began, those hugging their bags and each other for warmth were nevertheless relieved to see its anemic light, their faith that morning would come at all having been sorely tested throughout the long night, both in nightmares and waking, through child-fears, cramps and creeping cold, and the restless stirrings of an old man heart-sick and frail.

"It's not snowing anymore," Dwight reported to the others as soon as his senses could discern the featureless light. The news was well received among the waking, shivering crowd. Dwight had intended it merely as fact, not necessarily as good news, for he knew the fog, this different brand of white that now enshrouded them, was no friend and could remain for days thick as milk or could be the harbinger of more snow – heavier, wetter snow – yet to fall. He did not feel compelled to report these things to the others.

Dwight spent the morning playing with the children, keeping one eye on the weather, the other on his patient who was surprisingly stable, but deathly weak and perilously close to slipping out of reach at any moment. Mrs. Ramsey stabilized too. Peaks of terror and valleys of hope flattened to a dreaded sea of waiting. In some ways, drifting in these doldrums was more exhausting, life and hope slowly draining from the core of one's being, time the enemy against which there is no defense. Where she had gratefully and graciously received all gestures of encouragement, she was now dull and unresponsive. Gradually the others ceased giving them.

While the children had whined in the night, they now seemed content in the day, so long as they were not hungry for food or attention. Rochelle tended to the food. Dwight tended to the attention. The adults who had whined in the night (silently) were likewise pacified in the light of foggy day by food and attention shared sparingly with one another. A malaise blanketed them all. When they did feel, they felt that they could not go on another day, sometimes another hour, without something bursting within them and gushing out. Slight attentions to one another kept them just above that threshold.

Richard felt the oppression more than the rest, having been a person of action in both career and family, and he felt the circumstances strangely. It was his nature to take charge and force a change, but against weather and fate, he could do nothing. The resulting paralysis prevented him from lifting a finger, not even to do the little that he could have done. His discomfort and fear of death was compounded by a sense of dereliction. As he counted his failures and coddled them closely, as his and the others' hope diminished, his frustration grew and swelled in an involuntary regurgitation of emotions, upward, outward. He grabbed his cell phone, which had failed as miserably as he had, and stared at its useless face, its science as impotent as his, imprisoned likewise by the forces of nature. He shattered the silence and the shackles of professionalism as he flung the pitiful technology against the cold, real stones and stared at the instrument where it came to rest on the floor, its disemboweled circuits broken, its silicone entrails scattered in the dust.

"Oh, my!" whispered Mrs. Ramsey softly, holding a hand to her lips as if to stop that which had already escaped. She hung her head and pretended to disappear.

Rochelle started to scold but checked herself. Wishing instead to nurture and comfort as a mother would a wounded child, she clumsily tried to hold him, but she was unpracticed, there having been no need of it before. So she sat quietly beside him and worked her hands and stared at them as if something would appear in them for all their frantic activity. Awkward moments passed, and the children returned to playing.

"If we ever get out of here, I'm going to make all this up to you and the kids," he said at last with eyes fixed on something distant as if he were seeing the future itself. "If I ever get out of here, I'm going to spend less time making a living, and more time making a life."

"If I ever get out of here, I'm not coming back. We'll stick to campgrounds from now on," Rochelle said, feeling that her comment was somehow parallel to his.

"If we get out of here, I *am* coming back. This is not going to beat me. I'm going to learn what it takes to surpass it. We need more time out, not less. We need to go farther out, not closer in."

"When I get out of here, I'm going to have a big cheeseburger!" Adam exclaimed, sending a chuckle about the shelter, relieving the tension that was near the breaking point. Only Dwight noticed that he had said 'when' and not 'if'. When we get out of here, Dwight thought to himself, I will change nothing. A warm shower, meal, bed and then I'm picking right up where I left off.

"If we get out of here, I want to sell the shop," Rochelle interjected.

"What?" Richard exclaimed, the idea of a smile waited at the corners of his mouth.

"Yes, sell the shop. It takes up too much time. I'll need that time for you and the kids…and more time out here. How important can antique fabrics be?"

Richard's smile erupted. He had always wanted her to be a kept woman, but she had felt the need to have something she could control.

"Your customers are going to miss you."

"Well, maybe I could just scale it back a bit," she said as she thought of the satisfaction she felt when a happy client invited her to see the finished work or showed her a picture of it. No, she wouldn't sell it, but she would definitely scale it back.

"When I get out of here I'm going to buy a new cell phone," Richard said. This drew a chuckle again from the others.

"What is that?" Ashley asked Dwight.

"It's a mirror, silly!" Adam said superiorly.

"What's the hole for?" she asked, ignoring Adam and tugging on Dwight's jacket.

"It's a signal mirror, Ashley," Dwight said, holding it up to his eye.

"How does it work?"

"You use it to signal someone far away. You look through the hole to aim it." Dwight demonstrated.

"Can I try it?"

"No silly, you'll break it. Let me try it," Adam intercepted the mirror as Dwight was handing it to Ashley.

"You can both try it."

"Will it work better than Daddy's cell phone?"

A restrained laugh squeaked out through Dwight's pinched lips.

"Only when we can see someone."

The children took turns looking through the hole, pretending to summon make-believe rescuers. Dwight stood up to check the weather. He pulled Howard's tarp aside from the door and reeled at the brightness of the sun's early afternoon rays shooting through unmolested by snow or fog. Knowing he may have but one chance, he rushed back to the children.

"May I have the mirror back, please," he said holding out his hand.

"I haven't had my turn yet," protested Ashley.

"Later. I need it now, please!" He half-grabbed it as she half-handed it to him. He bounded through the door into the waist deep snow and made his way up the hill toward its nearly bald crest, high stepping with his feet and swimming with his hands against the drifts that held him back, stopping only when he had made it to the place where the trees were thinnest. There a great boulder protruded from the glistening snow, and he crawled up on it. He brushed the snow from his clothes, and looked in all directions like a radar scanner, straining his eyes and ears. The sun felt good on his face and body as it broke through the fog and the hoar-frosted trees. There's not much time he thought. His vigil was not in vain, for less than twenty minutes passed before he heard the droning beat from the east. He turned around and stood. The sound pulsed louder, echoing from the white slopes toward Rocky Top and Thunderhead. He aimed the signal mirror toward the sound. No good! The light is all wrong. He lay down on the stone, his feet toward the approaching throbbing, his head toward the sun. He aimed the mirror toward the zenith and rocked it from his feet to his head. Yes! That will work! The helicopter appeared, swirling the snow as it went. It's going too fast! he thought in despair, but he signaled steadily. The chopper slowed slightly, and out of its belly, two green duffels fell amidst the artificial snowstorm raging beneath it. The helicopter raced away and disappeared over the trees.

They did not see my mirror! We don't need supplies. We need help for Howard and for Kim's friend! He hung his head and felt the cold again. Then he raised his head.

The beating of the chopper grew loud again, circling to the northwest, appearing over the trees and hovering. They have seen my signal! Dwight signaled again, this time his SOS followed by the signal for medical emergency. The light was good. He signaled three times and the pilot flashed his lights and inched the chopper forward until it was clear of any trees, setting it down in a blizzard of its own making. Dwight ran toward it and met two men at the rotor's edge. He did not wait for them to speak.

"Elderly male, angina, possible MI," he yelled pointing toward the shelter now visible as the snow settled. The bearded, orange-clad rescuer signaled to Dwight with his hand and crouched back to the chopper. Moments later, he and another emerged dragging a litter and large tackle box.

Once away from the din of the engine, they could hear each other without yelling.

"We're not medics, but there's fog all over the area. We might not have time to get another chopper in here before it closes in. We can just get him out," the bearded one said loudly.

"I'm an EMT," Dwight said, "But I've got no supplies."

"Great! You'll go with us," said the other.

"There's another emergency. There's a girl on Thunderhead with a broken leg. Her friend was pretty bad off. She and my partner went back for her. She's been on the mountain three nights already."

"We're not equipped for that. We were just doing supply drops. We'll have to insert a team on Thunderhead. Let's get this man out now."

When the men in orange jump suits emerged through the door, grins went from ear to ear as the stranded ones stepped forward to welcome them. The rescuers made their way to Howard and greeted Mrs. Ramsey with a reassuring nod as they transferred him to the litter.

"Folks, listen. We can only take three. This man and his wife, and the EMT have to go. We've dropped supplies outside. We have to make more supply drops before we can come back for you. We'll get you before dark or in the morning if the weather holds. And the weather probably won't hold."

Four Bobo smiles turned to frowns, then flat lines. The end was in sight if not immediate. One more night was doable with supplies. Richard gathered his family under his arms and bade Dwight and Kathleen goodbye and good luck.

THE HELICOPTER LIFTED off before the door was even closed, and once clear of the trees, it sped forward and downward as if falling off the mountain. Dwight tended to Howard with what equipment he now had. That amounted to a stethoscope and blood pressure cuff. But there was nitro and epi in the box, though he lacked lidocaine. Never mind. Howard's pulse was weak but steady. His blood pressure was low and immeasurable over the noise of the aircraft. He started an IV. Nothing else needed doing except holding Kathleen's hand, for they were but minutes from UT Medical where doctors and nurses shivered as they waited on the helipad for the approaching dot in the misty sky. They landed, and Howard was transferred to the gurney and whisked indoors. Dwight followed. He felt a shudder as the warmth behind the double doors hit him. A nurse approached him, and Dwight recounted Howard's history. Dwight stood and watched his bald and ashen head disappear through the double swinging doors, his hands limp at his sides. Howard was his no more.

"Come on, Dwight! We have a rescue crew in the air now! They need to know where the girl is," the bearded rescuer urged and immediately thrust a topo map in his face. Dwight looked at it helplessly.

"Listen, I haven't been where this girl is. I just know where her friend *said* she is. She's on the other side of Thunderhead from Spence Field."

"You're the best compass we got, buddy," the bearded man's face changed from kind to dead serious. He folded the map to where only the vicinity of Thunderhead was showing. "Where do you think she is?"

Dwight studied the map. There is Spence. That line is the AT. There's the peak of Thunderhead. His palms were sweating.

"She must be right along in here, right along the AT," Dwight said pointing to the eastern slope where the trail cuts left and right in folded switchbacks.

The bearded one relayed the location by phone.

"He wants more details from you," he said, handing the phone to Dwight.

"This is Captain Cunningham," a gruff voice said. "We're going to try to insert four men on top of Thunderhead if we can get a break in the fog. They'll hike down to her tonight. They'll radio for a pickup from the top of Thunderhead when they have extricated her. That will be in the morning. Now how many are we expecting?"

"In the morning? That will be four nights that girl's been out there. We have to get her tonight. When do we leave?"

"We will get her out tonight if we can. And it's not we. You've done your part."

"There's nothing wrong with me a hot shower won't fix later."

"We can't let you go. It's policy."

Dwight told the man what he knew, three victims, male and two females, two may or may not have reached the third, broken leg, out three nights already, another girl and a guy, further east, don't know location. They promised to keep him posted.

When Dwight hung up, he felt drained, used up, overswept by a depression that made him want to cry, but he didn't. He just wanted to be up there, to find Roy. He felt loneliness swarming up within him. He sank onto the molded yellow plastic bench. A nurse approached him. He perked up, hoping she brought word of Howard's condition. She didn't know about Howard, but she had a clipboard and forms and questions, not about Howard at all, but about Dwight, all required for admission to the ER. He was now the patient. The bearded one had sent her. Routine she said. No choice. It took two hours to prove that he was all right. After that, they showed him a shower and a bed. Something for the interns, they said. He called his parents, then Roy's. The latter conversation wasn't easy. Somehow, they made it seem his fault. A tray of food appeared. As he ate, a sleepiness he could not resist overtook him, and he lay on the bed and closed his eyes. He surrendered.

27
Thunderhead

The light of day increased over their half-buried tent, and staying awake became easier. Freezing was now their constant peril, and Roy had commanded that they stay as wakeful as possible. There was little need of conversation. Daytime brought warmer temperatures, and Roy managed to keep his digits thawed, but there was a constant searing pain in his once-frozen feet as if they were submerged in hot coals. The skin on his toes was blistered raw and red. There was little hope now of his hiking out. Kim's feet were fairing much better than Roy's, though alternating numbness and pain kept her more aware of them than she wished. She wandered in and out of drunkenness, and fought off fits of shivering that shook her violently. Roy knew that she was hypothermic and did all that he could to hold her and Michelle close to his torso. Roy's hands and feet were useless. He could no longer use his hands to start the stove, to melt snow to drink or hot water for the bottles to warm them.

Thus, they passed the day, their minds wandering through the annals of their lives down below with alternating amusement and sentimentality, periodically returning to the sober present to renew hope and fend off despair. They were now beyond reckoning with death. They waited passively for something to happen, be it rescue or their last sleep. Kim could no longer think of Michelle; she was too far away to have relevance in her shrinking mind. Amber was but a memory. Roy thought of them both, and thought how cruel it would be for Kim to lose both of her friends in the same stroke of the scythe. He could not even speculate about Amber's state, but Michelle's he knew too well. She lived, but did not move except for shallow respiration. He was weak now, too weak to feel her pulse, though he knew that it still beat in her veins. He also knew too well that he might never come to know her as she was. She had sunk so low for so long, her brain having been deprived of its fair share of lifeblood. He had long since given up on her leg – it was her life at stake, and her mind, he feared.

They waited for something to occur, but were unaware when it did. The tent that separated them from the snow and wind and fog, also separated them from perception of the sun breaking through the fog and warming the air above them. The sun would make things worse before they improved, for its warmth melted more snow, wetting the trio further, chilling their bodies, dimming their minds. They did not sleep, nor were they awake, when voices calling reached their ears. Minutes passed before the sounds were perceived, and sluggish brains could dissect their meaning. Roy responded first. He told his body to sit up, but the message traveled only to the root of his neck, lifting his head momentarily before its weight brought it back down to rest. He opened his mouth to yell; only a whisper sounded in a voice he did not recognize as his own. He heard men's shouts again. This time his arm obeyed as he flung it clumsily against the ceiling. Time between shouts did not exist to him, distance meant nothing as the voices echoed in his ears. Each minute was an eternity, but all events were strangely compressed in time. Nothing seemed real until he heard the scratching of shovels about the tent. Dwight had come, he thought, and he said his name, but the sounds did not come out. A knife pierced the nylon ceiling and white light poured in, blinding him. His eyes began to adjust and a face took shape. It spoke.

"Y'all all right in there?" it boomed. "I got all three here. At least one's alive."

There was a flurry of activity about them. The snow was scratched away, and a knife split the tent from stem to stern, laying it open like a pea pod, revealing its three inhabitants.

Roy saw the man to whom the face belonged peering at them and barking out orders. He was a large man and loud, jumpsuited orange, which clashed with his red face. He spoke to Roy through a brushy Stalin mustache. He felt his clothes being removed. From the corner of his eye, he saw the same happening to Kim and closed them.

Another man was talking into a radio.

"We've got three Caucasians, early twenties, one male, two females, all severely hypothermic. One female comatose, tibia fracture right. Other two conscious, not lucid…"

The man with the radio continued passing on the information passed to him, and it all ran together, except for one phrase isolated to his ears, "…frostbite below the fracture." Roy's soul sank, and he glanced toward Kim, now wrapped papoose-like in blankets. She had not heard, he thought.

He felt himself being wrapped snugly in warm blankets. Warm packs were added. It felt good as his shivering calmed. How strange, he thought when he saw the bottle raised above Michelle's head, how strange to start an IV out here where it would freeze. Hot Sack. That was it. Someone placed a mask over his face and warmth flooded into him through his mouth and nose from a strange little box lettered Res-Q-Air. Soon he could feel his edge returning, his mind sharpening, honing in on what was happening to them.

Stalin was speaking with Kim, her voice but a raspy whisper, his voice booming resonantly in the trees. She was speaking of Amber. He nodded and said something to the man with the radio, who spoke again into it.

"Story confirmed. Another female and male, off trail near Lower Buckeye Gap. Separated before storm…"

The trees began to move above Roy's head, and he felt himself being lifted onto a litter. Soon they were sliding bumpily along the trail. He twisted his head, cocking it to the right, and he could see two men carrying the litter with the IV bag swinging above it, pulling away with relatively greater speed. Kim bumped along in front yoked to Stalin, and someone's broad orange shoulders swung back and forth in front of him like a metronome, hypnotic. His legs felt crampy. He tried to move them, but they were strapped down and held apart by the equipment piled between them. The warm packs combined with the metronome shoulders and dizzying tree above relaxed him. Relieved of responsibility, he slept despite the bumping. He woke when the motion stopped, and there were no trees over his head. He must be at the LZ. He had no perception of the time that had passed. Was it short or long? He could not tell. He would soon hear the drumming of rotors, and he calmly listened for them. They were still beating the air in the distance when Roy perceived a fading out of the orange evening light. Fog closed in around them. He felt its dampness on his face. His body felt warm now, though weak and limp. He heard talk of a bivouac until morning. Kim was sitting up, fighting with a medic who was commanding her to lie back on the litter. Roy could tell by the medic's worried face that he was losing ground. He was no match for Kim. She was going to be all right. Kim was now sitting on her litter, leaning halfway onto Michelle's, holding her hand beneath the blankets. She could will this fog away, Roy thought, as he closed his eyes and sighed. He heard beating again and thought it was his heart, which now raced each time he tried to hold this girl in his mind. But the beating grew louder and filled the air about them. The chopper descended through a break in the fog, rocking tentatively on the uneven rocks on the treeless ridge below them toward Rocky Top. He felt himself being lifted once more, and he knew the ordeal was over, for him at least. Kim, Michelle and Amber were possibly just beginning theirs. The helicopter whisked them off the mountain, above the fog and into the orange face of the setting sun.

Wednesday

28
Russell Field

The morning greeted Carrie with the smell of coffee. That and a pleasant orange glow warming through the snow tunnel and open gate filled Carrie with feelings reminiscent of her hours spent communing with the crackling fire. She pulled herself from her sack, and sat upright, pushing back her tangled mass of hair with two hands. The air was bracingly cold and exhilarating as it nipped at her skin beneath her Duofold top. It was the first night she had felt warm enough in her bag without wearing every stitch of clothing she had. When she was awake enough to remember Bob's presence, she covered herself with folded arms and looked about, discovering the shelter was empty. She reached for her pants and parka and made quick work of dressing while she looked about for the source of the sublime scent of coffee. She found a steaming billie on the hearth next to the unlit stove. She climbed off the sleeping platform into her boots, found her cup and filled it with steaming coffee. Beside the billie, there was a Harvest Bar, which she assumed was hers. As she ate and sipped, she heard voices outside, and then saw Bob's form lumbering through the snow tunnel.

"I was just coming to wake you, but I see you're up. We let you sleep because, well, Brian left it up to me, and I just didn't have the heart to wake you."

"Thanks. Where is Brian?"

"He's clearing some branches from the landing zone. As soon as you are through here, you'd better pack your things up. The helicopter will be in the air in fifteen minutes."

Bob packed his stove and billies, thrust it into his pack and returned to help Brian. Carrie noticed that Brian's pack was fully loaded and by the door, another sign that he could not wait to have this over with. She sipped the last of the warming coffee and sat on her log, scanning the scant dark shelter with misty eyes, sad after all these bittersweet days to part with the place of her awakening.

She did what she must and packed her pack, dragged it and leaned it beside Brian's. She felt a sudden urge to add something to the smattering of carved or chalked graffiti. A strange desire, she thought, unaware that it was born of a need to make something permanent out of such a transitory experience. Now that it was almost over, it seemed but yesterday that they were wandering through blinding snow and sleet, seeking this very place to save their imperiled lives. And it did. And now it was up to her to make a life worth saving. She had changed so much already. The shelter would go on unchanged when she left it, through thawing and spring, summer, fall and winter, over and over as it had done for decades, and will do until some fool with a little money and authority decides to improve it for a generation of pansy hikers, destroying it and what it stands for in the process. No one could design a place so beautiful in its simplicity, so harmonious with its surroundings, she thought.

Carrie went outside, climbing through the snow tunnel toward the orange glow at its end. Her eyes squinted and her brow ached, unaccustomed to so much light. Her vision cleared to behold a wonder world of snow and ice, frosted trees, and sunlight playing off pillows of lingering fog and sparkling from each frozen surface as though it were studded with jewels. She turned her back to see her shelter from without and laughed. It was scarcely there, just a few courses of stone and the outline of a gabled roof in the drifted snow that covered it, spilling downward at its eaves to join the drifts that hugged its walls. Her chimney was there above everything. She said goodbye aloud and turned to follow the broken path of snow. No sooner had she started than she was bogged down, mired to the hips, and her movements became more like those of a swimmer, struggling to make any forward progress at all.

Brian met her and laughed. She smiled an insincere smile, and returned to the shelter-cave with his assistance. Bob was just behind and all three entered the shelter and sat down.

"We're waiting in here until we have word the chopper is in the air. Apparently there was more fog down below," Bob explained.

"Have you heard about any others on the trail?" Carrie asked.

"I was supposed to hike on up to Spence Field, but they already got a chopper in there last night. There was a medical emergency. The rest are being picked up after you. Apparently there is a big rescue underway for some hikers who weren't in shelters around Thunderhead."

"Do you know anything about our thru-hikers?"

"I didn't get a lot of details. They were asking us to stay off the air unless necessary. Besides these batteries don't last forever in this kind of cold."

Carrie thought of Roy and Dwight, and hoped they were safe. She wondered if this was enough to turn them aside from their thru-hike. Pangs of uneasiness gripped her, not anxiety for their well-being, but for her own. She envied them their freedom and their passion, while she returned to a life she had not yet created, a life others were very eager to create for her with boundaries designed to exterminate her passions before they budded. It should be a time of such joy, she thought, of opportunity, but she felt as though a sentence had been passed, and the time had come for her incarceration.

Ah, the negativity. I must stop it, Carrie scolded herself. Brian is a wonderful man, and with time, he will come to understand…I will come to understand, and I will have the opportunities to know myself and my world, to experience what there is in it for me, and to leave it better when my short time in it is through. But we have to make a living and a home, and I want a family all in good time. There is nothing wrong with these. So chin up. There's a bathtub down there somewhere and a steak dinner just for me. Thus, she talked herself into joy – joy that the time had come to go home, and that her life would be her design, and Brian would be both the benefactor and the beneficiary of it. She felt the warm and tingling feelings for him again, and all was well.

"So how long have you two been married?" she heard Bob ask.

"Ten days I think," she heard Brian answer. "Ten days if I can still count. What day is it today?" An embarrassed grin twitched, his lips pursed, dimples showing and eyes flashing downward.

"Wednesday," Bob answered.

Brian counted on his gloved fingers.

"Eleven. It's eleven today at three," Brian said. "Eleven days of wedded bliss."

Carrie looked up and searched his face for the sarcasm she knew would be there, but she didn't find any. Could it be that he was sincere?

Was he glossing it over already? Was his tendency to remember only the good (for there was plenty of that early on) and to forget the bad, or to forget the parts he could not understand? Was confusion an amnesiac for him? Truly, they did not know each other yet.

"This has been quite a honeymoon," Bob chuckled.

"It's not exactly what we had planned, but I couldn't have been stuck here with a better woman."

Carrie blushed inside to have expected a condemnation where compliments were instead. She felt ashamed now.

"Most women would have complained and accused and wimped out on me," he continued, "But Carrie here is a real trooper." He smiled at her, and she smiled, blushed again and found her feet with her eyes.

"She's the prettiest thing in the firelight, too," Brian said, and cast a seductive eye her way.

She began to feel wet.

"And we saw plenty of the fire," Brian went on. "But that girl is tough. Most women would have been crying for their daddies. Not Carrie. Sure, there were times she got down, and I had to keep her spirits up. But she bounced back. One time I thought she was going crazy on me when she said she liked it out here in the snow and all."

Carrie tensed.

"Started talking out of her head about dreams and stuff. Delusions about becoming a great artist or something. She had me going scared on that one. But she came around. I guess a little stir crazy is normal, right Bob?"

Bob looked at Carrie. She looked up and met his eyes. He saw the surprise and hurt in hers, and suddenly he knew the whole story. He had seen her wit and tenacious spirit last evening. He gave a sympathetic nod and looked back at Brian as he continued.

"What with hormones and everything, women just aren't suited for this kind of…"

The radio crackled and popped and the announcement came that the chopper was in the air. Bob jumped up. Brian started to finish his sentence, but Bob cut him off.

"She's a fine woman. Let's get her and you on a chopper headed home."

Carrie felt embarrassed and betrayed. But mostly she felt foolish. How easily he had seduced her with words. Empty words from the sound of it. No, he was sincere. He spoke heartfelt words, but they were more suitable for a good horse or dog. They wouldn't do for her.

Bob shouldered Carrie's pack, and strapped his own to it. He left the shelter first. Carrie pulled on Brian's sleeve.

"Hormones?"

"Yeah, my father warned me about times like that. I'm glad he did so I could recognize what was going on before we really got into it bad. So after I figured that out, I just quit taking everything you were saying so seriously."

Brian had such an air of confidence and pride that for a moment Carrie almost took his point of view. Maybe she was a little stir-crazy or hormonal or something. However, a voice within said, "No!" and she gave leave to her anger, but the anger would not flare, for, as she stared into his arrogant and ignorant face with all its blunted perception, something would not work right with her feelings. They were an incongruous mix of anger, guilt, pity and loneliness. She felt like someone whose house just burned down, but she couldn't grieve because she just discovered that all she lost was things. Nothing in her mind would come together, so she let it go, and passed through the white tunnel walls into the open sun. Brian shrugged and followed. They slogged their way to the clearing above the shelter, Bob turning to lend a hand where the snow was deepest, Brian pushing a little from behind. Below them, the sound of beating blades approached, and their honeymoon was over.

Thus, their lives were saved, and, though Carrie did not know it yet and Brian would never understand why, he lost his wife on that mountain, for she had gone to a place that he could not.

29
UT Medical

They came and went throughout the night, but Kim was not aware of it. They noisily checked and charted, changed IVs and flipped the lights on and off, but they did not wake her. She was sound asleep; her sleep, however, was not the sleep of peace. Her mind and body tossed endlessly with unseen struggles until the morning came. Even before she opened her crusty swollen eyelids, she saw the color blue, and it returned her to the terror of the frozen tent half-buried in snow and tucked secretly under the shoulder of Thunderhead. She listened but heard no breathing but her own, and a tremor spread throughout her battered body at the thought that her rescue was but a dream, and she was the last one still alive. With much effort, she opened her eyes but still saw nothing but bluish blur. She tried to raise an arm to rub her eyes, but the arm would not obey the command to move. She furiously blinked her eyes, and only after what seemed an hour her vision began to slowly clear. At last, she could see that the colored light was that of the morning sun filtering through the Wedgwood curtains, and her arms were not frozen but tethered to boards for the security of the IVs that were in them. Only then did she know for sure that her vague memories of rescue from the mountain and treatment in the hospital were not merely a dream of comfort and deception while she became the third to freeze and die.

When an old and kindly nurse came, Kim pleaded to have the curtains opened so she could see the world. The nurse complied, and the sunlight filled the room with indistinguishable brightness, painful but welcome as she began the celebration of life.

Once Kim's eyes had adjusted, she could strain her neck to the side and catch a glimpse of the mountains. She could see their tops were white and hoary, and they looked soft, friendly and harmless in the slanted rays of dawn, which outlined each earthly fold in varying shades of orange or purple. There was one peak rising above the rest, still shrouded with a ring of fog about its middle. This she took to be Thunderhead. It could have been any of them, Cove or Rich, Clingman's or LeConte but she believed it was *her* mountain, the one that nearly killed her and her friends. Perhaps it had killed them, she thought with painful suddenness. Panic gripped her as she floundered in her mind, searching for a clue. Had she seen? Had someone told her? Her memory was blank. She searched frantically for the call button.

The elderly nurse entered, a sincere but perpetual smile etched in the granite of her Maybelline face. She at once detected Kim's distress and quickened her pace, moving more swiftly than one would have imagined, to arrive at Kim's side a moment sooner.

"What is it, dear?" she asked, leaning over the bed rail to draw closer, for Kim's voice was still but a hoarse whisper.

"My friends, what have you heard about them?"

"The young man, is he your boyfriend?" she asked, then continued before Kim could process the question. "The young man is going to be all right, dear. You aren't going to lose any of him. He's in a room down the hall, and you can go see him after awhile if you feel like getting out of bed. The doctor said you could move around a bit if you felt like it. Wheel chair, of course."

"What about Michelle Christensen?"

"I heard there was a girl with you. She's not on this floor though. I think they had to do some surgery or something, but I will find out for you."

"And Amber Johnson?"

"I don't know anything about Amber," she looked puzzled. "But I'll find out."

She rose and started to leave.

"Your breakfast is on the way. I hope you feel like eating something."

"Nurse?" Kim said, and then hesitated while she looked at the huge bulky bandages on her feet. She tried to move her toes, but she could not feel them move in their bindings.

"Yes, hun'?"

"My feet?"

"They're going to be OK the doctor thinks. Just some minor frostbite. You've still got five and five." She held up her hands with fingers outspread. "You're lucky, you know, Miss Lee."

"I know," Kim replied, looking away toward the window again, toward the mountains, the snow and Thunderhead. Was Amber still up there? Was she all right? She burned to know.

"I know," she repeated, but the nurse was gone.

* * * * *

Howard stabilized by midnight, and slept restfully through the night, waking midmorning to a sunny room. Somehow, Kathleen had coerced a young doctor into releasing him from intensive care by warning the timid physician of the moods she expected him to wake in, his presence being detrimental to the other patients. And, true to her predictions, he came alive, glad to have survived and feeling better, and expressing it in a feisty fit of minced expletives and commands barked at the nurses, present or not. They knew his type, and respectfully barked back, and set up a good-natured sparring, which livened up their otherwise mundane shifts.

"Kathleen!" he snapped, "Kathleen, you wonderful wife! I want to see that young man …you know…the colored one."

"Why, whatever for?"

"Never mind what for. I want to see him. If I didn't have all these tubes and wires going in and out of me, beep-beeping, I'd get him myself!"

Kathleen rose from the chair in the corner, laid aside the mustard colored hospital blanket she had wrapped herself in and strutted through the door. She came back without a word and settled again into the corner chair.

"Well?" he asked impatiently.

"Well, the nurse is going to find him, but it might take awhile. Just settle down, old man," Kathleen said, ending her sentence with a sharp downward nod of her chin, which Howard knew as an exclamation point, signifying that no further response on his part would be appropriate. Howard gave his assent with silence, and watched the blip on the screen as it bounced up and down, etching the peaks and valleys of his EKG.

That was an early battle won with the nurses, the right, that is, to have the monitor moved where he could watch it.

Kathleen was dozing, and Howard finally closed his eyes, still seeing in afterimage the jerky waveforms of the cardiogram on his eyelids, when there came a faint double-rap at the door. It opened before anyone could respond, and Julie, the prettiest but most sharp-tongued of the nurses entered. Her round, plumpish face was circled by thick straight brunette hair, which hung to her shoulders and bounced when she walked. Her skin was white and wintry, with thick red lips and rosy high-boned cheeks, and from between them and her heavy brow, her small impish eyes squinted seductively from deep-set sockets. She did not look at all forty years old, which she was, but she would not admit her age for all of Howard's persistent prying. She carried a tray with two hypodermics, which she proceeded to inject into his IV line without a word. She cast him a superior smile when she saw, out of the corner of her eye, that he was watching her face, waiting to gain the advantage of her speaking first. She withheld, and he gave in.

"Is that some sort of serum to make me more agreeable?" he quipped.

"Yes," Julie said, straight-faced and cocky.

"Well," Howard said, delighting himself in a successful setup, "Didn't you save any for yourself?"

"I'd pinch you good for that one, young man, but it might make your heart jump."

They sparred on until another knock on the door sounded, this one bolder, but the rapper waited for an invitation before entering, which Kathleen gave. The door opened, and Dwight entered, walking softly until he could see that Howard was alert and upright.

"Nurse!" Howard boomed in a voice not at all commensurate with his status as an ailing man.

She looked up, and Howard continued.

"This is one of the best men I have ever known! I wanted you to meet him."

"Howard!" Kathleen responded with surprise. "That's changing your tune."

"Hec! Even the most gnarled old twisted Tupelo tree can have a shoot of new growth occasionally," he said with an exaggerated and prolonged wink that began with Dwight, passed across Julie and ended on Kathleen.

"Well, I'll say that the new growth is always the comeliest," she declared.

"Dwight," Howard said, lowering his voice and sounding a bit sicker for the protection a little pity might afford him. His forehead wrinkled and he buried his chin into his gray-haired chest so that when he looked up, his eyes were almost hidden beneath his overgrown bushy brows. He somehow looked quite childlike for all his age-spotted leatheriness.

"I'm not real good at apologies, but you, young man deserve one if it's the last thing I do. I can't say much for many of the colored men I've known, but judging from the likes of you, I was wrong to ever lump them all together. You not only saved my life, but you opened my eyes. I swear to you and to God and the rest of 'em, I will never judge another man for what he looks like on the outside. You got character, you, and that's what I should go by. I don't have money to reward you with, but you will always be welcome at my house and at my table, and I want you there when I get out of here." He looked up, then continued, "Son…I need to know that you forgive an old man for his blindness and stupidity!"

Dwight shuffled his feet and clasped his hands in front of him. His look of surprise was frozen on his face. He searched for more eloquent words, but those he found were simple and noble.

"I forgive you, Mr. Ramsey." He thought of Martin Luther King's mountaintop speech, which he had memorized early in life. Here was a white man, Southern and from the old school, practically quoting it to him, at least its essence, and all he could do was restlessly shuffle his feet. Howard relieved the tension.

"You don't know how glad it makes my heart to hear these words, son. I wouldn't blame you if you hated me. But you are good through and through, I believe, and you helped me when I didn't have much regard for you. You heaped coals of fire on my head, boy, and then you put them out when you said you'd forgive me. Thank you, son."

The effort took a toll on the old man. He quieted down from fatigue and relief. The monitor beeped more slowly.

"One more thing I have to ask of you, Dwight."

"What is that, Mr. Ramsey?"

"Look at my chart and make sure this so-called nurse is doing right by me?"

"I'm sure she's quite qualified."

Julie grabbed the chart and thrust it toward Dwight.

"Thanks, Dwight, but you might as well do as he says. How many days did you spend with him in that shelter? It only took me half an early shift to figure out it was easier just to humor him."

"Right, nurse," he said with a chuckle, and took the chart and began flipping through it. "She's right on top of things, Mr. Ramsey. It looks like you are going to be OK. I'm glad of that."

"OK? They're going to split me stem to stern and rearrange my innerds. You call that OK?"

"Howard, they've needed rearranging for awhile. I'm just glad this has made up your mind for you to do it," Kathleen inserted.

Dwight leaned over and whispered in his ear loud enough for all to hear, "Mr. Ramsey, I think you're tough enough to take anything."

That satisfied him, and he closed his eyes to rest, a contented smile turning the corners of his mouth beneath the oxygen tube, which crossed his face under his bulbous nose and circled his oversized ears.

Julie ushered Dwight toward the door. Kathleen followed, stopping him in the hall. She spoke awhile, and then hugged his neck. He hugged her back, and turned to go. She watched him leave, and waved weakly as he disappeared at a turn in the hallway.

Dwight shuffled down the hallway toward Roy's room, fighting struggles welling up deep in his mind, uncertain of how he should feel, confused about how he did feel about Mr. Ramsey's confession. He did not understand why he held the man in such regard with concern for his welfare, but he did. Why should such a man be absolved so easily from a life of bigotry just because he had a few sentimental thoughts while laid low on a hospital bed facing the uncertainty of open-heart surgery? Dwight felt a surge of anger and nearly turned about-face to confront Mr. Howard Ramsey head-on. But the thought scared him: it was obviously wrong, and suddenly Dwight understood. His anger was not for Mr. Ramsey, or at least not for him alone, but for all the bucolics and urbanites alike who had snubbed him for his color since his earliest recollections as a four-year-old in Maryland. And not only those who had added to his personal experiences directly (they were numerous), but to all those he heard about, or read about, those who came before him, tormenting his ancestors. Howard had collective guilt, and Dwight had at last felt the collective rage of his people.

He stopped at the water fountain, taking a drink, and dashing a little of the icy water on his face. He was born after the days of segregated fountains, but he felt as though he could remember. Anger and rage were foreign emotions to Dwight, and they struck fear in him. He leaned against the cold sterile glossy tile walls feeling his own guilt for having had these thoughts. They were normal, but they were not him. He could never hold the enmity long enough for it to ferment into bitterness. He knew so many who had, and he saw what it did to them, holding them back, holding them down, providing a ready excuse for every failure, removing responsibility, spoiling them, souring their souls, germinating a murderous hatred, and killing them in the end. No, Dwight was not a bitter, angry man. Howard Ramsey was sincerely sorry, even if he lacked understanding of the extent of the pain he was capable of inflicting and had inflicted in another human being. No, Dwight was equally sincere in forgiving him, and he would not take it back even for a flood of knowledge or memories of injustices committed.

Dwight took in a deep breath and let it out in a long unvoiced sigh exhaled through clenched teeth and pursed lips. The battle was over, and he felt himself again. Dwight turned and continued toward Roy's room.

He rapped twice and entered. Roy was on the bed, alert and smiling.

"Morning, Chief," he said to Dwight. "Sit down, my friend."

Dwight sat down and looked him over, head to foot and back again. "Well, you don't look too much worse for wear."

Roy leaned forward and lifted the sheet from his feet. They were bound thickly in gauze and tape.

"How do you like my new hiking boots, *compadre*?"

"They look fine, Roy, but white ones? Why would you choose white ones?"

Roy took on a serious expression. "The doc says they'll be fine. They are kind of blistered as if I stuck them in boiling water or something, and they burn like hell. But he says it is all superficial, and they'll be good as new in a couple of weeks. Except one spot on the tip of my second toe. It was a little purple or black looking. He says we've got to watch that. If it grows, I lose my toe. If it sloughs and heals, well, good as new. It's just a little spot, so I'm optimistic we'll be back on the trail in a month."

"What did doc say about that?"

"He just looked at me and laughed. He doesn't know how quickly I heal though, does he?"

"I guess he just didn't know who he was dealing with."

A knock at the door sounded, with a strange bumping and clanging.

"Come in," Roy responded.

"What the…?" Dwight muttered as he rose to open the door.

"Good Lord!" Roy heard Dwight say, but he could not see what was there. He expected that another cart-pushing nurse had come to torment him. As he looked, he saw two feet appear, bandaged as his own, preceding their owner as she wheeled herself into the room.

"Kim!" he uttered, surprised and delighted. "How are you?"

"Fine, Roy. I'm just fine," she said, her hoarse voice much improved from when she first awoke. "How about you?"

They traded prognoses, pretty much the same, except Kim's repeated exposures had lead to a little more tissue damage. Her chances of amputation were greater with dying tissue on seven toes. But the doctor was optimistic that loss of digits could be avoided.

"What about Michelle?" Roy asked gravely.

"She's going to be OK," Kim said. "She's in surgery now. They said it was real touch and go, getting through the warming process. She was a lot colder than you and me, of course. They told me that when they start warming people up, many times that's when they die. But she made it through that OK, and she was conscious before they took her to surgery. She was asking for Amber and me. She doesn't know about you yet."

"Surgery?" Roy asked.

"They have to do a lot of work to try to save her leg," Kim answered with incongruous detachment. Then she began to cry. "She's going to be OK, though," she sobbed.

Dwight put an arm around her, and Roy took a hand. Kim regained herself and went on.

"They have to set her leg. The vessels are damaged though. And her foot is badly frostbitten. She's going to lose a foot at least, they said, if she doesn't lose the whole leg."

The three held each other for a time, and then Dwight withdrew and sat down. He was more tired than he realized.

When Kim could speak again, she said, "There's still no word of Amber. They didn't return before the snow, and they haven't been found yet. I gave the rescue guy the place on the trail where they left us, and they have a team up there now. I'm just so scared about her. I had such a bad feeling when they left us. And that was before the snow."

Kim and Roy looked at each other for a moment. There was really nothing to be said that their eyes could not say.

"Well enough about us, what about you guys?" Kim said when the silence became awkward. "When are you heading back to the trail?"

"What makes you think we're going back?" Dwight answered.

"Oh, come on. Get serious. I know you've probably got all your plans figured out by now."

"If the doc does his part, we'll be back to Spence Field in about a month I think," Roy said. "Taking up where we left off."

"Will you still have enough time to finish…before the snows hit up north?" Kim asked.

"A lot of people don't even start in Georgia until May, so we'll be OK if Roy here can keep up." Dwight said, teasing.

"Roy will have no trouble keeping up, you mongrel," he said, grabbing his pillow and feigning throwing it at him.

"I sure would like to hike the trail," Kim said, looking at her lap, then at Roy. "I need to get back on that horse as soon as I can."

"You don't like to be beaten, do you?" Roy said.

"Beaten? What's that?" she said with a great smile, which hurt her face. Suddenly she became conscious of her appearance, a vanity quite foreign to her.

"I hate you have to see me like this," Kim said, looking down and wrapping her blanket tighter about her, pulling its edges toward her face.

"Like what?" Roy asked insensitively, having never seen her except in a state of damage and distress, and having been quite impressed anyway.

"My face," she mumbled. "Dwight, got a mirror?" She had just realized that she had not seen herself since leaving the car a week ago. He did not, but he assisted her in standing to view herself in the mirror over the lavatory. She was not shocked. The face looking back was as bad, but no worse than she had imagined, her hair flat, dirty and stringy, pulled back and tethered behind her neck where it did nothing to hide her swollen, red and peeling face. Her eyes were but slits, and her lips were cracked and bleeding. Dwight helped her back into her chair. She suddenly wanted to return to her room and not face Roy, but that made no sense to her, so she resisted. Instead, she allowed Dwight to return her to Roy's bedside.

"I hate you had to look at this, but I thought you would want to know about Michelle. They said we could see her when she gets to a room," she reported without emotion, severing the warm connection.

Dwight opened the door, and Kim wheeled herself out and down the hall. Once back in her room, she felt suddenly so alone in the world. She thought of Michelle's mother and Greg, whom she knew were downstairs, but she had not seen them yet. Somehow, she could not face them just now, so she called her own mother, who could not make the trip. Hearing a mother's voice comforted her a little, but her need was for the others who were all so near, yet untouchable.

* * * * *

As THE MOUNTAINTOPS cleared, and the morning fog lifted below, every available helicopter was put to flight to evacuate those who remained in shelters along the Appalachian spine in the snow-laden Smokies. The first flight picked up a newlywed couple and their rescuing ranger at Russell Field and moved on down the line to whisk an eager family of four from Spence Field. As soon as a dense blanket of cloud slid off the ridges to the east, two more flights carried ground crews, inserting them at Silers Bald and Derrick Knob, the shelters on either side of Lower Buckeye, to search for a missing couple last seen there, then picking up a church group divided between two shelters. Another was hovering about the draws between Lower Buckeye Gap and Elkmont campground. All crews in fact had been alerted to keep an eye out for any movement, smoke or other sign that there were people stranded at any point over which they flew in route to their assigned pickups. Before the morning was half spent, the occupants of Double Spring were off the mountain and on their way to join the others at UT Medical Center.

As the three helicopters shuttled their survivors in, the victims were herded through the emergency department as a matter of routine, to assess their status as injured or healthy. Those who passed were directed to a room cordoned off with institutional wood grain finished moveable walls where they were given blankets, coffee, hot chocolate and turns at telephones in the hall. There were no strangers among them, human beings, otherwise separated by scores of social barriers, coming together in common experience that disrupted their lives, threatened them and forced them to think of one another as allies. Thus, the groups mingled and compared their stories and looked for ways to help one another, now that the need for help had all but passed.

Glen and his flock waited nervously by the door as they received word that Dave and Tammy would be joining them shortly. There was no word on their condition. Tammy entered the room first and without a limp, Dave following a few yards behind. They were greeted by hugs and praise-Gods. Tears were shed. Tammy looked about for Christie, and, not seeing her, burst into tears of grief, guilt and panic. Lori stepped forward to hold her. When Tammy could speak, she uttered Christie's name with an interrogative inflection.

"She's all right, Tammy," Lori comforted. "She was with us. She was very weak though, so they've got her back there somewhere. We'll see her as soon as they will let us."

At that time, an orderly entered, calling Tammy's name. Tammy responded sheepishly, and followed the orderly through the doors, down the hall and into the ER. He took her to a curtained off area and ushered her in where Christie lay upon a gurney tightly wrapped in white cotton blankets up to her neck. Upon seeing her friend, Christie sat up and smiled a great smile across her pale cheeks, and, disentangling her arms from the covers, reached out for Tammy who plunged into the embrace so fervently that she nearly rolled the gurney into the wall. They hugged and cried until words came, and when they finally did, they were spent in argument about who was at fault, each one blaming herself for the rift that had occurred between them. By reason of extreme fatigue, Christie wore down first and repeatedly declared that she was absolving Tammy of all wrongdoing.

The orderly broke in and insisted that he had orders to transport, and it was only Christie's refusal to comply until she had seen Tammy that this sweet little reunion was allowed to happen in the first place. "So let's get on with it, ladies," he said, as he opened the curtains and rolled Christie toward the elevator. Tammy said goodbye, gathered herself, and retraced her steps, stopping at the facilities to wash her face. Thus, she returned to her people with a measure of restored pride. As Tammy walked into the room, she was met with Dave's inquisitive look. She answered by casting him a smile and a nod of affirmation, and hope grew in both of them that Tammy was beginning a full recovery.

* * * * *

When Dwight, Roy and Kim received word that Michelle was out of recovery, they converged on her room, one walking and two rolling, eager to discover her state of body and mind. They found her there, groggy and nauseous, but reasonably communicative given the circumstances. Her leg was in a cast, smooth and white as newly fallen snow, elevated on piles of pillows. Her other foot was bandaged the same as Roy's and Kim's. There was a strange smile on her face as they approached her.

"Hey kids," she said, and giggled. The words were slurred as if her tongue would slide from her mouth at any moment. Dwight and Roy stopped inside the door. Kim pulled along side her bed and backed her wheelchair until their faces were parallel. She leaned and gave her a kiss.

"Hey, Kiddo," Kim said, and brushed the hair from Michelle's damp face. "How're ya doing?"

"Not so bad, how 'bout yourself?"

"I'm good."

"Hey Kim," Michelle's mother said from the corner chair. They had ignored her. She stood up and gave Kim a hug. "These must be the young men to whom I owe my daughter's life."

She hugged them, and withdrew, repeating, "Thank you! How can I ever repay you? Bless you!"

"Mom," Michelle said weakly. "I want to see Roy."

Roy wheeled himself to the foot of the bed.

"So you are Kim's knight in shining armor? I understand you saved us up there," she said, struggling with rebellious lips and tongue to get out the words. "Thanks. Damn, that's just a word. But what can I say?"

"You don't need to say anything. Seeing you here is enough," Roy said blushingly.

"How are your feet?"

"They'll be fine. Just have to be off them a couple of days."

"Did they tell you about mine?" Michelle asked.

"Yes, but I have a feeling you're going to surprise them."

"Everything is for a purpose, right?" Michelle said. "Like to keep us all here long enough for you two to figure out what love is, eh Kim?"

"What?" Kim exclaimed. Michelle's mother looked knowingly out the window, shaking her head.

Roy looked at Dwight for help. Dwight nodded back toward Michelle.

"I've been hearing about you two. You are a bit dense about this sort of thing, aren't you!" Michelle added.

"You guys are getting the wrong idea here," Roy objected as he turned toward Kim. "Right Kim?" The words stuck in his throat inaudibly as his eyes met hers. She had readied her objections in her mind, too, but as their eyes locked, she forgot them completely. Both blushed hotly.

A nurse came in and ushered them all to the hallway. Michelle's mother followed, and when they were in the hall and, out of earshot, she put an arm on Kim's shoulder, wheeled her a few yards and spoke to her alone.

"You know Michelle's not going to miss a chance to make a match for you. But you'll know when Mr. Right comes along," she smiled a wry smile. Then she became very grave. "Michelle lost all the toes on the broken leg. There was enough muscle and vessel damage that she will never run again, maybe never walk again, at least without a significant limp. There's still hope the leg can be spared if what's left heals well. There will be months of rehab. The other foot just had some skin removed. The bones and muscles were intact. It just needs to heal. One more thing. They were surprised to find that there was no observable hypoxia to the brain, no swelling, but her speech is proof that there was at least some minor brain damage."

They hugged and cried, and Kim joined the others in the hallway while Michelle's mother returned to the room.

The ringing of a telephone carried from Michelle's room into the hall. Mrs. Christensen appeared a moment later.

"They're looking for you, Kim," she said. "They'll call back at the nurses' station."

"Who is it?"

"Didn't say," Mrs. Christensen said.

Kim rolled on down the hall, declining the help that Dwight had offered. Roy, Dwight and Mrs. Christensen watched her answer the phone while trying to look as though they were not watching. They saw the receiver where it slid down into her lap as her hands went limp by her sides. They saw her twist her face with intense pain as if a saber had pierced her heart. She turned red and began to shake. Roy went to her, wheeling awkwardly and weaving. Mrs. Christensen retreated, closing the door behind her.

* * * * *

JACK BAKER PAUSED to catch his breath. Clambering down the steep drop off from Buckeye Gap had not been easy, crouching to keep his center-of-gravity low, lest a careless move send him, his 265 pounds, his pack and a whole mountain side of snow careening down the ravine ahead of him. He stood in the snow panting, his hands braced on the knees of his orange coveralls. He stood upright and stroked his beard, debating whether to call to the others to rope up, but decided against it.

And so the rescuers picked their way down into the hollow, stopping frequently to scan the snow-laden spruce and hemlocks for signs of victims, but found none. They reached the tiny trickling headwaters of Buckeye Gap Prong gurgling beneath the snow in the floor of the ravine and followed it. Gradually it peeked out from its snowy cover as it grew, gathering strength from the seeping sides of the hollow until it led them to a clearing, which was the old Backcountry Site 25, since abandoned. They rested, then donned snowshoes, and did a sweep of the area. From there they picked up a short section of trail, which led them to a confluence of the stream they had followed and its eastern branch. There they left the trail, and followed the branch upward, per instructions, toward Lower Buckeye Gap.

In some places, they had no choice but to walk in the stream itself, a treacherous undertaking due to the combined perils of icy rocks and miniature snow caves where the stream had undercut the drifts. They came to a place where it ran through a flattened area, and the going became easier for a spell. But Jack was exhausted. He sent the two younger men on a sweep, while he leaned against a tulip tree, and sipped from a water bottle between gulping mouthfuls of air. Stamina had never been his *forte*. Strength had. But he felt that if he were to deliver his strength where it was needed, he was going to have to get himself in better shape. He cursed every donut he had lovingly consumed; he could enumerate them now as he felt each one hanging from his middle. He caught his breath at last and wiped the sweat from his eyes. A pretty place, he thought, scanning the beech and hemlocks, rhododendrons and small red spruce. A fog was blowing through, wispy and surreal. It bent and scattered the sunlight, which glittered like jewels off the heavy-laden hemlocks bending low toward the snow-blanketed ground. Then something caught his eye, an alien hue amidst the kaleidoscope of colors refracting in the snow-jewels. Through the fog, in the snow bank by the stream, there shone an ashen gray tone, mute, sullen, marble, white…but not as the snow. Jack approached and the truth struck home. Adrenaline surged through his body, and he radioed to the others excitedly. There before him was the naked frozen body of a young man half covered with snow as if even in death he had insisted on a measure of modesty. His face had worn its paradox of peace and surprise for some days now. The rescuers fanned out, the search more difficult in the maze of evergreens, until they found the shredded tent, and its sentry, frozen in watchfulness as she waited eternally and hopelessly for the return of her cold-crazed lover. Outside the useless shelter caved-in with snow, she sat beside a tree, clad only in a singlet and warm-up pants many sizes too large, her fleece jacket cast onto the branches of a nearby spruce, a little green book in her porcelain hand.

Jack radioed to headquarters. Two victims, one male, one female, found, *not alive*. He spoke the words as he was trained, but their coldness disturbed him. The words were likewise not alive, but his heart was, pounding and leaping, and emotions were swelling up inside. He looked at the girl. Snowflakes still clung to her eyelashes. The tears came; he could not hold them back. The others heard him and turned to see his great hulk hunched in the snow, weeping. They wept too.

About the Author

Born in Atlanta, Georgia, **S.L. Baer** has lived in various places in the South including Florida (Jacksonville), South Carolina (Columbia, Greenville), Mississippi (Hernando), Tennessee (Memphis, Clarksville, Jackson, Knoxville), before settling in the Tennessee Valley in East Tennessee between the Cumberland Mountains and Great Smoky Mountains National Park. S.L. Baer has spent many years hiking the mountains of Southern Appalachia. He misses no opportunity to explore the cities and trails of North America and the European Continent, with an eye for the beauty of the nature, culture and history of the places he visits. He is a member of the Knoxville Writers' Guild and a life member of the Appalachian Trail Conference.

Printed in the United States
36310LVS00004B/181-189